THE PARADISE EATER

THE PARADISE EATER

THE FIELD TRILOGY

JOHN RALSTON SAUL

VINTAGE CANADA
A Division of Random House of Canada

Published in Canada in 1997 by Vintage Canada, a division of Random House of Canada Limited, Toronto, M5E 1G4. Published in 1989 by Ballantine Books of Canada.

Canadian Cataloguing in Publication Data

Saul, John Ralston, 1947–
The paradise eater

(The Field trilogy)
ISBN 0-679-30898-9

I. Title. II. Series: Saul, John Ralston, 1947–   . The Field trilogy.

PS8587.A3865P37 1997   C813'.54   C97-930923-9
PR9199.3.S28P37 1997

Cover design: Scott Richardson
Cover image of reclining woman: Kenichi Seki/Photonica
Inset photograph: Ed Pritchard/Tony Stone Images

Printed in the United States of America

10 9 8 7 6 5 4 3 2 1

For

John McBeth
who uncovered the Lao story

Sulak Sivaraksa
radical royalist

Father Joe Maier
of Klong Toey slum

Weave a circle round him thrice,
And close your eyes with holy dread,
For he on honey-dew hath fed,
And drunk the milk of Paradise.

Coleridge

CHAPTER 1

'Schizophrenia is merely a state of mind.' Dr Michael Woodward's voice was raised over the uneven heaves of the air conditioner jutting out behind him. 'Chemically based, in general. In my case, not.'

Known to the Thais as Dr Meechai Wuthiwat, he might have avoided joking about his own character had he not been with a foreigner – a *farang* – who was also a friend, John Field. The smell and the weight of the East, creeping through the walls and surging in with the mechanically cooled air, insinuated themselves as a reminder that, outside his own office in the Bangkok Nursing Home on Convent Road, Woodward would have been even less likely to discuss such a thing.

The Home had been Bangkok's first western hospital. It curved through two acres of garden with a nineteenth-century colonial air of long, low, slanting roofs covered by red tiles. The white stucco façade rose to an upper floor of ceiling fanned rooms open on to large verandas. These were furnished with wicker sofas and writing desks. The patients lived little in their rooms – unless chained by tubes to machinery – and much on their verandas, gazing in minimal or great agony out across the tropical, almost botanical collection of trees and flowers that were clipped constantly back into severe controlled shapes. Nature in Bangkok was still something to dominate or be dominated by.

Even lying down, the patients could pick out through their picket railings the cars carrying patients – if not friends, certainly known faces – as they weaved up through the trees towards the great porch, designed to protect them during the rainy season. This ability to identify the newly sick was central to Bangkok gossip. Between the porch and the hall there were neither doors nor walls. The Nursing Home had been built before fans and so everything which could be left open was, in the hope that air might be encouraged to move.

Along the street, just beyond the garden, lay Christ's Church, Anglican and Norman in style. In the other direction was, first, St Joseph's, a French-founded convent school for the rich, and then the Swiss Guest House, patronized largely by Baptist missionaries, down from the hills and in from the paddies. The Carmelites hid across the street behind a stone wall, recently raised still higher with corrugated plastic sheeting to preserve the nuns' isolation from the city growing taller around them. Convent Road was thus an island, one block long, crowded with devotion to God and to health. At either end, a sea of iniquity in concrete broke upon its shores.

From across Sathorn, the wide cutting avenue beyond Christ's Church, a five-storeyed massage parlour the width and depth of a department store, its façade decorated with Christmas tree lights, stared down the length of Convent Road. At the other end, beyond the Swiss Guest House and Silom Road, a hundred or so bars and smaller massage parlours jumbled against each other along Patpong, Patpong 2 and a series of other little lanes.

The Bangkok Nursing Home had lost its position as the city's only source of modern medicine decades before. The Thais had better hospitals and, for that matter, better doctors than the general expatriate variety. Still, the European community lent a great deal of importance to familiarity, even if it meant risking death. Familiarity was a form of religion: the Expatriate's Faith. Dr Woodward, in both his English and his Thai incarnations, was a good doctor, but it was his English half that earned the bread and butter by pandering to this faith.

'Don't be verbose, old man,' he added, ending the conversation, 'and pull down your trousers.'

Field focused on the neat figure before him; there was a spare elegance about it that could only have been Thai and must therefore have been inherited from Woodward's mother. Outlined as it was by a dark and very English suit, this Siamese half receded towards invisibility.

8

'You should know it by now,' Field complained.

'I have no particular desire to see your remarkably ordinary and diseased sexual organs, old man. You tell me the discharge has not cleared up. In that case I need a specimen. In which case I need to see the thing. The jewels, old boy. To hold them, in fact, distasteful though that is to me.'

Field didn't listen and let his friend slip out of focus. He didn't want to do what he was told. As to the doctor's needs, they were the furthest things from Field's mind. His eyes slipped up to the wood ceiling, down to the indifferent blue shining walls, soft with humidity and too many coats of paint, and round to the left of the doctor's silhouette where a group of photographs hung.

Woodward's father was there in the uniform of a captain of the Siamese Navy. The print was dated 1914. He had left England in 1912, having gradually realized that his Jewish blood, though apparent in neither name nor physique, was a hindrance to his career in the Royal Navy. A discreet hindrance. Nothing had ever been said; not within his hearing, not even at school. No one had ever called him Jew-boy or made him consciously feel an outsider. And yet he had felt precisely that. Curiously enough, the photograph made him look Thai, perhaps an effect of the photographer's style, because if ever a sailor had been cast in the Admiral Beatty tradition, Woodward was the man. In August 1914, immediately upon the outbreak of the war, he had renounced his citizenship, ceasing to be a subject of King George V, changed his name to Wuthiwat, a direct translation of Woodward, and had married a Thai from a good family. The girl had been immediately impregnated. The resulting first daughter was his real declaration of independence. He would not go back to England for the war. They hadn't wanted him when they didn't need him. He was now unavailable.

Field put his hand to his fly. The metal of the zipper was ice cold; like a pin puncturing his hot skin. Everything was hot. The air conditioning only made it hotter. The gusts of cold air, belching out from the rudimentary old machine which took up half the window, were little better than deodorant applied over old sweat. He looked down at his own hand. The nails were

9

cut in perfect quarter moons. Although a particularly clean man at all times, his standards of cleanliness rose still higher whenever he was infected.

'For God's sake, John. Get on with it.'

Field grunted – it was a form of laugh, indicating assent – and yanked both his trousers and his underwear down in one move. The rush of air against his genitals relieved the pain for a brief second. It was more the illusion of relief. He looked straight up at Woodward to watch him prepare a swab on a stick, then move forward. Field let his eyes slip back to the wall.

There was a second photograph, in a frame as baroque as that of 1914. It showed the father as an admiral, in 1942. His first wife had already died and so, with Thailand's entry into the Second War on the side of the Axis, he had married again, again a Thai, and had immediately shot out the seeds for Michael, the last of his nine children and the only son. The admiral was still alive – now ninety-five – and still strong enough to terrorize his married daughters and their husbands.

Two other photographs showed Michael in the robes of a Buddhist monk during his teenage retreat to a monastery and the same Meechai in a pin-striped suit at the University of Edinburgh medical school. Michael and Meechai both meant strength.

Field felt his penis seized firmly, pulled out and the stick twisting up inside. He managed to ask, 'How much pleasure would you think this equals on a weigh scale?'

'What a Catholic thought.' Woodward was too absorbed in twisting the swab to say more for a moment. 'I had enough trouble clearing you up last time. I want a bloody good specimen.'

'Nobody says bloody any more, for Christ's sake! I've told you that, Michael. Nobody! Not even the English.'

He went on talking to deflect the attack of white flame which the scraping produced within him. On the doctor's face there was the expression of a man baiting a hook. Field hadn't been fishing in thirty years. Not since his childhood. And certainly not since he'd left Montreal for Bangkok twenty years before. You don't fish in the Far East, he thought. People fish for you.

People do everything for you. Catching VD is one of the few things you can do for yourself; that and choosing the girl to help you catch it.

'You ever go fishing, Michael?'

'Whatever for?' Woodward asked this with the innocence of an educated Thai. He twisted the swab out and turned away to smear it on a circular glass plate six inches across.

Field looked down past his flat stomach; taut, he remarked to himself, but then muscle was neither a compensation for nor a protection against his problem. The penis appeared quite normal. A little red perhaps. He replaced the stained Kleenex in his underwear and thought about the three girls he had slept with the week before; that is, the week before the usual dripping and fishhook pains had started. Perhaps all three girls had made a contribution. Perhaps it was that miraculous combination – a meeting of germs never meant to meet – which had made the infection impervious to the first attack of antibiotics. He considered putting this theory to Woodward, but thought better of it.

'What did you give me last week?'

Woodward glanced up. 'Kanamycin. Two grams, last Wednesday wasn't it? A gram a day – Thursday, Friday, Saturday.' His voice took on a marginally reassuring tone. 'Now don't worry, John. I have been seeing a fair number of resistant cases. You're quite certainly not alone with the problem. And on the positive side, there are twenty-four antibiotics smeared around this plate. One of them will strike it dead. No. No. Keep your trousers down. Let's take advantage of the buttocks being bare to have a go at your little case with some Spectinomycin; fill in the time, so to speak, while the others are fighting it out on the plate. Why not? Think of it as Russian roulette.'

'What?'

'Except I pull the trigger while the germ waits to be shot dead.' He covered the dish and put it away in a cooler before searching through a medicine cupboard. 'Two shots of two grams each, one per cheek, straight away. A gram a day for the next three days, right or left buttock, your option. Marvellous. I'll see lots of you. You, I mean, not your lower parts in

11

particular.' He paced over to his desk, lifting his shiny, heavy, black shoes with care. Field's file lay open. 'This is your second gonorrhoea of the year.'

'The other was last year.'

'I'm afraid not. You came calling here on January tenth. The incubation period being less than two weeks, except in rare cases, you most certainly caught it this year. Now last year was quite a different show. Chlamydia was the star. Four infections.'

'One, Michael. They were all the same one. You know that. I couldn't shake it. Come on, for Christ's sake, give me the shots, eh, so I can get my trousers up. There's a wind in here. Why don't you get rid of that antique?' He was talking about the air conditioner. 'My fees alone would buy you a new machine.'

'No.' Woodward didn't move. 'Not by my calculation. You see, each infection counts separately if separated by a month. There was also a non-specific urethritis.'

'Nothing.'

'Almost nothing. And a gonorrhoea that ran over from '83.'

'You can't count it twice.'

'I'm not. Good grief, no. Wouldn't dream of it. Now . . . you have been in Bangkok twenty years. I, however, did not see you until May seventh, 1969; an emergency visit occasioned by an out-of-control gonorrhoea. You had been stuck in the hills for two weeks with no drugs. However, there were girls.'

'There are always girls.'

'I believe you had lost your previous records, leaving me ignorant regarding your first four years. However, as of today, you are up to eight gonorrhoea, one syphilis – '

'That was bad luck.'

'Extremely, I agree. You must have got it from a European. Six chlamydias. Five assorted non-specific urethritis. And that's it. There are at least eight infections you haven't even tried. Peyronie's disease, for example. I'd like to see one of those.'

'Would you?'

'Induration of the corpora, that's what you get. Swelling on one side of the penis. It can become very large and distorted

'... quite a trial, I understand. Requires patience. Or Reiter's Syndrome ...'

'Give me my shots.'

'No cure really. You have to starve it out. A bit like chlamydia, only this one inflates the surface of the bone. Little spurs. It might also damage those blue eyes of yours.'

Field ran a hand with frustration through his hair, thick and blond. Woodward noticed this gesture.

'Not the scalp. No. It doesn't affect the scalp, though I can understand why you might think the opposite. We treat it with steroids, which eventually make you moon-faced. Rather like a Chinese eunuch, if you see what I mean.'

Field swivelled round and bent over, presenting his backside as an encouragement. This drew Woodward's attention from the file.

'Oh, good. You're ready.' He got up to prepare the needles. 'You are not top of the list as yet. I've two patients running ahead, though you're closing fast.'

'Crappe and Sweetpie.'

'No. As a matter of fact, not. Henry Crappe is surprisingly careful and Sweetpie, as you call him, is very lucky. Here we go.' He jabbed in the first needle. 'Of course, you are only forty-four. You'll have lots of time to catch up once we've beaten this one.'

'I should write Wojtyla.'

'Wojtyla?'

'The Pope. Look, when I'm not sick, what do I want? Sex. Not voraciously, no more than most, but I want it when I want it, how I want it. That desire has got to be the most natural, irresistible and permanent thing in the world. Then I catch one of your drips and snap, I don't want sex any more. Snap. No desire. And that without moral questioning. Pain deadens desire. That's even a Christian concept. So VD is a friend to chastity. It conquers the temptations that make chastity difficult. Give every priest the clap and the priesthood's weakness for sins of the flesh would vanish. I should know, a Montreal lower town Irish boy. We're priest breeding stock.' Field never dwelt on the fact that only his mother had been Catholic and Irish. His father had been a Protestant Anglo.

13

'Except the pain doesn't last, John. You get the desire back and you're still sick. Now bugger off! Go and see the old duck outside. She'll give you some pills to build you up while the shots are dragging you down.'

'I'll buy you lunch.'

'No. They're waiting for me at Klong Toey.'

'I'll come with you.'

'Don't. My clinic lasts all afternoon. It's exhausting enough without your company.'

'St Michael among the poor, eh? I'll drop you off there.'

'No. Don't you have anything to do?'

'Not when I feel this way. I'll pay the taxi.'

'No. I've got to change.'

'Quite right. Savile Row in the swamp. Not the right image.'

'Get out, John!' He pushed the neatly-dressed blond figure towards the door.

The old duck – she was scarcely thirty and had long black hair – gave Field his pills and sent him off down the stairs. He ignored the pain in his groin as he moved, his legs marginally wider apart than in normal times, and paused at the bottom to examine the names on the patient board. All *farangs*. Mostly Anglo-Saxons. The board was lacquered white with thirty-five polished brass card holders fixed upon it in four rows; a white card had been slipped into each, the patient's name inscribed in an elegant black script. The whole thing was reminiscent of the seating plan for an embassy dinner. No. There was no one he wanted to visit.

As no wall divided the pillared hall from the garden and the drive, so a strong heavy smell of grass and flowers drifted in to mix curiously with the medical odours. There was a woman climbing from the rear seat of a BMW. A servant followed her, carrying a sick child. The driver came last with a small suitcase. Field didn't know her. The humidity and the heat reached to where he stood. He could sense these elements building up as they wove their pattern across the day towards the afternoon rain. Field stepped out into the sun. Curious. After all his years in Bangkok, he still felt a conscious pleasure each time the sun and heat and humidity struck him violently with a single blow.

14

This pleasure was not devoid of masochism. He could sense blood rushing out to the surface to protect him and his eyes shrinking in to escape the glare and his lungs measuring their expansion carefully to avoid exertion. Yes, it was pleasure he felt. Pleasure beneath a clear, hot sky. Revenge upon a child-hood of winters and marginal poverty. Had the sun wanted to strike him dead, he would have been quite happy to accept its judgement. He had always imagined that one day it would. Field walked gingerly along the drive, focusing on the narrow space directly ahead of him.

A voice called out from a balcony behind. 'John. Hello, John.'

He recognized it as belonging to a woman who checked in twice a year for a two week rest, her reason being that the Home was the best old fashioned hotel cum social centre in Bangkok, providing you had your food cooked outside and brought in. Field waved a hand over his shoulder without looking back or breaking stride.

On Convent Road his eyes automatically shifted away from the traffic and down to the pavement, or rather to the jumble of shattered cement slabs, sewer openings and refuse piles. He turned right and began to pick his way on the sunstruck side of the street. It was a three-hundred-yard walk to Patpong and to Napoleon's. There he would inevitably find someone to cheer him up while he ate a steak. Across the road a Chevrolet Impala, 1959, began to follow while still allowing the taxis and *tuc-tucs* to rush by. It was pale green and white and enormous, gleaming, and outlined by a mass of chrome that reflected the light with the force of a solar heating device. The rear window wound down and a woman's warm, husky voice called out.

'John. John. Come over here.'

Field continued as if he had not heard.

'John. Oh, stop!' She tapped her driver on the shoulder. 'Stop.'

The car eased up to the kerb like a galleon and an old Thai, dried on the bone, climbed out from behind the wheel to open the rear door. Mrs Norman A. Laker emerged as if from a stretch limousine on Park Avenue. The Carmelites' wall, with its corrugated plastic top, rose behind her to provide shade. Her hair was teased up into a stiff but perfect mountain of

15

white. A deliberate layer of make-up emphasized her bone structure, with a black line around the outer edges of the lips to accentuate their fullness. The face lifts were sensed without being concretely observable. She wore a pale linen suit and walked out into the sun in a highly articulated manner, though without adjusting her step. Even her pupils seemed impervious to the glare, scarcely bothering to contract. The overall result was a highly personal interpretation of beauty. A three-wheeled *tuc-tuc* screeched its brakes to avoid her, then swerved in an arc, honking as it passed.

'John!'

Field stopped and turned back, changing his focus as he looked straight into the sun. 'Good morning, Catherine.'

'What's the matter with you? Are you ill?'

'Nothing serious.'

'Then don't go into that place. You could catch something. You've been in there forever.'

'Had I known you were waiting . . .' He saw that she was insensitive to irony and so broke off. 'I was wasting Michael Woodward's time.'

'Stay away from him, John. He spends too much time in the slums. Diseases are very communicable. And what are you doing on foot out of doors? Come over to the car.' Her manicured meccano fingers beckoned. 'I want to talk to you. I've already been to your house. That dirty old woman you pay to do what? . . . I can't imagine what . . . sent me here.'

'She's not so old.'

Field allowed himself to be dragged across the road and pushed into the back of the car. Mrs Laker followed behind so that he was forced to slide the full distance to the other side of the tooled leatherette seat.

He patted the yellowing surface, 'When's the richest *farang* in Bangkok going to get herself a new car?'

'Norman ordered this Chevrolet!' She appeared to regret her outburst and looked down at the seat's intricate Mexican saddle pattern before continuing in a more intimate tone. 'It arrived, I thought it very strange, exactly sixty days after his death . . . in that place.' Without turning, she raised her right hand and pointed a finger through the back window towards

16

the Nursing Home, then flicked it forward, as if it were a riding crop, and tapped the driver's shoulder. 'Cemetery, Lek . . . this, this was the first air conditioned car in Bangkok . . . Sixty days precisely.'

The driver eased with the slow curve of a ship of the line out on to the road and floated along at twenty-five miles per hour. The car, although American, seemed perfectly suited to a city that still drove on the left. In any case, everything modern in Bangkok – and there was a great deal – quickly took on an awkward, clumsy, obsolescent air, so that the glass skyscrapers and the Mercedes immediately resembled pyramids and dinosaurs. Mrs Laker's Impala, therefore, fitted in very well.

'I want you to go to Vientiane,' she said.

'I was going to lunch.'

Mrs Laker considered his words. 'After walking in the heat? That aside, you shouldn't ingest food till the sun is down, John. Eat early and late. That's the secret here. I want you to go to Vientiane tomorrow.'

'I'm not going anywhere. And I've been eating lunch here for twenty years.'

'You'll suffer for it in the end. Ingest before sun rise and after sun set. I have an agreement on 100 tractors. All you have to do is tidy up the details and sign. It's easy money.'

'In that case, anyone can do it.'

'You know the Laos, John. You used to go there. Between tying up details and signing, a firm hand is needed.'

'There are lots of old Lao hands with firmer hands than mine.'

They sailed out on to the windless sea of Silom Road and banked left into the scrum of small taxis, *tuc-tucs* and buses, while Catherine Laker sat silent, apparently evaluating the depths of his resistance. Honking and fumes enveloped them like an ocean mist contaminated by a jam of old motor boats.

Annoyance seemed to overwhelm her and she shot out, 'You should have kept on as a journalist if you weren't willing to travel at the drop of a hat! That's how agents make money, John. Flexibility! Agility!'

Field gazed at her from as great a distance as he could manage by pressing himself up against the door on his side. She was staring hard into his eyes. Hers was an open, theoretically penetrating stare. He considered pointing out that for seventeen years he had done nothing but jump on planes to Vientiane, Saigon, Phnom Penh, the Plain of Jars, Chaing Rai, Mae Hong Son and every other place there was a battle, a coup, a drug snatch, a peace effort, a refugee camp, to say nothing of following endless American generals, anthropologists and senators through their brief appearances in the on-going struggle for South-East Asia. But then she knew all of that. And in general she kept herself perfectly under control. A sanitized, self-cooling, back-combed freezer, rolling with indifference through the heat and humidity. Betrayals of impatience were out of character. He thought about that before replying, 'So what's the big deal, Catherine?'

The freezer door swung shut, re-establishing the normal impenetrability. 'It is not big.'

'I mean, Catherine, what's all the excitement about?'

'Don't be childish. Money is money, John. And this is easy money.'

He shrugged and repeated himself; 'I won't go this week, Catherine.'

'Full fee.'

'So what?'

'Plus one per cent.'

'Next week, Catherine. I'll go next week.'

Mrs Laker fell silent while she digested her defeat, though her eyes at no time relaxed their stare on to Field. 'You must be ill, then.'

'Catherine, such powers of deduction.' He felt her, in turn, moving further away along the seat. 'Not contagious. And not the result of eating lunch.'

She looked away from him, abruptly, out at the traffic along with which the car was edging at ten kilometres per hour, a reasonable average for Bangkok. Field shrugged and followed suit, turning to his own window. The popular explanation for the city's lack of bank robberies was that a getaway car wouldn't be able to get away. You could run faster than you could drive, except that it was too hot to run. Silom Road was lined on both sides with three-storey crude cement façades stained black by the polluted rain. Interspersed among these was the occasional marble-covered bank tower. Throughout the business sections of Bangkok, the presence of massed, cheap, stained cement overwhelmed all other impressions. As Field found nothing else to distract him, his attention was drawn back to the pain in his groin.

'Where the fuck are we going?'

Before Mrs Laker could answer, they began edging left to turn down a lane between two undeveloped blocks. Each was enclosed by a high, crumbling wall. Only tree tops and the odd cross could be seen rising above them.

'The cemetery.'

'What for?'

'Norman.'

The entire Catholic, foreign community had been and still was squeezed into these two blocks, which had once been on the edge of town and were now deep within the centre. The car drew up before a small service entrance to the cemetery on the left hand side of the lane. The plot on the right was devoted to Chinese Catholics. Mrs Laker climbed out, without waiting for her door to be opened, and disappeared through the wall. Field found her standing just inside, surveying from safe ground a disorder and desolation that verged on jungle.

'Christ!'

She looked at him dispassionately. 'You haven't been here before?'

'I'm not dead yet.'

In the corner where they stood the guardian had built a small tin hut. Its walls were braced against four stone tombs. His family's laundry hung drying from the horizontal bars of the crosses raised above a dozen other monuments. Only in the area the guardian personally made use of had nature been kept in check. Everywhere else reeds and bamboo had sprung up, hiding the graves. A mango tree had forced its way between two ten-foot-high wood monuments and pushed them out at opposing forty-five degree angles. They remained standing only because branches and vines had entwined them in a protective net. Field sauntered over to look. A Royal Counsellor, Basil Southend, 1836–1889, in the service of the King of Siam, was being forcibly separated from his wife Emily by a wall of indifferent roots.

He turned back towards the entrance only to find Mrs Laker immediately behind him holding two pairs of rubber boots. Behind her the driver was carrying a bucket of water and a bottle of bleach. She held out one pair of boots.

'See if you can squeeze into these. Lek is getting too old for this sort of thing. Go on.'

He forced his feet in until his toes were curled up under themselves. Mrs Laker handed the driver's bucket to Field and Field's shoes to Lek, for safekeeping, then she set off down a raised and narrow overgrown path on either side of which green water lay, with reeds rising out of it, blocking the paths between the tombs, themselves islands in the swamp or actually submerged. Fifty yards along she abruptly cut to the right and plunged down into a foot of mud, where the green tangle of reeds was as high as herself. With a sweeping of her arms she pushed them aside and struggled forward. Field hesitated, but followed. It was twenty yards before she stopped at a slab of greenish marble, the surface of which was a few inches above the water level. The reeds immediately around the tomb had been scythed in a not-too-distant past and were only beginning to grow back. Field dumped his bucket down on the stone. The inscription was furry; partially obscured.

NORMAN A. LAKER
1916–1959

you are not gone
you are still loved

Only then did he realize that the slab of marble was not green but white, and stained by mould.

'How much do you come out here, Catherine?'

'Every Tuesday. It's not so bad in the dry months. The water goes right down to two or three inches. Now things are just about to get out of hand. Next month the whole stone will be under water. The walkway. Everything. Here.' She handed him a rough rag and a pair of gloves, then poured the bleach into the bucket of water. 'Go ahead. Put them on. It will eat your skin otherwise. If I don't use a strong mix the slime won't come off.' She plunged her own rag into the bucket, squeezed it lightly and began scrubbing at the surface. Field followed suit without enthusiasm.

'How would you like,' he remarked, 'to know the cobra statistics in Bangkok? This place looks like their headquarters.'

'Scrub, John. I don't spend any longer out in the sun than I've got to.' She worked energetically while she talked, her hair holding as firm as a helmet despite the agitation. 'Disgusting! Disgusting!' She plunged her cloth in again. Squeezed it. 'In 26 years I've only seen three cobras around Norman's stone.'

Field looked up. There wasn't a hint of humour or of sweat on her face. Of course, he thought, it's barely ninety-five degrees. The humidity can't be more than ninety-eight. He went back to scrubbing. 'How long were you married?'

'We're still married.'

'Yes. But I mean before the funeral.'

'Eleven years. Six in New York and five here.'

'And you come every week?'

'I have to, John. He wouldn't forgive me.'

'Why don't you just pay someone?'

'When Norman's stone was placed on this spot, I couldn't afford to pay someone. Now, coming here is part of our married life.' She looked up to catch Field's attention, thus emphasizing her point. 'You have the most beautiful eyes, John. Do you know that? Their colour is such a deep, penetrating blue. Thoughtful eyes.' She went on scrubbing as if this observation were part of a banal conversation.

The slime came off quite easily, no doubt because it was only one week old and had not been given a chance to eat its way into the stone. They worked in silence for another ten minutes. Field noticed that the pain in his groin had been drowned out by the cramps in his toes, curled up as they were within the rubber boots. He also noticed that Mrs Laker's fingers and hands moved over the stone with the same dissected articulation that she used in polite conversation; this detail led him by indirect logic to wonder just what he was doing out there in

21

tight rubber boots, thirsty and hungry as he knew himself to be. Field observed in a loud voice,

'So you loved him.'

She didn't bother to answer. When they were back at the passage, which led through the wall to the lane, Mrs Laker gave the guardian ten *baht* and, once outside, she allowed Lek to pull her boots off while she braced her shoulder blades against the car for balance.

Field had quickly freed his feet and was stretching his toes with relief. 'If you haven't got any other plans for a good time, I'll go to lunch now.'

'Do you want a ride?'

'You've already taken me for one.' Field walked back the few yards to the main road where he hailed a *tuc-tuc* passing out in the centre lane. It veered on to two of its three wheels and came careening through the rows of traffic.

'Patpong,' Field announced.

The driver peered out from beneath his cover to survey the prospect. 'Fifty *baht*, mister.'

Field laughed good naturedly and replied in Thai. 'I'm not a *farang*. I live here. Twenty *baht*.'

'Forty *baht*.'

'No. Twenty is already double the price. Come on.' He said this in an encouraging tone and smiled. 'OK. Come on. OK.'

'OK, mister.'

Field climbed up behind, only to hear Mrs Laker calling from a distance. 'I'll arrange Vientiane for Monday. Send your passport over.'

He didn't answer. He slouched on to the orange, blue, yellow and green striped plastic seat, spread his hands to either side to grasp the metal bars, which were his only protection against falling out, and threw his head back so that it escaped the shade of the plastic awning stretched above. The *tuc-tuc* leapt into the traffic, the roar of its little engine deafening Field, and its own thick stream of exhaust rising up in a circular path to blow on to the passenger seat. He let this and the fumes of the hundreds of other machines crowded honking around him fill his lungs and envelop first his body, then his mind. Somewhere ahead was the whine of Thai rock music forcing its way out of

22

the transistor the driver had strapped to the panel before him. Field closed his eyes, the pain in his groin suddenly distant and Mrs Laker dissolving into the carbon monoxide. This seamless web of filth and of noise filled him as always with a wonderful, meaningless sense of pleasure.

CHAPTER 2

Henry Crappe's was the only familiar face in Napoleon's, or rather, his was the only face that Field felt up to recognizing. Two traders he had once done business with – sold them a container of wicker furniture for export – were sitting in a corner. Field took care not to see them as he went through the room to slip down across from Crappe, of *Crappe at the Flicks* and *Crappe Reads for You* and *Crappe's Bangkok*; this last being a weekly analysis of new bars and new bar girls. All three columns appeared beneath his byline in the *Bangkok Post*.

Field tapped his fingers on the table. 'I thought you slept till midnight.'

Crappe looked up from his peanuts and beer. His eyebrows arched to emphasize concern. They were encrusted with dandruff. 'I'm over extended. I have to view two videos this afternoon for review, catch a few hours' sleep and come back out here to labour.' He waved at the chair in which Field sat. 'Consider yourself invited to join me. What's the matter?'

'Nothing's the matter.'

'You don't look right to me.'

'I'm fine. Just feeling a little off.'

Crappe examined him at length. As much as Field felt sympathetic towards the man, he had to avert his own eyes. It wasn't that Crappe was ugly. Not exactly. He had swollen into middle age by taking on the shape of a pear – both his body as a whole and his face taken on its own – an endearing characteristic, as was the innocent expression which he had managed to maintain despite twenty-five years in Bangkok. The man wasn't clean. That was the problem. Quite apart from the

24

eyebrows, his hair was thick and dark in an unwashed way and mined with particles of dead scalp. Field made a point of never looking that high. There was a cold sore on the lower lip and his fingernails were curiously brown, probably from fiddling with his personally blended pipe tobacco which, according to Crappe, had to be mixed at the last second, pipe by pipe. The slivers of fresh pomelo peel, sliced each morning by his Thai wife, made this essential.

At last the man removed his stare. 'You've got a dose of the clap.'

Field couldn't hide his surprise. 'Yes.'

'It's in the eyes. I can see it in the irises. Experience is very important in that kind of diagnosis.'

'You should have been a doctor.'

A girl came up and put her fingers softly on Field's shoulder. 'Hello, John. Beer?'

'No. Not allowed. Coffee. Steak sandwich.' He put out a hand to keep her at his side. 'And, Phet, turn the fucking air conditioning down, will you darling. I'm not hung meat.'

'What, John?'

'Cold. Too cold.' He made a turning down sign with his fingers.

'Music too loud?'

'No. Music's OK. Too cold. *Yen maak.*'

'OK, John.'

Apart from the Thai girls in silk dresses with number badges, Napoleon's resembled a comfortable bar anywhere in the world. Perhaps that was the secret of its success among the *farangs*.

'As a matter of fact,' Crappe said with a hint of resentment, 'I like it cold. However, as you are ailing, I will defer. Regarding medicine, it was indeed one of the two professions I considered. The other being history; that is, as taught at the university level.'

'And you settled for neither?'

'I chose communications. You cannot turn your back on the century. You cannot pander to your own sentimental fantasies when the heart of your epoch beckons.'

'The *Bangkok Post*?'

'I tell you, Field, I am without any question the most controversial and widely read journalist in this city. I'll admit that some people read me because they don't like me, but that in itself is a sign of success. My name is up on the walls of half the washrooms in Bangkok. Why is that? Because I touch something within each of these people. Why again? Because my opinions are based upon education, intelligence and experience.'

'Crappe, all you do is tell a lot of unimaginative men where to get a good fuck.'

'In a way, yes. Although I would submit to you: A, that most of the human race is short on imagination; B, therefore needs guidance; C, I am guiding them in one of the key areas of life. I submit this without even mentioning the advice I give in other columns regarding literature and regarding the silver screen. But let me put my own concerns aside. So you have the clap. That is hardly a reason to succumb to depression.'

Field shrugged. His coffee and steak sandwich arrived.

'There must be something else.'

'No. Nothing. Just a down week.'

'Who is living with you?'

'I threw her out last month.'

Crappe showed relief. 'So you are freed even from the need for an awkward explanation in the style – "No, not tonight, I'm tired" – or – "No, I sat on my balls and they ache." '

'What?'

'More common than you might imagine among men who wear boxer shorts, which are, on the more positive side, better for your sperm count than the tight variety. However, if you lean towards the boxer shorts you must never sit down rapidly on a hard seat. Never. It is, on the other hand, my preferred explanation for a sexual recess. You can only use it once every five years or so, as the unusual character of the complaint in itself makes the argument difficult of repetition. But when used, who would dare to disagree with you?'

'No one, Crappe.'

'That is correct. No one.'

'Your wife, for example, would she believe you?'

'My wife?' Crappe appeared astounded by the question. 'No.

26

But then belief is not what matters. The important thing is to give them an explanation of sufficient quality that they can pretend to believe it without appearing naïve or, indeed, stupid. An experienced woman will never forgive you if you make her look naïve. They hate it.' He emptied his beer and went back to picking up peanuts one by one. Crappe was known to prefer an invitation over paying for himself whenever possible, and could nurse a beer with a few nuts for hours while waiting for the inviter to come along.

'Can I buy you lunch?'

'No, Field. That is very kind. Just a beer perhaps.' When the bottle was safely in front of him he looked up with an air that combined both criticism and the imparting of knowledge. 'I'll tell you what your problem is. You miss the journalistic profession. You miss doing something meaningful.'

'Crappe, will you stop saying that every time we meet? You drive me crazy.'

'Thus you admit it. Over-reaction is invariably the proof of an accurate statement. What have you become, Field? You, one of the best journalists I know? You have become a money changer in the temple. Nothing more.'

'Thanks to which I bring in three times what I used to make.'

'Money is a temptation. No argument there.'

'I don't have to get up in the morning. I can take long holidays. I can keep my daughter in the best university.'

Crappe shrugged as if this information wounded him. 'Tempting. Tempting. All very tempting.'

'You,' Field persisted, 'are the one who gave up being the best narcotics reporter in town to write about bar girls.'

'Now there you slip towards imprecision. Let me go further. You are incorrect. There was no point in my wasting my time. The figures, for example, are illuminating. One day – while still devoted to the "drug scene" – I was seated at my desk reading the annual statistics and, by the time I had finished, something had died within me. I immediately wrote out my resignation. Thirty-two tons of heroin per year come out of this area. One half of one ton – that is the total amount seized by the police. Heroin is like a guerrilla force, Field, it passes by the paths of least resistance. The low ground. The endless valleys of human society. I personally might spend a year in print bemoaning the crimes of a particular dealer and the success of a particular conduit. The day the police finally got around to arresting the man and closing that floodgate, the flow would simply divert itself to a new valley. This parody of justice led me to view events from within my historian's mind. – Is there a desire to stop the flow? By you? By me? By our society? The circuit profits too many people now. We are like the Chinese one hundred years ago being forced to smoke opium by the West. The process is now reversed. Worse. Half the time we ourselves are forcing ourselves. Sex, on the other hand, is a positive subject; certainly more important than drugs. I deal in desire and gratification, Field; the most important and continuous of human weaknesses. I search within myself for the meaning of the bodily fluids.'

'And what do you find?'

'Suffice it to say that I am known as the fastest open field runner in town. I've laid a lot of Thai girls, but I've only married one of them.'

Field nodded vaguely, his attention having drifted away. He had always had difficulty keeping his mind on a conversation. There had been a time when he had made great efforts at linear concentration, but then he had lost his interest in public formalities, rather the way Crappe had lost his interest in exposing the drug traffic, and from then on he had allowed his mind to carry him wherever it desired.

Of course Crappe was right: Field found no pleasure in hawking wicker furniture and tractors around South-East Asia. It wasn't the writing he missed. No. It was the charge of adrenalin which had once come with each new story. But when he weighed that vanished pleasure against his desire to keep on living in Bangkok, the scales hung so unequally that the right choice was clear. There wasn't enough money to be made, writing the sort of things he had written, to guarantee survival beyond one's youth in a city like Bangkok. Not that Field now lived in any greater comfort than he ever had. If anything, less. He packed most of his money off to a tax free bank account in Hong Kong, keeping back in Bangkok just enough for his own life, his women, the upkeep of his daughter's mother and, of course, the upkeep of Songlin, his daughter.

She had been the result of his first love upon arriving in Thailand; an unintended result. His lower town Montreal working class Irish background had led Field to classify this pregnancy as a snare set by a poor, uneducated woman to capture a ticket for herself to North America. And so he had cast her off. At the same time he had begun to support her on a higher level than he supported himself, to ensure that his daughter was brought up properly. This fatherhood by remote control was the great success story of his life. Songlin had turned out to be smart. He had been able to get her into Mater Dei, the best private school for Thais, despite its Catholic origins. And when she had graduated in 1984, he had paid to get her into Chulalongkorn, the university for the rich and well bred. None of this would have been possible had she not been smart. In fact, Field was convinced that she was far more than merely intelligent. The money he had been accumulating in Hong Kong was set aside to buy her the freedom to do whatever she wanted in life: marry the right sort of Thai, go into business, join the diplomatic corps. Just as Field desperately resisted respectability for himself, he was determined to guarantee it for her.

'So where do I find the best new body, Crappe?'

'A lot of people ask me that. I would say go to the Fire Cat this week. The tourist season is so bad they have started dancing with their bottoms off.'

'Ah.'

This calm reaction disappointed Crappe. His mouth somehow shrank to a smaller size. 'Thank you for the kindness of a beer. The world of video awaits me.' He pulled himself out from the table and waddled towards the door. His trousers were cut high so that the belt appeared like a collar around the neck of his pear shape, or rather, in the place of a neck.

Field watched the silhouette disappear through the door and sat staring in indecision at the remains of his steak sandwich, until certain that it bore no message and so abruptly stood up to wander out into the heat. He stepped carefully over the half-metre-high flood dike, built in a curve before the entrance. This crude cement barrier had originally been decorated, but the previous year's rainy season had carried away the tiles. He hesitated in the sun while its rays scorched the air conditioning from his skin. According to Woodward, the best treatment for VD was rest and abstinence of all kinds. He considered going home to bed. The idea left him indifferent. Totally indifferent.

To his right, against a wall, someone had painted a flood level marker. 1983 held the record, with a yard or so of water rolling through the city in September. The problem was not, of course, the rising water, but the sinking city; up to five inches a year. The limitations of the municipal water system had led people to drill private artesian wells, some ten thousand of them in thirty years, and the city, built as it was on mud in the estuary of the Chao Phya River, sank with every opened tap and flushed toilet. After the '83 disaster, a gigantic flood control programme had been announced.

Field considered the marker. It was freshly painted. Perhaps it was a joke. Perhaps it was a protest. After all, August had come, leaving less than a month before the expected autumn overflow, and the needed dikes and control gates were still on paper. The only people who had the money and influence to make the emergency programme work were those who didn't particularly care, because they owned the few buildings that were not sinking; that is, the new skyscrapers which had been floated on deep set piles. Field laughed out loud. Cynicism was one of his easy comforts.

He stepped around a jumble of broken pavement and mud on to the road. Across Patpong an innocuous painted sign – PAGA'S APARTMENTS – hung out from an innocuous three-storey building. It was in this place that Paga, Queen of Patpong, had begun her rise fifteen years before. Now she owned a dozen bars and massage parlours and controlled more than five hundred girls. Field wandered up the wood stairs to a rundown landing where a bar, a barber shop and an office were glassed off to keep the air conditioning inside. The apartments were on the next floor. From there Paga ran her empire.

The bar girl waiting on the landing had begun to call while

he was still climbing. 'Hello, mister. Massage. You want massage?'

'I want to see Paga.'

'Paga? What you want?' She smiled from within her cocktail dress.

'Say a friend.'

'Big friend or little friend?'

'Why?'

''Cause she sleeping upstairs now maybe.'

'Big friend.'

'You come back later anyway, OK.'

'Go on,' he insisted. 'You know me. Tell her Field.'

He and Paga had both arrived in Bangkok twenty years before and had met, so to speak, almost immediately. She had been twenty and had arrived more or less barefoot from a village in the north-east with her three children in tow. She had left behind in the rice paddies a husband of seven years and had begun in Bangkok as a hostess in the Café de Paris at 250 *baht* a month; some ten dollars. Sleeping with customers doubled this amount. Field had contributed in a minor way to her income by taking Paga home a total of three times, but even then she had been looking for men to bankroll her. She had therefore tried to limit the wear and tear on her body to possible candidates. One look at Field's first apartment was enough to disqualify him. On the other hand, they had become friends.

'Field,' he repeated, uncertain whether he'd ever slept with the girl. 'Go on.' He gave her a tap on the rear. 'Take the message up.'

She looked doubtfully at him. 'You come back later, OK.'

At which Paga came running down the stairs from above. 'You see, John. All *farang* look alike.' She grasped him under the arm as she passed. 'You want to come with me.' It wasn't a question.

Field was swung around and dragged down the stairs. From the pavement she stared up the road with her chin stuck out impatiently.

'My son, he so slow! I should send him back to village. Where is he?'

'Busy day?'

Her chin went out still further. It was strong and wide. In fact, the whole face was like a flying wedge. Both her bust and her backside had grown with time to a comfortable size. Not so that she was fat. No. She had merely taken on the proportions of success, which also added up to a subtle declaration that her own body was no longer on offer. In any case, she had never been a great beauty. Her success with men had always stood as an argument for the value of content over form. She wore polyester slacks and a loose cotton blouse.

'There he is!' She rushed out on to the road and leapt into the back of a Mercedes sedan. 'Where you been? Where you been?' She slapped her son on the shoulder and the weak, angular boy melted down into his seat. He said nothing. He didn't even whimper. 'Petchaburi Road. *Soi* 37. Go on!' Her short, plump fingers moved on to Field's thigh and gave a warm squeeze. 'Busy day every day, John. This morning I spend training new girls.'

Field laughed.

'What so funny?' She aimed her chin at him. 'When I start first bar, you remember, business not so good. I try everything. I change many things, but still bad. Then I understand. Have to find right girls. Have to teach them how to please man. Sex is only twenty per cent. It last just a few minutes. Important, but the girl must learn the rest. How to make a man feel like a hero.'

'Come on, Paga.'

'Sure. All men want to be a hero. So I teach my girls everything. How to make love. That's easy part – how to move, how to make noise, when to moan, way to breathe. You know all that, John. Difficult part is how to make man feel good. You know, man, maybe he want to be smart, so girl she learn how to act stupid. Man want to be lion, she learn to be lamb.'

'You mean I've never given a second of pleasure to anyone? In twenty years?'

'You give her money, John. Money is a kind of pleasure if you don't have any. Friendship maybe. Friendship is a kind of pleasure when girl knows you well.'

'Great, Paga. Great. What's she feeling when she's with a man who has a bit of talent in his cock?'

'Oh,' Paga dismissed the idea of such abstract specifics, 'she feeling nothing. She thinking how to do better. You OK, John? You don't look too good.'

Field ignored the question. 'Half a million girls putting on a show?'

'Only the good ones. That's why my business like a big acting school. A good actress, she makes me money. I'm not smart. I know myself. And most girls, they just like me. They work hard. They know they can't count on man for anything. Men all bullshit.'

'What is this, Paga? I could do with a little encouragement today.'

'Oh, you OK. You bullshit too, but OK. Why you look so down?'

'Maybe it's because I haven't got a good actress running around the house at the moment.'

'You getting old, John. When I start, I was young. Now old too, but I learn. You don't learn anything, John. You still a child. Lesson one. Life is simple. All men want sex all the time. They not capable of it, but they want it. Women don't. Not all the time. They have to learn how to do it when they don't want it.'

Wireless Road was completely jammed beyond the intersection ahead, so Paga's son swerved left on to Ploenchit Road without looking first and had to screech to a halt in the middle of even thicker traffic.

'Idiot!' Paga cuffed the back of his head. They were across from the British Embassy grounds and Paga pointed towards the large statue of Queen Victoria that sat on a long sweep of grass half-way between the grille and the residence. 'She have to do it all the time.'

'It was worth it.' Field saw there were garlands around the statue's neck. 'If she hadn't been laid so many times, no one here would remember her.'

Queen Victoria was widely believed in Thailand to be a fertility goddess. Women with reproduction problems brought her presents.

'Don't be stupid, John. If sleeping with men is all it takes, I know lots of women like her.' Paga lurched forward over her son's shoulder and honked the horn. She pulled her lips back with impatience, uncovering two rows of very small teeth, even and tightly fitted together. 'I never like Bangkok. Bangkok a place to make money. But you know, dirty air make me sick. One hour in traffic, I sick for one month.'

'Go back to the rice paddies.'

'You laugh, but I go soon. You'll see.'

They were another half-hour in the car. The secret to life in Bangkok, if you were either busy or delicate, was to go to as few places as possible in one day, because each trip took between thirty minutes and an hour.

When Field saw they were pulling off Petchaburi on to a small lane parallel to the overhead expressway, he turned in surprise to Paga, 'You mean we're going to that Chinese hotel?'

She nodded indifferently.

'You're not tied up with them?'

'Associated, maybe is better word. Their girls, who can train them? If no one train them, they are no good when they grow up. What they do then? They got nothing then. You go there sometimes?'

Field shook his head. 'They remind me of my daughter.'

She registered this in a matter-of-fact way. 'That the only reason?'

'I also don't like it when a girl is locked up. It removes, let's say, the tiny remaining element of adventure.' Field saw that Paga hadn't understood this was a joke.

'Doesn't stop other *farang*.'

He shrugged. 'Or Thais. Are you suggesting a moral point?'

There wasn't time for her to answer. They were already in the courtyard and Paga was out of the car on her way towards a cheap cement construction three storeys high. The hallway and stairs were of unadorned cement, their only decoration being an old man in rubber thongs who waved them on upstairs well after they had gone by. The first landing was blocked by two men slouched in cheap armchairs listening to a radio. *Born in the USA* was screaming out and echoing up the stairwell.

'Zoo keepers?' Field asked.

Paga nodded as she climbed. On the second landing a dozen or so young girls crouched on the floor working on each other's hair or stood around chatting and filing their nails. They looked up when Paga appeared, and fell silent; a respectful silence. To the left and to the right a corridor stretched off with sixty or so doors opening on to it. Other girls wandered in and out of their rooms, sending a low babble of voices through the air. It was early for business and so most were dressed in jeans or shorts or sarongs. The odd one was already in her cocktail dress and heavily made up like an adult. When seen next to the others, undisguised, this masquerade failed. The effect was of a little girl playing at being a grown up. Their ages ranged from twelve to eighteen and they were all now smiling eagerly at Paga as she stared around looking for someone.

'They like me here. I'm popular. I come to give my lessons or sometimes I take older girls away, if they got talent, and give them decent jobs.'

'Decent?'

'Not locked up.' In a louder voice she asked no one in particular, 'Where's Yang?' There was no answer. 'Yang!' She clapped her hands twice in a sharp, hard way and the sound echoed along the corridor. 'Yang!' She clapped again.

A man appeared from one of the rooms with the rumpled look of someone who had been woken up. He shook himself into place as he came down the corridor so that by the time he arrived the impression he gave was of a smart Californian in white trousers and a collarless shirt open to show a smooth hairless chest and two gold chains. His expression was defensive. He whined, 'I've been waiting all day for you.'

The contempt on Paga's face cut through the complaint. 'Where's the girl?'

'Who's he?'

'Mr Field, he's Medical Inspector.'

Astonishment flooded over Yang's face. 'What do you mean, a Medical Inspector?'

'You don't understand English? Get the girl.' She gave Yang a sharp little push and when his back was turned she lifted her eyebrows in Field's direction to silence him.

Yang led them to a room, no doubt identical to the others

except that it had four chairs and no bed; a sort of reception area where customers could choose a girl. He gave Field a puzzled look and left them, closing the door behind.

Field whispered. 'What's this inspector business?'

'I make it up.' She was quite pleased.

'I know that.'

'Yang is a pig. You make him suffer. OK.'

The door opened and Yang pushed a girl in ahead of him. She was in a brown sarong and appeared innocuous, but then Paga's presence reduced everyone else to shadow.

She shouted at the girl in Thai, 'So, you sick again! How you do that? You not supposed to work. So! He make you work?'

The girl shook her head without looking up.

'You don't catch it in the air. So who is lying? Yang, you work her?'

'No!'

'You think I believe you? You would force her to lie.' She turned back to the girl. 'So, you in pain?'

'Yes. Hurts a lot.'

'Like the last time?'

The girl hesitated, probably trying to decide which was worse; the pain or the trouble it was getting her into. 'A little bit.'

'And you dripping?'

'Yes.'

'Stupid girl. Let me see your scar.'

The girl pulled up her sarong. She wore lace cotton panties and just above them a five-inch scar ran across.

'You can't dance with that.'

Field came forward to look. When he touched her skin, he felt it trembling and glanced up to find her eyes glued on to him, as if to anticipate a blow. It was the stare of a frightened child. He gave her a little smile and her eyelids snapped shut. It was a neat, narrow scar. Thai surgeons had very deft hands, but Paga was right. You couldn't undulate an abdomen, no matter how attractive, with the lights picking up a five-inch scar. Of course, she could become a massage girl. They didn't dance and they didn't undress except integrally and for action, at which point a scar probably wouldn't matter.

36

Had the girl not been so visibly terrified of everyone in the room, and in particular of Yang, Field would have admitted to himself that he had noticed her long straight legs and graceful thighs. She was taller than most northern girls – he assumed she was from the north – and instead of the normal round, soft look, she had wide shoulders and a long neck. 'What happened?' he asked.

Yang reverted to his defensive pose. 'She got infected like everyone. I mean, like anyone can.'

Paga broke in, 'Mr Field, he checking Bangkok VD. Police waiting for his report.' In answer to the question Yang was afraid to ask, she added, 'Police need my help.'

'It was just gonorrhoea,' Yang insisted. 'I mean nothing special.'

'So what's the scar, eh?' Field indicated the girl could lower her sarong.

'She let it get out of control.'

'Yang runs a dirty place,' Paga added. 'I find this girl in her room one day, half dead, so I take her to the doctor. He say, she so badly infected that something explode. I don't know.'

'This girl is not very careful,' Yang tried again. 'I think she is the dirty one. She catches things so easily.'

'Easily?' Field showed alarm. 'You mean she has no resistance to disease? We're concerned that AIDS may get into the prostitute population here. I think we'll have to close you down while we check her.'

'No, just the clap! The clap!' Yang rushed out of the room and came back a moment later with a large brown envelope that he forced into Field's hands. 'That's all she's got. Anyway, I don't want her anymore. She's out of here today.' He jabbed at the envelope. 'Look inside.'

Field glanced over the papers. There were hospital reports in Thai and X-rays. The medical terms meant nothing to him. Field handed it all back – but Yang refused to take the package as if the documents themselves were contagious – so he dropped it on a chair.

The girl had been listening in an obsessively careful way, no doubt catching only half of the English. 'I got nowhere.'

'You can have her,' Yang said to Paga, 'or she can go back

to her village. Your family,' he threatened the girl, 'will have to repay me three thousand *baht*.'

'My parents dead.'

'Liar!'

Paga's impatience resurfaced. 'Even so, you never get your money back.'

'How old is she?' Field asked.

'Seventeen,' Yang said bitterly. 'I got her on contract through a village agent three years ago. Twelve thousand *baht*. There's another year to run on the deal. They owe me three thousand.'

Field was beginning to feel a strong dislike for Yang and broke in, 'You make more than that on her in two nights.'

'That has nothing to do with the contract. And she's been sick four months out of the last six. She's always sick, this girl. She's no good.'

Paga shook her head. 'I can't take her. Too young for me. Not enough good experience. If she no have scar maybe I take her for bar girl. That easy job, but no can do with scar. You been to doctor this time, Yang?'

'No. She only told me she was sick yesterday. You took care of her last time so I called you. You take her and I'll give you the contract for two thousand five hundred.'

'So I pay the doctor again. And I put her up while she sick. No deal.'

The girl went down on her knees and raised her hands in prayer to Paga before moaning in a low voice, 'Khun Paga. Khun Paga. Please, Khun Paga.' Her expression of supplication belonged on the stage, which made it somehow even more pathetic.

The effect, however, was to infuriate Paga still more. She was beginning to see the whole visit as an attempt by Yang to trick her into taking on damaged goods. Of course the girl would beg. What else could she do? 'You make her better, Yang. Then we talk.'

'No. I'm going to throw her out if you don't take her.'

'Khun Paga! Khun Paga!'

Yang swung hard at the girl. 'Shut up!'

Field reached out to block the blow, but he was too far away and she managed to dodge the fist herself without lowering her hands from their position of prayer.

'Khun Paga! Khun Paga!'

Paga was on the edge of losing her self control and to avoid this she turned to leave, dragging Field behind her. Once in the hallway, he took a quick look back. The girl had swivelled on her knees as they left so that she was facing the door and still praying – 'Khun Paga!' – although Paga was already out of sight. The girl's eyes, however, did not follow the direction of her body. They were fixed off to the side on Yang's fist, still clenched and slightly raised. Her eyes were filled with terror. They were large and clear and her black hair fell straight to midway down her back.

'I'll buy the contract.' Field didn't realize he had said it until the words came back to him, as if in an echo off the walls of the corridor.

There was a short silence, eventually broken by Paga, still invisible. 'You stupid, Field. She's sick.'

'That doesn't matter.' He walked back into the room and stared at Yang with uncontrolled loathing. 'I want the contract.'

'Idiot!' Paga shouted, coming after him. 'The contract is worth nothing. He says he throws her out. You can take her for free.'

Yang saw suddenly that the *farang* was not a medical inspector, but just another customer. 'No, he has to pay. If he wants her, it's three thousand *baht*.'

'You say two thousand five hundred.'

'For you, Paga. Not for a *farang*. Three thousand for him. This girl is pretty when she isn't sick.'

Field lunged forward and grabbed Yang by his shirt. 'You shut your fucking head! Hear me. Shut it! Now get the contract and her papers. Get them.' He threw the man towards the door and Yang only just managed to catch his balance.

Neither Paga nor Field said a word while they waited. The girl had stopped chanting, although she still knelt with her hands up in prayer, her eyes moving between the man and the woman. Yang reappeared with a second brown envelope, out of which he drew the contract signed between the girl's father and the village agent. At the bottom it had subsequently been countersigned by the agent and by Yang, who now sat down to write an elaborate codicil on the back making her over to Field. This he signed before holding out the pen and the contract. Field scribbled his name on it. Only then did Yang smile. He drew out the girl's identity card and residential registration card. These he offered for inspection from a distance, keeping himself between the door and Field, who pulled out his wallet and counted off three thousand *baht* – one hundred and eleven US dollars, he mentally calculated – which were handed over in return for the cards.

'Get your things,' he said to the girl.

She half crawled out of the room on her knees with her hands still raised in prayer and the other three stood around in silence for five minutes; a silence broken only once, by Yang, who murmured, 'It's a good deal for a *farang*.'

Paga read some sort of threat into this comment, because abruptly she turned on him, 'If you go to the police, Yang, I fix you. OK.' He made no reply. 'OK!' she insisted. His silence began to indicate assent. 'I fix you good,' Paga said with satisfaction. 'Some night when you sleep, one of your girls, she cut your balls off. I fix you that way. Or another. You hear me?'

The girl reappeared with a cheap airline carry-on bag; the sort of thing companies give away. She wore a lime-green cocktail dress with frills around the bottom and had put on lipstick as well as mascara. Field thought the effect grotesque. He hated green at the best of times, but said nothing and snatched up the medical envelope before pushing the girl out ahead of him through the crowd of fifty or so teenagers pressed forward to hear the shouting. He towered over the girls as he made his way through. The two zoo keepers on the first floor watched them go by without curiosity. Field was moving on automatic pilot. In the courtyard Paga caught up and took his arm to stop him.

'Where you want to go, John?'

'I'll take a taxi.' Field pulled away and moved on.

He had no idea.

'See you,' she called after them.

He walked down the lane towards Petchaburi Road, holding the girl firmly by her arm, dragging her along at his speed. Once there, the full humidity and heat struck him at the same moment as the traffic noise and the thick mist of exhaust fumes. Together they all forced him back into the real world. He began to feel an idiot. What had come over him? He looked at the girl. She was grotesque. He hailed a taxi, still uncertain of where to go. The green made her look as sick as she probably was. A doctor. Michael Woodward, he thought. Woodward would still be at his slum clinic down by the port. The taxi driver was hanging his head impatiently out the window.

'Klong Toey,' Field said.

'Eighty *baht*, mister.'

He didn't have the force to negotiate and pushed the girl in ahead of him. Music whined from the radio. 'Headache,' Field complained, pointing to his own head. 'Turn off.' When they were up on the expressway far above the roofs of the city and heading towards the river, he looked at her again. 'What's your name?'

'Ao.'

'Ao,' he repeated.

'Ao,' she confirmed and put her hand out on to his thigh to squeeze his flesh.

He glanced down and noticed how small her fingers were. The nails were dirty beneath the mauve polish. He felt a fishhook pain in his groin and lifted her hand to place it on her own thigh. His gaze turned to the other side where he could watch the tin roofs of the city going by beneath.

CHAPTER 3

The taxi left Field and the girl on a stretch of barren land, down near the port at the edge of the Klong Toey slum. Prolonged gusts of hot wind drove the loose dirt around them into the air. The afternoon rain would come a few minutes behind this agitation and so Field took Ao's arm and dragged her quickly forward on to a wide, raised boardwalk, which snaked out through a mass of wood shacks built over a swamp on the edge of the Chao Phya River that divides Bangkok from Thonburi. The forty thousand poor who lived there were separated from dry land and from a relatively prosperous section of the city by nothing more than a wide road. They lived above an average of half a metre of water and reached their houses across a maze of elevated walkways built, as were the houses, upon a forest of wood stilts.

Field had pulled her on only a few metres before her high heels caught in the crevices between the planks.

'Hey, mister,' she pleaded.

He stopped long enough for her to remove her shoes. Field knew his way vaguely through the maze, which soon degenerated from a surface of solid, wide crossboards into uneven scrapwood with entire planks missing. This and the repetition of identical shacks on all sides meant that the only landmarks were the occasional solid, larger house. It was part of the slum ethos that when one of its own succeeded in life, he didn't necessarily move across the road to the cement Bangkok from which he was both physically and mentally separated. He often chose to stay where he was and to replace his shack with a new wood building balanced on new piles. While elsewhere in the city the resulting house might have appeared less than ordinary, in Klong Toey it was a palace.

Yet even with these markers, Field twice lost his way and had to ask for directions. Each time, he pulled Ao with him off on to a porch. Slum etiquette forbade standing still on the narrow walkways where a traffic jam could build up in seconds. They had been ten minutes winding along into the maze when the rain began, falling straight and intense and soaking them immediately. Field looked around for a porch, but somehow none seemed to suit him and he walked on, increasing his pace. He glanced back to be sure that Ao was keeping up. The rain water had moulded her dress tight to her body and the mascara had run on her face. The girl was so intent on doing what she was told that she betrayed no hint of protest.

The boards were soon slippery as if soaped and Field's own leather-soled shoes began skating from beneath him with each step. He stopped to pull them off, along with his socks, and held them in a bundle covering the girl's two brown envelopes, all of which was clutched up against his stomach to protect the papers as best he could from the rain.

Everyone else had disappeared inside, so that the two walked in isolation, surrounded by silence. The cars and *tuc-tucs* and buses that dominated Bangkok were far away; and quite apart from their absent noise, there was no exhaust. The air was clean and fresh. Curiously enough, the government had sunk septic tanks into the mud so that even the water didn't smell. And although the 40,000 residents did throw their garbage out of their windows, there wasn't much garbage in a slum and anything that might have rotted instead disappeared, probably eaten by fish.

Field found Michael Woodward near the centre of the district in a shack that ran along one side of a small square, itself only partially covered by planks. Even those had been laid in various directions and at various heights. A shop stall spread out across the opposite side and an administrative building closed the far end. The section by which they arrived was open on to lily pads.

Woodward's shack had no front wall – only a grille that was pulled back during the day – and so Field could see before he entered that a crowd of women and children were waiting on the floor, with Woodward in the front corner, his hands moving over a boy's mouth. Any evidence that he might have been an English doctor had disappeared. Instead he wore baggy, black cotton trousers and a loose, collarless, rough shirt. On a table at his side was a round straw hat and a large cloth shoulder bag. On his feet were sandals. This uniform of an upcountry peasant was the one Woodward wore everywhere and always, with the sole exception of inside the Bangkok Nursing Home.

'St Meechai, good afternoon,' Field shouted from the entrance, stopping long enough to run a hand flat over his own hair. The expelled water dripped down his neck. He dropped his shoes on the floor and began brushing the excess liquid off the two envelopes. 'I've brought you a patient.'

Woodward looked up, annoyed. When he saw Field's sodden state this changed to bemused frustration. 'What are you doing here?'

These five words in English caused a sensation among the women crouched on the floor. They had never heard Meechai speak English before.

'I've just told you. I've brought a patient. Where are your friends St Peter and the Virgin Mary?'

Field was referring to an American priest, Father Peter and a Chinese nun, Sister Mary, who had lived and worked in the slum for years. Woodward was the Buddhist newcomer, having been there only eleven years. He noticed Ao, standing behind Field. The high heels in her hand, the heavy mascara, the party dress; all confirmed what she was.

'Bring her to the Home tomorrow morning.'

'Can't.' Field held out the medical envelope. 'She almost died a month ago and she has the same symptoms now. Don't stare at me like that, Dr Meechai, just read the fucking papers.'

Woodward gave the boy he had been examining a pat on the shoulder and told him to wait with the others. He had a cleft palate. The papers inside the envelope were wet but the ink hadn't run. Woodward spread them across the table and read for a few minutes, then he twisted around to wave Ao in from the door, before which she was still waiting, just out of the rain.

'Where did you find her?'

'Chinese hotel off Petchaburi.'

Woodward nodded without comment. He looked again at Ao, now standing close to him. 'They let you take her out of there?'

'I paid,' Field said vaguely.

The doctor thought about that, then waved Ao into a corner where there was a high bed. He unfolded a cheap screen, leaving Field and the crowd of patients on the other side. Field glanced around at the Klong Toey women, all staring at him from the floor. After a time, Woodward and Ao began an inaudible conversation.

'So what's the story, eh?' Field called out.

He was ignored at first, then Woodward's voice came through the cardboard division. 'She had gonorrhoea, probably like you for the nth time. The papers don't say, but probably she had been taking antibiotics for months as a preventative measure, which simply built up a resistance to cure. This particular infection she did not get rid of properly. The germs spread. They got up into her Fallopian tubes and gradually formed a lump – an abscess, if you like. This lump would have been noticeable, at least to her, and the pain would have grown. She probably hid all of that and tried to cure herself. Then the abscess exploded and she had gonorrhoeal peritonitis; like an exploded appendix, only more dangerous and unpleasant. After that the hospital got hold of her somehow, pretty close to death I'd say. Given where you found her, I'm surprised her owners didn't just let her die. The hospital operated, scraped her out and removed the infected tube. I should think the other is as good as sterile after all of this, so it's another victory for our birth control programme. Not a very tidy victory.' He went back to questioning Ao quietly in Thai, then squeezed out around the screen. 'Well, there is no new abscess; at least none yet apparent. I suspect she's simply infected again. Quite badly. Perhaps in the other tube. She says she hasn't had a man since the operation, which is quite plausible. An explosion like that is a nuclear blast. The fallout gets in everywhere, making it pretty hard to find all the infection and clean it out. You bring her to the hospital tomorrow morning when you come in for your shot. I'll take a culture from her then.' Woodward turned away and waved the boy with the cleft palate forward again. When Ao reappeared, Field walked out without a word. He was in the rain before Woodward called after him, apparently as an afterthought, 'Have you gone nuts or something?'

'Me? Why?'

'You seem somewhat, shall I say, preoccupied.'

'Just wet.' Field spread his arms, with his palms up to catch the rain, but stayed out in the open.

'The girl says you bought her contract.'

'So?'

'Isn't that a bit crazy?'

'It was cheap.' When he got no smile, Field added defensively, 'What is this, Meechai's morality play?'

'I'm a doctor. Medicine has to do with bodies, not morality. I know that better than anyone. When I treat all these people,' he nodded at the patients on the floor, 'for nothing, Bangkok says I'm a saint. When I ask out loud why the poor don't have proper medical facilities down here, Bangkok says I'm a communist. No. No. It just seems a bit crazy.'

'I'm in the buying and selling business, Meechai.'

At that Woodward laughed and turned back to the boy with the cleft palate.

The downpour had slowed, but Field seemed intent on not waiting for it to stop and waved at Ao to follow him out on to the plank deck. Although the temperature had dropped, the humidity had risen, as it did after every rain, when steam came off the hot ground and the walls and the roofs. The whole city was transformed into a steam bath. It was curious, he thought, how the moment Woodward changed clothes and left the Nursing Home his English became lean and efficient.

Field lived on *Soi* 53 – Lane 53 – off Sukhumvit Road. It was a small rented house in a compound shared with five other houses. As Sukhumvit compounds went, this one was mediocre verging on rundown. The owner, a Chinese businessman who lived in splendour not far away, didn't waste money on the upkeep of the grounds. There was one ineffective gardener for

46

a space that needed four; the result was overgrown with a hint of jungle. The guardian on the main gate did not glance up when Field and Ao came through. He was busy with a pair of tweezers pulling individual hairs from his chin. Field lived off to the left behind a clump of trees.

The chief attraction of the house lay out of sight on the far side. There, the downstairs room – dining and living room combined – had a long screened wall separated from a canal only by a raised wood porch. Like most of the *klongs* in Bangkok, this one was now cut off from the main water system and therefore lay picturesque but stagnant, a breeding ground for water lilies and mosquitoes – more the latter than the former. Upstairs there were two bedrooms and a bathroom. Outside, beside the small rear entrance, was a little hut that constituted the servants' quarters. For most of the fifteen years Field had lived in this place, the quarters had been empty.

He had lived with a series of girls, each of them freshly arrived in Bangkok from villages, like all the girls who made up the city's marginal night life. If they were up to it, he also used them as cooks and laundry maids. This wasn't avarice on his part. After all, a maid could be had for forty dollars a month. But Field detested having to deal with servants. He found it difficult enough dealing with the girls who shared his bed. For a *farang* to live in such simplicity was considered unusual, if not unsavoury.

When Field had thrown his last girl out a month before, he had turned to an old woman who over the years had periodically done his laundry and could also cook decent Thai food. This time he had asked her to move in as housekeeper. He had agreed reluctantly to her bringing along a grandson, twenty years old, who was to act as night watchman. That cost a further twenty-five dollars.

Ceding to the need for paid help had struck him at the time as a giant step towards respectability, the last thing he was after. However the old woman had proved herself so untidy and undisciplined that his life became, if anything, more disordered than before.

The one miracle in all of this was that he continued to manage, as he had always managed, to leave his house every day neatly dressed in a style that might be called soft and clean; which was far more than most *farangs* were able to do despite their servants. But then they weren't truly happy in the tepid, polluted atmosphere of Bangkok. They crept from air conditioned rooms to air conditioned cars and the moment the real air got a chance to strike them, they and their polyester sweated, wilted and crumpled.

Field's obsession with his own cleanliness was inherited from his late-Depression childhood, when shined shoes and looking better off than you really were was at the heart of moral survival. It didn't bother him that this external rectitude stood in direct contradiction to his belief that overheated, exhaust ridden air was a form of perfume. In fact, he appeared to draw great pleasure from the contradiction.

He sloughed his wet shoes off beside a row of other shoes outside on the rear porch and banged the screen door open.

'Cook!'

No one came. He stamped about, throwing his soaked shirt into a corner of the kitchen alcove, then yanking open the fridge. He grabbed a beer and held out a Coke to Ao, who had come into the room almost on her toes and was looking furtively around. She accepted the bottle only to clutch it without taking a drink. Instead she began to creep from object to object, examining everything in the house. There was nothing in particular to see, but she opened each drawer in the little kitchen, looked into the cupboard in the dining room, took out a plate to examine it, put the plate back, went over to the living room area where four cane chairs with leather cushions were the only decoration apart from two walls of disordered bookcases. She pulled out a few books and examined them. On one of the shelves there was a black and white photograph of Field's father as a young man in railway gear, standing with the Rocky Mountains behind him. In the bottom corner a careful hand had printed – 'Banff 1928'. The photo was in a Thai frame, black and baroque. Field himself had never been west and he kept the image as much for the mountains as for his father. Ao picked it up and examined the subject. There was a path of wet footprints behind her. At the bottom of the stairs she stopped and turned to Field, who was watching her while he drank from his bottle of beer.

'Me go upstairs?'

'Go on.'

She disappeared with her carry-on bag. Field shoved open one of the large screen doors and dragged a chair from the dining table outside on to the main raised porch, which was covered but without any walls. There he slouched down and stared at the *klong*, covered by water lilies. It was beautiful, he thought. His eyes wandered up among the trees. They were no longer in flower. Earlier in the year they had been covered in white and red blossoms. He saw a white squirrel jumping from one branch to another. A family of them lived in the garden but he rarely caught a glimpse of them. Perhaps this sudden appearance was a good luck sign, like the King and his white elephants. Perhaps the gods were commenting on his purchase of Ao. He slouched lower. Why did he do such stupid things? He listened to the noise of Bangkok across the garden. The long squeak of a pile driver being raised not far away forced itself through the other sounds. Then it was silent, then came the soft thud of its impact in the mud. Various radios were playing. *Forever Starts Tonight* floated over before being swallowed up in an incomprehensible maze of songs. Voices came from the other side of the *klong*, voices invisible behind trees and garden walls of woven bamboo. Beyond it all was the uneven vibration of traffic and the branches of palm trees scraping in the wind. He sipped his beer unconsciously and fell slowly into a stupor until, with the falling light, the layers of noise began to peel away. Suddenly the mosquitoes were louder than all else and he got up to go inside.

Ao was crouched upon a living room chair, waiting. How long she had been there he didn't know. She had combed her hair, reapplied her make-up and wore the brown sarong. Without the cocktail dress, her make-up appeared even more incongruous. He looked down at her. She had probably been brought straight from her village to the brothel. This was, no doubt, the first modern house she had seen. She probably thought it was quite a grand place. If only she knew, Field thought. She smiled at him. He turned away and climbed the stairs to his room. Her airline bag was by his bed. Its contents were laid out on a table.

'Ao!' he shouted.

She came running up the stairs. When she was there, he took the bag and some of the make-up tubes and carried them through to the other bedroom. She followed.

'You sleep here. OK.'

'OK.' There was no expression on her face.

'OK?' he repeated.

'OK,' she agreed.

'John.'

'OK, John.' She gave him another smile. It was very large and tinged with shyness.

Why not, he thought. She doesn't know anything about anything except sex and getting sick. Why shouldn't she be shy? Most people seemed to think that knowing about sex made you worldly. That was crazy. Knowing about money made you worldly. And knowing about people with their secrets and obsessions. But sex. Sex was about as worldly as plumbing. He smiled in return and hers grew still larger. It was a pretty smile. The lips drew back full and soft across the slightly irregular teeth. She giggled and cupped a hand over her mouth. He went off to have a shower.

Before Field left the house that evening he gave the cook a lecture: Ao was both sick and a child. She was to be treated that way; firmly, but with kindness. She was not to be allowed out of the compound unaccompanied and was to stop wearing make-up. Field told her to take the girl early the next morning to buy two simple blouses and skirts, plus a couple of sarongs for indoors. Finally, he said that if her grandson came within three feet of the girl, he would personally beat the boy until he was maimed for life, in particular his reproductive organs. This last detail caught the cook's attention. Then he went out on to the road and took a taxi to Amara's house in Huamok, a new area to the north-east of Bangkok.

That part of the city was built on particularly low land and was therefore mosquito infested in the dry months and flooded in the wet. Why a whole section of the Thai rich had chosen to build elaborate compounds out there was an ongoing mystery.

Amara was a perfect example of this syndrome. She and her husband had come back, respectively, from finishing school in Switzerland and from Oxford, nineteen years earlier and had married. Both had been away from the country over eight years without a single visit home. Theirs was quite a common story among the upper classes. Amara came out of the greatest non-royal family in Thailand and her husband, Tanun, out of a close runner up. On both sides there had been endless regents, chancellors and generals, stretching back into the past. Tanun went into the Foreign Office.

They announced to their friends that they were going to live Thai-style. No one was doing that at the time. They took a piece of land they already owned out at Huamok, then but a stretch of rice paddies, and began combing the countryside for old raised wood houses with beautiful roofs and interesting carving. These they bought whenever possible and had carted back to Huamok to be reassembled and fitted together beside a *klong* in an enclosed pattern with a great raised deck built to join them all. In the heat of the day everyone retreated to the open ground floor beneath the deck.

Very quickly Tanun lost interest in his work. After a few years he resigned, saying he saw no reason to leave a perfect house in order to spend the day either in traffic or bored. Instead he concentrated on his real interest, which was jazz piano. He played well and he collected every record, tape and film that existed of the great jazz men. His days were devoted to playing or listening. As for Amara, she enjoyed her life in every detail more than anyone Field knew.

Field had met her not long after her marriage and they had become great friends; particularly after Amara discovered that a little girl called Songlin Prapanya, who had started going to Mater Dei School at the same time as her own daughter, was in fact Field's child. A lot of people in Bangkok knew this, but said nothing to him. They saved it for gossip among themselves. Amara had immediately cornered Field and he had admitted that he supported the mother and the child without legally recognizing them.

'I've seen the woman,' Amara insisted. 'She fetches your child every day. A real bitch, I'd say. Ahha! What's the point

51

in sending the girl to Mater Dei and leaving her in the hands of a woman who picks her teeth and scratches herself . . . well. The schoolchildren will make fun of your poor girl. You listen, she will be very unhappy.'

Once a week Field saw his daughter and he was forced to admit that the child was suffering. No one wanted to know her. She did everything wrong except her lessons and her mother couldn't understand what the problem was, let alone explain it to her daughter. All she could contribute was affection. Field was forced to admit that the affection was genuine. Why wouldn't it have been? The fact that without the child there would not have been the money didn't necessarily disqualify her emotion. Eventually even she had to recognize that something was wrong. Six weeks later Songlin went to stay for the rest of the year in Amara's house. She became the greatest friend of Amara's daughter, Dang, and spent close to seven years out of the next thirteen living there. But then the daughter was sent off to school in England, while Songlin stayed on in Bangkok for university.

Field was the last to arrive. There were already twenty or so people lounging around the raised deck on low cushioned tables. Amara grabbed him as he came up.

'Later than a Thai!' She let out a small raucous laugh. 'We'll have a funny dinner tonight. Take vodka. Go on.'

She always reminded him of a highly elegant but plump little buddha, with her thick black hair combed straight down when she was at home. He looked across the deck. Tanun was on the far side playing the piano that had to be dragged out for every party. His audience was gathered on a low Thai table before him. Nestled among the guests on each of the other five tables were large lacquer bowls filled with grey, oily caviare. And beside each, a large spray tin of insect repellent. The mosquitoes were already thick.

'What's this?' Field was looking at the caviare.

'Oh, so funny. So funny. Ahha! Here, vodka.' She topped up his glass. 'I have a friend in customs. You know all these Iranians are not allowed to take money out of their country. Oh no! So they bring caviare with them to sell. Like gold, you see. I said to my friend: you should confiscate some of that at customs. We'll have a party. Ahha! He overdid it.'

It was a perfect Bangkok story. Ten pounds of confiscated caviare. He took the vodka and glanced around. Tanun's audience was made up of a half-dozen well born Thai homosexuals who were joking and laughing as much as listening. Their studs had been brought along, but not introduced, and were seated on the floor along a wall whispering to each other and eating as much as they could. Most of them had shaved heads. Their clothes were cut to reveal muscles, while the fashionable queens who had brought them were swathed in baggy folds of linen and silk, as the Italian and/or Japanese designers dictated. One woman lay curled up in their midst being made a fuss of. Someone was stroking her hair. She lay like a true queen among her jesters.

'Who's that?' Field asked.

'General Krit's wife.'

'Krit!'

One of the queens shouted, 'What do you call a Thai queer who has AIDS?'

'A tied bannedaid!'

'You've heard it.'

Field turned away from the laughter. 'Is Krit here? Where?'

Amara nodded at a table where only two men lay.

'What the fuck is he doing here? Since when do you go in for power hedonists?'

'Ahha,' Amara laughed and cupped a hand over her mouth. 'Booboo. Is that right? You two don't go together?'

'That's it. I used to say things about him. On paper. For publication.'

'Things? Oh! True things? Oh! Booboo. Here, you come over with the boys.' She meant the clutch of homosexuals. 'He won't see you.'

'No. No. Why's he here?'

'This district is on low land. Right, Johnny boy? First place to flood. Right? General Krit has made a big statement. He's going to make sure the flood doesn't flood. He's going to make the controls work.'

'He said that?'

'Oh yes.'

'He's crazy. Nothing's been done and we've got a month to go.'

'Sure. But he has political power and he has pumps. Lots of power and lots of pumps. Thousands of them, but not enough for the city. So if they're going to pump out one part of Bangkok, it better be this part. Ahha! How is Songlin?'

'She loves university.'

'Why doesn't she come to stay with me? Dang doesn't need to be here at the same time. Songlin's my daughter too. You tell her. Come live here for a while.'

Field nodded, but his mind was on Krit, lying there unprotected for anyone who wished to cross-examine him, anyone who was still in the cross-examining business.

'Hey, Johnny boy, listen.' Amara pulled him close to her. 'Why not send Songlin to university with Dang? That would be better.'

'I've told you, she's Thai. I don't want her mixed up.' He pointed over at Amara's husband. 'Look at Tanun playing Fats Waller instead of working. If he's confused, think what would happen to a half-breed like Songlin.'

'She told me you won't let her learn English.'

'When did she tell you that?'

'Last week.'

'She comes to see you then. She doesn't come to see me.'

'That, Johnny boy, is because you visit her once a week. Ahha! Her allotted time. She's afraid to come to see you.'

Field rolled his eyes with disgust and refilled his glass. He was upset at the truth in the statement, not the falsehood. He had always seen her once a week, on his own terms. He had arranged things that way. 'It doesn't mean I love her less.'

'Come on over here. Eat some caviare.'

'She doesn't need to learn English,' Field protested. 'She's Thai.'

'Every other student except her is learning it.'

'Later, maybe. I don't want her confused. I don't want her getting any ideas.'

'No ideas! Ahha! No ideas.'

Field nodded again, then walked across to where Krit lay

and threw himself on the table beside the general. 'Hi there!' He pulled himself half up on to a hard triangular cushion.

Krit was in the midst of what sounded like a long exposé to a *farang* Field didn't know. There were always some foreigners at Amara's parties, but they were usually old Bangkok residents; more Thai than foreign. This Englishman looked resentfully at Field, who ignored the stare and repeated,

'Hi. Great to see you, General.'

Krit's attention gradually focused on Field. It was a curious but distrustful look. His eyes burnt from a combination of drink and ambition. There was a double brandy and soda in his hand. Until six months before, the General had been commanding the Mae Hong Son region up north on the Burmese border. This had been a form of political exile from Bangkok; punishment for the minor part he had played in an attempted coup. He had used this exile and the access it gave him to the border smuggling trade as an opportunity to build up his fortune. Then, quite abruptly, a delicate power struggle between two classes of officers in Bangkok had produced a miracle: the two groups were made up of graduates from two separate years at the military academy and each wanted one of their own as the new commander of the 1st Division; a key post because power lay in Bangkok and the 1st Division controlled the city. Rather than one side or the other ceding, the officers decided to give it to an outsider. Krit was considered a loner, with more friends in the opium armies than in his own. Suddenly he was recalled, promoted and appointed and there he was, back in the centre of the world. Not only that, his fortune now permitted him to enjoy himself. It wasn't enough to make him really rich, but it was enough. And money plus power equals more money; in six months he and his Chinese Thai advisers had got him on to a dozen boards and helped him to manipulate his contract issuing responsibilities to enrich those same companies. The crevices of disappointment, that had cut across his smooth skin when he was first sent into exile, had now softened and spread gradually over his face, giving him the appearance of an old, worn but relatively wise statesman. In fact, he was only in his mid fifties. The climb had been rough; that was what went through Field's mind.

'I believe I do know you. But forgive me. In this light.' He made an elegant gesture towards the candles spread around the wood deck.

'John Field.'

The beginnings of alarm appeared on the General's face.

'Ex-journalist,' Field added.

Krit repeated, 'Ex-journalist.'

They stared at each other while the General recovered his composure.

'You are no longer writing?'

'I'm in business,' Field replied. 'Like you.'

'Mr Field! Mr Field!' Krit was suddenly jovial. 'You do not write perhaps. But you do not change. Always very provocative. I am delighted to see you.' He seemed genuinely delighted. 'Old enemies make good friends. Isn't that right? Maybe we can do some business together. What do you think?'

'Great.' It was impossible to know what Field meant.

'And this is Mr George Espoir. He is here to research a book. He has been interrogating me about the border.'

Espoir smiled, picked up the can of mosquito deterrent on the table and sprayed his ankles, arms and neck. Only then did he nod at Field, as if to say, of course you know who I am. He was right. Field did, although he never read novels. He could even, with a little effort, have dredged up the man's real name; the one he didn't sign his novels with. The expression of serious self contentment on Espoir's face stopped Field from betraying any sign of recognition. Instead he picked up the can of insect spray and made as if to put a protective coat over the caviare. General Krit chuckled. The deck was ringed with dozens of smoking coils and still the mosquitoes circled thick around the tables.

The General pointed at the tin. 'This country's safety is as delicate a matter as the safety of your ankles, Mr Espoir.' He turned to Field. 'I have been attempting to explain to our friend here that while there is a genuine humanitarian problem on the border, nevertheless all these Cambodian refugees are but a footnote to what is really going on. And if westerners concentrate only on helping the refugees and forget that Thailand itself is at stake, plus the stability of the whole area and so much more, then we are all lost.'

'I'd go along with that,' Field said.

'Really?' the General exclaimed. He looked more carefully at Field. 'Really?'

'Sure. Half the people in Cambodia and South Vietnam want to leave. So who's going to take them? And why should the West take them, say, instead of Czechs or Poles or Ugandans or Ethiopians? So if no one takes them, you end up with X million refugees in Thailand, then the Viets come charging in here because the refugees are harbouring guerrillas. Right now you've got a recipe for disaster. And I happen to like living in Thailand. I don't want the Viets charging across the border. I don't want tanks on Sukhumvit. So everyone fucked up Vietnam, Cambodia, Laos. Doesn't mean we've got to go right on and fuck up Thailand.'

The General nodded. 'You see, Mr Espoir?'

'Of course. I appreciate the political problems are complex,' Espoir said kindly. 'Very complex, no doubt. But the human problem. Well, it seems to me we must never forget the human problem. Yesterday I toured a border camp. I found it very humbling.'

'That's an interesting reaction.'

'I'm sorry?' Espoir was trying to guess Field's meaning.

'Humbling,' Field insisted. 'What exactly does that mean?'

'Well, to see such massive human tragedy, it brought home to me the fragility of our own . . .'

'Sure,' Field cut in. 'Only, to be humble is to be in a certain state, Mr Espoir. Low self esteem. No self importance. Modest pretensions. The noun implies action; constant action in order to remain humble. Does this mean you've decided to give up the way of life of a successful novelist?' Field regretted immediately that he had shown recognition.

Espoir maintained his kind smile. 'There are contradictions in any life.'

'So you plan to devote yours to changing the Western world?'

'I'll certainly be writing about the refugees.'

'Yeah. We've all done that. Big deal.'

Espoir began to lose his calm. 'I'm describing to you an honest, emotional reaction before a massive human tragedy.'

'Sure. So, by humbling you mean you suffered a temporary, superficial shock; what we might call a facile and self satisfying emotion. Right?' Field felt the silence around him. He didn't know what had made him lose control. The man was annoying, but that wasn't reason enough. He got up. 'Words don't mean their opposites, eh. If you don't mind, General, I'll go dance with your wife.'

'Go on, Mr Field.'

'We'll do business, right?'

'Big business, Mr Field.'

He walked away, conscious that he had made a fool of himself and yet almost turned back to ask Espoir why he'd changed his name. Was the implication that he had hope? Or did he see himself as the hope for others? Field forced himself to keep on walking.

Mrs Krit was dancing with one of the well dressed queens to Tanun's version of a Duke Ellington tune. Field cut in and held her firmly, yet at a distance. He didn't say a word, but he danced very well and stared into her eyes the whole time. She showed disappointment when at the end of the song he handed her back to the lighter-handed homosexual. Field blew her a kiss and went off to fill a whisky glass with vodka. Amara came up behind him.

'Make friends with the General?'

'Buddies.' He nodded towards Mrs Krit. 'I danced with the girl who danced with the man – she must have, she's married to him – who's danced with half the crooks and drug dealers in Asia.'

'Ahha! And Espoir. He could write good things about Thailand. Think how many people read him.'

'Great.'

'You liked him?'

'It was a humbling experience.' Field's glass was half empty. He filled it again. Then he remembered Woodward had told him not to drink. Well, it was too late for that particular evening. He put his arm around Amara and began to dance with her.

'How is your friend Meechai?' she asked.

'Still slumming it.'

'Ahha! I hear that from his sisters.'

'You don't approve?'

'I think his sisters don't. Or maybe it's their husbands. They think he's crazy, walking around Bangkok like a peasant.'

'Walking for a start.'

'Ahha! Ahha! That's the worst part. His wife has the car and driver! He walks!'

'And what do you think, Amara?'

A little smile crept over her lips. 'For a Thai male, he's missing the boat. If he wants to be a good man, loved by the people, he should become a monk and give up everything. Otherwise he should make money and go with the girls like the rest of them. Ahha! He thinks he has invented a third way or something.'

Field danced faster, holding her in a hard grip, then abruptly stopped.

'Something wrong, John?'

'No. No. I'm just an idiot.'

He was unsteady by the time the evening ended. Espoir appeared from somewhere and offered him a ride in a hotel car that had been waiting below. White with smoked glass windows.

Field flopped on to the rear seat. 'Royalties pay for the driver?'

'That's it.'

They were silent for twenty minutes as they threaded their way back. Then Espoir said, 'I like Amara.'

'She's great.'

'I mean, beneath her social number, there's quite a bit of substance. She told me all about you. You know, I want to write something visceral about this place. I want to get to the heart of it. You're the kind of person who could steer me in the right direction. Would you mind if I picked your brains?'

'Not tonight.'

'Lunch tomorrow?'

'I've got a full week. Call me after the weekend.' Field didn't mention that he would be in Laos by then.

'I'll get your number from Amara.'

'Great.'

Field stumbled into his house and switched on the lights downstairs. The first thing he saw was two brown envelopes on the dining table. He went over and held one up, upside down. Ao's ID card, House Registration and his contract purchasing her services, herself in fact, fell on to the table. He examined the House Registration. Hers was individual. She was listed as the head of the household and sole occupant of apartment 212 in building 13 on Soi 37; where he had found her. He supposed that the single registration was useful because it meant a girl could be transferred anywhere without anyone else being involved. He picked up the contract and read it through. The money had been paid to the parents at the calculated equivalent of four years labour on the family farm. He could send her home. What for? She would simply drift back to town. He began to rip the contract in half, then stopped himself. He replaced the three documents in their envelope and slipped it into a drawer in the living room, along with the records of her medical disasters.

Then he pulled himself up the stairs and stripped, except for his underwear, switched on the ceiling fan and fell asleep.

Something woke him later in the night. He slowly realized that his left hand was cupped around a small, firm breast. A back was curled in against his stomach and groin. It was the erection that had woken him. He listened for a moment to the soft breathing of the sleeping girl.

'Ao, get out! Get out!' He pushed her away with his hands and feet. 'Get out!'

She disappeared into the darkness without a sound. There was a dull light beyond the screens and steel grilles on the seven windows that ran around two sides of his bedroom. Field lay still tracing the outline of the palm trees and banana trees on the horizon until he fell asleep. In the morning he found her wrapped up in a sheet and sleeping on the floor beside his bed.

CHAPTER 4

They arrived at the Nursing Home early enough to see Michael Woodward climb up the stairs in his peasant outfit and disappear to change. He kept five suits on the spot and all the shirts and socks he needed. A hospital maid was tipped to make sure everything stayed clean and crisp.

Field didn't particularly want to hang around in the waiting room to be observed by the other *farang* patients who had begun trickling in and sat moving their eyes from Field to Ao and back. She was now dressed in a white cotton blouse and a navy blue skirt. Without make-up she looked like a student. Not a brilliant student. No. Probably not even a smart one. No. But there was a certain dignity. Unfortunately the cook had followed his instructions precisely and, as he had not mentioned footwear, the cook had not bought the girl any plain, flat shoes. The first thing the *farangs* noticed were her pink spike high heels. In truth, Field paid little attention. His mind was on his groin. Clearly whatever good the antibiotics might have been doing had been negated or made worse by an evening on beer and vodka. He decided not to mention this lapse to Woodward.

Ao was called in first and kept for close to half an hour. Field then insisted that she stay in the office while he was given his shot.

'I don't want those creeps out there ogling her.'

Woodward made no comment. 'I've taken the culture and given her some kanamycin. However I fear, my friend, that she has more than a prolonged case of gonorrhoea. I would say there is also some chlamydia, some vaginal warts and some-

61

thing else. Very difficult, as you know, to sort it all out at once. Perhaps the unknown element is just a little thing. Next week we'll know better.' He said nothing about Field's increased discharge, except to remind him to get to bed early and not to drink. 'And for God's sake, don't touch this girl. She's a walking textbook of communicable diseases. A veritable Turkish cocktail.'

'What?'

'Balkan wars. The infidels sent girls in her state across the lines to run amok with Serbian morale.'

Not quite grasping what was said, Ao looked up with an angelic expression.

'I'm not crazy, Michael.'

'That would depend on how you define the word.'

When they were outside, in the Nursing Home's garden, Ao took hold of Field's arm with a warm squeeze. 'You buy me drink, John?'

'Sure.'

They walked over to Silom Road, where the *Saigon Bakery – Vietnamese Food and World Famous French Pastry* lay behind a jumble of caved-in pavement and a particularly high flood barrier. The Saigon Bakery was French Indo-China's principal contribution to Bangkok, despite its Vietnamese owners. Field chose a table near the window and made her drink a fresh mandarin juice rather than a Coke, which was what she wanted. Then he ordered two coconut tarts, because he considered them to be the best coconut tarts in the world; better than anything in Hong Kong or even in Saigon in its hey-day. They sat in silence, watching the nuns and priests and old Bangkok residents come slipping in to buy large rectangular loaves of bread so white they would have shamed South Africa. He was quite used to sitting for hours in silence with these girls. He enjoyed it. Their English was invariably bad, worse even than his Thai. Besides, there wasn't much to be said. There were no ideas to exchange, few emotions to share in the Western sense and Field wasn't big on small talk.

Instead he let his gaze follow the owner's son, a wafer thin, nervous boy who passed through from the back to the front and went out on to the pavement. His left hand was arched with the fingers pressed tight against each other. The right hand held a light straw broom with which he began to sweep the filth and dust in front of the bakery from each of the shattered slabs of upheaved pavement. His sweeping pattern was extremely intricate. The aim was to make the dust fall into the crevices between the slabs and not into the street.

Field bought her a second juice, then led the way over the swept pavement outside and hailed a taxi to Catherine Laker's office, where he was to leave his passport for the Lao visa. Mrs Norman Laker, as she thought of herself, lived and worked in a three acre compound half-way along Sathorn Avenue, which had once been a major canal and was now a large open sewer that separated three lanes of traffic running up the right side from three more down the left. A high colonial villa sat at the centre of her compound, with the East-West Trading Company functioning inside. Its exterior had been painted so often that the arches and shutters shone in a pulpy way beneath the sun. The garden was used for storing material, which meant that the house was surrounded by hundreds of tractors and graders and various bits of railway equipment. At the back of the compound, behind this forest of machinery, there was a high cement wall built in a small square. On top of the wall there was broken glass and exposed electric wires. The only opening was a single steel door. Inside, according to conjecture, because no one had seen it, Mrs Laker lived in a three room fortress. This involved another set of thick cement walls without windows and a generator on the roof to keep the air conditioning going in case the town electrical grid failed. She lived there with one elderly female servant. No one knew what she did with her spare time. Certainly she never appeared in Bangkok society, either Thai or *farang*. As for the colonial villa, it had been completely transformed inside so that the eccentric wood rooms now resembled those of an antiseptic Holiday Inn. Mrs Laker was careful about her health and therefore her surroundings. Infection was something which she imagined to be hiding in wait in the most unexpected of corners.

It was always difficult, when looking at this compound — sterilized indoors and a mess outside — to credit the rumour all Bangkok believed: that she had been the mistress of the CIA director for South Asia during the Vietnam war and had first built up her capital by letting him use the trading company to launder the Agency's funds. It was nevertheless a rumour with a long life. In general Mrs Laker did not appear from within her fortress until much later in the morning, so Field was able to simply drop off his passport and leave.

That night he again awoke to find Ao curled up beside him. Field switched on the light. It was three a.m. She had put a sheet over herself, but the heat of the night had made her throw it half off; that and no doubt the heat from his body. Normally he didn't sweat. It was almost as if he weren't a *farang*. But his body was dripping. He wiped his face and chest with her sheet. She had a narrow, elongated back. Sleeping as she was on her side, the small shoulder blades stuck out slightly. Her hair had fallen in disarray and was partially caught under her neck. He reached out to straighten it.

She rolled over on to her back and opened her eyes. He looked away from her breasts and stretched stomach.

'What are you doing in here, Ao?'

'I never sleep alone, John. Lonely.'

'There was always a man?'

'No. They never stay night. Girls sleep together because unhappy. No family.'

'All of you?'

At this she sprang up and sat with her legs to one side. 'I have my friend, John. I don't do anything with her. You know. I don't like that, but we sleep together. She one year older. Went away to Tokyo. She work there.'

'Doing what?'

'I no tell you. That a freecrit.'

'A secret.'

Ao nodded. Then she looked at Field, examining him in a clinical way. When she got down to his thighs she put out a hand to grasp one. 'You not too difficult for work. Some men so fat they have thighs like tree trunks. Very difficult for massage.'

'I'm not fat.'

She ran her hand over his chest. 'Strong man.'

64

Field felt desire stirring beneath the pain and removed her hand. 'You're sick, Ao, I'm sick. No sex.'

'Oh no, John!' She laughed with pleasure. 'I no want sex. Just lonely.'

'Great,' Field said in a sour tone. 'Then cover yourself.' He pulled the sheet up over her waist.

She slapped his wrist with a little scream of laughter. 'No look, John. No look. I know men. If they look, they want to touch. First time I fourteen.'

'Where was that?'

'Hotel. You find me there. You meet Yang. His father test girls. Fat man, John. He tell me lie on bed.' Her eyes grew large with the pleasure of telling the story. 'He take off his clothes. I just look at his big stomach hanging down and cock sticking out. Not big cock but seem big then. I just look. Then I lie there.' She threw herself down on the bed simulating her petrified position. 'No move. Too scared. Just lie there shaking.' She sat up with a smile. 'Not too bad. He expert on new girl. He tell me, not worry.'

'He would.'

Ao slapped his chest with pleasure. 'All cock same. Plop. Plop. In, out. Easy job.' She pushed Field. 'Lie on stomach.' He did as he was told and she began running her knuckle down his spine, then stopped half-way and with her thumb and finger yanked the skin out. 'Oh! No good.' She started over, running her knuckle down and yanked the skin out again. 'No good. Should go quack.'

'There's not much duck in me.'

She laughed and fell on him to pull his ears. Field had to push her away and arrange the sheet over himself. He let her spend the night on the floor again and the next day told the old woman to drag a mattress in. That afternoon he went off to the university to meet his daughter. Songlin was half-way through her first semester and yet this was the first time he had gone to see her on campus. He walked in through the small maze of streets off Rama IV and found her where they had agreed to meet — at the outdoor bar just within the university wall. Under a cluster of high trees there were twenty or so tables and a cart selling drinks.

She put her hands up, palms pressed together, as a Westerner would to pray, and bowed slightly. He returned the greeting. This *wai* was held to by both as a formal limit on their intimacy. They walked on through the grounds, with Field lagging slightly behind to get a good look at her. He found each time that she had become increasingly Thai, and yet not like her mother, which relieved him. He couldn't in all honesty say she was beautiful, but it seemed to him that she wasn't far from being beautiful. Dressed as all the girls on the campus were, in their uniforms of white blouses and blue skirts, it was hard to guess what she or they might turn into, except that Songlin always struck him as very much alive and curious and shy and all sorts of other things which made him feel better about himself for a few days after each meeting. Because he had forbade her to learn English, they were obliged to speak to each other in Thai, which put her automatically in a superior position. He didn't mind. It made him feel he had succeeded even by his own minor definition of the father's role. He noticed that she was not wearing black shoes, but white, the mark of a first year student.

Songlin had promised to show him her lecture halls. Instead she apologized and led him away towards the centre of the campus. 'I want to hear someone talk.'

'Who?'

'You probably wouldn't know. He's a Buddhist teacher.'

Field followed obediently. 'Amara wants you to go to stay,' he said. 'I think she's lonely without Dang there. It would be a nice thing to do.'

'Then mummy would be lonely.'

Field began to say something, but stopped himself.

'I would like to go.' She looked over at Field. 'Funny that I have two mothers.' She probably meant – 'and no father'.

Field ignored the suggestion. 'You might go for a short time.'

'All right. Sometime soon. What did you do this week?'

He had always told her about his comings and goings and while he was still a journalist there had been lots of stories to amuse her with. Now he was hard pushed to come up with something. He thought of Ao. What would Songlin think if he told her about that? Probably she wouldn't believe him. He looked at her again. The first change he had made in Ao was to dress her in very much the same uniform. What did the uniform mean? Ao knew nothing and everything. Songlin knew everything and nothing, or he hoped she did. He looked around at the students they were passing through.

'The boys don't wear uniforms any more.'

'Oh no. They come as they like and lots of them have cars.'

Field nodded. 'I'm going to Laos on Monday.'

'What for?'

'Just business. I guess it will be fun to see how everything has changed since '75.'

Ahead of them, beneath the shade of trees, a crowd of students blocked the way. The closer Field came, the larger the crowd seemed. Five hundred or so. The sound of a man's voice had been drifting over the grounds through a crude loudspeaker system for the last few minutes. Suddenly Field realized that the figure up on the steps of the Student Union Building, dressed in peasant's gear and wearing a round straw hat, was Michael Woodward.

'Don't tell me he's handing out his condoms here.'

'Oh, no. They wouldn't allow him to talk about birth control on the campus. Dr Meechai is speaking about Buddhism in a modern society.' Songlin's words were filled with admiration.

Field towered over the students so that even standing at the back he knew he would be noticed.

The phrases came out of Woodward's mouth in a quiet, almost whispered tone, with hardly a gesture to prove he was alive. 'Economists see development in terms of increasing the value of currency and all that is related to currency; thus fostering greed. Politicians see development in terms of increasing power, thus fostering ill-will. Together they measure results in terms of quantity, thus fostering ignorance. What are greed, ill-will and ignorance? They are the Buddhist triad of evils.' The delivery style alone was an illustration of Buddhist humility. Field thought of Espoir and his stagey humble pie. 'They would say I am not modern. But what is that? If modern means good, then it must be good for us. If modern means bad, then why would we want it? How do we make certain that it is good? By using it in our own interests. We must adapt it to our way. The Buddhist way. The Thai way. Westerners look down on a system that provides neither incentives to buy foreign goods nor is anxious to exploit natural resources to the maximum. Is that our problem? Why should our system do either? What is good in these notions? What makes these the criteria of modernism?'

Somewhere in the audience a voice called out, 'Dr Meechai, does that mean we must all dress like peasants?'

There was an embarrassed twittering.

Woodward dug his hands into the belt of his trousers and pulled it out like a clown. 'In twenty years I've seen the whole world come to wear western clothing. What is the result? Millions of constricted, hot crotches.'

The twittering turned into a wave of laughter.

'I am not allowed to talk about sex here, but I can tell you as a doctor, constriction is unhealthy.'

They laughed again, all constricted as the boys were.

Field pulled Songlin away. 'I hear enough of him. I'd rather talk to you.'

'You know Dr Meechai?' Songlin was amazed.

Field suddenly realized he had only ever mentioned Woodward by his English name. 'He's a good friend. Tell me what they're teaching you.' He had never been to university and so his curiosity was quite genuine.

They walked back down to the bar near the gate through which he had come in and there sat at a table. Field bought two soft drinks. The sun played through the trees on to Songlin's face so that he couldn't take his eyes away as she talked. He could scarcely listen, so great was the delight he felt in looking at her. Thai though she was, he could see hints of himself in her expression.

'Why don't you let your hair grow?'

She stopped in surprise and ran a hand through her short, Europeanized cut. 'Only peasants wear their hair long.' It was said without prejudice.

'Still, it would look nice.'

She appeared both embarrassed and pleased at the attention. As for Field, he was blushing, because he realized that he was accustomed to long hair on the bar girls, all of them peasants.

They had been there some time when Woodward came by with a small group of students escorting him. He saw Field and stopped to call out in Thai, 'You didn't stay for the end.'

Field shrugged. 'Come and meet my daughter.'

Woodward lost his teacher's pose and came to life, springing forward. 'I've heard about you for years, but your father keeps you hidden.' He turned back to the student delegation and thanked them, saying he would go the rest of the way on his own, then he sat down with Field and Songlin and whispered to her, 'I think he loves you too much.' She blushed. 'But then he is an impossible man.'

Songlin fell silent in respect, an attitude she had never adopted towards her father and which he had not encouraged. But now she waited, as if expecting Woodward to do all the talking and Field was amazed to see how his friend managed to accept adulation with modesty.

Later the two men left Songlin and walked down to Rama IV. As soon as she was out of hearing, Woodward said in English, 'What did you think of my talk? You haven't mentioned it.'

'What do you want me to say?'

'You usually have an opinion on everything.'

'Sure. If you want to get the back of your head blown off, you're going about it the right way.'

'Really? I'm just talking religion.'

'I may be without purpose in life, Michael, but I'm not naïve. Don't tell me you are more of a child than your audience.'

'I don't follow.'

'No? Listen. Minister to the slum dwellers if you want. No one cares about them. But leave the students alone. The people you hate are terrified of the universities. Terrified. Because they would have to shoot their own children if the students rose. They can't do that. But you; that would be easy.' Field reached out to hail a taxi.

'No,' Woodward stopped him. 'We'll take the bus. I'm going to Klong Toey. You can come part way.'

They waited in the heat until a bus came along, its windows and doors wide open and Thais crowded into the aisle. Field couldn't stand without his head bent against the ceiling. They had been lurching in the traffic for a few minutes when a man, who was shoved up against them, began to stare at Woodward's face.

'Meechai,' he said quietly.

Woodward looked down and smiled.

'Meechai! Meechai!' the man said to the people standing around him. He had tattoos on his chest and the look of a workman. The word spread among the passengers until everyone was turned their way and commenting.

Woodward abruptly shoved a hand into his cloth bag and pulled out a fistful of plastic packages which he began throwing up to the front of the bus. 'A condom a day keeps the doctor away,' he shouted. In each package there were five condoms: red, blue, yellow, green and black.

The people on the bus took up his call and chanted it back, laughing at the same time. 'A condom a day keeps the doctor away. Meechai – condom. Meechai – condom.'

Woodward turned to a woman on a seat beside where he stood. 'How many children do you have?'

'Four, Khun Meechai.'

'What! Your husband did that to you?' Woodward feigned horror. 'Where is this monster?'

Everyone, including the woman, laughed. 'Where is he?' someone shouted. They began chanting, 'Where is he? Where is he?' Meechai made a sign for silence. The woman had a hand over her mouth to keep from laughing.

'You send him to me,' Meechai said. 'This man needs a vasectomy.' The woman nodded in agreement, her hands still over her smile. 'You send him on the King's birthday. Last year,' he announced to everyone, '1,202 smart men came on the King's birthday. 1,202 vasectomies in one day. A world record. 1,202 men who are richer today because they were smart. This year I want a new record. You can all come. Do it for the King.'

Field thought of Ao, probably sterile at seventeen thanks to a very different process. The next morning he took her back to the Nursing Home for their shots and Field found Woodward particularly solicitous.

'Let me have a little look at the thing.'

Field turned his back on Ao before complying.

'This filthy discharge hasn't slowed up?'

'No. I can't say it has.'

'Pull it then, and squeeze.'

Field did as he was told and watched Woodward collect the liquid on a slide. He examined this, and washed it away.

'Well, old boy, at least the stuff is still clear.'

'What do you mean, still clear?'

'Well,' Woodward said slowly, 'after a time it can turn yellow, then green. At which point, I suppose we're in trouble.'

'Trouble?'

'We haven't come to that.'

'Trouble?' Field insisted.

'The infection gets into the blood stream, the joints. Causes septic arthritis. Pus in the joints.'

'Pus in the joints. I'd rather die.'

'You might, in that case. What I need now is a new sample.'

'What for?'

'Well, John, your first sample just gobbled up all twenty-four antibiotics on the plate. It grew stronger on them. So that's no good. I think the spectinomycin must have had the same effect. So what I need is another specimen.' He went away to prepare two swabs, came back and twisted the first one in. Field hadn't remembered it being so painful. 'We'll go for two trays this time. We're bound to find a good one.'

'In the meantime?'

'We'd better leave your body to fight on its own for the moment. I'll give you some more vitamins.'

This delay pushed Field into a depression from which he couldn't escape. The pain hadn't mattered so much when he knew it would be gone in a few days. Instead, on Monday – another three days – he would be off to Laos where there wasn't a return flight until Thursday.

That evening he went out to the Grand Prix on Patpong, as he did on most Fridays. The girls weren't the most beautiful nor the atmosphere the most surprising, but it was the original *farang* bar, run by Rick, an ex-US supply sergeant who had begun sixteen years before. The travelling salesmen on holiday didn't go there. It wasn't flashy enough; the music not quite new enough. The old hands, mostly journalists, were its mainstay. He skirted the booths and the oval bar where four girls danced up in the centre. Henry Crappe was down at the far end. Field slipped on to a stool beside him. Crappe raised his eyes to the dancers, all of whom had seen lengthy service.

'Noodles and time, I'd say. Hey Rick!' Crappe called over his shoulder to the owner. 'Noodles and time, it gets to the best stomach muscles and calves eventually, that's what I say.'

Field greeted the handful of other journalists around the bar; some married to Thais, which didn't stop them coming out on their own; others like Field.

Crappe was staring at him. 'I see that you are still suffering.'

'What?'

'Your illness.'

'Yes. It's hanging on.'

'I am a great believer in the medicinal powers of papaya.'

'I hate papaya.'

'Always satisfy your deepest emotions.'

Only then did Field notice the First Secretary of the Canadian Embassy sitting alone a few seats away. Barry Davis had been in Bangkok longer than any other diplomat and longer than most journalists. His third tour had just begun. How he managed to stay no one understood, except that he knew his files and said he would resign if sent elsewhere. He caught Field's eye and nodded at him to come over.

'What are you doing here, Barry? This isn't your territory.'

The diplomat smiled. 'I like to change bars from time to time.' He was not married. 'Nice to see you.'

'Sure,' Field said. 'What's up? Have I done something wrong?'

'You? What makes you think I'm here to see you?'

'All right, you're not. You're here for the beer. We all are.'

'I hear you're doing well in business.'

'If by well you mean money, yes.'

'That's good, John. They tell me you've even got deals in Laos.'

'Who told you that?'

'You're going to Vientiane on Monday.'

'Who told you?'

'No one.'

'So?'

'So, John, there are three planes a week to Vientiane. Not many *farang* go on them. Not non-Communist *farang*.'

'All right. You read reservation lists. Since when do embassy wankers read reservation lists? What's up?'

Davis smiled patiently. 'You wouldn't mind saying hello to someone for me, would you? No big deal. Just say hello. We haven't got an office there, you know.'

'Who's that?'

'A couple, actually. They're in Vientiane on a UN aid project; forest management to be precise. I guess they've been there two years. They haven't come out for nine months. That's a long time.'

'So just check they're alive?'

'Yeah. Well, I know that already, John. They're not my responsibility, you understand. I mean, they're UN. Only I got a message the other day via an Italian trader. From him. The male half. I told you they were a couple, eh? A funny sort of message. Couldn't make it out really. I figured it was just to pique my interest, you know. To make me say hey, what's going on here? So you go. You say hello. You find out.'

'What's his name?'

'Well, you'll laugh at this.' He stared at Field with a mournful Protestant air. 'Charles Vadeboncoeur.'

'Charles?'

Davis looked up at the girl dancing before him. It was a polite way of missing the alarm on Field's face. After a time he replied.

'That's right.'

'And his wife's there?' Field insisted.

'Well, yes. Diana, you mean. I met her when they came through here on their way in two years ago. He told me he knew you. In fact, he asked me not to mention to you that I'd seen them.'

'Sure he would. His wife and I . . .'

'I understand,' Davis cut in quickly. Despite his life of worldly delights in Bangkok, he was capable of reverting abruptly to the perfect, discreet, introverted Ontario Orangeman.

'Before they were married,' Field insisted. 'I mean, it was before that she and I got together. In Montreal. But just before, you understand. He knows that. He doesn't want to see me. He told you he doesn't want to. Right? And you want me to look them up? So you've gone screwy?'

'Well, I just think you might. Just to check. We're not talking about youthful screwing, for Christ's sake, John.'

'What are we talking about?'

'I don't know. It might be something . . . I don't know . . . Make sure . . . That's all you have to do – make sure.' He gave Field an appraising glance. 'She's still very beautiful.'

'You don't need to tell me that.'

'No. I suppose I don't. You'll do it for me, John. Won't you?' He put fifty *baht* in the cup before him and pushed over a scrap of paper with an address and a phone number in Vientiane written on it. 'See you next week.'

Field went back to Crappe, who caught his arm before he sat down.

'I want your opinion on something.'

'I just want to sit here and drink my . . . my Coke.'

'Come on. It's not here. You can buy me a drink across the road.'

'Where?'

'At the Fire Cat. You must be aware of the Fire Cat. Upstairs. I told you about it earlier this week when you sought my advice. Well, listen to this, Field. There is an Amerasian dancing there. Oh yes. And that's not all. Half black. Think of it. Fresh out of the rice paddies they tell me. Just think of it. Cotton fields and rice paddies bred into one strain. We must see this phenomenon while it remains unspoilt.'

He dragged Field off outside, where the temperature rose by thirty degrees. They were immediately set upon by pimps.

'Massage, sir. Sex show, sir.'

'This way, sir. Right inside.'

The smell of grilled pork and exhaust was in the air as they stepped carefully over the fragments of pavement into the road and across to the other side, where a row of doors swung open to greet them. Crappe disappeared through one and led the way upstairs. The temperature dropped thirty degrees while the music rose an equivalent amount. There wasn't much difference between any of the bars in Bangkok unless one measured the quality of the girls. Also, in general, whatever happened upstairs was more overt than whatever happened downstairs.

Three girls were lying on the bar with blow guns in their vaginas and their hips raised. Someone threw a balloon into the air, one of the girls snapped her knees together and the balloon popped.

'Christ,' said Field, drawing back. He had seen all this so many times.

'No, come on.' Crappe pulled him forward. The moment the staff saw the official chronicler of night life come in, they cleared two of the best places at the bar.

'I hate freak shows,' Field complained.

'Come on. It's nearly over. One beer. One papaya juice.'

'I don't want . . .'

'What's that, mister?' The girl leaned over the bar, her breasts firmly encased and resting on the wood surface.

'Papaya,' Crappe insisted.

'We no got, mister.'

An older woman corrected her in Thai. 'You wait, Mr Crappe. We get for you.'

'I don't want . . .'

Crappe stopped Field. 'I would appreciate your leaving me to handle the situation.' He had to shout because the music in the Fire Cat was several decibels higher than in the Grand Prix. 'What is more, once through a door, I must stay a minimum quarter of an hour. One must be seen to be even handed.'

The girls on the bar now had long horns inserted and were blowing them with vigorous thigh action.

'Christ, Crappe, you lead a shitty life.'

'I'd appreciate your showing more enthusiasm. You might help me find the purpose of our visit to this place. The young Amerasian, in case these worn delights have diverted your memory.'

Field was happy to do anything other than watch the show, so he began searching about. The first thing he saw was George

Espoir eyeing the girls from across the bar. His intense intellectual bearing had been stripped away to reveal an equally intense lascivious ogling. Field immediately looked in another direction. He saw no one who resembled a cross between cotton and rice. Then a hand fell on his shoulder. He looked up, although he knew who it was.

'I'm on the old research path,' Espoir joked. 'What about you?'

'Me? I'm a dirty old man like everyone else in this place, except you.'

'Wonderful.'

Field sensed the man was taking mental note of the exchange for future use on the page. The stool next to him was occupied by a large Australian with a little snub-nosed girl balanced on his lap. One hand was cupped over a breast. The other was kneading a bare buttock. The girl sucked at a straw as fast as she could, emptying the ounce of Coke already shortened by a mass of ice.

'You wanna fuck, mister?'

'Maybe,' the Australian said.

'You buy me another drink?'

'Maybe.' He went on kneading, his mind apparently separated from his body and somewhere far away.

Espoir, being quite thin, managed to squeeze in between the couple and Field far enough to get his left arm up on the bar. He placed his mouth one inch from Field's ear to avoid shouting. The breath had a sweet, cloying edge. 'I've come across the most extraordinary business. What do you think? I've met a Thai who has offered to help me buy a kid. Male or female, 8, 9, 10, for any purpose. Of course, we've all heard of these things. I mean, there are periodic articles in the papers. In London, I mean. Certainly it would make the most extraordinary background for my story. I mean I could do it, then free the child. Return it to its mother.'

'Background.'

'Well, yes. But I've also been thinking of creating some sort of foundation. Here or in Central America. Where my money could be put to good use. Perhaps child slavery would be the perfect thing.'

'Great PR for your next book.'

'I wouldn't be doing it for PR reasons. This Thai seems to feel I could do quite a bit of good.'

'How much?'

'Five thousand dollars. I've given five hundred to show good faith.'

Crappe was impatient at being left out. His eyes were on Espoir, as if trying to place him. 'Field, who is your friend?'

'George Espoir.'

A light came into Crappe's eyes. A fast light. 'I am Bangkok's reviewer of books.'

Field nodded. 'Books and Porn. Henry covers the field.'

'The arts,' Crappe insisted. 'What brings you here?'

Field saw that Espoir was hanging back with distaste. The dandruff in Crappe's eyebrows was highlighted by the flashing lights.

'Research,' Field shouted. He got up and pushed Espoir over next to Crappe, then added, 'He's bought a child.'

'Not exactly. A down payment.'

'Exposure business?' Crappe looked warily at the older man. 'Are you using or being used, Mr Espoir?'

'I'm sorry?'

'Who is the middle man?'

Espoir pulled out a card and handed it over.

'Vichit!' Crappe exclaimed. 'Another sucker for Vichit.'

'What do you mean?' Espoir's eyes were clouding over.

'You'll be his third. His first novelist though. He got some London pinko front page hot shot last year. No one said a word because the guy's lawyers issued writs all over the place. A veritable scandal. Now you, Mr Espoir, need better guidance. Doesn't he, Field?'

Espoir was hanging back as far as he could from Crappe's mouth and its cold sore. Field pushed him forward and agreed.

'You're just the man, Crappe. Just the man.'

'There she is!' Crappe pointed a brown nail up at the stage.

The show was over and four dancers had begun their stint; among them was a girl larger, darker, rounder than the others; with crinkly hair. Crappe watched in rapture. After a moment their tops came off, then the bottoms. They danced on in high heels and bobby socks. Despite all her Thai mannerisms, the girl stood out as quite different.

'I must get her story,' Crappe exclaimed. 'I'll make her dancer of the week.' He put an arm around Espoir. 'The finer points of the performers here become apparent after some years of observation. The sheer quantity of them causes the newcomer to believe that all is the same. All is not the same.'

Field slipped away from this instruction, leaving the writer to pay, and went out into the street. He noticed Espoir's car and driver waiting at the kerb and sighed. Normally he would by now have chosen a girl for the night. It was eleven thirty and at twelve the girls could be taken away without any extra payment to the bar owners. 'Tonight I'll go home alone,' he thought, then remembered Ao. She would be asleep on the floor at the foot of his bed.

CHAPTER 5

The Russian-built Lao Aviation imitation Fokker heaved into the air on time on Monday morning. Field was a model traveller. He looked at none of the scattered passengers. He said nothing. He concentrated what energy he had on the *Bangkok Post*, reading every line about every prince cutting ribbons, every daughter of every general getting married, every office block being blessed by monks and opened. In the second section he found that Pong, General Krit's principal Chinese Thai businessman-cum-backer had been named President of the Siamese Bank, one of the largest in the country. The old man who had founded it was still Chairman and his son, married to one of Woodward's sisters, was still Managing Director, but Pong Hsi-Kun was being parachuted right into the centre of the vault, which could mean only one thing: Bangkok's money men were putting their bets on Krit for Prime Minister.

'Ah, Pong Hsi-Kun. Pong Hsi-Kun.' Field slouched back and murmured the name. 'What a pile of shit.' He threw the paper aside and took out the notes Mrs Laker had delivered to him.

The tractor import deal he was being sent to negotiate seemed as good as signed. It had been held up by the Lao Trading Company only because they wanted a quid pro quo: the export of five tons of Lao coffee over a two year period. Communist organizations were always big on quid pro quos. His instructions were to agree to the coffee after cutting the tonnage down as much as possible. He threw the file aside. 'For Christ's sake.' This was aimed at no one in particular. He put a hand over his genitals but moved it quickly. Nothing was to be gained by focusing on problem areas.

There was no one to meet him at the airport. Nor were there many taxis. And what there were moved very slowly, though not because of traffic. There wasn't much. Nor were there many people about on bicycles or on foot. It was all very different from Field's last visit in 1975.

The Lane Xang hotel was ten minutes away in the centre of town, with only a road to separate it from the Mekong River, which flowed high and at a solid speed from the cumulated effects of the rainy season. In the dry months it was a minor stream and you could climb down the long uncovered bank, planted with temporary vegetable gardens, and wade across a few hundred yards to the island in the middle. On the far side of the island, another wade and a few strokes would get you over to Thailand. It was August however and the water was so deep that on either side of the island the river was a kilometre wide.

Before the hotel's main door there was a small In and Out drive which had once been abundant with flowers. No one came out to help, but then Field didn't want help. He stretched and looked up at the long three-storey cement facade, then strolled in and asked for room 215, which he had always had in the old days. That didn't appear to present a problem. Vientiane had never been the sort of place you had problems, not even in the hot days of war. Now the city had shrunk from 500,000 to 50,000 or so and the hotels, well, they were certainly empty, apart from those lodging Russian experts. Tourism was forbidden and there wasn't much business to be done. It was an extremely quiet town.

Field liked room 215 because it looked out behind the hotel across the garden that stretched a hundred yards to the main road. It also had a windowless sitting room with a small fridge and a completely separate bedroom.

He picked up the phone to let Mr Som Nosavan of the Lao Trading Company know he had arrived. The line was dead. He tried tapping on the connection lever. Nothing happened. He smiled to himself and wandered back downstairs. The man behind the desk tried to telephone for him and seemed surprised that the line was dead. Field wasn't. He asked for some paper and took it out into the overgrown garden.

Curiosity drew him to the left where there had once been caged bears to amuse the guests. Now there were just cages. He headed out to the swimming pool in the centre. The low wood beds for sunbathing were still there, in need of paint. He found a proper chair and pulled it up beneath a frangipani tree where he scribbled two notes. One to Som Nosavan. The other to Charles Vadeboncoeur. Field made a point of not mentioning Diana. 'Barry asked me to say hello. Am here till Thursday.' That was it. Your service, he thought, and took both messages to the front desk clerk who called taxis to deliver them.

In fact, the Lao Trading Company was no more than five minutes' walk away on the main street that ran along the foot of the garden. Diana's house was a bit further – fifteen minutes perhaps – down the opposite way towards the old Australian Club. Field was in no mood to rush people. It wasn't that sort of place. He went back into the garden to his chair by the pool and waited.

Strange, he thought, to be here like the sole survivor of a tidal wave which a decade later redeposited him on the same chair in the same garden to be visited by the ghosts of other times, other lives. In '75 the hotel had been filled with Americans and others on their way out. Souvanna Phouma's neutralist coalition government was on its short road towards collapse, in a mirror image of Saigon. Good old Souvanna Phouma. Everyone's definition of a nice man. The Pathet Lao was closing in with a gentle sort of thrust. None of what was happening bore any relationship to the violence of Vietnam and Cambodia. Field had shuttled back and forth between Bangkok and Vientiane to chronicle the steps of the decline. He had seen Father Peter, now of Klong Toey, come down out of the hills, forced to abandon his ministering among the tribes by the Communist advance. And Matthew Blake, having left his Meong guerrillas at the very last moment, had suddenly appeared. Field and he and Pop Beulle had spent a drunken evening together at a French restaurant of the sort Vientiane specialized in; the colonial check tablecloth variety, which was all Field and Blake had ever known. The other Americans in the hills had already left. Even Anthony Smith had flown in from Singapore to attempt to collect on a contract and had got back on the plane the moment he saw it was impossible. In the midst of that constant disorder, the swimming pool had been covered over once a week to make a dance floor.

Field looked around, unsure whether it was he or all of those people who were the ghosts. At the far end of the garden he could see a double wooden gate standing open. It had been closed in the old days, to keep the uninvited populace out. Now there was no one to come in.

He stared hard at the opening and imagined Diana appearing as if by chance for a swim. She would still be everything he wasn't. And she still wouldn't want him. But that didn't matter now. He held her image in his imagination, there, half-way through the gate in the shade of the trees. She had the sort of skin that freckled and burnt. After her, he had spent his life with girls whose skin was smooth and even. And whose hair was dark. He blinked to make her go away.

A new, yellow Toyota came through the rain in the afternoon to pick up Field and take him to the Lao Trading Company down the road. The few other cars he saw were, with few exceptions, ten years old; that is, pre-revolution. Most of the buildings in the street, the commercial thoroughfare of Vientiane, had a ground floor plus one or two storeys. The lower variety were pre-second world war. The higher were in classic cement, modern and dated, like the cars, from the short period of American glory. The trading company belonged to this superior category. Behind plate glass windows, the wares of the corporations they represented were displayed. The driver led Field in past these to a corner and into a small toilet, scarcely large enough for both of them, once the door was closed. A second door was opened and they went through to a windowless boardroom where the air conditioning functioned at a sub-Arctic temperature. A large Thai television sat up in a corner beside a bar stocked with twenty bottles of western alcohol.

In the centre of the room an overweight man in an American cut safari suit was waiting with a pleased smile. He waddled forward on his sandals and began exclaiming in exuberant and perfect English that leaned towards a New York dialect, 'Welcome! Welcome! You're not as good-looking as Mrs Laker, but welcome anyway. What'll you drink?'

'A Coke.'

'Oh, no! I have everything here. Even bourbon. What'll you try?'

'I don't drink.' Something about the man caught Field's eye.

Som Nosavan showed honest disappointment. 'Well, if your idea is to keep your mind clear for our tough talking, you're going to force me to stick to tea.' He drew Field to a round table at the far end. 'So what do you think? Has Vientiane changed much?'

'I've never been here before.'

'No? I thought Mrs Laker had said you knew Laos.'

'No. Vietnam. Not Laos.' Field slouched down and indicated the road beyond the windowless room, 'Very quiet out there.'

Som nodded vigorously. 'Oh yes, very quiet.' He rolled his eyes. 'But not in here. Oh no. I've got a small Bangkok going inside these walls. I turned over seven million US last year. In a country of sleepers, the wakened man grows rich.'

'Marx?'

Som looked at him, amazed, and repeated, 'Marx,' as if trying to place the name. Then he saw it was a joke. 'Marx! Marx! There isn't much of that here. Just the same old sleepy Laos and a few hot shots like me. They are driving the Russians crazy, Mr Field. Or is it John?'

'John.'

'Crazee. It's the funniest thing you've ever seen. Even crazier than they drove the Americans.'

'You're Lao then?'

'Me?' Som was amazed by the question. 'What else? You're surprised at my energy. Well, lucky for you. We'll get some business done.' He patted his own stomach fondly. 'Money, John, that's what makes this stomach grow. Now why don't you want my coffee? Five tons is nothing. It's the best in the world. We'll try some later.'

They spent the rest of the day arguing out the details and at six the door from the toilet was thrown open. A young woman in a Paris dress came through leading two men. It quickly became obvious that she was Som's object, while one of the men was his partner and ran both a state brewery and a state detergent factory. His name was Iem. The other man was introduced as the Prime Minister's private secretary. Kamphet, as he was called, and Iem spoke only French; as did the girl. Field thought she had a Vietnamese accent. From time to time they slipped into Lao, which Field could follow, although it was not for that reason he had denied having been in Laos before. He simply saw no reason to admit knowing more than the essential minimum.

They drank whisky for an hour, then a Chinese meal was produced and the three men continued on whisky while Field and the girl nursed Cokes. All this time he was trying to place Som. Field was certain they had met. People went through such radical personality changes during Communist takeovers that he might have been anything under the old regime. The theme of the evening was life on the outside. The girl had been to Paris to shop a few months before and Som had made a trading visit to Hong Kong two years earlier, but otherwise they had all remained 'in our sleepy prison', as Som put it.

They were astounded to discover that Field had never been to Europe and refused to go back to North America, even for visits. This limited their questions to Bangkok, about which they already knew quite a bit since they could illegally watch Thai television, beamed from across the river.

Tuesday morning Field had free. He strolled over to the Café Pagode on Sam Sen Thai Avenue. Behind lowered bamboo blinds it was still turning out coffee and croissants. Field ate two and wandered back to the hotel. He negotiated again in the afternoon while it rained, refused Som's invitation to dinner and went off to the French restaurant where he had last eaten with Blake and Pop Buelle. The menu seemed unchanged. That night he noticed as he undressed that his discharge was no longer clear. He considered this for some time, wondering if it had now reached what Woodward had called the yellow stage. On Wednesday morning the deal was closed. Three tons of coffee over two years. There was still no message from Vadeboncoeur.

Field took a trishaw down the river to the Australian Club

with the idea that he might run into Diana there. He passed the King's palace, closed up since '76 and the King's disappearance, either into a Vietnamese prison or quite simply to his death. Beyond that was the old official residence of Souvanna Phouma, who had been allowed to stay on there until he died in 1984. The centre of town was already behind and the houses were strung out along the river bank in a rural way, separating the road from the water.

The fresh pink paint covering the cement of the Australian Club was its most remarkable feature, lying as it did low to the ground beside its pool. The girl on the desk didn't seem to mind him taking out a temporary membership. Field wandered around the pool examining the wives and the children of western diplomats for whom this was the heart, the core, the very social centre of Laos. Any one of the children might have been Diana's. Barry Davis hadn't mentioned a child, but logically she and Vadeboncoeur would have had some. In fact, their creations might already be off at university. Field stopped this examination. It was only that he hadn't seen her since before her marriage. Time therefore should have stood still. He went inside and ate a club sandwich while it rained, then came back out and stretched on to a deck chair in the shade at the end of the garden by the bank of the Mekong.

From where he lay, the centre of Vientiane could be seen about two miles upstream on a bend of the river. And straight across the water from him Thailand sat apparently indifferent to this Marxist-Leninist capital and to the Australian Club with its clean and brittle Anglo-Saxon air.

He was woken by a hand tapping on his arm. Only slowly did he realize who was staring at him in silence. The first thought that came to Field's mind was that Charles Vadeboncoeur had waited until the last possible moment to materialize, thus limiting the time they spent together. Charles was in a bathing suit, although he didn't appear to have swum.

'Long time,' Field said.

Charles nodded. 'I'll just get changed. I'll take you home.'

He disappeared, leaving Field to stare out over the Mekong, where the sun was low and red on the far side. He had slept through the afternoon. Charles reappeared and paused long enough to look down the river bank.

'Usually a policeman is posted here. Officially his job is to protect the club. In reality he's supposed to stop Laos swimming across the Mekong.'

Field looked over to Thailand. 'It's a long way.'

'This is the favourite spot. The current is not so bad. At night there are always two or three boats for those who don't swim too well and have a little cash. Fourteen thousand went over last year.'

'The club should rent binoculars and bleacher seats.'

Charles laughed. 'Not all of them cross right here, thank God.'

Only then did Field register that they were speaking English, Charles with just a hint of his elegant Quebec City accent. In the past they had always talked in French. As they walked back towards the clubhouse his tone changed to one of social pleasantries, which struck Field as quite false. And there was something else. Something more than that. He remembered Charles as a fragile, pale person; that was what Diana had seemed to want – a man who believed in things, a man not merely educated, but for whom ideas were a prerequisite to beliefs. Field looked over at the healthy, tanned figure beside him. He had thickened out into the essence of the physically wired man of action.

'Diana is going to be delighted,' he said in a clear voice as they came through the club, at the same time waving to four women who played cards.

Outside, a driver was waiting beside an old Ford. The two men said nothing while they were driven the short distance to a house on a street running off Sam Sen Thai. It was a little street. The driver honked and a watchman pulled the gate open. There was a garden inside; the watchman's house was by the gate and the main house set back twenty yards. It had two floors and was not particularly large. The garden was filled with flowers and with orchids hung in the trees. Charles shouted as he walked towards the door.

'Diana. Viens! Viens voir qui est là.' He glanced back at Field with the smile of someone pleased by his surprise.

She appeared from around the side of the house. 'Charles, qu'est qu'il y a?' Then she saw Field and stopped, gave a little laugh and came forward calmly to kiss him.

Of course she's cool, Field thought. She was always indifferent to me. The skin of her cheek brushed against his. It was warm with a film of damp from the heat. He stood back to look at her, conscious that Charles was watching. She hadn't changed a great deal. Laos had brought out her freckles, but they went well with her relaxed self-confidence. She was wearing baggy shorts and sandals. Her legs were as he remembered, as he remembered touching them.

'Come on in,' Charles interrupted. 'I'm assuming you're free for dinner.'

'Free,' Field said. 'Very free. Very, very free.'

Charles called out and a young girl appeared 'Whisky.' The Lao turned to go before Field could ask for something else. 'It's ridiculous really,' Charles went on. 'I come here as a forestry expert, which I'm not, and they give me five servants to do the work of one, or for that matter, the work Diana and I would be happy to do. Well, there you are.'

'What are you doing here then?'

'Forestry expert. I now am. So it's fair to say that I'm here doing good.'

They sat down in a living room certainly furnished by someone else. It all had a functional unchosen feel to it, while he remembered Diana as someone obsessed with the details of her surroundings.

'Yes, but what are you doing here? I mean what?'

Diana echoed, 'What?' and sat down beside her husband with her arm loosely laid on his shoulder. 'More to the point,' she added, 'what were we doing in Montreal? Getting richer like everyone else. Complaining bitterly about everything as if our problems were the worst in the world. There were some problems to be dealt with, of course. But apart from that, it was a pretty cushy, easy, free place to be.'

'We all thought there was going to be a revolution,' Charles broke in. 'You remember what we all thought. Everything was going to be overturned.' No one could have looked less revolutionary. 'Then a few elections went the right way and a few laws changed everything without great difficulty. I mean, compared to . . .' He trailed off.

'So you switched to forestry?'

'I decided it wasn't good enough. Or rather, it was too good. I resigned and got a job with UNDP. Five years ago. At first they wanted to use me as a lawyer. It took a while to kill that idea. Then they got another one – Canada equals forests. So I converted. Now I spend my time outdoors. We were in Lagos for two years. Deforestation is the big deal in Africa. It's not so bad here. I'm up in the north a lot of the time.'

'And you don't miss . . .'

'Complaining? No.'

'Winter, yes,' Diana added.

'You never go back?'

'A couple of times,' she said. 'Just before we came here. For funerals mainly.'

'I've never been,' Field couldn't help saying.

'Never?'

'Twenty years. Not even for funerals.' There was a hint of satisfaction in his voice.

As they had had no experiences in common for those twenty years, the evening was spent talking about the Montreal they had known, which required some care to avoid anything embarrassing. It was almost an aberration that the three had ever met, let alone slept together and married. Field had slipped straight from school in lower town on to a newspaper, while Charles had been on the other side of the mountain at the Université de Montréal when Diana had come down from her safe toehold on the English slopes of Mount Royal to discover the world.

Field was surprised that there was no mention of the message sent to Bangkok. Towards the end of dinner, he said, 'Barry Davis seemed a little concerned about you. I can't think why.'

There was a servant in the room at the time and Charles waited until she was gone before replying mildly, 'Was he? Barry is a bit of a worrywart.'

'So everything is all right?'

Charles gestured and smiled as if to say, of course.

'Good.'

'A little bored, perhaps. Laos is, how shall I put it . . .'

'Quiet,' said Diana.

They laughed and sat silent. The silence of the night outside was complete. There were no voices, no traffic, no hum of men working as they did twenty-four hours a day in Bangkok.

Charles jumped to his feet. 'I'll give you a letter for Barry. There are a few things here that might interest him. Would you mind? I'll go write it now.' He left the room deliberately.

Field sat silent, looking at his hands. He could feel her examining him.

'We heard about you being in Thailand. I was surprised at first. It seemed so improbable. Last year a journalist came here who had just been through Bangkok and had spent an evening with you. He entertained us for most of a dinner with a description of what had happened. I felt like a peeping Tom since he didn't know I knew you.'

'I can't think I've ever done anything that interesting.'

'It wasn't that exactly. In his story you had the role of the old Asia hand. You know. Cynical. Seen it all. Gone native. I'm quite surprised to see you looking quite so unchanged.'

Field shrugged. 'Are there no children?'

'No,' she said quickly. 'I couldn't . . . For a long time I thought Charles would mind, then we left Montreal and it all made much more sense.'

'Sense.' Field repeated the word. 'I've never thought of sense having much to do with anything.' He was about to volunteer that he had a daughter at university, then didn't. Instead he stared at her quite unapologetically. Twice he had talked and coddled, in fact dragged, her into bed with him. She had come out of kindness. Even at the time he'd realized that. He simply didn't have the qualifications for the position as she had imagined it.

Diana interrupted his examination. 'I don't suppose when I got married that happiness was at the top of my list. I mean that was way down. The funny part is, I've had a great deal of happiness.'

'Here?'

'Particularly here.'

'But what do you do with yourself? When Charles is out in his teak forests, for example?'

'I used to play bridge with Souvanna Phouma, well, almost every day. He was an old sweetie. This place is such a village, we'd only been here a week before he found out I played well. Bridge was the sort of game we all learnt to play in Westmount. Bridge and tennis.'

'Proper games. While we Irish down the hill played hockey.'

She smiled and for the first time Field noticed there was a tired edge to her face. Something buried quite deep.

'The old man has been dead a year. So what do you do now?'

'Oh, lots of things. There are other wives. We have keep-busy projects. And I look after Charles. He is quite different from us.' This was said matter of factly, as if Field's and her own inferiority were self-evident. 'He has his personal views of proper and improper games.' She blushed. 'So he needs to be taken care of.'

'OK,' was all Field said.

The servant girl came in to refill their coffee cups and Diana waited until she had gone before saying more. 'The letter he is writing. You must be careful with it.'

'Of course.'

'No. That's not what I mean. Charles plays everything very low key . . . You must take care with it. Particularly on leaving Vientiane.'

'All right,' Field repeated, this time putting conviction into his voice. 'I'm an old Asia hand, remember. I know the ropes.'

'Very improbable,' she said and laughed again. The background of fatigue or worry was still there.

They talked for another half-hour before Charles reappeared and apologized. 'I haven't quite finished. I'll give it to you tomorrow morning at the club, all right? Say at ten. Your plane isn't till midday.'

'Fine,' Field said.

He refused a ride back to the Lane Xang. It was only a fifteen minute walk which somehow he needed. The peace in the streets was quite wonderful, with only the sounds of occasional birds and the air soft and restful. He crossed the grand avenue that ran from the King's palace to the Victory monument. One of Vientiane's three traffic lights was red. He crossed anyway.

There wasn't even a cyclist. Someone in search of calm and peace would have been very happy in this place.

The next morning he took a trishaw to the Australian Club and was there shortly before ten. He ordered a coffee and sat outside in the shade, where he could watch the children learning how to swim. There was a policeman in an army uniform sitting below the club on the river bank. Of course, it was highly unlikely that anyone would try to cross in daylight, so the policeman's role was more theoretical than real.

Charles still hadn't appeared at ten forty-five and Field was beginning to worry about his plane. The thought of another three days in Vientiane with his groin aching and nothing to do was a terrible prospect. He went outside and took a taxi to their house. There he asked the driver to wait.

The watchman didn't answer when Field rang the bell. He rang a second time and tried calling. There was no answer. The gate, although shut, was unlocked, so Field went in and called. He was relieved to see the old Ford sitting outside. That meant he hadn't crossed with Charles on his way there. The house shutters were still closed. Diana had probably slept in after what by Vientiane standards must have been a late night. No one appeared, so Field went over and banged on the door of the house. The maid didn't answer. He called and tried the handle. It was open.

Inside there was perfect quiet. The air was cool. Only after his eyes had adjusted to the half-light did he notice that there were things strewn on the floor. He pushed the door closed behind him and walked slowly into the living room. The chairs had been turned over. The books in the bookcase had been scattered on to the floor. He went into the kitchen. There was no one, but every cupboard had been emptied. Plates and frying pans were all over the counters and floor. He went back out to the main hall and paused to think. Perhaps the best thing he could do was raise the alarm. He looked up the wood stairs and listened to the silence, then began climbing step by step. There were four doors at the top. Two were open. One led into a bathroom where the linen had been scattered about. The other was a small bedroom in disorder. He went out to the landing. There was a cheap Chinese rug beneath his feet. It swallowed up the sound of his footsteps on the wood floor. He examined the two doors in front of him, considering which to open. He chose that on the left and opened it slowly. The room was quite dark. He found a light switch and turned it on.

The first thing he saw was Diana's foot, on the floor at the end of the bed. Then he saw the other. He walked forward two paces and stopped. Charles was lying half-hidden behind the other side of the bed. Field's eyes came back to Diana. She was naked. There were slash marks across her groin. Her arms were stretched out. They had been bound and then cut loose. The sheet that had held them was still attached to each wrist. The fingers had been hacked off. He forced himself to go on looking. The breasts had been removed, almost surgically. He looked up at her face. The ears were gone and there was something raw stuck in her mouth. Even from a distance he could see that the blood everywhere was fresh, not even dry where it lay on the floor. Her eyes were wide open. They hadn't touched her eyes. He could tell from her expression that she had been alive through all of it, even when they had stuffed her mouth. And yet she seemed to lie quite calmly.

He looked away quickly at Charles. A cloth had been tied sharply around his head so that it cut into his mouth. He had been mutilated in the same way. His hands were still bound but the right arm had been half severed, perhaps in self-defence. And his genitals had been cut away. They, Field realized, were what had been stuffed into Diana's mouth. His whole body was arched and contorted.

Field managed to turn around and walk to the landing. He closed the door behind him. The air was quiet again. He put a hand out to steady himself and swallowed to stop from retching. There was no one in the house. That was the first thought that came into his mind. No one. He put a hand out on to the banister and carefully made his way down the stairs. There was a mirror at the bottom. He avoided looking into it.

Outside the birds were singing. He walked across the garden to the main gate. The taxi driver was still there. No one else. Raise the alarm, he thought. He looked back into the empty courtyard, then pulled the gate closed and got back into the taxi. 'Hotel.'

They drove by other houses where there were signs of life. No feelings, he thought, no feelings. Reason it out. He thought his way back into the house. Five servants. None of them there. He hadn't checked all the rooms. Perhaps they were dead or bound up. No. It wasn't possible. Not so many people when there were houses on either side. They weren't there and the alarm hadn't been raised. He saw the bodies again. They hadn't been murdered. It was torture. And the house had been searched. He looked at his watch. The plane was in an hour. The next in three days, with him stuck in the middle of something he couldn't control. 'Get on the plane,' he said, half out loud. The driver turned around at the sound and caught his eyes, as if something were photographed in their reflection. Field looked away.

He sucked in his breath and tried to calm himself. Had it been an accident that he was the one to discover the bodies? If not they would never let him on the plane. Fall back. Fall back. The British Embassy covered for the Canadians in Laos. It was two sides of a triangle to the hotel and to the embassy. He looked out. They were almost at the hotel. All right. All right. Step by step.

At the hotel entrance he leaned forward to the driver. 'Wait here. Don't go.' The man nodded. Field ran up the steps to the reception. 'Key. Bill immediately. I'll get my bag.'

The man handed him a small thick envelope with the key.

'Who brought this?'

'Come this morning, Mr Field.'

'Who?'

The man shrugged. 'Messenger.'

Field ran up the stairs to the second floor, fumbled with the key, stood back and pushed open his door. All was calm inside. He ripped open the envelope. There was a cheap notebook inside. He flipped through it. The writing was small and careful, in English. He fell on 'Pong Saly: June '84, while on forest inspection observed large poppy production unaccounted for in official figures . . .' It was Charles' letter. Cover the angles, he thought, call the embassy. He rushed to the phone in the first room. It was dead. He slammed it down and ran to the bedroom. He had left the window up and his things packed with the bag still open. He flipped it shut and headed for the door. Embassy first, airport second, he thought. It's safer.

Behind him there was a shout. He turned towards the window. Yes, there was shouting. He ran back to look. Through the wood gate at the far end a crowd of soldiers or police were running with machine guns. He dashed towards the outer room, stopped. Opened the door slowly and listened. There was running on the stairs. He looked down the corridor for a fire escape sign, then stopped himself, stepped back in, closed the door and locked it. He stood quite still, trying to think. He could hear the feet in his corridor.

The notebook. The notebook. It was in his pocket. He pulled it out and stared stupidly at it. Was that what they wanted? He opened it. ' . . . state detergent factory in fact used as drug laboratory . . .' He snapped it closed. What would they do to him if they thought he had seen it? He stared quickly around the room. Down the toilet, he thought. No. It wouldn't go in one flush. There wasn't time for more. He ran over to the fridge, ripped open the door. It was empty. Someone started knocking behind him. He pulled down the freezer cover. There were two ice trays. He slipped the notebook into its envelope and put it flat at the back under one tray. The other he put in front and closed the door quietly. They were shouting for him to open. He walked half-way back before answering in a calm voice.

They seemed not to hear him and kept shouting. When Field was close he registered that they were shouting in French. He asked,

'Qui est là?'

'Police! Police!'

'Attendez.' He unlocked the door and turned the handle slowly.

As it released, they came pushing in and shoved him up against the far wall. He raised his arms and tried to look perplexed. They searched him and rummaged quickly around the room.

A small, neat man, apparently in an officer's uniform, came forward. He might have been a teenager, he looked so young. 'Votre valise?' He nodded at Field's suitcase.

'My plane is at noon,' Field said.

'Monsieur Vadeboncoeur?' the officer said.

'British Embassy,' Field replied.

In halting English the officer insisted, 'Why you kill them?'

'British Embassy,' Field repeated.

The officer sent his men to search the bedroom, apparently for arms, then had Field pushed back into that room along with one soldier and closed the door. There was no chair, so Field sat on the edge of the bed. The policeman stood nervously at the door with a Kalashnikov across his chest. Ten minutes later the officer came in. He had Field's passport.

'Why you come here?'

Field stood up. 'Business.'

'Business?'

'Lao Trading Company. Tractors. Som Nosavan.'

'Tractors,' the man repeated. 'Why you kill these people?'

Field looked hard at the man and guessed this was his first murder. Probably it was the first murder in Vientiane in years. 'I didn't. Please call the British Embassy.'

'Neighbours see you go in. Come out.'

'Who else did they see? I went to say goodbye. They were friends. I found them dead.'

The officer nodded. 'Why come here, say nothing about murder?'

'Please call the British Embassy.'

'Murder two hours before plane, escape before discovered.'

'Who told you?' Field said.

'Phone call.'

'How did they know?' Field raised his voice. 'How did they know?' He felt himself losing control and sat back down on the bed.

The officer turned and left the room. The door was closed behind him. Field looked up at the young soldier on the door, who averted his eyes. They waited for half an hour, when the sound of a plane going over came through the window. Field got up to look at his return flight disappearing, but the soldier rushed across to keep him away from the opening.

'I'm not going to jump, for Christ's sake.' Field sat back down and waited until he couldn't bear it. 'L'officer!' he shouted. 'L'officer!' The soldier threatened him with his weapon but Field hadn't moved. He kept shouting, 'L'officer!'

The door opened. Through the opening he could see that the other room was being ripped apart.

'L'Ambassadeur Anglais!'

'Over there.' The officer pointed to the corner by the window. 'Stand over there!'

Four of his soldiers came in and began searching through the room. They stripped the bed, turned over the mattress, removed everything on the walls. That meant they hadn't yet looked in the freezer. Field glanced out through the open door and saw an overweight figure following a soldier across the room. Then someone shut the door. It was a few moments before Field registered that the figure was Som Nosavan from the trading company.

'Hey!' he shouted at the police officer. 'The man I am doing business with is out there.' He pointed towards the door. 'I saw him there. Let me talk to him.'

The officer seemed to ignore this and left the room. A few moments later Nosavan came in looking very embarrassed. Field wasn't in the mood for delicacy.

'Listen. I've asked them to call the British Embassy. I have a right to that.'

'I'm sorry, Mr Field. I don't understand what's going on. They sent someone to get me. Did you use my name?' There was a resentful edge to the question, as if to say, in a country like this you don't involve other people. 'They tell me you killed a young couple.'

'Just tell them what I'm doing here.'

'I told them. But coming for business doesn't rule out killing someone. They say the house was ransacked. They asked me to find out what you took.'

'I didn't take anything. They were friends. Look, will you go to the embassy? That's all. Just warn them I'm here.'

Som's embarrassment was getting out of control. 'Please don't ask me, Mr Field.'

'Just phone them. Two words.'

'You don't understand.'

Field tried to be reasonable. 'Surely I have the right to let my people know what has happened.'

'That's just it, Mr Field. I don't think you understand. You have no rights. We have no legal code in Laos. The discretion of the government is absolute. None of us has rights. We have obligations.'

'Well, what's happening then?'

Som shrugged. 'They're trying to decide, I think. The police are asking for advice from other levels.'

'Well, for Christ's sake . . .' Field was beginning to lose himself between frustration and anger. So far he had managed to close out any other emotions. 'Will you try to find out what's going on?' He waved his hands vaguely and sat back down on the bed.

'Of course. I owe that to Mrs Laker. And you must not worry, Mr Field. This will not affect our agreement. This is merely a personal matter.'

Field looked up bitterly. 'You have a law that separates them, do you?'

Som smiled in an understanding way and left. Then nothing happened. The soldier remained at the door. Field drew his feet up on the bed and held them bent up against himself. At one point he dozed off, only to be woken by a nightmare of Diana being murdered. There was a light on in the room and it was dark outside. The guard had been changed for another, who had left the air conditioning machine off and the window open, so that mosquitoes had invaded the room. Probably the man had never seen anything more sophisticated than a fan.

CHAPTER 6

Shortly after two a.m. the door opened. The officer called his soldier out and sent Som Nosavan in. During that instant, while the door was ajar, Field thought he saw the Prime Minister's private secretary staring in with curiosity; the man called Kamphet, who had dined with him at the trading company. The door closed. Som smiled at first, then wandered aimlessly, indecisively through the room on a path that left him, at its end, looking out of the window. After a time he said, without turning around,

'You haven't thought of anything you might have been looking for or have happened to find in that house?'

Field ignored the question. 'Did you call the embassy?'

'I discussed the matter with some friends. If I call the embassy, the matter becomes official. Then a process would begin which might go on for months. And where would it end?' He turned around and came over to sit beside Field. It wasn't hot in the room but there was sweat on the fat man's body. 'I'll go to the embassy if you ask me to. But I have talked to these police, talked you know, with my friends as well, and,' he betrayed a small smile, 'made certain offers, out of friendship for Mrs Laker, and the question in their minds is, do they really want to try a foreigner for murder? Right now? Of course, it is up to you, but many people leave Laos informally, you know. Quietly. They just cross the river. And if you could do the same it would ease everyone's embarrassment. Mine included. Imagine how it would look for me in this small town having to testify on behalf of my client, who has just slaughtered two people.'

'I told you . . .'

Som put up calming hands. 'I'm just trying to explain that even I have reasons for wanting to see you gone. So if you agreed, then the police would retire downstairs for five minutes or so. They would wait outside the front door. And you would go down and out into the garden. The gate at the other end of the garden would be open. There I would have a man in a car waiting to take you twenty-five kilometres down river to Tanaleng where there is a ferry. It opens at eight a.m. I have friends on the customs post there. They'd get you through and across to Nong Khai in Thailand. By then you would have missed the first train for Bangkok, but there's another at six p.m. You could even rent a car and driver. About the same time you were crossing, the police would discover the bodies. You would have evaporated from this complicated business without a word being said or a shot being fired. That would be much cleaner for everyone.'

Field looked carefully at the man, but could think of nothing to say.

Eventually Som appeared to find the silence unbearable. 'We can't wait too long. If they keep you in here much more, everyone will know. Then it will be official . . . You could be in Bangkok tomorrow night.'

'And if I go, the police will say it is proof that I killed them.'

'You care what they say? I wouldn't in your place. Anyway, I don't know what the public line will be. That's a political decision. Out of my hands. Out of my friends' hands.' He shrugged. 'I would prefer you went, but I can't force you to go. Perhaps you would prefer the route of justice.'

'What about the witnesses who saw me go into the house; didn't they see anyone else?'

'Apparently not.'

Field thought about that. He looked around the hotel room. If he stayed, this unbearable space would be changed for something far worse in a jail. And for how long? Eventually they would find the notebook in the freezer. Then they would know that he knew. What would they do then? Once they had him locked up, out of sight, anything could happen. He looked over at Som, who stood up and walked discreetly away, towards the window, out of which he stared pensively, as if contemplating the outer world. It would be even neater for them, Field thought, if there were an accident during his escape. He glanced up and caught Som's eyes fixed on him.

'What do you think?' the man asked.

'I don't know.'

Som nodded sympathetically. 'It is very difficult.'

'There are risks both ways.'

Som nodded again. 'Perhaps.' He appeared to be considering the odds. 'Of course, I live with uncertainty, just by doing business here. I'm a capitalist in a socialist world. You can imagine. There are always risks when there are no rules. Perhaps . . . perhaps less for you in crossing the river. I did it myself once, a few years ago, then I came back a few months later when things were quieter.' He shrugged. 'There are always risks.'

Field stared at him in silence, unable to concentrate. 'All right,' he said eventually. 'I'll go.'

At first Som seemed not to have heard. Then a hint of relief showed on his face. 'You stay here. When the door to the hall slams you wait a few minutes, then come out.'

'What about my passport and money?'

'Everything will be waiting in the next room.' He went over to the bedroom entrance, where he stopped long enough to give Field an encouraging smile. 'Good luck.' And disappeared.

Field got up and walked around the room. He tried to think and walked around again, wishing he had opted to stay. Well, he could still stay. They would come back in ten minutes and find him there. But what did that accomplish? If their idea was to kill him, they could as easily do it in the room as in the garden. Easier in fact. He wouldn't have a chance. So the choice was really between Thailand and some unknown bogus accusation.

The door slammed. It was a deliberate sound. Field turned out his light and crossed to the window. It was a dark night. There was a slight glimmer from the swimming pool, but he could not see the wall and the gate at the far end. He crossed back to the bedroom door and turned the handle. They had left the lights on. His passport was sitting on the table. His bag was on the floor beside it. Beneath his passport were two thousand *baht*. There should have been close to twenty. So he had paid for his own escape. That simply showed Som was a careful businessman. Field stuffed the passport and money into his trouser pocket and crossed over to open the hall door. There was no one in the hall. He walked down the corridor to the landing. No one was waiting. He went back to the room, opened the freezer and lifted out the notebook, which he slipped into his other pocket. It was cold against his skin and made a wet rectangle on his trousers. Field took his bag and left the room, rapidly this time.

In the lobby downstairs the receptionist had disappeared. Through the front doors, the police jeeps could be seen, but no policemen. The patio leading into the garden was lit by multicoloured lights, as if for a dance, beyond which was darkness. He pushed the glass door open and stepped out, pausing despite himself in expectation of a shout and of gunshots. There was nothing. Only the frenzied circling of mosquitoes in the glare of the lights.

He moved quickly off to the left and skirted around the garden edge towards the bear cages. The grass made no sound beneath his feet. At the cages he stopped and listened again before moving forward, still close to the garden edge where he could weave between bushes and trees. The wall at the far end was hidden behind thick planting. He skirted to the right, along the front of this tangle, towards the gate. It would be about fifty yards. After thirty or so he heard a sound and stopped. That would be Som's driver. He crept forward again until something glinted in the night. It was hard to judge the distance. Ten yards perhaps. Field cut out a bit to get a clearer view and went slowly forward. There was nothing. The man should have been in the open. He moved back in against the wall and lifted his feet carefully. A vague outline of the gate began to separate itself from the darkness, ahead to his left. It was indeed open. A clutch of frangipani trees partially obscured it. Gradually he made out, in beneath the trees, two human forms.

He put his case down and waited. They were well in, out of sight from the central path. There was another glint. He looked down and saw, in the right hand of one, a knife. Field concentrated on the other man. He also held a knife. It was faintly outlined against the light colour of the gate. The blade had a curious curve. He followed the line up from the metal across the clenched fist to the muscles of the arm. The shoulder was unusually wide for a Lao. Where had he seen shoulders like that before? And those blades? In Bangkok. With Woodward. Down at the pig slaughterhouse. A good part of Bangkok's murderers were hired there. In an instant he could see the place and hear it.

Pigs with hooks wedged into their jaws being dragged screaming – with exactly the scream of a human – towards the slaughter table. Four semi-naked men flipping it up on to its back. One of them raising a knife and cutting an x in the throat. The blood pouring out into a barrel and the scream with it, before the half-dead carcass was seared with steam and the hair scraped off with cleavers. Then they began slicing. And suddenly Field saw Diana being sliced. He saw her whole body again, just as he had found it, the ears, the breasts, neatly cut away. Vientiane would have a slaughterhouse. And they would kill him quietly. No gunshots which might have to be explained. No witnesses among the hotel staff. Or more likely they wanted him somewhere isolated to question him as they had Diana.

He left his case on the ground and crept carefully back along the edge. The night closed in around him again until he felt safe enough to stand upright and to examine the wall. It was three metres high, with broken glass along the top, but the trees had been allowed to grow up against and higher than the wall. There was a large tree with low branches just off to the left. Field eased in among the bushes that surrounded it and began searching for a foothold. His leather shoes slipped on the bark, forcing him to go very slowly, thinking all the time that the two men would be wondering what was taking him so long. The glass had been planted so thick along the cement ridge that he knew he would be unable to lower himself over. Instead he climbed higher, until his feet were on the level of the top of the wall. He couldn't see the ground on the other side, but assumed it must be a cement slab pavement or a ditch. Whatever it was, he would have to jump over the glass because the sound of it breaking would certainly be heard by the men. His landing on the far side might not.

He leapt with his legs crouched up. The fall seemed far and silent before his left foot hit uneven ground and sent him rolling into a ditch. He lay still. There were no shouts.

He climbed to his feet and loped away to the left, away from the gate. At the first intersection he looked down to his left. The expanse of the Mekong could be seen reflecting dull light as it flowed at the end of the block. The soldiers would be waiting around to the left again, in front of the hotel. He crossed the street and cut up to the right, still undecided. The British Embassy was up that way, and the Australian. But how would he get in? There might well be police outside. It wasn't worth the risk. He turned right at the first intersection, along Sam Sen Thai, the other main road parallel to the river, and began running. At the next intersection he looked right towards the Mekong only to see a man standing in the middle of the road a hundred metres away, staring. There was a shout and the sound of running. Field pushed himself faster and at the following intersection turned down towards the river under the trees of the main avenue. It was blocked from the Mekong by the old palace grounds. He skirted around its walls listening, but the sounds had gone. Perhaps they hadn't seen him cut off Sam Sen. The river was at the end of the next block. He crossed over the quay and ran down along the edge of the bank. Charles had said there were boats smuggling refugees across from below the Australian Club. That couldn't be more than two kilometres. He ran back up on to the quay and on past the hospital grounds and then the dark spires of a Wat. There was still an island out in the river. It wasn't far, he kept thinking, not far. Then from somewhere he heard a voice, followed by an answer, echoing off to his left behind the buildings. His eyes shot around. There was no one. When he looked ahead again something had changed. Something was unclear. It was a few seconds before he realized that the blur was a man running towards him along the quay. In his right hand there was the morse code flash of a knife rising and falling as his arms pumped.

Field stopped himself and stood watching the signal come

closer. There was no point in running back upstream. None. He looked out at the river, then ran down through the few metres of weeds and dived in. The current was strong and even. He took a few strokes, kicked off his shoes and swam further out before looking up. The man stood on the bank staring at him, no more than ten metres away. He raised the knife, hesitated, to gauge the speed of the water and threw it. Field saw the blade coming, the metal luminous in the night. Its flight seemed locked on to his eyes as if they were magnets which also fixed his head in place. He waited in the current for the flash to arrive. Waited. Then the blade slipped by him on the upstream side. He looked back at the bank where the man was watching without a word or a further gesture while his quarry slipped away.

Butchers don't swim, Field thought and struck out again to avoid rocks or snags or whatever he couldn't see along the edge. Then he let the water carry him in a smooth flow. The islands disappeared behind him and he could make out a vague line off in the distance which was no doubt Thailand. The outlines on the near shore were hard to distinguish. There was a dark bulk which he thought might be Souvanna Phouma's house, in which case the Australian Club and the boats would not be far ahead. He swam closer to the shore and only then noticed the loose drag of his trousers. He reached down to his pockets. They were hanging out and the notebook was gone. His passport and his money were gone from the other. The shock of diving in, then kicking off his shoes must have done it.

A low form whirred suddenly out of the night and he was swept crashing against slimy wood and on under the thing. Seconds later it was gone. He came up coughing and gasping for air. There was the echo of shouting which died away into darkness. The boats, he thought. He was already past the Australian Club. In any case, without money they wouldn't take him. He would have to swim across. He struck out towards the centre and the fast current with the idea of letting it carry him down towards Nong Khai where there was a train to Bangkok. The water seemed to be running close to ten kilometres an hour. That meant there would be light before he had to swim the rest of the way to the far side.

The liquid had a thick dark quality, charged as it was with silt, and this plus the evenness of temperature between the river and the air removed all sense of physical contrast. The flow out in the fast stream carried him as if he were a child wrapped up in a blanket, on and on past meaningless shapes in the distance to either side. There was nothing there, he knew, just trees and the occasional building and the wide stream that emptied his mind of time and of images. Once the memory of Diana, butchered on the floor, swelled into his imagination, only to be swept away by a small wave that rolled over his head. Much later the silence was broken by a distant thumping which he registered as a drum calling for prayers in a monastery. That would mean it was four a.m. and he had been floating an hour and a half.

When the outline on the Lao side began to lighten, Field started kicking in the direction of Thailand. His main worry was that the customs sheds and the ferry of Nong Khai would flash suddenly into sight and he would be carried past them. At the first signs of scattered buildings, he swam hard for the shore. It took him five minutes, but when he reached out for something solid to take hold of, his hand slipped like jelly across a rock and he was rolled over, taking in mouthfuls of water. He coughed violently, then summoned all his energy to rush the bank in an attempt to get his feet down. They seemed boneless when he tried to wedge them in, but his hand caught on to a root and wrenched his arm. This he held to and levered himself forward until he lay in the sloping mud.

He could not stand or even crawl and so stayed there watching the light grow across the river. After a time he felt strong enough to drag himself up to higher ground, where he rested again, this time on his knees, and then pulled himself on to his feet and began walking haltingly along the edge of the fields towards the town. His chief concern was to find soft ground for his bare feet. When his knees were steady enough he climbed back down the river bank, stripped and washed the mud out of his clothes. Then he set off again.

After a time he saw fencing ahead and, behind that, huts. Those would be the Thai customs sheds. He cut straight inland until they were out of sight, then back again towards Nong Khai. Off to his left he could see a train waiting near the small station. There was no reason why the Laos would not also be waiting for him there. A single shot was all they needed. He cut back through the fields and over the tracks in order to get to the train on the opposite side from the platform. There were passengers waiting inside. He crept across the stones to the rear and looked carefully around the other side, then walked as quickly as possible to the first open carriage and climbed up. There had been a handful of people on the platform and had they noticed him, he would certainly have stood out. His clothes had already dried in the morning sun, but they were filthy and creased and he was barefoot. He locked himself in the toilet beside the carriage entrance and crouched there.

When he awoke the train was moving. He looked into the small dirty mirror on the wall and saw a web of scratches across his temple. His face was filthy and his hair matted down. These meaningless details were the first things he allowed himself to find upsetting and he set about trying to remedy them as best he could with water and with his fingers. Then suddenly Diana, as he had found her on the floor, filled the mirror and he began retching, again and again, into the basin, until there was nothing more inside him to bring up. It was a good half-hour before he had recovered enough to slip cautiously out of his cage and into the first seat in the carriage; a third-class compartment, only half-full. He shoved his feet as far under the seat ahead as possible and tried to sleep again. He was woken twice. First when the afternoon rain began. And later when the ticket collector arrived. Field went on to him about a friend in Bangkok who had his ticket. The trouble would be handled at the other end.

Indeed, as they pulled into Bangkok twelve hours later, the official reappeared with another and they stood over Field to make sure there was no escape, then escorted him through the crowds in the great tunnel-shaped hall to a policeman. Field felt the soles of his feet, dirty though they already were, gritting against the filth on the floor. The policeman took him to an office where he was allowed to telephone. He got Mrs Laker, who was about to leave her office for her bunker. She began immediately to bawl him out like a schoolteacher with a late child, but he cut her off. 'I'm at the train station. Get the fuck down here with some money.'

She arrived an hour later, chaperoned by her driver, and paid for Field's freedom without any comment on his appearance or his predicament. Once they were sailing along in the Impala he told her the story, leaving out any reference to the notebook. She said, 'My goodness,' when he came to the bodies, which he described only as mutilated. It was a distancing exclamation. Then she said nothing until the end. 'I'm surprised Som tried to help.'

'If that's what he was trying to do.'

She digested this. 'What about the contract?'

'My copy is in the hotel garden along with my clothes. You'll have to get it from Som.' She looked at him questioningly until he added, 'Three tons of coffee.'

'Good.' She patted Field's arm before realizing how dirty he was. After examining her palm, she added, 'What a horrible story. Horrible. How young was the girl?'

'My age.'

'Horrible!' There was a long silence. Five minutes, perhaps more. Then she repeated in a voice quite transformed, soft and quavering, 'Horrible. The human race is bestial. Bestial, John. How little we know. How little we want to know.'

He looked over. Her eyes were closed and there was a tear at the edge of the lid on the side that he could see. Nothing more was said.

When he shoved open the screen door and stamped into his house, there was an air of calm, which he could not ignore. Ao was curled up on the floor in the living room looking at a comic book that the cook had bought her. She smiled. Field scarcely saw her. He was already on his way upstairs, pulling off his shirt as he went. A moment later he was stopped by a hand that took over the unbuttoning. He looked down and focused on the girl for the first time. To his astonishment he felt a hint of pleasure at seeing her. It was the first thing he had felt since finding the bodies. She slipped around to the back to finish easing off his shirt.

'You OK, John?'

'No.'

'What happen?'

'It doesn't matter.'

She seemed not to hear this and pulled off his trousers. His underwear was caked with yellow stain. 'Oh, you sick, John.'

He felt his pain again, for the first time in thirty-six hours. 'That's right. I'm sick.'

She pushed him into the bathroom under the shower, tucked up her sarong and began to wash him carefully all over a first time, then a second, then dried him and led the way back to the bedroom where she massaged him until he fell asleep. Just before losing consciousness he asked,

'Did you go to the doctor every day?'

'Yes, John.'

'Well?'

'I still sick.'

He woke at six on Saturday morning, rolled over and found her at the foot of the bed. The sight filled him with a curious sense of warmth. He went downstairs and telephoned Barry Davis at home.

'It's Field.'

At the other end there was mumbling and a girl's voice in the background. Davis raised his own voice over the interference. 'Would you like to have a beer tonight?'

Field hardly let him finish. 'Get over here.'

'Listen . . .' The girl could be heard complaining. With Davis there was always a girl. '. . . I'd like to, only . . .'

'Just get over here!'

He hung up and went out to the cook's hut where he banged on the door. 'I want coffee.' Then he stood under the shower.

Davis didn't live far away. He was there in half an hour and sat down at the dining table, refused a cup of coffee from the cook, rested his elbows and his hands, clasped expectantly, on the surface and offered an expression of monk-like patience – which was his own interpretation of the diplomatic pose – while he listened to Field's story. This included a detailed

108

description of the bodies and of the lost notebook; the little Field had seen of it. At the end there was a thoughtful silence, then Davis asked for it to be told again. This time he fiddled with his moustache.

'I'll get you a new passport. Perhaps I will have a little coffee.' When this was in front of him he drank it very hot, the way only Celts and Anglo-Saxons can. 'Let's take it step by step. Our Embassy has not as yet been informed by the Laotian government that there are two murdered Canadians in Vientiane. Therefore we do not know anything. I'm going to wait twenty-four hours to see what the Laos volunteer. If there is silence, I'll start enquiring discreetly through the British and Australians, who are on the spot. And the French. They're still plugged in. You let me know if the contract with your Mr Som is confirmed, will you? And don't say anything to anyone.' He got up to leave.

Field put a hand across the table to stop him. 'What's going on, Barry?'

Davis raised his eyebrows as a sign of confusion. 'Drugs, I guess.'

'Don't give me that shit. Who was Charles working for?'

'What?'

'Was he working for you? Come on. What is this?'

'You tell me, John. You know more than I do now. Sounds like he might have been working for himself. Good citizen time. You know. Public spirited.' He walked over to the door and paused. 'I'm sorry.'

'Sure,' Field said. 'We're both sorry. In general, I'd say we are both very sorry. Specifically, me more than you, eh? Me, I'm extremely sorry.'

Davis listened to this with his hands held behind his back, as if frozen in embarrassment. 'I'll call you.' He went out.

Michael Woodward was at the Nursing Home every Saturday morning. It was a popular time for sickness and for treatment; so popular that Field and Ao found a room full of people waiting when they arrived. Instead of going into the waiting room he stood outside Woodward's door in the hallway, and when a young woman came out with her child, Field and Ao slipped in. Woodward looked up from his desk.

'If you insist on barging in, shut the door behind you.'

'What's the news, Michael?'

Woodward took on a commiserating air. 'I'm afraid, old boy, that there isn't any.'

Field sat down across from him. 'None?'

'Forty-eight, old boy. Forty-eight of medical science's finest antibiotics and your little dipococci just gobbled them up. Quite remarkable.'

'Remarkable?'

'Well, I mean, old boy, I've never come across it. You've produced some sort of new strain. I don't know how you've done it. And the world will certainly want to know about you if we don't start succeeding soon. Of course, we shall. Out there in the laboratories of the United States, the United Kingdom, Italy, and I don't know where else, there is an antibiotic waiting to pounce on your unusual monsters and shatter them.'

Field just nodded.

'I've already sent off some letters. Well, not letters actually. Speed is what we're after, if you are willing to pay, on which assumption I've sent some telexes. We could have a few more trays' worth out here in two weeks.' He looked at Field's depressed expression. 'Well, a week if they're sent by air courier.'

'The discharge is yellow.'

'Ahh. And the pain, it wouldn't happen to have moved back up the penis?'

'Yes.'

'Anywhere else?'

'Not yet.'

'Good. I think we'll just fall back on sulphonamides to see if we can't slow it down. What do you think?'

'What do I think? What are you talking about?'

'Sulpha drugs. They were used before the war; before antibiotics I mean. They did have some effect on gonorrhoea.'

'Before the war?'

'Well, John, we are somewhat beyond the beaten path now. All thoughts are of interest.' As he went about preparing a bottle of the white pills, he smiled over at Ao, curled up on the examining bed in the corner. 'Your friend is in slightly better shape than she was. The chlamydia, I should say, is on the retreat. Strange thing is, it was the gonorrhoea I treated. You must be looking after her well. And, of course, beneath all her disgusting diseases there does lie the strong constitution of a peasant. As to her gonorrhoea, it responded quite well to kanamycin; not in an absolute manner, but I've produced a number of clear knockouts from her culture and so she's already off and running on a series of cefutoxine. That little body of hers has no doubt seen a remarkable variety of medication, but my guess is we've surprised those nasty dipococci with this one.'

'Can't you talk like an adult, Michael?'

'Not in English, old boy. That's not the way they teach you in public schools. Now get your trousers down.'

'What for?'

'A specimen, dear boy, a specimen. I've got a few more brand names to play with while we wait for the exotic stuff to come in.'

Field turned his back on Ao.

'She's a sweet girl,' Woodward said.

'That's right.' Field was concentrated on the process.

'Now I'd say that the sceptre and the orb of western man are technology and rampant emotion. Wouldn't you? What would western man make of her, do you suppose? She doesn't fit the bill, old boy. Not by any description. Come here, Ao.' He turned away from Field and gave her her shot, which she accepted without question.

'Don't start talking at me, Michael. I'm not in the mood.'

'No, of course not. Anyway, it is just as bad here. Next month, you know, is my father's 96th birthday. Eighth cycle. Quite remarkable.' Woodward added sourly, 'My sisters want to give him a big party.'

'What's the matter with that?'

'It's not him the party is for. Their husbands want to show off the power of the clan before he moves on to his next reincarnation, or whatever. My father's friends are all dead anyway. The party is for the banker husband to ask bankers, the manufacturer to ask manufacturers, the general to ask generals . . . What else is there? A Police Assistant Director General. A senior director in the finance ministry. A property developer. And two Ambassadors. So they trot my father out and congratulate themselves.'

'You're not going?'

'Not if I can help it. If one of the Offensive Surgery Groups is being flown into a hill village, I'll get myself invited along.'

'That ought to win you a few more friends in town.'

'Do you think my brothers-in-law like me?'

'No. I suppose they don't.'

'Precisely. They will be happier if I don't come.'

'And your father?'

'My father doesn't tell anyone what he thinks. He's past that stage. He's not past thinking. He just doesn't want to talk about it any more.'

Field took Ao off to lunch at the Thai Room on Pat Pong 2, a restaurant noted for its mediocre Mexican, Italian and Thai food. At the next table a tensed Englishman was negotiating with a boy on the basis of the number of *baht* he would pay per position, stretched out over a weekend. The young man looked increasingly depressed as his future partner haggled with near viciousness over these positions, detail by detail, each of which was repeated two or three times to ensure there were no misunderstandings as to the deal.

On the other side, a carefully dressed Thai businessman and a Brooks Brothers-suited American were semi-whispering.

'As crudely as that?' the American said.

'You mustn't think of it as a bribe. Think of it as a special form of influence.'

Field looked around at the other tables of large, overweight, reddened Europeans picking at the food on their plates across from tiny, smooth Thai girls eating fast. He suddenly thought that it really wasn't a suitable place to bring a seventeen-year-old girl. That made him smile.

'What's so funny, John?'

'Private joke.'

'You tell me.'

'No.'

She pinched him under the table and when he jumped, she laughed. 'You tell me.'

'I'll buy you some ice cream.'

'Ice cream.'

'And Monday morning you go with Cook to your old District Office. Take your House Registration form and say you've moved. Then I'll write a letter for you to take to mine. You might as well be legally registered in the right place.'

She indicated agreement but hadn't understood. He didn't bother to explain in Thai.

The next four days went by without a word from Davis or a word in the press. Field combed the *Post* every morning before he set about his day, which, because he wasn't looking for business, consisted of doing nothing and trying not to think about his problem. In the afternoons he sat on his porch watching the rain. In the evenings he stayed home, since neither women nor drink, his two normal entertainments, were allowed. Even idle conversation would have struck him as an enormous effort.

On the fourth night he woke to find Ao wrapped in a sarong and curled up in his arms. He turned on the light and nudged her.

'What are you doing here, eh?'

'You make noise in sleep, John, so I come near you.'

'What noise?'

'Bad noise, John. Unhappy. Last night too.'

He was amazed. 'You slept on the bed last night?'

'No, John. You have bad dream all night. This time I come close. You stop.'

Field thought about that. He pulled himself up with a pillow behind his back. So the images were still there. He had succeeded in driving them out of the day and into the night, nothing more.

'What happen, John?' She had rolled on to one side and drawn her legs up, covering herself carefully with the sarong.

'Someone died.'

'Girl?'

'That's right.'

'Your girl, John?'

'No.' He looked at Ao. Her face was so young. Again he saw the sheen of purity, which made him forget what she was.

Untouched womanhood about to blossom. Eyes filled with questions, yet lacking fear. He wanted to take her head in his hands. 'No.'

'You love her, John?'

'Love? What do you care about that? For Christ's sake.'

'I know about love, John. They have TV at hotel. I see love all the time. Every day when I no work. TV all about love.'

'Shut up, Ao.'

'What you say, John?'

'Oh fuck.'

'You love her?'

He looked at the girl again. 'Sure. Sure. That's right. I loved her.'

'Like on TV, John?' Ao's interest was growing.

'Sure. Like on TV. Only more. A lot. I loved her a lot.' He sat staring at the girl. He saw nothing. His stare was unfocused so that he saw only the vague outline of a small dark body before him, an island in the night of crude electricity. Something alive but unseen. He stared and stared. 'A lot.'

The darkness of her body became larger as she came close and pulled herself against him. Ao lifted a hand full of her own hair and wiped the tears from his cheeks. 'It's OK, John.' She switched off the light and let him hold her tight until the human warmth sent him back to sleep.

On the third page of the next morning's *Bangkok Post* he found a small report under 'COUPLE MURDERED IN VIENTIANE.' 'Shock waves have swept through this small and peaceful Communist capital . . .' was how the article began. Charles Vadeboncoeur's driver had been arrested and had confessed, stating that he hated his employers, who had treated him badly.

Field called Davis at home. The diplomat immediately said, 'So you've seen the paper.'

'That's right. What's up?'

'Nothing. Absolutely nothing. We haven't had a word from the Laos. Yesterday I made an enquiry via the Brits saying we hadn't had contact with two citizens in Vientiane for some time. Twenty-four hours later comes the reply in the paper.'

'Which is a load of shit.'

'As you say.'

'So, Barry, what now?'

'Leave it with me.'

Field hung up without a word. He stamped around his house for a time, even picking up the photo of his father in the Rockies. The young man, who resembled Field himself, was wearing a checked flannel shirt with a leather, sleeveless jacket over it. Cold, Field thought. He stamped outside to look up into the trees but couldn't find the white squirrels.

'Ao!' he shouted. 'Come on. Time for your shot.'

When they had finished at the Nursing Home, they went over to the East-West Trading Company, where Ao was left on the porch downstairs while Field climbed up and insisted on seeing Mrs Laker. He was sent in only to find her on the telephone, a mask of studied patience and contempt upon her face. The voice at the other end had a shrill quality which carried so that Field could hear it.

'Now that he is in such a position, people can't expect me to drive around in a BMW.'

'No, dear,' Mrs Laker reassured. 'Of course they can't.'

'Bangkok isn't the provinces!' the voice whined.

'Well, then,' Mrs Laker cut in, taking charge of the conversation, 'what would you like to be seen driving in?'

'A Rolls.'

'What colour?'

'White, Catherine, and convertible.'

'All right, dear. Would you mind if we traded in the BMW against it?'

'You can have the thing back any time. I don't want it.'

'I understand that.'

When the phone was again in its cradle, Field asked, 'Who was that?'

'Krit's wife. We're up for some of the flood equipment contracts that he controls, so she wants a new car.'

'At least she doesn't waste time beating around the bush.'

'No,' Mrs Laker said. 'That she doesn't . . . Where have you been? I've tried to call you all morning.'

Her office was a symphony of nylon and polyester, the peculiar odours from which hung in the air despite a blasting

115

installation of air conditioning. The shutters were all closed and the neon lights on. She sat behind her desk, an American middle executive model, herself like a piece of the furniture.

'Let's put it this way,' Field replied. 'You haven't been trying to call me all week. And I've been at home.'

'Why should I call you, John, when I have nothing to say? You are such a sentimentalist. The Lao contracts came in this morning with a nice letter from Mr Som. Apparently he enjoyed doing business with you.'

'Enjoyed? Did he enjoy the murders?'

'Don't be silly. You know his mail would be examined on its way out. Besides, I saw the *Post* this morning, as I'm certain you did. The matter appears to have been cleared up.'

'Cleared up?'

Mrs Laker looked at him sympathetically. 'I understand, John. I do understand. You forget that I also have known pain. Known pain even to this day. And yet the lesson I carry with me is that pain will continue and must therefore be separated from the details of practical life. Now, for example, you have earned a good commission on this business. Remarkable. All around you, at the very same time, people have suffered and been in pain. People you love. You yourself have been emotionally scarred. And yet what is the result? A handsome profit for you personally. That, John, is the meaning of life. Don't you think I have discovered the same in my relationship with Norman? Do you know, I went to the cemetery yesterday and found the water flush with his stone. Oh, it is disgusting, John. Disgusting.'

Field nodded rather than comment.

'I have consulted the tidal charts. This month they will wash up the river at record heights. And the rain is heavier than it should be. Mrs Krit wants a car so that I can sell flood equipment to her husband, but the flood has already begun.'

Field nodded again.

'In one week this rain will have covered his monument as if my emotion did not matter. Norman and that stone are symbols of the American dream in Asia. Do you understand me, John? You talk of tragedy. What of our great tragedy here? Our loss of moral worth in the eyes of these people. For a start the stupid war we fought. Why? Why did we waste all those lives?'

At that Field rocked forward. 'Don't talk garbage, Catherine. You made your fortune out of that war and so did most of the Americans living in Bangkok.'

She moved her hand well up into the air, with fingers spread and nails glistening, and on in a wide sweep to dismiss his words. 'Where do you want your money? Hong Kong as usual?' There was a wounded edge to her voice.

'Yes,' Field replied. 'Hong Kong.'

'It'll get to your bank this week.'

He was jammed with Ao into the rear of a tiny taxi on his way home when Field noticed the policeman on the corner of Rama IV. He was wearing a white cloth face mask. That was new. At the next intersection he noticed the same thing. Perhaps all the traffic police had been dying of lung cancer. Or quite simply of asphyxiation. The afternoon rain began a few minutes later, which was two hours early for the season. After a short time the gutters stopped swallowing the water and the edges of the street began to fill. 'It's started,' Field mumbled. The traffic stood still and they were an hour getting home.

He found it impossible to stay cooped up inside that evening and went out to the Grand Prix. There were a few regulars there, but none of the journalists. They were all off covering the return from Vietnam of a US team sent to dig up a crash sight in the hope of identifying American soldiers listed as missing since 1975.

Field chatted with Rick, the owner, about this searching for remains. 'With a bleached cheek bone,' Field said loud enough for a number of people to hear, 'they can reconstitute on a computer the man's whole face, but they can't win a war.'

No one answered, so he concentrated on joking with the few girls who were reasonably recent arrivals at the bar, as opposed to those who had been dancing there for years. Then his attention drifted away and, as they knew him, they left him alone. His eyes were nominally on the legs dancing up on the centre of the bar, but in reality were on nothing, when he noticed the front door at the far end swing open. A Thai came in. Thin. Poorly dressed. Field reflected that he was a bit old to

117

be a shoeshine boy and went back to gazing up at the girls and sipping at his mug of Coke. Something made him glance down again and he found the Thai looking at him, just for a second, because the eyes flicked away the moment Field noticed. There had been an element of recognition in the man's stare. He began to work his way past the girls, who offered him a seat, and on up the side of the bar. Field watched this progress discreetly. There were rubber thongs on his feet and he wore a multicoloured shirt that fell loose outside his trousers. His hands hung down at either side.

Suddenly Field understood. Of course. It was clear. He knew exactly the type. From the docks or the railway yard. A fifty-dollar job. The standard Bangkok elimination. Field glanced at the man's averted face. No. He wasn't of the desperate bottom of the barrel quality. Perhaps a hundred or a two-hundred-dollar job. The man had paused five yards away and looked up at the girls as if interested. Field sipped his Coke and waited. He glanced round. There was no one on the stools to either side of him. Rick was behind his counter in the corner talking to a drinker. He looked back and found the man almost up beside him. Field's eyes were down on the hands hanging limp. The fingers were long. The nails short and dirty. The right hand moved up casually beneath the shirt as if to scratch the stomach. The man breathed in, loosening his belt, and the hand clasped something and jerked it free, then paused before lowering the pistol into sight. He flipped it up towards Field's head. As it came, Field threw his drink in the man's face and with his other hand grabbed the gun. He was stronger than the assassin and twisted both the hand and its weapon up on to the bar where he whacked the knuckles with his empty mug. The man made no sound and Field didn't look at his face. He whacked again and the fingers opened, letting the pistol slip away on to the bar top.

Field looked up at the man. The face was filled with fear. The lips were drawn back a fraction revealing a mouth that lacked its side teeth. The man yanked his hand free and ran for the door. When he was gone, Field asked for a Mekong neat. Only then did he notice that everyone at his end of the bar was silent and staring.

'What was that all about?' Rick shouted above the music from his corner.

Field dropped the pistol into his own pocket. 'A friend.' He emptied his glass of Mekong.

It was a ten-minute walk from there to the *Bangkok Post*. He cut across Soi Sala-Daeng, where it was quiet. And there, beneath a street light, pulled out the pistol. His hands were trembling, though not wildly. It was an 11 mm., the sort of gun a professional would use; unlikely to hurt anyone except the victim; noisy enough to cower bystanders while the man escaped. Field slipped it back into his pocket and walked on quickly.

CHAPTER 7

Field didn't notice the girl at the main reception, although she nodded to him when he came in. He cut through a rabbit warren of offices to the news floor, a large, almost windowless area where, across the open disorder of tables, Henry Crappe had a corner. As midnight had passed, he was there, typing behind an elementary school desk. It was a piled up, dirty desk. The middle drawer of the filing cabinet against the wall beside him was open a few inches, with Crappe's socks hung from the lip. Various tins of tobacco were set up along the desk front like a medieval defence, behind which Crappe slouched, his belt undone, his zipper lowered, releasing the full possibilities of the pear-shaped stomach that swelled out, pushing his shirt aside and revealing white boxer shorts. Crappe looked up, displeased.

'I am writing.'

Field threw himself down in the metal chair placed for supplicants and waited. Crappe stared at him. 'You've still got it. I told you to drink papaya juice.'

'Henry, I've got a problem that makes the clap look like applause.' He dropped the pistol on the desk.

Crappe stopped typing and gave Field a wary look.

'Have you ever heard of a man called Som Nosavan?'

'No.'

'He's a Lao, or claims to be. I've just done business with him . . .'

'That murdered couple,' Crappe cut him off.

'What do you know about it?'

'What I read in my own paper. Primo, chauffeurs, I can

120

assure you, Field, do not kill foreign employers in Communist countries. Secondo, nothing else has happened in Laos for six months, if not a year. Ergo, you are talking about the murdered couple.'

'All right,' Field said. 'This person, Som, I'd seen him somewhere before and my guess is it was a drug story.'

'Well, then,' Crappe said, turning to remove his socks from the filing cabinet drawer, 'we ought to look through the drug files.'

'That's why I'm here.'

Crappe slid the drawer open. 'What did he look like?'

'Plump. Short. Casual clothes. Good English and French. The full salesman.'

'The name you are giving me is wrong. There has never been a Som Nosavan in the drug business. Not that I have heard of. That is to say, not at all.' He swung out a thick file. 'Look through this. '84–'85. We'll have to hope there is a picture.'

Field turned the file round and opened it. Apart from published articles, there were all Crappe's private notes and unpublished photographs.

'I thought you wrote on sex now.'

'This is my stamp collection. I have the right – you are aware of the concept of inalienable rights, no doubt – to maintain a hobby.'

Field looked up, surprised at his vehemence. 'Who said you didn't?'

'No one. No one.' The dead tone of Crappe's skin was slightly flushed. He abruptly began typing his article again while Field flipped through the file. After a time Crappe stopped typing and picked up the pistol still lying on the desk. 'And where did you come across this?'

'The Grand Prix. Someone pointed it at me.'

'Pointed it. Ah. Unpleasant.' He sat watching Field turn paper.

'Don't you have an article to write?'

'Absolutely,' Crappe mumbled. 'Absolutely.' His enthusiasm came back. 'The Duke's Den is my subject. And it is a delicate matter to explain the full attractions of the place without mentioning the miraculous ejection of razor blades from private parts or the young couple who express their physical involvement so eloquently on the stage.'

'The bar top you mean?'

'Well yes. You know the place. As a matter of fact I took your friend George Espoir with me. I felt he was grateful for my guiding hand.'

'Good.' Field went on turning through endless stories of a kilo and a half of heroin seized at the airport while strapped to a German tourist's stomach; five kilos under the seat of a Chinese Thai's car parked outside the French Embassy; one and a half grams in the pocket of an American student; one kilo in a radio carried by an Italian model; eight kilos in a sofa being moved to the United States along with a junior diplomat's furniture; a plethora of false suitcase bottoms on their way to Hong Kong; rice trucks carrying acetic anhydride, the essential chemical in the drug chemist's life, up north towards the heroin mixers; pseudo battles between the Thai border police or army and Lao Sa's drug army; and, of course, declarations by ministers that the 'dark influences' must be wiped out. These declarations included several veiled references to the 'dark influences in senior positions', which sounded like General Krit was the one they had in mind. Field skipped through most of this. His eye was watching for an image or for a reference to Laos. Curiously enough, there weren't any. He finished the file and handed it back to Crappe. ''82–'83 please.'

Crappe nodded and reached over to the cabinet. 'I hear you've got yourself a young girl.'

Field looked up sharply, 'What do you mean?'

'Nothing. You know. The word is around. You've been dragging some young Thai beauty about with you. Here.' He dropped the file in front of Field. 'Very young, I hear.'

'What is this? Suddenly Bangkok is wallowing in morality?'

'Oh no! You misunderstand my interest. First, I have nothing against the King David principle. Let the fresh virgins warm our failing bodies if they are willing. Second, sexual deprivation in young girls immediately after puberty causes physical damage that probably explains why many western women cannot experience orgasm.' There was a gleam of missionary sincerity on Crappe's face.

122

'You mean sexual deprivation after the age of ten? Come off it.'

This was apparently the sort of response Crappe had been expecting, because he threw himself forward into a preaching pose. 'Apply to the sexual sensory system the facts known to apply to virtually all other body senses; viz, lack of use, at a critical period of development, causes degeneration. Take chickens, for example. Hatched in the dark and kept in the dark for 5 days, they will immediately begin to peck grain once the lights go on. But! But keep them in darkness for 14 days and they lose the pecking response. They will proceed to starve to death in the midst of plenty. Now. In western societies girls spend roughly six years after puberty without having their sexual receptors fully and regularly stimulated. I would describe this period as one of sexual deprivation, comparable to the chicken's period of light deprivation. Statistics, both eloquent and tragic, tell us that only 53 per cent of American women have experienced orgasm by the age of 20. There has just got to be some damage to the underlying nerve mechanisms by then.'

'All right. If you say so.'

Crappe reached forward and pressed his hand down on the second file to stop Field turning pages. 'It's not enough to stimulate the outer structures. I refer to the labia and clitoris. Because the deeper vaginal receptors and their nerve connections aren't getting anything.'

'So you don't disapprove?'

'Of you? No, Field. I do not. Though your condition might suggest some restraint vis-à-vis this girl.'

Field nodded. 'It might.' And went back to his search.

The picture that emerged was one of failure, just as Crappe had described it a few weeks before. The multitude of minor seizures added up to a few hundred kilos, while tons were getting through. And with few exceptions those caught were the 'mules': truck drivers, students, the poor and the stupid. If any trend emerged it was of the growing power of the Chinese networks that could distribute the drug from its opium stage in the Shan States right through its conversion near the Thai border, its transport out of Asia and its commercialization in

Europe and America. The traditional Mafia and other organizations seemed to have been pushed further and further down the stream in the process. Only the actual distribution in western markets remained a monopoly for them. He came across a profile of Shirley Chu and, a few months later, an interview with her. General Chu, her father, was the Kuomintang leader and had once been a major drug dealer; but his daughter had rejected this past and was calling for repression of the drug trade.

There was nothing in '82–'83 or in '80–'81. By then Field was slowing. The pain in his groin rose to interfere with his concentration. He began scratching first his arms, then his chest. When he focused on this and looked at his skin, it had come up in a low rash that seemed to be spreading from his joints out across the body. 'Oh, Christ,' he mumbled and stopped, his palms pushing hard on to the paper to keep the nails away from the skin. He sat immobile, his eyes open but unfocused.

'What's the matter?' Crappe asked eventually.

'Nothing.'

'What do you mean, nothing?'

'I don't know.' Field lifted his hands from the file for a second. 'I don't want to know all this. I don't want to know.'

'Debasing?'

'What?'

'Debasing?' Crappe repeated. 'You find it debasing?'

Field looked up at him, surprised. 'Sure. I mean, I don't want to know these things any more.'

'You think I do?' Crappe's tone was defensive.

'I didn't say that.' Field looked down at the file. 'You collect it, eh? So why do you do that?'

They stared vaguely at each other for a moment, then Crappe turned away deliberately and went back to his typewriter. Field began turning the pages again.

Crappe was finishing the fourth draft of his Duke's Den review and the morning light was outlining the news room windows when Field came across a ten-year-old photo. The plump, relaxed figure seemed not to have changed, except for his name. Somchai Pamak was what the article called him. He was a Chinese Thai and his story, the moment Field saw it, came back in a flash. 'Somchai Pamak,' he said out loud.

'Somchai!' Crappe exclaimed. 'But of course! Arrested March 9, 1974 along with four friends from Hong Kong, who were charged and sentenced. I suppose they're still in prison. But 84 days went by and the Public Prosecutor had forgotten to charge Somchai. Eighty-four days being the maximum you can hold a man without a charge, he was released. My article revealed this peccadillo which no doubt involved the exchange of considerable funds. A new warrant was issued. Too late. Our friend had disappeared for ever. Almost. My only satisfaction was to have forced the firing of the Public Prosecutor, who no doubt could by then afford a very comfortable retirement.'

'And Somchai just disappeared?'

'Yes. Now I know where. His wife and children got into the US during the big refugee rush. How, I don't know. And Somchai's businesses still exist. In whose hands I am not aware. He had a restaurant in Paris. A trading company in Switzerland. Another one in France. I assume they're dormant. And you, you were introduced?'

'He's running a trading company for the Lao government. I was selling him tractors and buying coffee.'

'Beautiful. And I suppose this couple had come upon something more.'

'I suppose. Henry, I'll make you a present of the whole thing. It's a great story and a little publicity will get them off my back.'

'And on to mine,' Crabbe said regretfully. '1960 to 1985. Forty-seven journalists shot dead.' He pointed at the pistol on the desk. 'What do you have? One fact. Somchai lives. The rest is rumour. You have no idea who is in charge at this end and that, that is what counts, because the individual in question, you understand, is the one who sicked this pistol upon you. Therefore, no thanks. This is not my birthday.'

Field scratched himself. 'Well, what the fuck am I supposed to do?'

'As I remember Somchai, he had fairly set habits. He was a family man when he wasn't out at a club. Sweet's I believe. Now Sweet's used to belong, at least in part, to Paga, of whom you are an intimate. Perhaps by that route you might unveil the Bangkok end of Somchai's trading business. But wait. Surely you didn't meet Somchai alone. Give me the context.'

'He has a partner called Iem. I didn't register the family name. And there was a Kamphet; his protector in the government, I suppose.'

'Kamphet . . . no. But Iem. Iem. Yes. Perhaps. A physical please.'

'Pretty ordinary. Short. Dry.'

'Dry. Stop. That's enough. Dry. Iem! Yes!' Crappe reached into his filing cabinet and shuffled for a moment before pulling out a file. 'Iem.' He shoved over a photo.

Field looked at the innocuous face. 'Yes. Probably.'

'Yes. Yes. Iem Norasing. Today 61. Chemist by profession. Formerly employed by General Ouane Rattikone. You may remember. Commander-in-Chief under the old regime. Also originator of the Double UO Globe Brand heroin business. The General, of course, has been benefiting from re-education in some rice paddy in picturesque rural Laos. Marxism in this case struck a just blow. However, I had lost sight of Iem.'

'He runs a detergent factory.'

'He would. How convenient. And he didn't change his name. Well, you see why I prefer to write on art and gratification. Nothing changes with drugs. There I thought old Rattikone and Co. were defunct and some new, raw, exciting chapter packed with new actors had begun; then out of the woodwork oozes Iem and off he goes again.' Crappe ripped his story from the typewriter. 'The Duke's Den offers endless novelty. Even if the act is repeated, those razor blades pop out of a new, unexplored vagina every week.'

Field got up. 'Thanks.'

'Ask Paga,' Crappe reminded him.

'Maybe.' He was thinking of Mrs Laker, who, after all, had somehow put a business deal together with the man. He turned to go.

'Hey, Field. I forgot to ask. What have you heard about the coup?'

'What coup?'

'Everyone is talking about it. The officers out of Class 5

126

believe, it would seem, that Krit is on their side. So much so that they're gearing up for a takeover. And the officers out of Class 7 also believe Krit is with them. And Krit, I would suppose, is raking it in on both sides. Amusing, don't you think?' Crappe betrayed a tremor in his voice.

'I thought you hated coups.'

'Oh,' he forced a laugh, 'I try to get used to them. But I do find it very upsetting. They are unpredictable, Field. Quite unpredictable.'

'Thanks, Crappe.' Field turned to go.

'Already the sugar is disappearing. You don't know a good place to buy sugar, do you?' Crappe had opened one of his file drawers and was staring in. 'Three large bags will do.'

'Thanks again.' Field repeated, scratched himself and left.

He dozed in the taxi and scarcely managed to keep his eyes open while walking from the gate to his house through the few centimetres of water that lay on the low ground. The first hint of morning heat only made him feel more exhausted and itchy and the pain in his groin more insupportable. His mind was clouded.

Ao sat facing him from across the dining table. She saw him come in and smiled with delight. Another girl in a white blouse and a blue skirt sat facing Ao, with her back to the door. Field at first thought one was a reflection of the other. He paused in the entrance. At the sound of him entering she turned to look. There was an expression of relief on her face. It was his daughter. She seemed unrecognizable because she had never before been to the house.

A rush of fear surged through him. He put out a hand to steady himself. 'What's happened?'

Songlin got up. 'Nothing. You were supposed to come to the university yesterday. I was worried.'

He came across the room slowly and dropped on to a chair as if to say, is that all. In truth it was the first time he had failed to appear without warning her. His mind clouded up again. He realized it had been clouded all week.

'I forgot.' He looked over at Ao. What had they been talking about? He didn't want Songlin in his house. He didn't want to be judged or shamed or responsible except on the territory he laid out. 'You shouldn't come here.'

She put her hands up above her head in a *wai* and went down on to her knees beside him. 'I'm sorry.'

'You shouldn't come here,' he repeated, without meaning to. He saw no way to explain. And the last thing he wanted now was for people to associate him with her; not now when some nut was trying to kill him. 'You mustn't stay here.' He saw dimly that there were tears in her eyes but he couldn't focus on them. He was too tired. Too confused. He couldn't deal with them. Instead he shook his head and looked away. There was a clatter, then the door slammed and when he looked up she was gone. The photograph of his father in the Rockies was lying on the table before the chair on which she had been sitting. His hand lashed out to knock the picture to the floor. He stopped it in time and instead struggled to his feet to telephone the Nursing Home.

Woodward had just arrived. He said the rash was quite common; an allergy to the sulpha drugs. 'Stop taking them,' was all he could suggest.

Ao came up from behind and pushed Field towards the stairs. He let her wash him and put him to bed. Then she sat on the mattress and watched until he was asleep.

The telephone woke him late in the morning. There was rain thundering against the leaves outside. He stumbled over Ao who was asleep beside him and on down the stairs. An imperious yet warm voice skipped any greeting.

'John, what are you doing now?' It was Mrs Laker.

'I was asleep.'

'That's good. It's good to nap during the day, but afternoons are better. I need to see you, John. Right now.'

'Well you know where I am, Catherine.'

'No. I daren't leave here. I can't trust the elements to remain in place. You must come.'

'Where?'

'The British Club.'

She hung up. Field had been about to say that he, on his side, also wanted to see her. 'Bitch,' he mumbled, then showered and dressed and went out. On the street he almost turned back to ask Ao what she had said to his daughter, but somehow he felt happier not knowing.

The British Club was a low stuccoed villa on a few acres lost in behind modern buildings between Silom and Surawong Roads. Bangkok had swollen around them, but the members had refused to sell. The clubhouse had once had a certain colonial charm. Only the Number Ones of British trading companies had been allowed to join. More liberal policies had led to more members and that to renovations and those to a lobotomized atmosphere not unlike a Trust House Forte hotel. Mrs Laker's Impala was outside, but there was no sign of her beneath the *salas* at either end of the pool. Field went into the clubhouse and stopped in the wood hall to brush the rain off his hair. The dining room was on the left.

Most of the tables were taken by men in white shirts and dark ties without jackets; the *farang* uniform. He looked around. In the midst of this anonymous crowd an old man sat alone at a table. He was slight and short and he wore his jacket. It was of a cream linen suit that had turned a soft gold with age. The suit and the stiff collar and the rest were extremely elegant. The man sat bolt upright. A wide straw hat lay on the chair before him. It was Michael Woodward's father. The ninety-five year old Admiral. Field went over to greet him.

The Admiral was concentrating on a plate of half-eaten steak and kidney pie. He looked up immediately and before the younger man could say a word, barked out, 'Hello, young Field. Sit down.'

'Thank you, sir. Just for a moment.'

'This,' he said, pointing at the remains of the food on his plate, 'is as disgusting as it ever was. Don't let them tell you different.'

Field peered at the dark floury mess. 'I'm sure it is, sir.'

'Nevertheless, I've been coming here once a month since 1912 and always order this stuff. Truth is, Field, I hate it.'

'Well why do you order it, sir?'

'Same reason I come here. Not because I'm British. 'Cause I'm not. I'm Thai.' He said this quite loud so that the other tables could hear. 'I come to this place to remind myself that I once was British. And I order that,' he pointed again, 'to

129

remind myself how disgusting it is. Steak and kidney pie is just the sort of thing an Englishman abroad might order to remind himself of home, don't you think? Nostalgia is a dangerous beast, Field. It can sneak up on you from behind. Now in my day we fought face to face.'

'So you come here to meet the enemy?'

'Correct. The enemy of life is nostalgia.' He stabbed a square of overcooked meat and chewed it with satisfaction. 'Now beginning to congeal.' He pushed the plate away. 'How is my son?'

'He's fine. I saw him two days ago.'

'Good. I like what he does. Stirs it up, don't you know. I like that. Not for me to do. Do you know, I came to this club in '41, the day after the Japs landed. There was a meeting here for all the British. Crosby, an idiot, was the Ambassador; Minister Plenipotentiary we called him then. He told us, "Sit tight, I've got it all in hand." They all agreed that Crosby was a good fellow and if he thought everything was in hand, well, it was. So I got up and said, "I'm here as a Thai who knows what is going on and you better get the hell out. All of you. Fast. Right now." 'Course they didn't trust me and they sat tight. Next day they were rounded up. Spent three and a half years in a prison camp.'

A Thai waitress removed his pie and set before him a bowl filled with trifle. He looked at her with a discreet but appreciative eye. There was a deep yellow quality to the custard. Admiral Woodward picked up his fork and speared deep into the bowl, causing the custard to jiggle. He came up with a soft, white cube and raised it beneath Field's nose.

'Note. We live in the country of the pineapple. It grows whichever way you look. Examine this cube. Tinned. They use tinned for their trifle. It's done that way in England, so that must be best. That, you see, is the colonial mind: an unassailable sense of superiority no matter how inferior one really is.' He popped the cube into his mouth. 'I shall finish this alone. You run along, young man.'

Field looked in the billiards room; it was empty; then climbed the stairs which rose up around the hall to a reading room, air conditioned and devoid of real smells. There were no books. Mrs Laker was waiting there alone in an armchair; her knees together, her arms laid out on the rests to either side and her eyes closed. She wore a green linen dress.

When Field was near her, she looked up. 'Sit here, John.' She indicated the chair beside her. 'Do you feel strong?'

'No,' Field said, 'and I want to ask you something.'

She put out a hand to stop him. 'John, listen carefully. Evil has greater power here because it is more openly used. We must therefore act vigilantly against evil. Now I am going to tell you things which you must never repeat.' She looked at Field for agreement and maintained her stare until he gave a nod. 'When my husband Norman fell sick in 1959 it was diagnosed as polio. He was taken to the Bangkok Nursing Home, which you know, and put in an iron lung on the ground floor. It was in December and it was cold, John. Cold the way I have never known it to be. I wore my fur as I sat beside him, enclosed as he was in the machine, and I listened to the terrible sound of his rasping breath. That cold was the final sign. It was a hand put over this country. Do you understand? He was five days in the iron lung. I never left his side. Then on Christmas morning, as I was wiping spittle from his mouth, he suddenly smiled, not at but past me, smiled in welcome and died. Or seemed to die. I was so cold, John. Then the doctor came and took me out on to the balcony. There was no nurse. We left Norman alone. I never saw his body again, you understand. The doctor led me from the balcony straight out to my car. At the time I thought he was trying to spare me the grief of seeing Norman dead. Now, Venus had been high three weeks before and during the two weeks between that date and he being struck down, I was constantly thinking the same things as Norman at the same time. Already I was becoming his cipher. Everything was in preparation for my takeover.

'Then, after his death, I was prevented from crying. I was prevented from killing myself, although I wished to. I thought of nothing but that, and yet my mouth was held by some invisible force in a grotesque grin. For weeks, John. For weeks. I ran away, back to New York and there on February 22nd I received a message from Norman.'

'A message?'

'I was lying in the bath trying to gather enough courage to cut my wrists when suddenly all of my fear slipped out into the water and with it the artificial smile. Then Norman's force rose up through the vapours around me and I received a message. He was with a group in the Andes. I don't mean he was a spirit. Not at all. He was and is of this world.'

'In the Andes?'

'That's where he is.'

'Why don't you go there to see him?'

'It isn't that sort of group. The message was that I should return to Bangkok. So I came back here and I found our company almost bankrupt. But every day he gave me instructions. I have been but his instrument. Since that day, John. And, in a sense, I suspect that he himself is but an instrument.'

'Whose?'

'I can't explain that. After 26 years I still don't understand their intentions or my purpose. But I want to understand. You see,' she paused to make certain he was listening, 'the body in that tomb out in the graveyard is not his. No, John. Some force removed him from the hospital. Remember, I went outside with the doctor. No one was there. We thought him dead. But some force came and removed him alive and replaced him with some organic form. And now Norman has given me new instructions. I must remove the organic substance from his grave before the waters cover it again. Those waters are imbued with the forces of evil. I wonder, John, if this urging does not arise from a certainty that the Vietnamese are coming. That the Vietnamese are going to invade, and if they do, they will be in Bangkok in hours. The army here will never stop them. You know that. They are so corrupt. Norman, Norman always hated the Vietnamese. He would never leave this organic substance in their hands. It is, without being his own body, nevertheless an integral part of his group. That is only a speculation on my part, I admit. My instructions, however, are clear. I must cremate the substance and preserve it. My calculations show that today may be the last before the flood and so we must do it now. I need your help, John, in case I am not strong enough. In case there is some manifestation which would require your calm and strength. They are waiting for us at the cemetery.'

Field had fallen into an ever deeper silence. He didn't want to have to deal with any of this. 'All right, Catherine. But first you tell me something. How did you get together with Som Nosavan?'

She blinked at him in amazement. 'I don't want to waste time over business.'

'I do.' He sat solidly in his place to make it clear he wouldn't move.

She said abruptly. 'The Lao Embassy approached me with the deal.'

'Som himself?'

'No. A trade officer. Then a government official came to Bangkok to see me.'

'Who?'

'I don't remember.'

'Come on, Catherine. Don't give me that.'

'Kamphet something. Kamphet Panyajak.'

'So you'd never come across Kamphet or Som before this deal?'

'No. What's this all about?'

'Nothing, Catherine. Let's go.'

As they appeared outside her driver quickly sprayed the back seat for mosquitoes. It had stopped raining momentarily.

'We're not driving,' Field said. 'It's five minutes on foot.'

Mrs Laker ignored him and got in, so he followed. The whole car was filled with the odour of DDT.

'It stinks,' Field complained.

'You have got to be careful.'

Nothing else was said until they reached the cemetery, where eight men and a truck were waiting. Silom Road was partially under water, as was the lane between the two sections of the cemetery. They waited in the back seat until the driver brought them the rubber boots from the trunk, then stepped out into five centimetres of murky water. On the inside of the cemetery wall there was a further step down a good ten centimetres into what looked like a green sea. The guardian had moved his household up on to a covered platform a metre above the water level.

The eight workmen were in shorts and bare feet and were crowded together waiting for instructions. Mrs Laker surveyed the swamp and struck out through the water with the tops of her boots rising a scarce few centimetres above the surface. Field followed and the workers trailed behind with crowbars and ropes. They passed the wood monument of Basil Southend, Royal Counsellor, who was afloat and held in place only by the vines which entwined him. His wife's monument had escaped and drifted off among other, more solid, graves. Fifty metres along, Mrs Laker stepped off to the right and screeched as she plunged up to her thighs and pitched over on her face. Field jumped down and lifted her upright. There was thickened water running off her face and through her set hair.

'We should have come yesterday,' she said.

Field took off his shirt and gave it to her to wipe her face and arms. 'More to the point, you should have brought waders.' He looked behind at the Thai workers who were still up in the shallow water, giggling.

'Mah Nee!'

They obeyed immediately, jumping down into water that reached their waists. Field struck out ahead of them, leading the way. The tomb was under eight centimetres of water. He told them to pry the lid off, but himself stood back without knowing quite why. As it came loose there was a sound of liquid rushing in to fill the void. He thought it curious that the cavity should have been so well sealed and looked for Mrs Laker, who was behind him and seemed to find it quite normal. No doubt she had gone to great efforts to make it airtight.

'It's a steel coffin,' she announced.

The Thais were already poking around in the submerged cavity to see what was there. It took them half an hour to get ropes underneath and begin lifting, while they complained that it was too heavy.

'Of course it's heavy,' Mrs Laker said. 'It's steel.'

The casket that rose from the depths was enormous.

'Was he fat?' Field asked.

'Of course not. That would have been unhealthy in this climate. I felt he needed a generous size. To give him room.'

Just then the coffin came above the water and a pungent smell filled the air. It wasn't a putrid smell or any other identifiable odour. And yet it was unbearable at close range. The men tried to cover their faces as they worked to get the bulk out. Field moved away. When he saw them attempting to lift it to their shoulders he told them not to. 'Drag it. The smell won't be so bad if it's under water.' Through all of this Mrs Laker stood firm, as if the air were filled with perfume. Field didn't wait to watch the transporting of the organic substance. He went out and climbed into the rear of Mrs Laker's Impala with his boots on. The leatherette was sticky against his bare back.

'Turn the air conditioning off, Lek.'

Ten minutes later the men appeared with the casket on their shoulders and one hand covering their noses. Mrs Laker was immediately behind, both hands at her sides, as if in a funeral procession, the mud-filled, back-combed hair leaning heavily to the left over her smeared face. She waited until the casket was loaded on to the truck before coming to join Field. The driver bent down to remove her boots, but she said it didn't matter and let her sodden form fall on to the back seat.

From there to Wat Tat Thong, where she had arranged for the cremation, the traffic was solid. Silom Road was dry, but the lanes running off it were all under six inches of water and cars had stalled here and there, slowing things up. In fact this was a blessing as it meant the workers could climb off the back of the truck whenever they wished to get away from the stink. It was almost two hours before they got there, during all of which Mrs Laker sat silent, her eyes closed in concentration. Field noticed there was water inside her boots up to the top. Then he realized the same was true of his own, so he emptied them out of the window. He stripped off his socks and rolled up his trousers. She still had his shirt in her right hand. He took it, wrung it out and put it up to dry on the ledge beneath the back window.

Wat Tat Thong was a popular place for cremations, so it was designed to ease the arrival of bodies. The workers were able to put the coffin on a trolley and take turns at pushing it. It was only a matter of minutes before they had it in the courtyard and on the table in front of the oven, which was just below the fifty-foot white chimney. They were about to take their distance and leave the rest to the monks when Mrs Laker rushed up shouting,

'Come back! Open it. We must open it.' They showed no eagerness for this so she turned to Field who had been standing at a distance in his stained shirt and trousers. 'I must see it, John. I must be certain. Please.'

He made no reply, but pulled his shirt up over his nose and walked across to the casket, which had a seal at each end. He pried one back. There was a scraping sound. He walked around and began to pry the other. Mrs Laker came up behind him. He said to her through his muffle,

'Cover your face, Catherine.'

She ignored him, so he flipped back the seal and with a sudden heave shoved open the lid. It rose straight up as if on a spring and the smell overwhelmed Field. He rushed backwards until he could breathe, then saw that Mrs Laker was peering down into the open shell.

'My God,' she murmured. 'My God.' And she fainted.

Field forced his legs forward and picked her up. As he did he couldn't stop himself looking in. The body was bright green and, apart from that, perfectly preserved; it might have been alive. It, he was a large man. An extremely large man. This couldn't have been a problem of swelling because his double breasted suit sat upon him as if just pressed. There was a welcoming smile on his face and his hair was brushed.

Mrs Laker was as light as air so he carried her back out to the car, leaving the monks to get on with the cremation. She regained consciousness on the back seat, but said nothing. She just lay perfectly still. An hour later the monks appeared with the *ghod* containing the bones and ashes and handed it to Mrs Laker. It was one she had been forced to buy at the last moment as her decision had been sudden. The silver container was in the shape of an elaborate phallic symbol and was covered by the most common of Thai designs. She took the foot high *ghod* and held it at a distance, staring with wonder.

'It wasn't him,' she whispered.

'What do you mean?' Field barked.

'It wasn't Norman. It was nothing like him. Nothing at all. I'd never seen the man before.' She held the silver container on her lap with a care verging on adulation. After a time she added, 'Cellular biology.'

'What?'

'Cellular biology. If I learn how my cells work, I might be able to control what they do, thereby avoiding the manipulation of the stars.'

CHAPTER 8

The water had risen earlier in the day, just enough to wash across Sukhumvit Road from the low side to the high where Field lived, though this minor wave had come nowhere near his house and had quickly sunk into the ground.

Field stayed home the time it took to shower and change and, more to the point, to lecture his night watchman about security. When this made no impression, he turned on the boy's grandmother, the cook, and explained that the doors must be kept locked and she and her grandson must beware of any stranger coming into the compound. Ao listened to all these warnings impassively.

Then he went back out into the falling darkness of evening only to find the rain had begun again. He ran up the lane towards Sukhumvit and jumped into the first thing that passed – a *tuc-tuc* with plastic semi-transparent curtains which somehow drew the water in rather than closing it out.

'Patpong,' he said.

'Sixty.'

'No, no. Thirty.'

'Bangkok too much traffic. Fifty. One way system. One way.'

'Thirty,' Field said and sat stolidly smiling until the man turned up his radio and surged ahead. The drums from the music vibrated into his plastic tent and around him as if the whole thing were a wired conductor. Behind the drums a voice half-sang, half-shouted: 'Made in Thailand, not in Japan.' It was the latest Bangkok hit and had picked up on the nationalist surge of which Meechai Woodward was a part. The humidity and heat outside acted upon the rain cover the way a burner would upon a steamer, with Field the morsel being steamed.

As they passed the British Embassy grounds, Field saw through the deformations of the plastic that there was a party going on inside the residence. And before it, Queen Victoria sat, lit up, with a dozen or so garlands around her neck. He could never understand how the women of Bangkok got past the Gurkha guards on the gates to hang their wreaths. It would have been quite a different matter in the early days when the British Legation had been down on the river along with all the other foreign embassies. There had been no roads in Bangkok and the King, out of sympathy for the tastes of the *farangs*, had filled in the canal that ran along behind their houses to give them somewhere to ride in their carriages. Outside the British gate on this New Road, the Queen's representatives had placed several tons of Victoria, staring at all passers with the full power of the Empire. This imperial threat didn't impress the Thais. Instead, her reputation for personal fecundity attracted sterile women, who began bringing presents, lighting candles in her lap and saying prayers. In no time at all, she had become a minor local goddess – the word 'spirit' would have been more accurate, but her size and shape ruled it out. In the twenties the legation had moved up to where it still was on Ploenchit Road and the statue with it. But this time the Queen was put fifty yards inside the gates; theoretically because imperial attitudes were out of fashion. But beneath this discretion lay a feeling among British diplomats that Victoria as a fertility goddess was not quite the image they wanted to project. Still, her reputation lived on. When the Japanese occupied Bangkok in 1941, they ordered her boxed in. The Thai workmen who built this cover cut a slit in the right place for her eyes.

It was seven p.m. and dark by the time Field reached Patpong. On the landing at the Paga Apartments, the girl in place was the same one who had refused to recognize him the week before.

She called down the stairs, 'Hello, mister. Massage. You want massage?'

'I want Paga.'

'Paga? What you want?'

Field waited till he was on the landing and came up close to her. 'I'm Paga's big friend. Remember? We went through this last time.'

'Sorry, mister.' She smiled.

'Is she upstairs?' Field strode by towards the stairs.

'No, mister. She not here.'

'Where is she?'

'Out.'

'Where?'

'King's Castle maybe.'

'Good girl.' He gave her a pat on the top of her head, which was at his chest level, and ran down the stairs. The gutters had flooded out towards each other without quite meeting in the centre so that it was worthwhile edging along the pavement in search of high ground.

The King's Castle was on the other side and it was Paga's newest revamp of old quarters. All her bars had been where they were for years, but each had resurfaced again and again under new names with a new décor. Four girls were up on the island in the centre of the oval bar and four more were at the far end; all dancing in bobby socks and pumps. Another sixty or so were on the floor encouraging the *farangs* to drink for a cuddle and to buy a drink for the cuddled. Well over a hundred people were jammed into the room. Paga was behind the bar, huddled over the cash and the receipts, beside the cashier, a pretty, efficient-looking girl.

Field leaned across so that she would hear him above the thumping music, 'I didn't know you did front line service any more.'

Paga looked up without smiling. The figures held her engrossed. 'Spot check, John. Come inside.'

He slipped under the counter door and dropped on a stool at her side.

'How is girl you buy?'

'Still sick.'

'Ohh.' Paga considered this with sympathy. 'That's no good. Why you buy her anyway?'

'Whim.'

She slapped him on the hand reprovingly. 'What you want?'

'Mekong soda.' Rice whisky wasn't on his official diet but he felt beyond doctor's constraints at this point. If medicine couldn't do anything for him, why should he co-operate?

'Eat your liver up,' Paga warned. 'Make you go blind.'

'So does masturbation.'

'Who told you that? Better drink beer or whisky.'

'I owe my liver nothing.' He grabbed the bottle, from which a girl was about to pour his drink, and put it down near Paga's accounting light to look at the date. 'This week's, for Christ's sake. Find an older bottle.'

The girl thought this was very funny and handed him another bottle of Mekong, which he rejected. She went on handing them over, one after the other, and Field kept sending them back.

'Here,' he said. 'Here's a good one. August 15th. Two weeks old. The poison should have settled.'

'Sorry about sick girl,' Paga said. 'I make you a present. You take any girl in the place except the cashier and I no charge take-out fee.'

'Thanks, Paga.' He slipped an arm around the cashier. 'Nok is the prettiest one here and the only one with money.'

'Two hundred *baht* present. You just pay girl.'

Field shook his head. 'I've gone off it.' He saw Paga looking at him doubtfully. 'I don't know why. Abstinence maybe. It's nice to look, but I've gone off it.'

She examined him carefully. 'You got a problem, John?'

'If I don't want a lay does that mean I've got a problem?'

'A man came to ask for you today. Not a nice man.'

'What was he like?'

'He came here before me so I not see him. That girl see him.' Paga pointed at a young dancer whose bathing suit was cut away sharply at the waist, leaving only a narrow electric green strip to dive down over her crotch and around between her bare cheeks. She was stuffing a ten *baht* note into a miniature temple on the bar and bowed before it.

'She must have a heavy date,' Field said.

'Pin. Come here.' The girl floated up to Paga. 'Who was man who ask for John Field?'

The girl put a hand out on to Field's arm. 'I not know. Never see before here. Not Thai man. Chinese man.'

'Great,' Field said.

'Not nice man.'

'What did you tell him?'

'I not know you.'

'Great,' Field mumbled and patted her bare backside before turning to Paga. 'You remember Somchai Pamak?'

'Sure,' she said. 'In the old days he come to Sweet's once a week and spend lots of money. Two thousand *baht* a night. Drinks for friends. Drinks for girls. Take girl to back room. Pay her. Pay me for room. Big spender.'

'Have you seen him?'

'Oh no. He disappeared. His friends I see sometimes. I see them for a while after he disappeared but not now.'

'Why not?'

'Somchai big dealer. You remember that?'

'Sure.'

'His friends little dealers. Thavorn; they catch him with lots of kilos long time ago.'

'Before or after Somchai disappeared?'

'Maybe one year after. Firing squad shoot him dead.'

'That's right.' Field remembered the incident. 'And he was a friend of Somchai?'

'Good friend. Then Hu Tien Sing and Hu Tien Phu, brothers you know, and some Vietnamese got caught in Paris. I heard after. Then Somchai's brother get caught in Bangkok. He was good spender too. I think he bribe someone because he's already out of prison but I not see him. Then Tasanai. Not too long ago. He's pretty smart. Ship lots I think. And one or two more get caught but I don't remember.'

'So Somchai is still in business, you think?'

'Sure, John. That's why he disappear. That your problem? Somchai. Watch out, John. If he got one friend in prison he buy new friend; six friends in prison, he buy six new friends. Look, John.' She pointed at a shy girl trying to dance before the half-indifferent, half-lascivious audience beneath. 'New girl. You want her?'

'I told you. I've gone off it.' Her face was overcome with

concern. 'It used to be more fun, Paga. The quality of the acting has fallen. That's your fault.'

'Not me. I run the best school. Too many *farang* now, John. Too much money. Not my fault.'

'Anyway, I have my sick girl.'

'What you want her for?'

'Conversation.'

Paga decided she was being teased. 'Go away now. I got my books to do.' As an afterthought, she added, 'I ask around for Somchai, OK?'

'Sure, Paga. You ask.'

Outside he paused and looked along the pavement to the left. The rain had stopped. Two or three stripped-down girls waited before the entrance to each bar. If their bit of pavement had given away, they were balanced on squares of plywood placed over the crevices filled with water. This crowd obscured his view, which was further blocked by the Whites and Japanese and Thais who prowled slowly along, pausing before each door while it was swung open for them to see the shape of the dancers within. During each pause, the girls outside tried to entice them. Anywhere in that mass, he thought, Somchai's friends could be waiting or prowling in search. No. Not in search. He wasn't hidden, after all. Any idiot could find him. Anywhere. Whenever they wanted. So they were there, merely waiting for what their own private interests might call an appropriate time and place. He let his eyes swivel out in a slow arc from the pavement on to the street and across to the other side, which was equally crowded, and on down to his right. Anywhere in this crowd, he thought. Any of these people. For the first time he felt a concrete, conscious fear and wanted to step back inside the bar where he could limit the faces. Where a gunman might stand out. He forced himself to remain immobile.

A girl beside him took his arm. 'You come back in, John?'

'No.'

She eased him to one side so that he didn't block the door.

'No,' he repeated, though it went unheard. 'I'm not coming back in.'

The next day was Saturday and the sky through his bedroom

windows was a clear, light blue. He took Ao out early to the Nursing Home and noticed as they drove that the streets were empty, the city still quiet. No one had been lurking outside his house. No one was following his taxi. Life was the way it had always been, except for the pain in his groin, which had been with him, after all, only five weeks; a short, a very short time, a mere blink in the years he had spent living in this place and the years he would go on living there. He had seen other blinks; not exactly like this one, not exactly like Somchai, but harsh little moments. And they had passed.

Woodward had no positive news for either of them. The new selection of antibiotics had not arrived and when he looked at Field's discharge he made absolutely no comment. It was to any eyes very yellow. He squeezed here and there and asked if it hurt. In general Field was obliged to admit that it did. As for Ao, he made encouraging sounds which amounted to nothing specific.

'In any case, I'm afraid she'll be sterile, which is perhaps a blessing in disguise.'

'Sterile,' Ao repeated. It was apparently the only word she had picked up.

'I'm afraid so,' Woodward repeated.

'Sterile,' she said again, with more tragedy in her voice.

It struck Field as a curious outbreak of emotion from someone whose life had been so narrow and brutal in all things related to family and sex.

'I could do with your help this morning,' Woodward said to Field, 'if you're free.' There was a quizzical little smile on his face.

'Sure.'

Field took Ao downstairs and put her in a taxi home. When he got back to the Nursing Home, Woodward had changed into his peasant outfit and was waiting under the porch.

'We'll walk,' he said.

'What did you want me for?'

'Not exactly want, John. You seem jumpy.' He turned right on Convent Road.

'I am.'

'You mustn't worry about your infection.'

144

'It's only five weeks, right? I'm not worried. I'm resigned. Which makes Ao a dream mate.' He chuckled at that. 'Unfortunately I've also got some loonies on my tail.' Woodward looked at him, blank. 'Oh, you know. Some drug types who fear my intimate knowledge, right. Bang, bang. Right.'

Woodward considered this pantomine seriously. 'And they have reason to fear?'

'Sure. They think so. I'd like to tell them my memory has gone. And my eyes. Blindfield, that's my name. I'd sign an affidavit of silence if they'd give me the chance, but things don't work that way.'

'Well, what are you doing about it?'

'Keeping a small distance between my good friends and myself to minimize the wounded.'

Woodward put his arm through Field's and drew him close as they crossed Silom Road. 'I thought this might amuse you.'

'What?'

'A sexathon arrival. Twelve days, $1,400.'

'A what?'

'Fifty Dutch men. A package deal.'

He said nothing more until they had walked the full length of Patpong and crossed over to a large new hotel where a few hundred students were massed silently before the entrance. They held fifty or so signs in English. Woodward left him on the edge of the crowd saying only, 'Wait for me here,' and walked along the front of the quiet demonstrators. When they saw him, they cheered and he raised his round straw hat on his cane. Field moved out enough to see the placards.

'Syphilis Tours Go Home,' was the most original. Ten minutes later an airport bus rolled up. The front and rear doors opened and men began to spill out, laughing and talking with each other, weighed down by duty free bags of alcohol and cigarettes. They were middle-aged and generally overweight. Field thought of Ao massaging the tree trunk thighs. At first they didn't notice the placards. They were all out of the bus before a group of students ran up and began to photograph them while the others shouted, 'Sex tours go home! Sex tours go home!' The men suddenly realized that this crowd had been waiting for their arrival. One or two tried to slip through to the hotel lobby, but the students had joined arms and these large family men couldn't bring themselves to use force; not against such innocent-looking children, because with short hair and uniforms, the impression was more one of twelve-year-olds than of university students. Instead they blushed and turned in confusion. Some ran back towards the bus, where the photographers stood clicking their cameras. Within seconds they were all in a crowd trying to climb back on board. Once inside an argument began with the driver about what to do next. The students had circled the bus and were laughing. Field himself was laughing.

Then he saw Songlin in the middle of the crowd. She didn't have a placard, but a boy was holding her hand and in the other hand he held a sign, 'Thai Girls For Thai Men'. Field thought the handwriting was like his daughter's. He slipped back so that she wouldn't see him and stared at the young couple until he was overcome by a fit of depression. 'She has no right to think anything of me,' he mumbled to himself, and walked away.

The humidity was building, but not enough to break into his funk. He wandered up to the intersection and turned along Rama IV where he walked and walked, much of the time beneath a row of skyscrapers. His left foot was lower than the right because these new buildings with deep foundations were not sinking while the road was, so that the pavement hung around the skyscrapers like a billowing skirt. Once he looked back just to see if someone was following. There was a crowd around him, but not one from which he could pick a particular face or peculiar action. He shrugged and walked on. At the corner of Sathorn Avenue he waited for the light, which lasted three minutes. Out in the intersection three policemen were whistling private symphonies to encourage the cars on. They weren't wearing pollution masks.

His eye picked out one of the officers. He knew the man but couldn't place him. Then he remembered and walked up to the edge of the road. 'Seni! Seni!' The man looked round and peered through the traffic and fumes before waving to Field. When the light changed he loped over, calling out cheerfully,

'Hi, John!'

Field said in a teasing way, 'What in Christ's name are you doing directing traffic? Did the Drug Squad throw you out?'

Seni laughed. He was a wiry man and wore white gloves. 'I go there afternoons. Half time. Mornings I direct traffic.'

'As a plain cop?'

'To make money, John. The narcotics squad is all honest, like me. And an officer's salary wouldn't pay my dinner, let alone my wife and children. I work with ordinary police part time to make extra money.'

'Crooked money.'

Seni smiled. 'You know. We pick up people who haven't got the right papers. We can arrest them or make them pay. So they pay for my son's school. This is a good corner. I've been here two weeks.'

'I didn't notice. You all had masks on.'

'That was better. I can hardly breathe out there, but the Minister of Tourism said we can't wear them. Bangkok is an exotic oriental city, he said. That's why tourists come. Pollution is not exotic. So there is no pollution. Therefore masks aren't necessary. In fact, they're forbidden.'

'When do you finish?'

'Ten minutes.'

'I need to talk to you, Seni.'

'Wait a minute.'

With Field following, the officer walked out to tell his partners that he was going, then led the way over to Wireless Road and into Lumpini Park, a great stretch of green with a canal weaving round beneath its trees. Field began his story as they followed the curve of the water. Off in the back there was a small nineteenth-century pavilion, empty except for an old woman whose job it was to guard a few shelves of books and some aquariums filled with exotic fish. There was one ceiling fan. Stationary. Seni led the way in out of the sun and examined the fish while Field finished explaining about Somchai Pamak.

'That's good,' was the Thai's first comment.

'What?' Field complained.

'You've filled in some holes.'

'Great. Now fill in some for me.'

'We knew about Iem but not Somchai. Now I understand. Iem is a technician, not an organizer. Somchai is an organizer. So we know Laos is back in the business, but how do we prove it. They used to produce a hundred tons of opium. In the sixties. With the fighting, that went down to forty, even thirty tons. The Pathet Lao forbade it in the Communist areas. Now it's all Communist and we think they're back up to seventy-five tons or so. We are also sure that there is no illicit trade by the peasants. In April every year government helicopters fly in to official pick-up zones and take it all away. They pay the peasants with barter. So all the opium goes to government warehouses. And there . . .'

'What?'

'There the mystery begins. For example, Laos signed the UN Convention on drug control in the sixties. Now they violate it by consistently forgetting to declare what they do with their stock. We think about twelve thousand tons go to the Russians and the Soviet bloc. Their Commerce and Industry department won't say what happens to the rest. This government man you saw . . .'

'Kamphet?'

'Yes. I'd never heard about him.'

'I've told you everything, Seni. All I need to know is about this end. Who runs it all?'

'Sixty tons. Say six tons of heroin. Someone big. More than a businessman. We don't know. A general perhaps. Up front anyway.'

'Come on,' Field insisted. 'I can't live on that. Look. I'm out doing your job for you for nothing. I don't even get paid off at the traffic lights and my risks are worse than exhaust fumes.'

'I can't help you. Honestly. We can't say a word in public until we're ready to close down the whole show. There is a man we picked up seven months ago coming across from Laos with twenty kilos. He had it in a lumber truck, but I don't think he's the truck driver type. We put him in Bang Kwang prison to make him suffer and he's been trying to bribe his way out ever since. I think he might have the answer, if I could get him to chat. We've been working on him, but you say Somchai also has six friends serving in there, which explains why we haven't been able to relax him. He's probably terrified. I'll go out next week and give it another try.'

'Thanks,' Field said without enthusiasm; and thought, if I'm still alive.

'I'm sorry,' Seni murmured.

Field was concentrating on a tank of little blue striped fish. 'Don't worry.' There weren't many bubbles coming up from the air tube on the bottom of the tank. The fish would die, he thought, if they left it that way. Suddenly Henry Crappe came into his mind. And Crappe's hobby of collecting information he didn't want to know. Debasing. That had been his word. 'You think I want to know?' he said quietly to Seni, without looking round. 'You won't tell me something I want to know. Is that it? Eh?' He turned, overcome by a desire to scream at him. 'Is that it? Stick and carrot time? Right? Is that it? Well, fuck you! I don't want to know. You understand? My problem is perfectly banal. For practical reasons of survival I need to know. Nothing important. Nothing moral. Nothing metaphysical. I just want to get on with my life. I wouldn't live here if I wanted to know things. I'd live somewhere I belonged.'

Seni betrayed no signs of having heard this outburst. He simply disappeared in silence, only to reappear a moment later. Field was still staring at the blue fish.

'There seems to be a woman involved.'

'A woman?' Field repeated.

'At the top. It's a rumour we keep getting.' He disappeared again.

'A woman,' Field murmured to himself. 'That cuts the suspects to twenty-five million.' He went over to browse through the book shelves. They were entirely filled with pre-Second World War novels. English and American. Hundreds of them. Not one of the titles or authors meant a thing to him. They left thick dust on his fingers. He slapped his hands together, which caused the old woman caretaker to stand up in a panic. Field made an apologetic *wai* in her direction and headed off towards the *Bangkok Post*.

Henry Crappe was not behind his desk. Field hadn't expected him to be there at that hour; in fact, the news room was virtually empty and, in the corner, Crappe's filing cabinet was denuded of socks, with its drawers closed. Field jiggled the drawer that interested him and pulled. It was locked. He searched around the desk for the keys, without success, then stared at the scratched green metal in frustration. Abruptly he threw himself against it in a violent shove, followed by a few kicks. All four drawers popped open.

Someone across the room shouted, 'Hey. What are you doing?'

'Hi,' Field waved back. 'Nothing to worry about.'

Three of the four drawers were filled with bags of sugar, rice, powdered milk, salt, cans of vegetables, boxes of eggs. Crappe was preparing for a long coup. Field wasn't surprised. Everyone knew that Crappe and his family moved into the newspaper building the moment a coup began and re-emerged when it was over. Only one thing did surprise Field. If three of Crappe's four drawers were filled with food, then he kept no files except those devoted to the drug trade.

Field shuffled through the fourth drawer until he came to the file for 1984–85. A dozen or so sheets in from the front he found the clipping about the man arrested with a load of teak and heroin while crossing on the ferry from Laos to Nong Khai, in Thailand. Attached to the article were police identity photographs. Field took both and left an apologetic note on the desk.

The rest of the afternoon was spent wondering how to get beyond the visitors' section in the prison and, once he had worked that out, trying to track down Woodward, who was neither at the Nursing Home nor down in the Klong Toey slum. Field wandered around the University in the hope that he might find the remnants of the anti-sex demonstration and therefore Woodward, but not his daughter. He found nobody. That left him little option but to phone Woodward's house and leave a message to call back urgently the moment he came in. Field waited at home all evening for the call and in desperation telephoned again at eleven p.m. Woodward was there, but the servant who took the message had gone to bed early and forgotten to pass it on to anyone else.

'Michael, I need to get into Bang Kwang prison urgently. You go there.'

'I was there all afternoon.'

'Shit.'

There was a pause before Woodward asked, 'Is it really urgent?'

'The little matter of guns I mentioned to you.'

That provoked another silence, until Woodward stated in a matter of fact way, 'There is a cholera outbreak at the prison. Today thirty were sick and a couple have died. I've been out checking the *farang* prisoners, theoretically on behalf of a few embassies. In fact all the sick are kept together. I could go back tomorrow.'

'What about me?'

'Perhaps if you came as a pastor I could get you in. Could you manage that?'

'Christ, Michael. I told you I'm lower town Irish. I was born to be a priest.'

'Have you had cholera shots?'

'Do you die of it?'

'Not if we catch the symptoms in time.'

'You'll catch them, Michael.'

The maximum security prison was upstream from Bangkok at Nonthaburi on the banks of the Chao Phya, an hour's drive along the autoroute. It was an attractive site for a fortress, marginally undercut on the outside by five strands of barbed wire running round the top of the walls. The surrounding gardens were intimate and informal, giving to the place an air of comfort and friendliness. This impression was maintained by the smiles that greeted Doctor Woodward on his way through the seven successive barred doors that constituted the outer security. Field had put on dark trousers and a white shirt. He held his hands behind his back and adopted an expression of devout authority, which was his childhood memory of how priests met the world. In this way he followed close behind his friend. Woodward was dressed for the role of the English doctor, in his English suit. It was the first time Field had seen this personage out of doors, but as Woodward's role in the prison was that of occasional doctor to the foreign prisoners – all 129 of them behind bars for drug offences – he chose to dress the part. Curiously enough, he had also insisted on stopping at a doughnut shop on the way and buying a shopping bag full of chocolate-dipped doughnuts.

Beyond the gates was a long and narrow open courtyard. Down each side was a double row of bars which separated visitors from prisoners. Visiting hours had not yet begun and so the impression was of an abandoned zoo. The men waiting before the steel gate at the far end were a mixture of guards and of prefects; trusted prisoners who dressed in blue shirts and blue shorts and carried billy clubs, theoretically to beat, if necessary, their fellow prisoners.

On the other side of the gate, through which the two men were ushered, lay a village green with bamboo administrative huts and an abundance of flowers. They waited on the inside while the guards poked the doughnuts with long pins. Prisoners wandered about in uniforms; except, that is, for the whites, who had refused to wear prison clothing, just as they had refused to work. The charming image of the place was marred only by a passing prisoner in leg irons, which were joined with a chain and held up out of his way by a dangling rope fixed round his waist. But then two young and blond Frenchmen in sporting clothes strode by lost in conversation and re-established the atmosphere of a country hotel.

'Where's the garden party?' Field whispered.

Woodward looked at him wryly. Both knew there were quarters for three thousand prisoners occupied by six thousand, most of whom were locked up for fourteen-hour nights in windowless, fanless and therefore very hot cells where they slept stomach to back in a single row. The rest hardly needed elaboration, except that there was more heroin inside than out. The guards and the prefects and even those prisoners with money and initiative, who acted as dealers, made it hard for anyone to stay away from the temptation.

They were escorted to the right, where behind a hedge there was a large *sala* with bars all round from ceiling to floor, the whole building itself in a small playing field enclosed by bars. Beneath the *sala* were prisoners laid out on mattresses, the Thais on one side, the foreigners on the other and the latter divided again among the few Chinese and the handful of whites. Two prefects, a young American black, who clearly did a lot of muscle building exercises, and a plumpish Thai, were on the gate, unlocking and relocking it with each passage. The American swung the gate open wide in mock respect and Woodward pitched the bag of doughnuts to him on the way through.

'Spread them around, Willy.'

The man caught the package with genuine pleasure. 'Who's this guy, Doctor?'

'A friend, Willy. A pastor. He has come along to give a little cheer.'

'Good, man.' The prefect didn't seem to mean it and he glanced at Field with an indulgent contempt which implied that doing good wasn't much good to anyone.

'Willy,' Woodward said quietly, drawing him away from the Thai prefect, 'do you know Phoumi Boussarath?'

'I guess I do. A sucker, right?'

'Will you fetch him for me?'

'Hey, Woodward, you know I can't leave the gate.' He carefully locked it before looking over quickly at Field, who was clearly listening. This time the prefect's eyes were filled with suspicion.

'I know, Willy. Just get another *farang* to fetch him. He can say he has some fever. He's a Lao. That makes him a foreigner, just like you. So I am within my rights to check him.' The prefect was still hesitating. He had turned his back on Field. 'Come on, Willy. I'll give you a package of Valium. All right?'

He smiled like a little boy. 'Sure, Dr Woodward, that's OK. Hey, I'll fix it. You know me.'

Willy shouted at another *farang* who was walking along twenty yards away in a daydream; a thin, unhealthy-looking man. The prisoners seemed to divide into two groups: those who exercised and were candidates for muscle competitions and those who were wasting away, partially from drugs or illness, but also from idleness, boredom, frustration, unhappiness.

Field followed Woodward beneath the *sala* – through its open gate. 'Valium?'

'If you're going crazy behind walls, there are moments when

153

the only solution is withdrawal. Valium is not a bad way of doing that. A lot better than heroin. There aren't any medals for spending ten years with a clear mind in a place like this.'

'I know, Michael. I know. I'm not criticizing.'

'Good,' Woodward said and went off to look at the cholera victims.

They were each rigged up with transfusion lines putting liquid into them to fight the dehydration by which cholera kills. Field followed him and stopped to talk with the few *farangs*. There was an Australian hairdresser who had tried a drug run with his boy friend, a footballer. Now they were locked up together; a form of bliss, he said, except that the price of drugs in the prison had doubled. There had been trouble after a German inmate sent an envelope full of heroin by registered mail from the prison post office to a friend in Cologne. The German police had opened it. Now the Thai governor was cracking down, a bit.

In a corner there was a bearded Frenchman who stank. When Field backed off, the man explained that he was philosophically opposed to bathing.

'What is more, dear sir, I am the only innocent foreigner in this prison. Innocent. Completely. In addition, I am one of four among the entire white population here who is not on heroin or any other form of drug.'

Woodward came up as this was being explained and cut in, 'We know you're innocent, François. On the other hand, you sold extremely young Cambodian girls to Europe for ten years.'

'That, dear doctor, was not illegal in this country.'

'So?' Field interrupted.

'One of them came back and planted a kilo of Number 1 in his suitcase.'

'But I detest drugs. You know this, Doctor.'

'I know it, François,' Woodward agreed.

There was a man shuffling in through the gate and Willy, the American prefect, was pointing him towards Woodward. Field went over to waylay him.

'Phoumi?'

The man glanced nervously at the cholera victims as if to see who was watching, then tried to look at Field. His eyes were those of an addict who wasn't getting what he wanted. Although he verged on bulkiness, the impression he gave was of a wasted man, or rather of someone who had lost control over the relationship between his mind and his body. This decrepit state encouraged Field.

'You don't get enough money for drugs?' he asked and drew him to an inside corner of the *sala*. There he blocked the man's way, so that Phoumi leaned back within the plaster angle as if looking for support from the walls. To either side of them the rows of floor to roof bars stretched away, cutting the green outside into slices.

The man's expression changed at the mention of drugs to let through a gleam of hope, but he answered carefully. 'Why do you say that?'

'I mean,' Field whispered, 'that Somchai doesn't take care of you.'

'Somchai?'

'Yes, Somchai. And Iem. He doesn't take care of you either. Does he?' The man made no sign. He stared at Field in a frozen, blind way. His pupils were transparent. He was petrified. 'Seems unfair when they're the ones who got you in here. And Somchai's other friends – Thavorn, Hu, Minh, Tasanai – are they looked after?' There was no reply. 'Are they here?' Field nodded towards the floor of the *sala* behind them. 'Are any of them with the sick? You can tell me that much, eh? Come on.'

The man didn't take his eyes off Field. 'No. None of them.' He neither looked nor sounded like a truck driver.

'And Somchai's brother is out. Free.'

'I know that. Of course I know that,' the man muttered. 'He was here.'

'Somchai paid to get him out. But none of them give you money. What did you do? You must have caused them some trouble.'

The man seemed unable to move his lips.

'Does no one give you money?' As there was no reply, Field poked his gut lightly with a finger. The skin gave in a slack, empty way. He poked again. 'Your family?'

'They are in Laos. They can't help.'

'How can you pay for your drugs then?'

The man hesitated. 'I can't.'

'Well, why doesn't Somchai help you?'

'I was tricked,' he mumbled. 'And now I am here. But I don't want to die.' He glanced around through the bars at the gate from where the Thai prefect was watching them. The prefect held his stare and Phoumi looked down. 'I don't want to give anyone a reason to kill me.'

Then Field took his leap. 'But you worked for Kamphet. Why did he betray you?'

The man started in terror. He was unable to lift his eyes to Field. His right hand went up inside the other sleeve and he began to scratch himself.

'Sure. Look at you. You're not some crummy drug dealer. You were a bureaucrat. A desk boy. Sure. It shows all over you. Where? Commerce and Industry? Foreign Affairs? Come on, for Christ's sake. The longer we talk, the more people will notice us.'

'Foreign Affairs.'

'Well, why did Kamphet betray you?'

'What will you do if I tell you?' He glanced up at Field, then down. He didn't deny the central question – Kamphet's involvement.

'First,' Field said, 'I'll give you five thousand *baht*. That will buy some happiness. Second, I'll get Kamphet and Somchai. You understand? I'll get them for my own reasons. But no one will know it was thanks to you. Third, I'll help you get a King's pardon.' Half of number two and all of three were lies. Field knew that the most he could hope for was to call the dogs off himself. And that would mean paying. In the process he would keep the man's name out of it and out of whatever followed, then he would make peace with whomever it was necessary to make peace. That at least was how he imagined things happening. And yet, instinctively he knew it was true that every minute this sucker, as Willy had called the man, went on talking, the more certain it was that Somchai's friends in the prison would find out and would make the man pay. Given his terrible state, there wasn't much more they could do except kill him. Field pushed any sympathy or pity aside. 'Come on. Make it quick. Come on.'

'I was on the UN Desk.' It came out convulsively, as if he were belching. 'One of my jobs was the UN Narcotics Control organization. We had contravened the reporting treaty for years so I was asked to prepare a report aimed at New York. I went to Commerce and Industry. The man in charge of the legal opium crop and its sale was Kamphet, but he stalled me at every corner. I had to be careful because he also worked in the Prime Minister's office. Every time I got information it was incomplete. And the rest, he kept telling me, was secret.' He glanced round at the Thai prefect, who was still watching but could not possibly hear. Phoumi started again in an almost inaudible whisper. 'It took me a while, but I figured it out; a few men were involved in the drug trade and they wouldn't tell. One day I found out about Iem and his background. Then I came across his import permission for acetic anhydride and I knew. I went to Kamphet. He confessed a bit and offered me a chance to make a fortune. All I had to do was drive a lumber truck into Thailand. He was buying me off gracefully and I was a poor official. Now I'm here where they can control me.'

'Who were you supposed to deliver it to?'

'No one. I wouldn't have seen the transfer. I was just to leave the truck on an agreed street.'

'But who controls the Bangkok end?'

'I don't know.'

'Don't give me that shit. Everything you've told me I knew already. It's the Bangkok contact I want.'

'I don't. Really.' They looked at each other in silence. 'You won't give me the money then.' He said this in a heartbroken voice, as if it were what he had expected all along. His hand came out and rested on Field's hand, so that the skin at the crook of the man's elbow was uncovered. It was scarred like sheet music.

Field grabbed the arm. 'That's not six months' worth of shooting.' The man said nothing. 'So you were an addict before.'

'Why do you think I needed Somchai's money?'

'And why should I believe what you tell me?'

The man was even more wistful. 'Your problem, I'm afraid.'

Field suddenly felt his energy drain away. He let the arm drop and looked over towards the gate, as if to leave. Instead he saw the Thai prefect's gaze, which even at that distance seemed malevolent. 'Oh, fuck.' He turned his back on the gate and counted out five thousand *baht* as discreetly as possible, then gave the man a half-hearted hug so that he could slip the money into his pocket. 'Don't eat it all at once.'

Phoumi missed the joke and, once he felt the bulge of the money in his trousers, lost interest in the conversation. He began to slip out of the corner without a further word, his mind no doubt already consumed by plotting who would sell him his heroin at the best price.

'Wait,' Field blocked the way. 'Listen. If Kamphet works for the Prime Minister, does the Prime Minister know as well?'

Phoumi drew upon what remained of his civil servant dignity. 'If a member of a government is involved in the drug trade, is the government involved as well?' He melted to one side round Field and on out of the *sala*. At the bars he waited without raising his eyes until the Thai prefect had opened the gate. Neither of them said a word. Willy, the American prefect, was eating a doughnut off to one side. He seemed to have forgotten about everything else. He took large, unconscious bites, not unlike an animal who must fight for his food. The chocolate had melted on to his fingers.

'Shit,' Field mumbled. 'Wouldn't you know? A fucking junkie.' He turned in frustration and saw the thirty mattresses laid out on the floor with Woodward moving between the victims like Bonaparte among the plague victims of Jaffa. 'Shit.'

Woodward heard this and came over to take Field away. 'Well?'

'He told me everything. Everything useless. Everything I know already. The only information I'm missing is the bit I need.'

Woodward put an arm around his friend. 'Come on. Let's get out of here.'

158

CHAPTER 9

The first of the season's high tides came flowing up the Chao Phya from the Gulf of Thailand while Field was out at the prison. It reached Bangkok in early afternoon, just as the day's rain began, and surged up over the river bank, across the lawns of the French and Portuguese Embassies, through the lanes to the old Portuguese church and the pseudo Norman-French cathedral, over the King's landing and in around Wat Mahattat and on right up to the walls of the Grand Palace, where the massing of pumps stopped its advance by driving the water laterally into adjoining districts. Field and Woodward got back to Bangkok just as the unabsorbed rainwater uptown began to creep from the gutters on either side of first Silom and Surawong Roads and then Sukhumvit Road until it met in the middle of each and then edged down the barely perceptible slope towards the river, only to be met half-way by the tidal water coming up.

That meeting was like a gentle clap of thunder, reminding the city again of its folly in listening to the insistent advice of western urban planners over the preceding forty years. Bangkok had been built on an estuary with *klongs* in place of roads, but these canals had always played a second role which had nothing to do with communications. They flowed with the tides and drained the monsoons. They were an imperfect but essential flood control system. Now the *klongs* were either filled in or, worse, covered over, so that, blocked, they sat stagnant until the rains came. At that point, they filled until they spilt out into the streets.

The difference between Bangkok's floods and those of other

cities was that none of this water moved violently. Far from it. Instead, a tepid, murky soup oozed up to cover the city with a foot of water and mud and refuse. Only the Grand Palace and the King's residence, Chitrlada Palace, along with the surrounding residential district where many of the generals lived, were kept dry by a concentration of pumps. It wasn't simply because Krit lived there that the area was protected. His real and potential allies also lived there.

The sinking of the city's land did make the flooding worse than it had been in other bad years, but not dramatically worse, and the cars continued to creep through the ten centimetres of water in the streets, while sand bags materialized to block the few shop entrances that for some reason did not already have a permanent flood barrier rising thirty centimetres around their door. The merchants sat just inside, dry and calm, waiting for customers who continued to wade bare-legged along the pavements.

Field dropped Woodward off at the Nursing Home, where raised planks had already been set in place to carry patients and visitors dry out of their cars to the stairs. From there he went on around the corner to the Saigon Bakery. The taxi got up enough speed in the intersection to have to skid into the kerb, creating a little wave that rolled across the pavement, up over the flood barrier and on into the bakery.

Field picked out the solid bits of pavement through the murky water and waded in behind. He ignored the furious looks of the owners as he slopped across the freshly drenched floor, past two French nuns who sat in white, drinking coffee and eating croissants with soft nostalgic nibbles. There were a dozen coconut tarts on a tray. He bought them all and slopped back out.

The flood had made its way by then across Sukhumvit Road to the higher side and he found his entire *soi* under a foot of water that stretched on into his compound. He held the box of tarts high and strode towards his own house, which seemed to stand on an island, with the ground floor still fifty centimetres above the water level. Across the room through the screens Ao was crouched on the covered porch. He walked over and threw the screen open. The *klong* had disappeared. The veranda had become a dock from which Ao stared out at the water. She looked at him and smiled.

'I've brought you some tarts.' He held out the package but his eye was drawn to the far end of the porch.

Two cobras lay side by side, almost straight, like two canes, also staring out at the water. They were a metre long and a stone-grey colour. The snakes paid no attention to Field and obviously had been paying no attention to Ao. She saw his frozen stare.

'Live under house. No place to live now.'

Field reached down for a shoe to throw, only to find he was barefoot. The box of coconut tarts was in his hand. He considered throwing it. After all, cobras swam. They could swim off to someone else's porch. 'Fucking nuthouse,' he mumbled before giving the tarts to Ao and going back inside, carefully closing the screen behind himself. 'Cook! Cook!' The old woman appeared from upstairs. 'Beer.' He flicked on a ceiling fan and sat down on a wicker chair to wait for the mug, which he emptied. Then asked for another.

It was curious. The pain in his groin was there. No doubt it was worse than it had been. No doubt if he analysed it carefully, he could measure how far the infection had moved back up into his system. And yet he had not thought of the pain all day. It had become part of the day. And it was true what he had said in joking to Paga: he had lost his interest in sex. It was, quite simply, unavailable; therefore his body turned away from physical gratification. The pain and the lack of physical pleasure; what were they but details in comparison to the possibility of another middle-aged shoeshine man slipping up beside him out of the night, or out of a crowd, with an 11 mm. pistol and in a single shot rendering irrelevant forever his little pains and desires. Perhaps that threat also could be dealt with by growing accustomed to it; growing naturally wary; living with the threat, as if it were quite normal, like sex and good health. He forced his mind away from that possibility and tried to think of what he could do, whom else he could turn to.

The afternoon went by with him drinking one beer after

another and gradually slipping from his real problems into daydreaming. Life, after all, was still as pleasant as it had always been. He looked up at his father, padded in his layers of clothing so that the mountain cold came reverberating out of the photograph and down across the room. For a brief second he felt the cold beneath his skin, but quickly pushed this twenty-year-old memory away. No. He was warm. And a sweet, beautiful girl waited on the porch. And a daughter was out in the city somewhere, unhappy because she thought she loved him more than he loved her, while he knew the opposite was true. And his life was his own. Everything else was detail.

By nightfall the tide had receded enough to leave Field's compound a clear but sodden mass, while the *soi* was still beneath three centimetres. He had a last beer and stumbled upstairs, where he threw off his clothes and slumped down to sleep. It was still light outside. He woke a few hours later to find Ao curled up in his arms. His right hand was on her shoulder and it slipped down to cover an innocent, firm breast. He pressed it lightly and felt the nipple nudge up between two fingers. She pressed back up against him so that a surge of desire went through his body, followed hard by a wave of regret. 'How can such a sweet little body be so rotten inside?' he said half aloud. She didn't move at the sound and he rolled over to occupy the distant side of the bed.

The next time he woke it was without knowing why. Ao was still asleep, with one leg stretched over to touch him on the side. He ran his hand over her toes, splayed wide from a childhood without shoes. The ceiling fan made a light whir above him. There was no wind outside and the leaves therefore did not rub against each other. He leaned up to look at the clock. It was only eleven. He should have felt hunger, but there was none. His eyes slipped closed again, but then, in the silence, he heard a low sound. It was a moment before he identified it as human. He rolled his head to look out of the window at the tree tops. They were still.

Field got to his feet and moved to the screen. There was silence at first, silence apart from the noise of bugs. Then he heard a voice again. Low. A few words. He thought of the night watchman; perhaps he was talking to his grandmother, but a few whispered sounds hardly constituted a conversation.

The pistol, he thought, where did I put the pistol?

He crept back towards the bed and stood in the darkness, trying to clear his mind from the thick cloud of beer that still hung over it. With my clothes, he thought. The pistol is somewhere with my clothes. He crept round the bed and eased the drawers open one after the other. Among his socks he found the gun and held it up to catch a hint of light. His finger eased the safety off, then he walked lightly to the corridor and out to the stairs. Half-way down he caught the outline of two men bent before the catch of the sliding glass door. The screens had already been pushed back. He stopped where he was and watched them until he could make out their movements, which involved some small instrument being manipulated against the lock. He could hear the scratch of metal within metal, searching for a release. The sound stopped while the hand withdrew and the fingers moved, before reinserting an instrument. The scratch this time was marginally different. Field was mesmerized by the sound, then he heard the latch click back and the door slide open.

He threw himself down the stairs two at a time. 'You fucking bastards! Get out! Get out!' He came running across the room towards the frozen shadows and stuck his pistol in their direction. The trigger pulled and pulled again before he heard the first small explosion. 'You bastards!' He went on firing and shouting, but they were gone. He went towards the door, scarcely able to see, his eyes clouded by anger. Then the noise of the shots came back to him. Five or six explosions. He hadn't thought or counted. Stupid, uncontrolled sounds. And the noise of breaking glass came back and of feet running on the deck.

He crept leerily on to the porch. There was no one. Not even the cobras. With the low tide they would have gone back under the house. He looked out into the night. The men might have run off or just have taken their distance to wait for him. He slid back inside and stamped across the dark house, unlatched the door by the kitchen and strode over to the servants' hut. There was silence inside. 'Cook! Open up!' There was no reply.

He tried the door but it was locked. He thumped on it and when the silence persisted kicked it with a bare foot. He kicked again and again until the door was opened by the cook's grandson, the theoretical night watchman. Field grabbed him by the neck and pulled him outside. 'You idiot! What are you doing in there?' He threw the boy on to the ground. 'You idiot!' The boy lay on the cement path, inert. 'For Christ's sake!' Field stamped back into his house and upstairs. Only then did he realize that he was naked and that when he had shouted at the boy, he had been pointing at him with the pistol in his hand.

Ao was sitting up on the bed. 'What happen, John?'

'Get dressed!'

Field fumbled through his cupboard in the dark until he found some trousers and a shirt. Behind him Ao switched on the light.

'Off! Turn it off. Get dressed, Ao.'

He ran downstairs and called the watchman, who came crawling into the house on his knees with hands up in prayer asking for forgiveness.

'Get a taxi. Quick. Taxi.'

Field waited with Ao in the dark by the kitchen door until the boy came running back, having left the taxi outside the compound gate. The distance between the house and the gate suddenly seemed to have stretched into kilometres. Field poked the boy. 'Bring the taxi to the door.' Ao hadn't made a sound, but once the boy had gone to organize this manoeuvre she came up behind Field and took his arm.

'Where we go, John? Late now.'

'I need Paga.'

There was a silence while Ao considered this. In a voice strained with neutrality she asked, 'You give me back to Paga?'

He paid little attention, then realized that her voice had been trembling. 'No. I have a problem. Paga can help me. That's all.' The little Fiat reversed up to the door. Field shouted at the driver, 'Turn off your lights.' He grabbed Ao's arm to drag her outside across the soggy gravel and pushed her to the other side of the back seat. 'Patpong.' His legs were squeezed up behind the driver's seat so that his knees approached his chin.

'Hundred *baht*, mister.'

'Sure. Sure. Lights off till we're on the street.' The car crept out through the gate, past Field's watchman, his hands still raised in apology, and past the compound guard, who lay half-awake on his platform. Once outside, Field said, 'Go fast.' He looked round. In the lane there was a car starting up. 'Jesus Christ,' he mumbled, 'a hundred fucking *baht* to get killed. Hey!' he tapped the driver on the shoulder. 'Thirty *baht* to go slow. Hundred *baht* to go fast!'

The driver looked back. He was Chinese Thai and in Field's experience a high percentage of the city's Chinese taxi drivers had a streak of lunacy in them that revealed itself through a particularly personal form of driving – something to do with mathematical minds attempting to calculate irrational circumstances. All motor skills went wild. The moment the instructions were given, the man thrust his foot to the floor and careened half-way across the pavement, then back again and came flying out of the narrow *soi* into the six lanes of Sukhumvit by darting between a *tuc-tuc* and a BMW then back across the front of the BMW. All this was done in silence, without the hint of a horn. Around the man's neck was a white handkerchief tightly rolled from point to point so that it hung like a flat string. The man suddenly released both hands from the steering wheel to seize the two points and surgically whipped the handkerchief up and down his neck removing sweat, which could only have been imaginary, as his car was crudely air conditioned to match a butcher's cold room. Field looked back at the stream of anonymous traffic behind them, all of it aggressive. He shrugged and sank down into the broken springs of the seat. They had bumped across beneath the elevated highway and flown on a hundred yards, when the driver released his wheel again and snapped the tautly stretched handkerchief over his head to run it tight, like a razor, down the bridge of his nose.

At the Silom Road end of Patpong, the taxis and *tuc-tucs* were gathered in a few inches of water where they could wait for closing-time customers. Outside Paga's Apartments Field shoved the car door open and splashed across the stagnant water, pulling Ao behind. The girl upstairs recognized him and insisted that Paga wasn't there. She did this in an embarrassed way, so that Field felt obliged to push by her and up to the second floor where he barged one by one into the five short-time rooms kept for rent at 500 *baht* an hour. Only one of them was occupied and Field didn't stop to apologize to the couple whose attention was on other things. The girl below insisted again that she didn't know where Paga was, only that she hadn't been in since Friday, two days before.

Field thought of the cashier at the King's Castle and dragged Ao back down the stairs. He paused in the doorway. There was no one standing idle on either side, apart from a girl calling out to those who passed, 'This way, sir. Inside sir.' Whatever attention she might have got was lost in the mud and water through which the prowling men had to pick their way. Field stepped over the flood barrier and rushed across the street to the solid little docks built before each door on the other side.

Inside the crowd was thinner than usual, but the temperature was as low and the music as loud. Field squeezed round the oval bar to the left so that he faced the cashier and, over behind her, the door.

'Where's Paga?'

The girl shook her head. 'Hasn't been since you here last time.'

'Come on, Nok, where is she?'

'Don't know, John. She here once a week to collect money. You want a drink?'

Field's eyes were on the door. He saw two Thais come in. They didn't have the slow, inquisitive look of men coming into a bar in search of short term fun. No. They had a very direct manner. They stared. Field shoved Ao around him and in behind the bar before leaning over to the cashier again.

'Listen, Nok. You keep my friend here with you. Give her a badge. Just keep her with you. Don't let her talk to any man. Don't let her work. I mean she can wash glasses or something, but no men, eh. I'll be back later.'

'We close soon, John.'

'Take her home, Nok, if I'm not back tonight. Take her home.'

Ao had a panicked look. 'You leave me, John?'

'Don't talk to me! The men will notice you. Just stay here for now. I'll be back.'

The aisle on the other side of the bar was squeezed between one row of men sitting up at the bar and another row lounging back on the banquette along the wall. This passage was littered with girls moving from man to man in search of drinks. The two Thais had pushed their way in through this flesh, examining the customers as they went. Field turned his face away and slid towards the door. They didn't see him until he was a yard from the opening and they, four or five yards. Girls shouted in protest behind him as the men shoved them out of the way. Field didn't look back. He slipped by the two people between himself and the pavement, paused a second outside in a desperate attempt to remember Paga's other bars, ran a few yards to the right and cut up some stairs before the Bunny Club barkers could do their enticing.

It was a small grubby place with dim lighting. Rolls of toilet paper sat on the bar and across from that a girl danced nude. There were only two customers, each enlaced with a girl. Field leaned over the bar and asked for Paga. The cashier said she hadn't seen her. Field's eyes were drawn to the large black man seated to his left, a girl down at his groin working with her lips on a very small penis.

'That's encouraging,' Field said and started back down the stairs.

Behind him he heard, 'What'd you say, man?'

Just inside the door Field stopped to think. The Kangaroo. That was Paga's. He waited for a crowd of men – Australians – to pass, going back the other way, before melting out into their midst and one door along melting in through another opening without any sense of being followed. The girl downstairs rang a bell and upstairs the door opened into a small living room, comfortable and seedy – a bar along one side, a tiny stage facing and comfortable chairs on the other two sides. The stage was filled by an older girl, with a scarred face and a muscular body, who was dancing nude, five lit candles clutched in each hand for the benefit of half a dozen men. She ran the flames over her breasts, pausing when the nipples were at the centre of the heat, the candles held at such an angle that the red wax dropped in gushes of liquid on to her skin. The breasts were encased before she moved the flame to her abdomen and then on down over her vagina, where the pubic hair miraculously did not catch fire while the wax encased her inner thighs. This molten wax held Field transfixed. It was like a second layer of diseased skin that suddenly reminded him of his own pain. He passed a hand over his groin, as if to put the reawakened pain to sleep, and leaned across the bar. 'Paga. Have you seen her?'

The cashier hadn't, but she thought the girl shut up in the room behind with a *farang* might have.

'Not long now. She work fast. You want drink, John?'

He took a Mekong soda and sat at the bar. Six of the seven girls in the room were busy being seductive and massaging male crotches just enough to produce drink orders from men who wouldn't have got a female glance in their own countries. Most of the girls were sniffling with colds caught from the air conditioning. A policeman in a uniform decorated by two rows of campaign ribbons sat in the corner. His pistol seemed inordinately large in such a small room. Field indicated him to the cashier.

'Friend?'

'Expensive. He come every night for money.'

The lady of the candles jumped off the stage, the wax cracking on her body and the free girl went up with some bananas to be used in the role of leading man. She was in the full flood of her performance when the downstairs bell rang solidly and a second later a Thai rushed up, his pistol drawn. Field threw himself to one side and spilt his drink. But the man ignored him. He was already up on the abandoned stage collecting the used bananas and shouting at the door of the little dressing room, behind which the performer had locked herself. He also held the bottom of her bikini and therefore her badge.

Field pulled himself together enough to ask quietly, 'Who's that?'

'One Two Three Squad. He got her badge. Big fine. Thai police no good.'

The district policeman sat quietly. He was paid not to

interfere; that didn't include interfering with flying squads of anti-corruption police. The man went away carrying the badge and the banana in a newspaper. A few moments later the naked girl came out of the dressing room crying. The fine would account for a month's earnings. Field gave her five hundred *baht* and asked the cashier to interrupt the couple in the private room long enough to ask where Paga was. He was nervous about leaving Ao any longer than need be.

'Sure, John.' She came back a few minutes later. 'Maybe at Duke's Den. You try there, okay.'

Paga named all of her bars after royalty or animals. She had never explained why. Field went carefully down the stairs and looked outside. The rain had begun to fall again, lightly. He couldn't see the faces of the passing people or of those waiting under awnings and so moved quickly out and along the seventy-five yards to the Duke's Den stairway.

Upstairs, a young couple were on the stage in calm intercourse, standing, she with her back to the audience and one leg up on his shoulder. The stage, like the large room, was painted black and the hundred or so men and bar girls were seated in respect. The man pumped methodically three times, lowered her leg and lifted the other, pumped three more times, then swung her sideways into the air, horizontal, and gave three more pumps. He stared out at the audience with a glazed look of indifference while she simulated passion with some skill. There was a Rolex watch on her wrist.

Field couldn't see the manager. He asked one of the girls and waited at the back while she disappeared.

'John! John!'

From near the front Henry Crappe was waving. Field made his way over before he realized that George Espoir was also there.

Field sank down and asked, 'How's the research coming?'

Espoir gave a bashful smile. This was followed by a conspiratorial look of contempt for Henry Crappe. 'Coming along,' the writer replied.

The man on stage had the girl from behind, gave three pumps, then her hands went down to the ground and her legs curled up around his waist. Three more. That was the finale

169

and they disengaged discreetly before leaving the stage, with him holding his penis in his hand so that no one might see it.

Crappe said, 'Thais are always discreet.'

'Discreet,' Espoir repeated, as if to say, I could make a thousand rude comments, but breeding holds me back. In fact he seemed to have drunk enough to be beyond any fast wit.

'Still suffering?' Crappe asked. When he got no reply, he asked, 'Did you find what you wanted in the drawer?'

'Yes, Henry. Sorry about your filing cabinet.'

'They were good locks,' he said plaintively. 'You didn't take a bag of rice, did you?'

'No, Henry.'

'I wasn't certain. I hadn't counted the rice. How about Somchai?'

Field cut him off. 'I don't want to talk about it.' His aim was to kill the story. Put it to sleep, if only he could find the right man to reassure. The last thing he wanted was someone like Espoir gossiping it about. 'You keep it to yourself, Henry, eh.' He insisted, 'To yourself.'

Espoir listened to the exchange with interest but said nothing. It was only a few seconds before the show began again with four plump girls putting on a lesbian performance. It must have been their first night on stage because they kept bursting into embarrassed giggles and turning their backs to the audience.

The manager, one of Paga's younger sisters, appeared from somewhere. She smiled uncertainly at Crappe while she asked Field, 'What you want, John?'

'I need to see Paga. Urgent. Where is she?'

'Don't know.'

'Can you find her?'

She nodded. 'You wait here.'

'Who is Paga?' Espoir asked.

'A friend,' Field answered and turned away, his mind slipping into the vague neutrality which he used as a public defence.

'If you come back here in two weeks,' Crappe said, to change the conversation, 'these girls will be polished pros. It is quite remarkable. The rice paddy fades faster than you would imagine. You must think of it all as a medieval guild with apprentices and masters. The pecking order almost defies explanation. 398 bars. 119 Massage Parlours. 96 places to dance, etc. 56 restaurants with quote hostesses unquote. All of those girls stand somewhere in the pecking order. There are a few expensive call girls; ex-beauty queens, that kind of thing, who trade one night at high cost not for the man's pleasure but for his prestige. There you find the full expression of male cupidity. Rising generals in particular are susceptible to what I would call prestige sex. Now massage girls, as you might imagine, are the great middle class of the industry – body massage, upper middle class; hand massage, middle middle – all solid professionals, working out of a stable establishment, usually married with children. Then come the bar girls. Lower middle class. At that point it becomes more complicated. You have a separate upper sub-class for the Japanese, because they pay more, and a lower sub-class for the other *farangs*, plus a third for the Thais. Unlike the Japanese, we don't in fact get better girls than the Thais, we just pay more for what we get. Then there are the performers. Then the brothel girls, semi-voluntary rated above involuntary. Then the riffraff working in cheaper places and a whole panoply at the bottom of those who work outside, on the street, so to speak. Of course, there is a separate cross rating which runs through each of these categories based upon the question of age . . .'

'Shut up,' Field ordered.

There was an awkward silence that Espoir filled with an attempt at humour. 'Babbling on the Babylon.'

Field silenced him with a glare, then caught the arm of a girl going by. 'Mekong soda.'

The four lesbians trooped off stage with hands hiding breasts and pubic hair. They were replaced by a girl who popped a spool of thread up into herself, pulled out the end of the thread, knotted it in a loop and offered this to a German in the front row who put it between his teeth and backed away across the room unravelling the invisible spool as he went. The girl danced like a fish on a line. She finished her act by inserting ping-pong balls and dropping them into beer mugs. Field followed none of this. His eyes were down and concentrated on his forbidden drink. Well, he thought, it may not do me any good, but it doesn't make me feel any worse.

Then he saw the two Thais appear at the top of the stairs and they saw him at the same moment, half-lit as he was at the front of the room. Field emptied his glass and watched them work their way forward. He reached into his belt and pulled out the pistol, which he held up half-hidden in his hand but pointed at the men. They saw it and stopped. No one else was watching him. They were cheering the dancer each time a ball dropped into her mug.

Espoir nudged him. 'What do think of that?'

'Eh?'

'What do you think of that?'

'Of what?'

'That.'

'Ping-pong?'

Espoir looked at him with doubt, then laughed. 'Yes. Ping-pong.'

'Hate it.'

Paga's sister reappeared and whispered into Field's ear, 'Not sure, John. Maybe she at Golden Panda.'

Field gave her thigh a soft pat and stared at the men. Even if he got out of the room first, they would kill him before he reached a taxi. He looked at Espoir with distaste and whispered so that Crappe couldn't hear, 'Is your car downstairs?'

The man was surprised at this attention. 'As a matter of fact it is.'

'I'll take you to an interesting place, eh.' He gave a suggestive tug at Espoir's arm and leaned over to Henry Crappe. 'I need to talk to your friend alone, Henry. See you.' He pulled the Englishman up and pushed him gently ahead, hiding himself behind and away from the Thais. They were waiting near the top of the staircase, but at the last second Field slipped in front of Espoir to lead the way down. Although the two Thais followed close behind, they couldn't get near Field because he kept himself just below his shield, who negotiated the stairs in a bulky way. At the bottom, at the last moment, Field ran out and leapt into the rear of Espoir's hotel car; the smoked glass obscured him so that the Thais couldn't see whether his pistol was drawn and aimed at them. The driver began to protest, but Espoir climbed in a few seconds later. Field could see the two men hesitating on the pavement. The bulges in the small of their backs were scarcely visible beneath loose shirts. Then they ran for their car. It was a little Fiat parked fifty yards away.

Field gave the hotel driver instructions in Thai and told him to go fast. Very fast, he repeated, or Mr Espoir would change drivers the next morning. They peeled away from the kerb and bore left on to Silom Road, caught a green light turning red, which might give them a three-minute lead on the Fiat and swept by the great statue of Rama VI, the fairy King, who liked uniforms and boy scouts. The grass round his image was littered with a few hundred aimless solitary males.

This burst of speed caught Espoir off guard and Field saw he was about to complain. 'Don't worry about the driver. I told him to go fast.'

Espoir's bleary eyes focused on him. 'You did?'

'Yes. Just leave him alone.' Field looked stonily ahead and there was silence for ten minutes.

Then Espoir revived. 'Where are we going?'

'Golden Panda.'

The silence lasted until they arrived. It was a high rise that resembled a modern, expensive hotel. Young men held the doors open on to a great expanse of thick brown broadloom supporting soft armchairs upholstered in lighter brown. On one side of the room was a glassed-in cage holding a hundred or so girls. Field led the way up a step towards the back corner and collapsed into one of the armchairs. He asked for the manager. Instead, a sleek little man appeared; one of those who helped clients make their choice.

'Hello, sir. You come late. You want some special service, sir?'

'No. No,' Field cut in.

'Young girl maybe?' He gave them a lookover. 'Boy maybe?'

'I want to see Paga. Is she here?'

'You want something from her?'

Field stood up so that he towered over the man. 'I'm a friend of Paga's. I want to see her. Urgent. Okay? John Field. You send her or you send the manager.'

'Sit down, sir. Take a drink. You want a girl first?'

'No!'

When the man had gone, Espoir slouched into his cushions and tried to surmount the effect of all he had drunk that evening. 'Funny place this town, you know. Doesn't make any sense dramatically. It's all too easy. They love their King too much and he's too good. The politicians and generals are too corrupt. And these girls. All these girls. Of course, it's wonderful for the ego to have them all around. An endless choice. Too many really. Doesn't it break you down in the end? I mean you can have them all, but none of them want you for any special power you've got. Just for the fee. Where is the emotive element? Nothing works dramatically unless there is an emotive element.'

Field forced himself to reply. He didn't want Espoir sulking out of the place. 'It's more complicated than that. Anyway, I wouldn't be caught dead sleeping with any *farang* women. All that syphilis and herpes and AIDS scares the shit out of me.'

'Really?' Espoir looked at him curiously. 'You wouldn't? And because of disease?'

'Looks. Because of looks. And feel.' Field knew he was making a fool of himself.

'Feel?'

Field glanced at him with anger. 'Maybe that's what you call emotive.'

His sarcasm seemed to cause Espoir to belch and the writer added, as if the words were part of his indigestion, 'Of course, it doesn't make much difference to my book. I mean, I'm out here to get a bit of the colour. The plot's all done anyway. Has been for months. What I need,' he managed some urgency as he leaned over to breathe in Field's face, 'is the moral aspect. I always need that. The rest, frankly, is just a bit of the old one, two, sleight of hand, soft shoe, now you see it now you don't routine. Mind you, I'm no worse than a Balzac or a Dickens. Each one has his touch, you see. Mine is to dress it all up in a sort of convoluted upper class verbiage that sounds like an Oxbridge crossword puzzle; if you see what I mean. That makes them all feel good; well, either good or impressed. Either way, it sells. Then you shove in some seedy spies for the *bas monde* and the moral aspect for the intellectuals.'

Field had only half-listened to this formula, although bent forward as Espoir was, a few inches from his face, it was hard to blot out the sound. His eyes were moving back and forth between the entrance and the stairs near the back, up which the sleek man had disappeared, theoretically to find Paga. Since then a few Thai and *farang* clients had gone up with girls, but it was late and most of the traffic was coming down the stairs, the men looking clean and relaxed with a cocky edge to their step. Espoir was still bent forward and seemed to be waiting for a comment, so Field said, 'Henry Crappe can give you that.'

Espoir looked to see if he was being teased. 'I don't think so. I fear he is missing the emotive element.'

'You don't know him,' Field said. 'He's very complex. Like everything here.'

'Who cares?' Espoir threw himself back on his cushions. His eyes wandered over to the glassed-in cage of girls and he shook his head slightly. 'How big is this brothel?'

'The building,' Field asked, 'the city or your mind?'

'Ha.'

Field saw the front doors being swung open for the two Thais. Perhaps they had gone back into the Duke's Den and questioned the manager. He seized Espoir by the arm and dragged him towards the stairs at the back, out of sight. They could have run up to the next floor, but the commotion would have attracted attention. He went to the desk and put down a thousand *baht*.

'41 and 47.'

'We have no 41, mister. She sick.'

'Must be 49.'

'49 no have, sir.'

Field glanced back, straining to read the numbers on the girls over in the cage. The two men still hadn't come that far forward. Perhaps they were questioning the men who waited to guide the clients. In the front row there was a big girl wearing glasses.

'24.'

'You pay for extras now, sir.'

'No.' Field kept looking over his shoulder. 'Not now.' He pulled Espoir up the stairs.

'Hey, did you pay for me?'

'Sure. Why not?'

'I didn't see.' He stumbled on a stair. 'Slow up, man.'

'Quick. Come on.'

The cashier at the desk called out, 'Wait, sir. Wait for girls.'

He stopped half-way up until the women were in sight. Neither was a marvel, but Espoir was too drunk to notice and Field gave him 47, the better of the two. They were put in adjoining rooms on the first floor. Once Espoir had disappeared inside, Field said he wanted to be on a higher floor. The women waiting in the corridor to change towels and sheets began to chatter when he reappeared and headed for the stairs.

'You haven't seen me,' he said in Thai, 'if men come looking. OK. I'm a friend of Paga. You haven't seen me.' He gave each of them twenty *baht* and headed upstairs with the girl following.

On the third floor he stopped and again gave money to the women waiting in the corridor. Once inside the new room he threw off his sweaty clothes. His eyes caught a green tinged stain on his underwear. He threw these down and dropped into the empty bathtub.

The girl was surprised at such speed. 'You friend of Paga?' she asked.

'Yes. Is she here tonight?'

'No. She not here. You in trouble?'

'Yes. And I'm sick.' He showed his inflamed penis.

'Oh. You sick.'

'No sex. Just wash and massage. I'll give you five hundred anyway.'

She set about her job diligently and Field looked at her for the first time. She was thirty or thirty-five. Her best days were over and she had begun to spread into matronly folds. There were grey roots to her black hair. On the positive side, she made up for age with professionalism and he began to relax. The room was an extension of the luxury hotel theme. Both the tub and the bed were oval.

'What your name?'

'John.'

'You married, John?'

'No.'

'I was. My husband, he killed in motorcycle accident.'

'You have children?'

'One girl. If my husband no die, I no come to massage. My mother look after baby. I live near airport with her. She not know I work in massage . . . You first man today.'

'The day is over.'

She shrugged. 'Sometime little people. Sometime big people.' She added more bubbles to the bath. 'Soap not good for me. This soap it make me scratch. Bad for my skin. All the girls use same. Make them scratch too.' She held up a bottle to show Field. 'You see. Badedas. Bad for me.'

When she had finished, Field sent her out to find the manager. He was a man, who resembled Paga, and even seemed to know who Field was. He was also sympathetic to Field's story or at least pretended to be. On the other hand, he had not seen his aunt for a week.

The massage closed at one, but he agreed that Field could spend the night there if he didn't mind being shut up in a sealed building with the air conditioning off. It was a form of torture, but Field accepted.

At one a.m. the girl dressed and left him lying on the bed. 'I go home now, John.'

'Say hello to your mother.'

She giggled and went out. Five minutes later the air went off and he began to sweat.

CHAPTER 10

The Golden Panda Massage was locked up until noon the following day, when Field was released by a sub-manager who must have imagined that this rumpled, sweaty person was a client left behind by mistake the night before. He took a taxi to the Dusit Thani Hotel, bought a shirt and a razor in the lobby downstairs and spoke to a friend on the reception desk who let him use a room long enough to bathe. Then he rode the elevator to the top floor and walked the last few steps up to the Foreign Correspondents' Club, with its walls of glass overlooking Lumpini Park, the Polo Club and, in the distance, his daughter's university.

Field had gone there with a very specific idea. He still wanted to put Somchai and his friend back to sleep. But how? He had no idea. He couldn't even find Paga. The other option was to get the right person to blow the entire story open. Not many journalists could do that for the simple reason that not many knew the drug scene well enough to find the missing pieces. And without those, Field's bits of information were useless; useless, that is, from Field's point of view.

He wandered over to the bar and fell into conversation with a New Zealander, who knew the Thai military backwards, and a Swede, who knew as much about the Shan States. Field bought everyone a beer and life seemed to return to normal. It was as if he had never left that bar; was still writing words for people to read; was still one who evoked events, not participated in them. It was a kind of peace. Half an hour later the man he had been waiting for came in; an Indian who specialized in Vietnam and its satellites. Field went over to stop the man and drew him to a sofa near the windows, where he explained his story, without dwelling on the attempts to kill him. He mentioned threats. No more. He didn't want to appear frightened. That wasn't the way he saw himself. The man listened carefully and thought for a moment before saying he couldn't help. His career was built upon access to Vietnam and Laos. If he wrote that story, he would never cross the border again. 'It isn't worth blowing my contacts for one drug bust.'

Field explained that it wasn't a drug story. It was political in that the Prime Minister of Laos had an assistant who was running the trade. By extension, the government itself was involved. Besides, all the journalists knew that drug stories were no longer just drug stories. How could they be when Thailand had gone from fifty thousand addicts to five hundred thousand in one decade, while the western democracies had seen drugs rise from their status as a minor amusement for rebellious youth in the sixties to become the largest medical problem facing that part of the world. If a Communist government was selling six tons of heroin a year into the illegal trade, the story was not only political, it was ideological.

Field said all this and the journalist listened politely, although he was smart enough to figure it out for himself. If he didn't it was because he, like most other journalists, still looked upon drug stories as appendages of ignoble journalism, not far removed from crime reporting and chasing fire trucks; the stuff for beginners or failures. The seizure, for example, of ten kilos of heroin could never compare in dignity or importance as a story with, say, a protocol visit to a tense border area by a known politician. That nothing would come of the border visit was irrelevant. The worth of a journalist was determined by the class (widely recognized) of the stories he covered.

So Field did not insist. He wasn't even disappointed. Instead, he went down into the street and walked over to Chulalong-korn University in search of his daughter. There the flood had receded, at least until the next coincidence of tide and rain, leaving the campus like a freshly drained marsh. It took him a good part of the afternoon to track down Songlin as she came out of a literature class on to the wet ground.

She raised her hands and gave him a forgiving smile. When

he saw this, he was filled with a desire to speak to her in English. He could have done that to any of the hundreds of students in sight, even if they understood only a few words, any of them except her.

'I knew you would come today,' she said.

He smiled. 'They teach you to read cards?'

'Oh, no,' she laughed. 'Yesterday I saw one of your friends and he asked if I had seen you lately?'

'A friend?' His voice exploded. 'Who was that?'

The abrupt change of tone frightened Songlin into silence.

'Who was that?' Field seized her arm protectively, although it must have seemed more of a threat.

'A man. A Thai. He came up to me on the street.'

'What do you mean, on the street?'

'I was in a queue for a film and he came up. He recognized me.'

Field forced himself under control and pulled her close to him, closer than he had in years, since her childhood. 'He couldn't have been a friend, Songlin. Now tell me, were you alone?'

'No. I was with a boy.'

'A boy?'

'A friend. We have some classes together.'

'What was this man like?'

'I don't know. He was Thai. Part Chinese I think. He had a tie on. Like a businessman, I guess.'

Field sensed that things were getting out of control. 'Do you have everything you need with you?'

'I don't understand.'

'I want you to go home now.'

'I can't. I have classes.'

'Forget them. I'm in some trouble and these people . . . these people might hurt you.' He gave her a pile of small *baht* notes. 'You take a taxi home. You pack up a little case and you wait for a call from me. If I tell you to go somewhere, you go. If I tell you to go with someone, you do it. No discussion. Don't let anyone into the apartment. You hear. No one. You leave your mother behind. They won't harm her.'

'Why don't I just go to Amara's house?'

180

'Sure, Songlin. We'll see. But you stay put till I tell you. I'll call Amara today. Just don't move unless I telephone or she comes to pick you up. Now go on.'

She walked off towards Rama IV with dutiful enthusiasm and, as he watched, he began to regret not having apologized for being so rude when she came to his house. He was never very good at excusing himself. And if he had, it might have started a conversation about Ao. No. It was better to say nothing. Why had she fallen in with his plans so easily? Because it was a chance to be drawn into his world; the one he carefully shut her out of. Be careful, he thought. Minimize. Minimize her expectations of him. When she was out of sight behind buildings and trees, he set off in the other direction to the Dunant Road entrance. If anyone was following Songlin, he would be drawn away after Field. Dunant wasn't a good road for taxis and just as he reached it, the afternoon rain began.

'Shit.' He looked around and saw a man coming towards him across the campus with a plump, easy waddle. 'Shit.' Field started walking up the road towards Ploenchit Road more than a kilometre away and looked round to see that the man was quietly running. He had cut the distance between them in half. 'Fucking idiot.' Field stopped talking to himself and began to run at a steady pace. The length of his legs alone would keep him ahead. By then the rain was falling thick and heavy and flowing in a stream off the pavement. He placed his feet carefully and looked round every thirty seconds to see that the man was still at the same distance. It was a ten-minute run to the main road where the rain was gathering deeper. There Field saw a bus ploughing through the water and leapt ahead to catch it. A hundred yards on, the traffic came to a halt. He jumped out and crossed to the covered rabbit warren of the Siam Plaza where he cut back and forth among the corridors lined by stores before going into a pastry shop. It was a white bread, white cake bakery. The walls were white. Shining. There was thick sugar icing on everything. Multicoloured icing. Field bought a jam bun and placed himself near the door to one side. He ate the bun with his left hand and kept his right on the pistol out of sight in his belt. If the man came, he would be confronted on Field's terms. But no one came and the water

181

began to run through the corridors. Moments later the electricity was cut to avoid any risk of electrocution.

He was already soaked, so there was nothing to be gained by waiting in the dry darkness. Field walked slowly out through the moving black liquid to the main road where he stood in fifteen centimetres of water until a free taxi appeared. It took them two hours to get to Patpong and the King's Castle. He held the car and splashed inside.

The first thing he saw was Ao, still dressed in her blue skirt and white blouse, being jiggled up and down on the lap of a man known around Bangkok as Sweetpie. He made his money out of soft drug dealing and advertising; in any case out of marginal deals, and his life was divided between a chemical haze during daylight hours and an alcoholic haze at night. Field detested him.

He was frozen by the sight of the man growling into Ao's ear. Sweetpie had a silent movie star style about him and a sense of humour that was perfect for girls who couldn't understand a word of English. He growled again and jiggled her. 'You feel it. Feel the tiger's tail.' Then he growled with great baring of teeth. 'See, my darling. I'm a tiger.'

Field rushed forward and wrenched her off his lap. 'Leave her alone. She's my . . . my . . .'

Sweetpie loved this. 'Oh, oh yes, I saw that immediately, John, immediately. She is your . . . um, your . . . ah. Of course.'

Field pulled her away. Behind he heard the voice going on.

'Let's burn the bar down. No evidence. No evidence. No evidence of his ah . . . um . . . his my . . . Who has a match? Who will help me?'

Field shoved Ao violently across the back seat of the taxi and crushed in beside her.

She protested, 'You leave me there, John. Just having fun.'

His hand came up and slapped her. She had not seen it come. She drew her legs on to the seat and wrapped her arms around them with her head down in silence.

From there to Amara's house was over an hour, almost all of it through thirty centimetres of water. Everywhere the traffic was slowed by stalled cars, but as they advanced the rain thinned and eventually stopped when the night fell. It wasn't until they were five metres down Amara's lane that the flood deepened and the taxi motor began to sputter. Their driver threw his car into reverse before it was too late.

'Stop!' Field shouted. 'Stop here.' He jumped out into calf-deep water. Above, the sky was so clear that the stars reflected on the black surface around his feet. Field stood motionless, thinking. Then the sound of a piano floated towards him. He looked to the side and saw a dozen cars abandoned in the shallower water. They were all Mercedes and BMWs. 'Amara! Amara!' The house was only ten metres on. 'Amara! Transportation!'

Moments later a flame appeared out of the darkness and then an elegant fishing skiff materialized beneath it, with one man standing at the rear, poling. Field lifted Ao from the taxi and placed her aboard before hopping up himself.

'Wait here,' he shouted to the driver as they slipped away in the direction of a Jack Teagarden tune that gradually took on the form of Amara's house, floating on the horizon like an exotic oil rig.

The boat sailed in across the open ground floor and under the raised deck until it was caught by a servant standing on the main stairs. Amara was peering down from above.

'You're late, Johnny boy!' she shouted. 'Late even for a gatecrasher. The meal is over. Ahha.' She gave him a kiss. 'And you're soaked.' She brushed away the water that stood out on her silk-covered arms. 'You can't dance with me. And this, ahha, a friend.' She focused on Ao.

'A friend,' Field confirmed. He shoved the girl towards the dishes of food laid out on a table – 'Go and eat' – before looking back at Amara.

'What's the matter, John?' She pulled him away from the food and from the tables littered with guests.

'Nothing.'

'So why did you come? Ahha! That is the question.'

'Just a visit, Amara. And General Krit. Is he here?'

'Can't swim, they tell me.'

'Then he didn't pump the area dry.'

'Oh! Oh! How many ministers live in this district? How many generals? How many police colonels? None. I couldn't pay so much as all of them combined for their districts. Instead I have become an expert on island life and, oh, and on earth subsidence. Archimedes' principle. I don't blame Krit. Oh, no! Never. He's just the general for us, my dear. So mediocre. So stupid. So manageable. He's the sort of man who would sell out his country for three nights with Miss Universe. Oh yes. I am still a Krit supporter. Oh yes. Perhaps then he will pay to repair my house. Do you think so? No. Oh no. Now look over there. Meechai's wife. That's why you weren't invited.'

'And not Michael?'

'He doesn't go to parties. You know that, John. Ahha. Not your condom king. He's in the slum every Monday night. All night she tells me. At the slaughterhouse, he tells her. Surely that's the wrong spot for a doctor. And you're to blame.'

'I've got nothing to do with it.'

'Tell the abandoned wife.'

Field looked over at Woodward's whisper thin wife, elegant in a piece of silk that left her shoulders and back bare as if there were no mosquitoes. In the same moment he caught a glimpse of Ao, suddenly solid and thick in comparison, still piling food on to a plate. Amara caught the glance without a word being said.

'Why did you bring her here? That child.'

'I had to. What does it matter? You let your queens bring their muscle boys.'

Amara dismissed this. 'Boys don't matter. The wives like it. The boys help spread the rumour that AIDS is in town and that makes the husbands a little more careful. Oh. Oh, anyway, I don't care. There is nothing wrong with prostitutes. They,' she indicated her women guests, 'do the same thing with men of their own class. Prostitutes are part of liberalism just like my friends' modern behaviour. It's monogamy I'm against. Once we brought that in, minor wives were finished and prostitution was bound to rise. 1935 was a very black year for female job security. Ahha.'

Field allowed a smile to show. 'Will you take Songlin in?'

'Of course I will.'

'I mean tonight. I'll telephone her and you send your car.'

'The telephone is dead. Drowned, I should say.'

'All right. Will you send your car? You must keep her here twenty-four hours a day.'

'So you see, I was right to ask what was wrong.'

'It doesn't matter, Amara. Just don't let anyone near her.'

'Of course it doesn't matter, Johnny. Nothing matters.'

'Will you send the car now?'

'Of course I will.' She had the driver sent up to her and gave him instructions. 'Now we also must go. And you must come with us.'

'Not tonight, Amara.'

'Oh yes, Johnny. Come with us. I've worked it out. A boat trip. The water is high enough to get all the way to a country place where they have the most marvellous catfish stew. So, big adventure. The first time since they filled in the canals that we can try to go by boat. The first time in years and years'. She broke away, shouting, 'Time! Time!' Linen table cloths and baskets of champagne were carried out from one of the pavilions and down the stairs. 'The noodles and catfish are good,' she said apologetically to Field, 'but the rest . . . oh no! Ahha! Not good enough! So you must come.'

'No.' Field walked over to the table covered with rows of dishes – coconut milk curries, crisp noodles, steamed dumplings, poached fish, banana flowers with pork, steamed prawns. He picked out and swallowed a few pieces, then gathered up Ao and carried her down to the boat. There were now five more skiffs waiting in a line, each with a torch. 'I'll send it right back,' he called up to Amara and when they reached the taxi he told the driver to head for the Klong Toey slum.

'Deep that way,' the man protested.

'Just try,' Field said. 'Come on. The tide is going out now. The water is dropping.'

They crept back towards the centre of Bangkok, where the traffic had thinned, and weaved their way around stalled cars and *tuc-tucs*. Some areas were dry again. Others, victims of the pumps that kept the influential districts dry by emptying water their way, or simply on lower ground, still lay beneath a stagnant sea. The taxi cut down through the warehouse district towards the river, where they skirted along the edge of the slums built on stilts above permanent water. Curiously enough this wooden maze was one of the few parts of Bangkok to make sense in the monsoon season. Its walkways were always above flood level.

They cut around the Foundation for Unclaimed Bodies. The unknown dead, most of them murdered, were brought there and kept a few days in case any relatives materialized. Outside, a neon light shone on a window decorated by colour photos of the dead, each of them deformed by some gash or swollen blue concussion. Pong Hsi-Kun, General Krit's businessman, had offered this charitable service to the city a few years before as proof of his good intentions and the gossip mill had immediately pointed out how appropriate was his choice of gifts.

The pig slaughterhouse lay just beyond, past the Catholic school. The area was dry because it had been flooded for three months in 1983 and the Chinese meat wholesalers had lost a fortune. An Asian city without pork was like an Italian city without pasta. The merchants had personally financed dikes to ensure the supply of meat was never again interrupted. Apart from that modernization, the whole place was locked into some distant century. The slaughterhouse itself was divided between two single-storey low shed-like buildings that stretched on and on towards football field proportions.

As the taxi edged its way down the dirt road that ran along the side of the main building, a smell of damp, cloying rot seeped in through the windows from the piles of bones and refuse left outside.

The taxi driver insisted the moment he stopped, 'You pay me now, mister.'

'I want you to wait.'

'I no wait here. You pay me.'

Field shrugged and gave in. He opened his door on to a long human scream. A scream, in fact, beyond the human, produced as it was by death removing reason. Hard on the tail of it there was another scream from another direction, then a chorus of them. Field had to pull Ao from the car and drag her forward. Inside, the neon lights lit a series of small pens. Dozens of them. Some were filled with enormous pigs roaming nervously about. Others were equipped with a steam fire in the centre surrounded by a cement table. In each of these pens there were twenty or so pigs, that had been separated out from the others, and five men dressed only in shorts. The pigs were invariably cowering in the corner furthest from the slaughter table.

The sight held Field so completely that he hardly noticed the animal slime through which he was walking. The pigs cowered like human beings. They lay packed up against each other for reassurance, heaving as if they could not catch their breath, drooling saliva with fear, their eyes out of focus. One of the men in the closest pen, his own skin running with the mucus and blood of the animals, strode over, a foot long iron hook in his hand and struck a pig on the head. Involuntarily its mouth opened. The man thrust the curve of the hook in and yanked so that the sharpened end came out through the flesh of the under chin. With the hook thus locked into the jaw, the man began pulling and the animal screamed a long steady human scream. The pig was half the man's height and a good deal heavier, but he made no attempt to fight back, only to balk and to scream. When he was near the steam oven, four men caught him, one by each leg and flipped him up on to the table. Another man flashed a knife and cut a great X in the throat. They rolled him over so that the river of blood flowed into a barrel; the scream petering out as the liquid emptied from his body. Then they pushed him into the steam, scraped his skin clean and halved him, gathering the innards up for a separate market.

Field looked down to see that Ao was waiting, already adjusted to the place and indifferent. She had probably seen endless slaughtering in her village, although on a minute scale in comparison.

The men noticed Field staring and asked him what he wanted. The question was not particularly friendly.

'Dr Wuthiwat.'

They pointed across to the other side of the shed. Field led the way through the slime past successive pens of animals screaming and behind them, successive rows of other men and other pigs. There was a honey-like smell of death in the air. It wasn't surprising that the slaughterhouse was one of Bangkok's sources for cheap contract killers. Woodward had once remarked that if you have been slaughtering pigs all night, there is no great difference in slaughtering a man.

All around the inside walls of the shed were makeshift rooms suspended five or six feet above the outer pens. The butchers' families lived there. Just outside the shed there were some food stalls. Michael Woodward sat at one of them in his peasant clothes. The rough wood table before him had a cloth thrown over it and was set up to deal with minor medical problems. Woodward, however, was seated alone on a wood stool with his head in both palms staring off into space. The mud beneath him was yellow in the crude lighting. He appeared neither pleased nor displeased to see them.

'My faithful walking wounded,' was all he said.

'Even unto hell,' Field added and sat down across from him. 'How would you like to help an old friend?'

'Why not?'

'I need some protection.'

Woodward waved towards the inside of the slaughterhouse from where the screams were still floating. 'The cream of the crop. Two, perhaps three hundred of the city's finest knife men. And all good Catholic boys. Perfect for you.'

As Buddhists, on principle, were against killing, the slaughterhouse was staffed by Christians, mostly descendants of Vietnamese immigrants converted originally by French priests.

'What would you like, John? Two to take home, cleaned and dressed?'

'Sure. Maybe not tonight. I don't feel up to going home right away.'

'Well, in that case I can offer you, both of you in fact, a bed in this hotel. I have the most charming digs above the stable.'

'Above?'

Woodward pointed. 'There.' It was one of the rattan partitions hung over the slaughter pens. 'The music of the sows' swan songs stops at two. Then the meat goes out and the men are free for me to examine. I'll have already looked at the women and children by then. Anyway, the bed is free till four, when I myself have a little rest, as it would disturb my family to return home at such an hour. How are the diseased jewels?'

'Jade extract coming out.'

Woodward nodded. 'Do not, I repeat, do not panic. Keep off the firey liquids and help will be here any day. Your lady didn't come in this morning for a shot.'

'She was caught up with me. Fleeing.'

Woodward waved Ao close to him and prepared a needle.

'I saw your wife tonight,' Field said.

'Dear thing. At Amara's that would be.'

'I'd say she wishes you were there, not here.'

'Yes, she would. When you came out, I was sitting where you find me, drinking my deliciously iced Ovaltine and thinking that every Monday night for eleven years I've been sitting on this stool drinking deliciously iced Ovaltine. Conclusion: Eleven years is a long time. But then I saw myself as in a vision ministering to nothing but the wealthy sick at the Nursing Home or in a private practice over by the Palace or perhaps, why not, in London in Knightsbridge charging a pound of flesh, and a perfectly natural desire to vomit presented itself to me without prompting. So I drank some more Ovaltine.' He emptied his glass and filled it up again by pouring tea, from a large tin pot sitting on the table, over his remaining ice.

'That is the tradition here. You pay for the Ovaltine. The iced tea is on the house. Of course, in my case the Ovaltine is also free; in exchange for services. I'll stand you some.' He waved to the woman behind the counter and asked Ao if she wanted a Coke.

An accidental concentration of pigs screaming as they were dragged towards tables, invisible from where the two men and the girl sat, stopped them from talking for a moment.

Woodward said quietly, 'What bothers me, you see, is that as I get older, I find it harder to accept that I do not stop death. All I do is delay it. And working here you cannot pretend that death is an occasional accident. The reminders. The reminders. Perhaps that is good. Take you, for example. There you were, plodding along from gonorrhoea to chlamydia as if life would never end and suddenly these people materialize, the ones I have not been introduced to, and remind you daily of your imminent demise.'

Field didn't smile. 'Sure. I don't mind about that. Why should I? It's just bad timing.'

'Bad timing?'

'From my point of view, eh. The fact is, I never understood that business about life being short. I'd say it's long. Very long,' Field repeated. 'And most of it doesn't matter. I'd say only a few seconds of it matter – the big moment, the big choice. But those seconds are never marked out, so you can charge right on through them without even noticing. Then there you are. You've had your big chance, your final, determining test. You didn't even recognize it, let alone seize it. You probably won't notice for years. But you have failed. Irrevocably failed. And after that, all the rest is an interminable wait for the end. Waiting for nothing.'

Woodward had an inquisitive look. 'You think this is your determining test?'

'Oh no!' Field laughed. 'I failed long ago. But it would be inconvenient to die now, just when I'm close to working out precisely when my big moment was. Life for me has nothing to do with success. I suppose that's why I left North America. What matters is coming to terms with my failure. You like that? Now your father is the man who defies time.'

'And he is never sick,' Woodward said. 'Never. He eats a lot of green chillies. He says they keep the digestion running and the rest is detail.'

'When is his party?'

'Next week. I had worked it all out to be away. There is an outbreak of koro up on the northern border with Laos. A team of doctors are going in tomorrow morning.'

'Koro?'

'You don't know it? Hardly surprising in your case. A primarily social neurosis which comes in times of political troubles and takes on the proportions of an epidemic. Its characteristics: both males and females believe their sexual organs are shrinking, or, more properly put, retracting. You, being antisocial and too lazy to have nerves, are, no doubt, immune. Besides, if yours retracted, you couldn't infect them. Of course, it is entirely psychological; the interesting point being that human beings are perfectly capable of, in fact, retracting their sexual organs; it is a talent which we retain from our animal past and which is consciously used by certain warrior groups who have not been introduced to the jock-strap. However, in the case of koro they actually believe there is retraction, while there is none.'

'But you aren't going?'

'My father wrote asking me to attend his party. He says his sons-in-law have turned it into such a business get-together that he won't go himself unless I'm there. Because of the rain we can't have it at his house, so they suggested the Siam Bank. Can you imagine? They settled for a hotel.' Woodward dismissed the subject and gave Ao a smile. She sat with a foot up beneath herself on the small stool and sipped her Coke. 'You had better go to bed now, both of you. None of the sick will come to me unless I'm alone. Besides, not everything here is what it appears. That lady,' he indicated an extremely fat woman behind a small soft-drinks wagon, 'was caught last year with three kilos of heroin. The term was life. She's already out. Now I wouldn't have much influence over her. Nor over the wholesalers who come down here every night. They're all Chinese and tied into any sort of thing. For a start there is a racket on weighing the carcasses that's worth hundreds of thousands every day. But so long as you stay within the slaughterhouse walls you're all right. I'll spread the word around. Now off you go.'

Field led the way in past the pigs and the slaughter tables to a rough plank staircase that led up to Woodward's room. There was nothing there except a bed and a small window with canvas over it. The smell within was the same as that outside and the small enclosure had trapped all the daytime heat. Field threw off his clothes and collapsed into a stupor. In the background there was the screaming of the pigs, which his dreams converted into the murder of Diana in Vientiane. And yet the nightmare didn't wake him. It was as if he needed to see the scene, needed to see it again and again.

At seven Woodward woke them, saying that he had been lent another room and so had let them sleep on. As for Field's safety, the butchers wouldn't let anyone near him. If he wanted to go home, there were two men who would go with him and stay as long as he needed them. Woodward said he would check in that evening.

But Field was in no hurry to go. He left Ao dozing and went out on to the stairs. The pens below were washed down and empty. In the other rooms built around the slaughterhouse wall, the families were sleeping. The silence of the place was such that he could hear their snores. Only one young man, in a shirt and trousers, sat indolently at the bottom of the steps. He gave a warm smile which tensed the muscles in his neck and got up to follow Field to the food stand. Field bought him some noodles and they ate together in silence. Then he went back and lay quite still on the bed, thinking.

The story was useless to a reliable journalist. What he needed, if he was going to publicize it, was an unreliable journalist. There were lots of Thai language scandal sheets, but they would be as immobilized with fear as anyone by the number of journalists shot dead each year. Only an outsider would take the risk. An unreliable outsider. It was then that Field thought of George Espoir. An article by him would be front page material in every western country. Just the man, Field thought, if I can't put Somchai's friends back to sleep.

'John.'

He looked over to the side. Ao was wrapped up in the sheet and half awake.

'We go now?'

'No. Not yet.' He turned on his side, away from her and went back to thinking.

Then noises drew him out on to his steps, where he could see children creeping from the length of suspended rooms on either side. They were clean and dressed in blue and white uniforms, as if they had slept in a little suburban house outside some European or American city. Field sat on the steps for the rest of the day, staring across the empty pens. The rain came down outside and its sound echoed beneath the roof; although without the flooding it seemed a distant, abstract music. He wasn't really thinking. He was trying to empty his mind. In fact he was remarkably happy for the first time in, he counted back, three weeks. Perhaps he was happier than he had been then. How could he measure the two? In the afternoon he daydreamed about Diana as he had known her twenty-five years before in Montreal. Then he went inside and had a nap.

Ao was there on the bed. She had refused to leave the room all day.

He was woken in the early evening by the sound of the pigs being herded in from somewhere outside. Thousands and thousands of them moved along the aisles in a river of flesh and were separated a hundred or so at a time into the waiting pens. When the slaughtering started, he retreated back inside. The screams didn't seem so bad to him this time. Ao reached across the bed to squeeze his thigh.

'We go now, John?'

'Not yet.'

'What we doing here?'

'Waiting,' Field said and caressed her hair. It was thick and coarse.

A while later he heard two voices arguing just outside in Thai. He peeked through the canvas-covered window. It was his young guard arguing with a Chinese Thai who, despite his sandals and ordinary white shirt, had a prosperous air. There were two gold rings on his fingers and a big gold watch on his wrist. His prominent set of teeth shone with the cleanliness of love and dentures. It was hard to follow the conversation.

'There was a *farang* here last night.'

'I don't know.'

'You must know. I saw him hanging around.'

'You mean the doctor?'

'Not the doctor. Don't be an idiot. I know the doctor. I just want to know where the other man is.'

'Who?'

'The man. The other *farang*.'

'I didn't see him.'

The Chinese was keeping his distance from the Thai, who swung a slaughtering knife in one hand as if playing with it.

'Look, I'll pay you to tell me.'

'How can I tell you what I don't know?'

Everything had to be repeated five or six times before the man withdrew. When Woodward turned up after nine p.m. he already knew about the conversation. The same man had been asking questions all over the slaughterhouse. He was a fairly large wholesaler.

'You might as well come out, John, and eat something. They know you're here, my friend. It's merely a question of what they can do about it. Not much, I would venture to say.'

Field followed him down into the sounds of the dying pigs, but Ao refused to move. 'I'll bring you something,' Field said.

'We go soon,' she replied.

'I'll bring you something.'

They sat on their stools outside and Woodward ordered two glasses of chilled Ovaltine. 'Your little Ao is a good girl. A good Buddhist. She won't come down because she doesn't believe in killing and she's afraid if she did come, that she might grow used to the violence.'

'You're the Buddhist teacher, Michael. What are you doing here?'

'Me. I think of it as a test. Like the big moment you were talking about last night. I force myself to come here and not to grow used to it. Would you like some meat? Pork?'

'No,' Field said. 'I'll skip that.'

'How long would you have to stay here before you could order roast pork? Now tell me that, John. Each time I come, I look at that crackling skin on the counter, quite delicious actually, and I ask myself that question, and I say no. Just because of the visible link. Of course, I eat pork at home. How I adore hypocrisy. Particularly my own.'

Field glanced back towards his room and saw the wholesaler who had been looking for him come into the slaughterhouse. There were two men with him.

'They're here.'

Woodward looked to see. 'Quick.'

They slipped inside and crouched behind the wall of one of the pens. They were forced to stand in a drainage gutter, filled with water carrying lost blood and wastes. The confusion of pens and of butchers between them and the three men was so great that they could watch over the top of the wall.

The wholesaler and his friends were half-way across the slaughterhouse to the room where Field had been sleeping before they stopped to question a group of butchers working in a pen. The men turned their backs on the questions and so the delegation moved on towards Field and Woodward, stopping now and again, but apparently learning nothing. When they were twenty yards away, they came upon the young man who had been guarding the room that afternoon. The wholesaler recognized him and motioned him over to the edge of his pen. Field's butcher ignored the summons and instead went with his hook into the opposite corner and dragged out a screaming pig that his friends set about slaughtering. All five were naked except for shorts. Their bodies shone with the grease coming off the skin of the pigs, outlining their muscles so that they seemed both powerful and deformed. They were misshapen men who worked in the least respectable of places. The wholesaler and his two friends waited patiently at first, then began to grumble and moved round to the entrance of the pen and went in with a menacing air. Field recognized one of them as the man who had followed him at the university, but this time the plump and easy swagger seemed familiar for some reason.

'Somchai,' Field whispered to himself. 'Somchai's brother. He must be. Yes.'

Woodward didn't know what this meant. He was straining to hear the argument that had begun in the slaughter pen. It was the same argument Field had overheard earlier, only this time the wholesaler had two protectors.

'Well if you don't know where the man is, where is the doctor?'

'He's not here tonight,' the guard answered.

'We've already been told he is here.'

The oldest of the butchers pointed his knife at them. 'Get out of here. Go on. Get out.'

'Stupid animal,' Somchai's brother shouted at him. 'You're as stupid as your pigs.'

'Get out.'

Somchai's brother whipped his hand in beneath and behind his shirt and produced a pistol. 'We'll pay you to tell us where he is or we'll make you tell us.'

His friend pulled out his pistol in imitation, but then the two men could only stand there like idiots, waving their weapons in a B grade movie way.

'Get out.' The older butcher came close to them with his knife. 'Go on.'

Woodward was becoming restless. 'I can't let them get killed. Stay here. I'll stop them.' He slipped out into the open.

'Michael, don't!'

Field tried to grab him, but he was already striding up the aisle towards the argument, past other pens where the men had stopped working to watch.

'Wait,' Woodward called out. 'I want to talk to you.'

The five butchers and the intruders looked over in astonishment. Woodward came round to the pen entrance and went in. 'Now listen, the man you are looking for has gone.'

Somchai's brother slipped behind the doctor and pressed his gun hard against Woodward's head. 'Now . . .' he began.

But the young butcher with the hook, who had been Field's guard, shouted, 'Don't touch the doctor!' He came running forward. 'Don't touch him!'

A kind of stomach noise rose up in protest from the other four men and spread to the adjoining pens. Somchai's brother was so astonished by this cry, half-human, half-animal, all around him, that he lowered his gun for a second. The butcher flung out his hook and struck him on the temple. He staggered backwards and fell down among the cowering pigs in the corner of the pen. His pistol was still in his hand but he was too stunned to use it. 'Don't touch the doctor,' the butcher screamed. 'You hear me! Don't touch him!' He ran forward in a frenzy. The stunned man tried to raise his pistol, but before he could the hook had crashed into his mouth, twisted and been yanked forward with the sharp end ripping out through the skin of the neck to lock around his jaw bone. The butcher yanked him again and he came on all fours, trying to hold himself back by pressing his palms into the slime-covered floor. His jaw was stretched forward and his larynx opened with this dragging so that a scream came out of his throat quite indistinguishable from that of the pigs a moment before. His eyes were flashing in panic to his friends, but they seemed unable to move and a second later the butcher had dragged him to the slaughtering table and heaved him up on his back beside the steam machine. The pistol was still in his hand, but it hung useless, like a prehistoric claw. The butcher seized a knife and as if to stop the man's scream cut a deep cross in his throat and pushed him sideways so that the gush of blood went into the usual barrel and the scream slowly petered away. The other butchers hung back, and came forward to interfere only when they saw he was going to go on and split the man like a pig.

No one said anything at first. They all stared at the drained and blanched body on the table, then the older butcher waved his knife at the remaining two intruders. 'Get out. I told you. Get out.'

The wholesaler turned and ran from the pen, slipping in panic and on down the aisle, with the other man close behind him. When they were gone, the older butcher bowed slightly to Woodward and suggested that he leave them to deal with the body.

CHAPTER 11

Field knew exactly what to do, now that there was no choice. He went forward, took Woodward by the arm and led him outside.

'You have to go right now, Michael, to the Oriental. There's a man staying there, I don't know which room, but his name is George Espoir. Bring him here. Do you have some paper?'

The air was so humid that his pen would scarcely write. Field scribbled – 'I have your emotive element. Come immediately.'

Woodward was back before midnight leading Espoir by the arm to encourage him through the slaughterhouse, although he tried to give the impression of merely showing the way.

'I once visited a place somewhat like this,' Espoir forced this out as a jovial greeting, 'in Zaire. I had an idea for a book that didn't work out. It was all emotive, if you see my point. Too emotive. A stormy sea. There were no railings to which your average literate public could cling. An overly rough sea for a novel reader.'

Field took him outside and sat him down at the Ovaltine stand where he told his entire story, with Woodward listening in. Espoir interrupted only once to say, 'Now I understand the Golden Panda Massage mystery.' And at the end, 'How very unpleasant.'

'Yes,' Field said, 'but it's a fucking good story. You could put it in a newspaper that counts and everyone would pick it up. I'd say you could do it in such a way that you might look quite a hero. In fact, exposing a Communist government would make you more than a star.'

'It is a good story, I'll grant you that.' Espoir was attempting to disguise his excitement, probably afraid that Field was holding back some catch. An unexpected tension appeared in his loose jowls. 'Anyone in London would take it. Or in New York for that matter.'

'Speed is what I'm in need of.'

'That is no problem.' He waited, still expecting some impossible condition, but Field merely stared at him nervously. After almost a minute's silence, Espoir smiled in relief and added, 'I'll do it tonight. The hotel can telex it for me after I've spoken to the right editor. A good story. A very good story!'

'Will you get a copy to Michael at the Nursing Home?'

'Of course, of course.' Suddenly Espoir had all his self-confidence back. 'And this mysterious woman somewhere up there in the Olympian clouds, controlling it all, who is she?'

'I don't know.'

'A pity really. That would have rounded the story off. Now you,' he turned to Woodward, 'as a Thai, how do you feel about all this corruption?'

'What do you mean, feel? I don't feel anything. What have feelings got to do with it?' Woodward's tone was cold and devoid of his Nursing Home pluminess.

'No. Of course. I express myself poorly. How do you interpret all this corruption?'

'Communists are corrupt not because they are Communist, but because they are human. Most Thais live off unofficial earnings because officially they are paid next to nothing. A captain earns 200 dollars a month. A sergeant earns 90. The captain needs a car and money for his children's schooling and a house, just for starters. So he does what you would expect. He looks for other sources of income. As does the civil servant. A first interpretation of corruption would therefore be that wages are too low. You see, assigning Brownie points to one side or the other in the Third World doesn't get you very far. The problem is not financial corruption, it is the corruption of the leaders' minds. For example, I am a great monarchist, but once the Kings started sending our young élite abroad for education, they were turned into modern brown British. I assume you know this phrase.'

'And you?' Espoir began.

'I am a prime example. So now the King thinks he under-stands the country. But how can he, honest and good as he is, when our leaders, his advisers, do not understand it and hide that truth from him in order to hide their own ignorance and corruption. They try to use the King as an instrument and they turn the country away from its Buddhist principles. The solution is not to end corruption but to change the leadership. That is, change the King's advisers.'

'Good,' Espoir said. Boredom or fatigue seemed to have suddenly overwhelmed him. 'Very interesting. My car is wait-ing. Would either of you like a ride?' He left as fast as he could, stepping gingerly across the slaughterhouse floor.

'So that is George Espoir,' Woodward said.

'You knew who he was?'

'Oh yes, brown British that I am. And also he told me on the way here. What was it he said? Oh yes. Very interesting things about himself. I must tell you sometime. And what do you suppose he will put in his article?'

'Any shit will do, just to get the ball rolling.'

'And you?'

'I have to wait for it all to happen. I'll wait here I guess. They're unlikely to come back.'

'Highly unlikely. I wonder,' Woodward mused, 'what will happen with that barrel of blood to which your friend has recently contributed. They sell the liquid for blood sausage. Do you eat blood sausage, John?'

'Not this week.'

'No. Neither do I. Would you like another Ovaltine?'

'I'd like a Mekong.'

'That would be bad for you.'

'Everything I do is bad for me. I'm dying of life.' Field looked up at the sky. It was clear again that evening and filled with stars. He was always relieved to find the big dipper absent. That alone was a reason for living in the East. 'No fucking dipper,' he said.

'What?'

'No dipper. The big work symbol in the Western sky. The heavenly equivalent of Jack and Jill.' His eye was drawn to a bright patch down on the horizon. 'What's that?'

Woodward looked the same way. 'A fire.'

'You'd have to work at it to start one in this weather.'

Woodward was still staring at the floating light. 'Klong Toey,' he said suddenly. 'Klong Toey!' A second later he was running through the slaughterhouse.

'Wait!' Field shouted and went after him. Woodward was in a wholesaler's car, explaining why he needed a ride, by the time Field caught up. He banged on the windscreen, 'Wait. Michael. I'll come.'

They were almost there before the road began to fill, first with children milling about and then with women who were carrying bundles. They had a surprised, aimless look. The crowd became too thick to drive through so Woodward abandoned the Chinese businessman, jumping out to question one of the women. She seemed to be frightened as much by his insistence as by whatever had happened, and was unable to speak. He pushed his way past her with Field keeping close behind. Over the heads Field could see only more heads against a background of uneven orange light. Suddenly the crowd ended and there was an opening. Woodward paused. Twenty metres on was the edge of the swamp and the beginning of the wooden walkway that led off into the maze of the slum. The jumble of tin roofs was lit up, as was the stream of women and children pressing off the walkway and melting into the crowd. There was no panic. They walked slowly and carefully over the rough planks that swayed on their pilings under such concentrated weight. The flames could be seen leaping up far into the centre of the slum.

Only then did Field consciously realize he had left the slaughterhouse without his two guards. The thought passed quickly through his mind, then he was off again, running behind Woodward along the walkway, the women making room for them as they came. His feet slipped on the wet planks but there seemed to be no time, no place to stop and bend to remove his shoes. A murmur followed behind them. 'The doctor. The doctor.' But Woodward gave no sign of noticing. He ran blindly forward with an urgency Field had never seen in his restrained friend. It took them ten minutes to reach the concentration of men passing buckets from the water towards the edge of the fire. Ahead of them was a ring of flame eating its way out through forty or so houses and in the centre of this was the remains of the central square and of Woodward's clinic, where the fire had already consumed itself. The two men stopped.

'I'm sorry,' Field said.

'That doesn't matter,' Woodward replied. 'I can work anywhere. It's the houses.'

'No,' Field insisted and he understood himself only as he spoke. 'No. I'm sorry. It's my fault, I think.'

Woodward looked round, suddenly confused. 'You think so? Yes. Yes. Perhaps it is.' He looked back out at the fire and caught the shoulder of a man passing a bucket. 'Where did it start?'

'Your clinic, Doctor.'

'But how?' The man was too embarrassed to reply. 'Come on,' Woodward insisted. 'How?'

'Someone, I think. There was an explosion.'

Woodward let the man go back to work and stood in a collapsed way.

'I'm sorry,' Field repeated.

'So I am very innocent, John. I don't understand how things work.'

'Perhaps, Michael, but they can rebuild this.'

'With money. No one will give them money. I've worked here for eleven years to help them and now I cause their houses to be burnt.'

Field was no longer listening. It struck him that while the fire could be a cheap form of revenge, it was also a way to draw him out into a crowd. He looked around. There was an unevenness to the advance of the flames, labouring over the soggy outsides of the buildings before finding a new opening and leaping suddenly forward, sucked inside yet another house where everything was dry. Among all the men pushing and throwing water there was a mongoloid teenager dressed only in shorts, who was rushing into the burning houses with a kind of linear frenzy, carrying out armfuls of belongings which he shoved into the hands of the women who were hanging back to witness their homes being devoured. Then he would rush back in, although people were screaming at him to stop. The more they told him it didn't matter, the more he rushed into flames to rescue bedding and photographs and pots; anything that came into his hands.

Field watched, hypnotized by the flames and the darting boy, whose heavy awkward face was tensed in concentration. I could do that, Field thought to himself, I could do that. But he stood and watched until his eye was drawn to another face only a few metres away. It was the surviving gunman, who had come to the slaughterhouse and had left, running with the wholesaler after his partner was slaughtered. He was easing his way up to Field and his hand was down under his shirt, clenched on to something in his belt. Field stared at the man, who was unable to look away, as if hypnotized, while his eyes grew small and filled with fear. One word, they both knew, one word would be enough to turn this whole crowd of slum dwellers on to the man. They would kill him. There. Before Field's eyes. They would kill him. And that would be his second execution of the night. Field motioned with a glance to indicate that the man should raise his hand from under his belt. There was a hesitation, but he brought it out empty. Field went forward until he was hard against the man's chest, pushing him against the railing of the walkway.

'Tell me. Come on, tell me.'

The man stared up, too terrified to say a word.

Field leaned down close to his head. 'Tell me who. Quick. You want to die?'

The man shook his head. 'They killed him at the slaughterhouse.'

'Not Somchai's brother. Who else? Come on.'

'I don't know anyone else.'

'I don't believe you.' Field turned his head, as if to call others over towards them.

'No! No! I don't.'

Field looked back at the man. He had a loser's face. The face of a man used by others. Field raised his hands and gave a sudden shove that sent him backwards over the railing into the shallow water below. Neither of them uttered a sound. Field looked behind to see Woodward caught up in the fire-fighting. The mongoloid boy was still dashing in and out of burning houses. I could do that, Field thought again, but turned towards the shore and began pushing his way through the stream of women who were going the same way, but not fast enough for the obsession with survival which was beginning to overwhelm him.

Beyond the crowd he found a *tuc-tuc* that delivered him back to the slaughterhouse. The men had finished and were sitting around the bars outside eating and gambling. He gathered Ao, half-asleep, into his arms, and went in the *tuc-tuc* uptown towards his house. For some reason, the idea of bodyguards no longer seemed relevant. If necessary, he would barricade himself in until Espoir's article appeared. Ao dozed across his lap. The roads through which they drove were mostly dry. Here and there, fifty centimetres of water was caught in lower stretches of land.

They were stopped at a red light on Sukhumvit where a newspaper boy was walking up and down selling papers. Field bought a *Post*. The picture on the front page showed the worst flooding, out near Amara's house. Field turned through the pages in the first morning light. It was curious. All the stories seemed so clean, so abstract. Even the flood waters had a smooth, silky quality on the printed page. A photograph in the sports section caught his eye. It was Paga. He folded the sheet back. It was a photo of her swinging a golf club.

'Miss Paga Kampisom, well known to Bangkok residents,' the caption read, 'swings the first club to open her new golf course, the Pattaya Country Club. Eighteen holes of sport and comfort on the road to our most famous beach resort. In the background are her honoured guests, General Krit Sirikaya, Commander of the First Army Division, American Ambassador James Gunther Dean and the Minister of Sport and Tourism . . .'

'Ao, wake up! Wake up!' Field lifted her from his lap and leaned forward to the driver. 'Here, okay. Stop.' He leapt out while they were still moving and flagged down a taxi. 'Come on, Ao. Hurry up.' She stumbled from the *tuc-tuc* still half-asleep.

At that hour, the highway out of town towards Pattaya should have been empty. But it crossed the great river plain, much of it below sea level and so spongy that the tarred surface had been sinking ever since it was constructed. After years of work the outgoing lanes had been raised by two metres, but the incoming still lay as low as the rice paddies, that is to say, under a metre of water. This was further complicated by the trucks that were not allowed into the city until ten a.m. each morning and therefore sat in a thirty kilometre queue filling one of the dry outgoing lanes and leaving little room for traffic going either way.

The ride was like a prolonged bumper car session, with drivers weaving from one side to the other of the highway around the parked trucks and the cars stalled here and there in the water and dodging oncoming traffic, everyone with their hands on the horns. This lunacy was limited to the length and width of the road, while on either side the inundated paddy fields stretched out of sight in perfect peace. Field was too tired to be upset by anything so banal. His sole aim was to keep his eyes open so that he wouldn't miss the exit for Paga's country club.

It was seven hours, over a distance that should have taken two, before they saw the painted sign rising out of the water off to the left. Everything in sight was flooded with the exception of a new, narrow dirt road heaped up even above the level of the main road. This causeway led, after some kilometres, to an enormous unflooded island. Paga had taken perfectly ordinary rice paddies and dug out a network of deep lakes to drain the land in between, which became her new fairways. She had used the surplus earth to build high dikes around her entire eighteen holes. Pumps had been placed at fifty metre intervals, emptying any unwanted water into the neighbouring rice paddies. Behind these dikes, her golf course lay dry. There had been no trees for kilometres and so everything was small and freshly planted, except for a single clump of tall eucalyptus on slightly higher ground at the end of the new dirt road. Beneath these trees lay Paga's clubhouse; a *sala* built out of cement in a vaguely Thai style and painted very bright colours. The walls were open and the moment Field released his door he heard Paga's voice carrying from the only occupied table.

It was an after-lunch voice. 'Well then, you have seen the world, Colonel.'

'Yes, ma'am, been around twice for pleasure, if you don't count the fighting trips.'

'But you've never seen the world with Paga.'

The American hesitated, at a loss for words. 'Why no, ma'am.'

'I make a toast to the USA,' Paga said, to help him out. 'Without you I still be a poor woman.'

The end of her phrase tailed off as she looked up at Field and Ao walking in. The little party of American officers in uncreased polyester golfing clothes followed her eyes and all five of them stared with a curious intensity until Paga jumped up and came forward.

'I need some sleep,' Field said.

She led them round the clubhouse to a changing room where Field saw for the first time that he was covered in grease stains and black smears from the fire. His trouser legs were discoloured from a mixture of pig guts and mud. Paga left him to shower. When he came out his clothes had been replaced by a sarong and Ao had been given instructions to lead him through the grove of eucalyptus to the other side, where there was a handful of new monks' houses raised up a metre above the ground. She took Field to one of these. It was a single small room with four screened walls. He lay down on a straw mat on the hard floor and for a brief second wondered why there were monks' houses on a golf course, then noticed the singing of the birds and the breeze rising to cross his face, then fell asleep. He awoke once in the night to the sound of rain, rolled over and came to a second time early the next morning.

Ao was asleep beside him on the mat. Through the screen he could see a small, open cookhouse under the trees. Paga was in it with a woman in white whose head was shaved. She belonged to an Order which was the closest that a female could come to being a monk. Field looked round through his other windows. An old monk sat on the porch of the next one-roomed house. After a time the woman in white brought the old man food. She moved very slowly. None of this peace seemed to make any sense. Field retied his sarong and went out to the cookhouse where Paga was drinking rice soup. She gave him a big smile. A stream ran under the wood floor and flies swarmed round the food. She threw a piece of meat from her bowl to a mangy dog.

'You sleep okay in my place?'

'Looks like it. What is this, Paga?'

'Monk contemplation centre. I spend four million dollars on golf course. Make myself a big present huh, so I can retire to country. So I make merit too, I give the monks a place next door. Fifty acres for them. I could make a *wat*, but need more monks. We only got three.'

'Who's the old man?'

'My father.'

Field nodded. 'You've got the only dry place in Thailand.'

'Sure I have. I'm a peasant girl. You see my dikes?' She gestured towards them with her chin. 'I know about water. Two hundred fifty thousand dollars to move all that dirt. I can afford it. You want soup?'

Field considered the flies and the dogs prowling around the edge of the porch. 'Sure. Do you mind if I stay a few days?'

'You still got problem?'

He nodded. 'I was looking for you, Paga.'

'So?'

'I wanted to know more about Somchai.'

'He know you come here?'

'No. How could he? I mean, I don't know. I don't know who his friends are, so I don't know what they know. That's what I wanted from you.'

'Me? Why you think I know them still?' she said stubbornly.

'Doesn't matter now. I don't want to meet his friends any more.'

'Why not, John?'

'I don't want them to forgive me any more. I'm going to blow them out of the water instead. Kapow. You know, Paga, kapow! A big artillery shell. And if they take me with them, too bad.'

'How you do that, John?' This came between two long drinks from her bowl. She seemed scarcely interested.

'Secret, Paga. My secret. One thing I did find out. One of his friends is a lady.'

'Not me, John. I'm a woman.'

'Doesn't matter anyway. So I can stay?'

'You're my friend. You stay. I got to go now. I got a class with monks.' She got up and thrust her solid body forward on through the trees towards a decorated pavilion.

Field went for a walk on the mud dikes and stared out at the flooded landscape, then came back and napped for most of the afternoon. When he awoke Ao was there. It seemed to him that he had always been in that small pavilion, smelling the cookhouse on the breeze and listening to the birds. And Ao, it seemed that she had always been with him. Nothing more. Just there, with him, an essential feature should he have wished to complete a picture of his own life.

In late afternoon Paga reappeared beneath a golf cap and Field went to join her while she told some little girls how she wanted dinner cooked. The flies, if anything, were thicker.

'So why did your father become a monk?'

'My mother die fifteen years ago. He alone. Ten years ago he become monk.'

'Because he was alone?'

'Being alone make him think. People together can't do that. No time. He think: people born, people die, born die, born die. Same people keep coming back. Born, do evil, die. Born die. But the problem starts with born. So he decide to give up everything. He decide to try to die last time. To escape.'

'How's he getting on?' That didn't sound quite right, even to Field. 'I mean, do you think he's going to make it?'

'He try pretty hard. I start to try, too. Now I'm out here alone pretty much. I walk around all day alone. No bars to run now. My family do all that for me. Now I go to the monks every day for two hours to learn. One thing I learn fast. Easy to talk but hard to give things up. Bullshit is easy.'

'Well, what about your bars? You don't run them but you still have them.'

'I don't think about them.'

'But you get the money, Paga. That can't be earning you much merit.'

'Why not, John? I do good in my places. You see those dogs. When I find hungry dog I bring him here. All the time I build this place I bring dogs. One time I stop in restaurant by the

208

road and dog comes up to me, very hungry. I have a chop. I give him. Then I ask the waiter for two more chops. I not tell him chop is for dog or he cook badly. So I see Thai woman who have children. Husband go away. She need money. No good jobs to find. I say to her; "Why be unhappy? Massage good chance for you. You make thousand, two, three thousand *baht* a day. Maybe you find new husband at massage." My Buddha very smart. He understand that body doesn't matter. Body is like everything; just water, dirt and fire we say. That means blood, flesh and energy.'

'You learn this today?'

'Yesterday. Body not matter. Buddha understand that mind is most important. Must learn to control mind. Not enough to stop fucking; must stop wanting to fuck.'

'I've done both,' Field said. 'And no lessons.'

'So why you buy that girl?'

'Because you wouldn't, Paga.'

She laughed. 'Good thing you not in massage business. Bad businessman. *Farangs* all the same. They like Thai girls because they so small. Makes man think his prick is bigger. Makes him feel he's going to make a big impression.'

'Did your monk teach you that? No? Well, that has nothing to do with me as I've given it all up.'

'That why you buy sick girl?'

'Maybe.'

'Why you so unhappy then? That's no good. You still think you will be happy sometime in this world. You have to give up that.'

'So I give up being unhappy and I give up being happy. What does that leave?'

'You stop wanting, John. That's all. You stop wanting happiness like you stop wanting girl. Stop dream life. You're a big romantic, John. No compromise. Big dreamer. What kind of girl you want anyway? Not that little girl.'

Field shrugged. 'Why not?'

'You think about dream girl, right?'

'No. She's very specific.'

'So where is she?'

'I never got her. I saw her. I even had her. But I never had her the way I dreamt I would, simple and perfect, so how could I still think it might work out better later? I mean, if it didn't happen when I was at my best, young eh, so that you don't think too much, you only feel, with a girl who was in the same shape and who I loved with senseless passion, so that when I slid into her body it really was part of the same passion, then why would it happen now?' Flies had landed here and there on him and he paused to wave them off.

'What went wrong with this dream girl?' Paga ignored the flies on herself.

'She wasn't interested. Men are funny about that. They think all you have to do is convince her. I'll tell you, Paga, there is no mythology in religion compared to sex. Look at the romantic types. They say, if you love her, the physical details don't matter. Well, if the physical details don't matter, then we're just like your dogs, Paga; we'll do it any old way anywhere with anyone. That's me, right? Just a two-legged dog. Then the jock types, they say, when the light's off, every cunt is the same. Those guys must have asbestos for skin. The funny part is, they're saying the same thing as the romantics. Neither of them want to talk about the possibility of something perfect. They're all terrified either of the body or of the soul. And fear always sounds like hate. You'd have to hate women to say that their bodies don't matter or their cunts are all the same. Now what I was after was both. How could I still want that? All I've got to offer now is wisdom.' Paga laughed at the word. 'All right, call it experience. Who cares. I mean experience is the loser's prize. Experience is a form of measure. Now passion, that means impossible to measure, not because it's too big or too anything. Just because there's nothing in it to measure. This girl, Paga . . .'

'Your dream girl, right.'

'I knew exactly what it would be like with her before I touched her. Exactly. There was no difference between my imagination and the reality. Her breasts would be like half moons, just right so that my hand could cup them, full and soft. And soft hips, quite full. And poreless skin. And when I was in her, she would feel a certain way. I can't explain it, but a certain way. I knew exactly; like a secret of heaven. I had her

210

three times. Three. Each time I had to convince her. I had to try so hard. And each time there was this great act of passion that I felt would be enough to persuade her for ever. Only it didn't. So I had to start convincing all over again. No. It was all wrong. Horrible. Like a torture, to find what you desire and to find you could get hold of her by a constant conscious and fucking intellectual effort, while your passion actually drove her away. Anyway, I knew she existed, even if she didn't want me. And I figured out that you don't seduce that kind of girl. And you don't buy her. She has to want you.'

'What happened to her?'

'She's dead. She just died. Someone killed her.'

'So that's what's wrong with you.'

'With me? Everything is wrong. Half my time I spend with girls I sort of love who are all wrong. They smell wrong. They feel wrong. A hard mouth. How can you kiss a hard mouth all your life? Or inside, they're like a cavern. I don't know. Then I still have the other half of my time for all your ladies; the creatures of physical perfection. At least I can pay for that. I mean, here you can really order up your tastes. Anyone can. So you lie to yourself. You limit your demand. You go for the physical and you agitate yourself around within the perfect body while she acts out – oh, in an honest, well meaning, friendly way – that you are transporting her to heaven. None of that has much to do with what I originally wanted. Simple passion, right? No needs, no expectations, no agendas. Just a kind of fusing together. And I didn't want it for long. Just a little while. A year, a few months. A week would have done, just so long as it was perfect while it lasted. In that case time doesn't matter. Time doesn't matter if you get what you want. It's an over-rated quality anyway. And I got everything except what I wanted.'

'Maybe you didn't want it enough.'

Field realized he wasn't making any sense, not to Paga at any rate. 'It has nothing to do with wanting. That's the point.'

'That's why you buy the girl?'

'That's not exactly what I did.'

'No? What did you do?'

'I don't know, Paga. Listen, I've got this animal on my back.

Somchai. This pig of an ex-friend of yours. I didn't put him there. I didn't seek him out. I just want him to go away and leave me alone. You understand? I want him to get off my back. I want to go back to my boring little life where I happily plod along not getting what I want. That's all. That's all I'm thinking about.'

'Sure, John. I understand. Somchai was always a creep. We'll eat in the clubhouse, okay.'

They sat all evening under the high peaked cement roof, three of them surrounded by a sea of empty tables. Field and Ao ate silently while Paga described in detail the construction of her country club and the radio played Thai rock in the background. *Made in Thailand* was being sung for the third time in an hour when the radio went dead. A few moments later the national anthem came on, several decibels higher, then an announcer introduced the Commander of the First Army Division, General Krit Sirikaya.

'A vast coalition of His Majesty's senior officers have tonight taken action to restore honesty and efficiency to the affairs of our Nation.'

'Christ,' Field said, 'the fucking robber is in the bank.'

'As Commander of the Army Division assuring the safety of Bangkok, I have deployed my troops to ensure the security of all government buildings, centres of transport and communications. I shall be meeting in the next hours with the full committee of officers, for whom I am but a spokesman, in order to allocate the specific responsibilities which each of us must assume in order to assure that this step towards full democracy and freedom is an unqualified success.

'May I say only that our action, so long restrained, has been provoked by the inhuman mismanagement of the capital's flooding. No government can claim the legitimate mandate of the people when it has contempt for the people's comfort and safety. Yesterday's uncontrolled fire in the unfortunate area of Klong Toey is yet a further example of the need for change. The first action of our national renewal should be to provide alternative housing for the forty-seven families left homeless, thereby showing concrete proof of our desire to work for the good of those among us who do not have enough. As a

212

temporary measure of security, an absolute curfew will go into immediate effect. You may sleep in the knowledge that the national well-being is again in firm hands. Long live the King.'

The national anthem was played again and followed by a programme of classical Thai music.

'The robber is in the bank,' Field repeated quietly.

'You don't like him?' Paga asked. 'He's like all the others. I think he was scared they would fire him over the flood, so he fired them first.'

'It's just like old times, eh,' Field laughed suddenly. 'Just like old times.'

'Coups are bad for business, John. Curfew means bars close early. I lose money.'

Field walked over to the entrance of the *sala* and looked up at the sky. There was a *geko* calling out in the distance. Field counted. High, uneven numbers were lucky, seven being a good score. On nine the animal stretched out the 'tooh-kaay' as if too bored to go on, but rallied enough to give two more.

'Must be a big one,' Paga said.

'An alligator,' Field mumbled. 'Been eating golf balls.'

'Every coup, I lose money. The men spend all their time making coups, but they don't like to fight. No one dies in a coup. The Vietnamese are different. They fight all the time. If Vietnamese came here, they beat Thai army; but after, they cannot beat Thai people.'

'They'll close your golf course, though.'

'I don't care. I born poor. I die poor. But Vietnamese man fight like lion, so he need Thai girl.'

They sat idly by the radio waiting for news while the music whined on and on. At last Field said, 'He's got a problem,' and began rolling the radio dial. The bands were silent until suddenly he picked up another voice speaking on behalf of an Army Division stationed across the river from Bangkok at Thonburi. They also had taken action and its officers were also in meetings to discuss how best freedom and democracy might be served. It wasn't mentioned, but Field knew that their general was a Class Five man. As the night wore on, a more and more confused picture emerged from radio stations popping up all around Bangkok. Some of them were military controlled. Others were broadcasting illegally with all sorts of gossip. It was clear that the entire army had moved to take over the country, but they had done it division by division and now they were all in meetings. With whom, nobody would say. It was Krit who held the jewel, but he was encircled by divisions commanded either by Class Five or Class Seven generals and each of their radios was attacking not only the government but also, by innuendo, their rivals from the other Class. Only Krit was mentioned by all of them as an ally of freedom and democracy. Curiously enough, nothing specific was said about the Prime Minister, Pa Prem, a quiet, honest, compromising retired general. Nor about the King. Every general had announced he was acting for the King and against the Prime Minister, but both men had disappeared.

Friday, the next day, no one came to play golf and it wasn't until late in the afternoon that a radio originating up north in Chaing Mai began to broadcast across the country via relays. Apparently the Prime Minister had escaped to the northern capital and the Royal Family with him and they had rallied the army divisions nearby. Pa Prem was now calling for all divisions to go back to their barracks. Instead, the Class Seven and Class Five radio stations replied violently that the 'former Prime Minister had kidnapped the nation's beloved monarch'. It was the fury of the beaten. Krit in Bangkok went silent. His station ran through its entire stock of classical music, broken only once by an ambiguous announcement about Communist agitators in the Klong Toey slum trying to prevent the relocation of those left homeless by the fire. It sounded as if he were trying to slide into a new attitude which would make him a defender of stability rather than a revolutionary.

Field lay about all Saturday, outside until the showers began in the afternoon, then within his breeze caressed monk's house while the rain beat upon the roof. Early on Sunday the music was broken to announce that General Krit would speak in an hour. This announcement was made again an hour later. Then again at noon. In fact, it was early afternoon before the General finally came on the air, his voice betraying scarcely a hint of the impossible squeeze from which he was trying to extricate himself.

'My position as the officer responsible for the safety of our nation's capital has forced me to act in order to ensure that the disputes dividing certain elements within our Armed Forces should not be allowed to bring violence and destruction to the streets of Bangkok. It is therefore with humility that I have held our city safe for the return of His Majesty at his convenience. While the nation's armed forces may differ as to the details of how best to serve our people, these differences are minor and temporary. More dangerous are the elements within our society who would exploit the opportunity of any divisions to violently attempt the seizure of power. We have identified in the last twenty-four hours a secret organization which showed its hand first in the long-suffering Klong Toey districts. Worse still, the people behind this organization have used the confusion now reigning in the country as an excuse to attack our most revered institutions in the foreign press. I have therefore ordered that certain charges of lese-majesty be immediately laid. Long live the King.'

Early Monday morning Paga sent her pliable son into town to find out what was going on. Field asked him to stop at the Nursing Home in the hope that Espoir's article had appeared. The young man was gone all day and when he came back it was with a pile of illegal Thai news-sheets, that had sprung up during the uncertainty, and a collection of English newspapers. He had tried to go to the Nursing Home, but found it encircled by soldiers, so instead he had gone to a big hotel and bought every foreign paper available.

Field spread the pile out on a table in the *sala* and ploughed through. In the London *Times* of Saturday he found a front page story on the attempted coup. It was a special report by George Espoir, 'the well-known British novelist who has been in Thailand for some time investigating its bitter and divided politics'. Field skimmed through the first part. There was nothing about Somchai. Nothing about drugs. His eyes darted back to the beginning. There was nothing. Nothing. Only some quotes from 'my recent conversations with the enigmatic General Krit Sirikaya, who now holds the key to stable power in this Asian kingdom'. The article was continued on the second page. He turned nervously and there his eye was stopped by a name. 'Dr Meechai Wuthiwat, well known as the Condom King for his colourful advocacy of birth control and as a devoted slum worker, whose eccentricity leads him to adopt peasant's clothes in Bangkok despite his high birth, has chosen this moment of crisis to attack a number of his nation's most cherished institutions. He sought me out at my hotel late at night on the eve of the revolution and insisted that I come with him to a slaughterhouse in the heart of Bangkok's most lurid slum. There, in a setting evocative of all that Karl Marx deplored in the European nineteenth century, he spoke to me of the humanity of Communism and the corruption of both Thai politicians and bureaucrats. When I questioned him as to his feelings about the dangers of experimenting with political systems, given the tragedies that we have already witnessed in Cambodia and Vietnam, he replied that you could not "assign Brownie points to one side or to the other in the Third World" and that personal feelings do not enter into the matter. In particular he attacked the "corruption of the minds of our leaders" and their use of Thailand's revered king as an "instrument". "The solution is not to end corruption," he declared, "but to change the leadership." This call for revolution on the eve of the current events may have been particularly well-timed and Dr Meechai would appear to be preparing himself for a move up from the position of Condom King to that of real political power.'

'Holy Christ,' Field murmured to himself. 'The fucking idiot. The idiot.' He looked up to find Paga standing behind him. She dropped a Thai scandal sheet down in front of him. There was a large photograph of Michael Woodward in hand and foot chains being led into police headquarters. Field couldn't read Sanskrit. He felt as if he were about to vomit, but forced out, 'What does it say?'

Paga ran her finger along the headline, 'Condom King Arrested for Attacks on His Majesty.' And then, the cut line, 'General Krit acts to protect the monarchy.'

Woodward had been arrested in Klong Toey where he was organizing the fire victims to rebuild their houses. Soldiers had tried to prevent them, saying that if they wanted to rebuild, they would have to do it further out in the swamp where the water was two metres deep. The Port Authority had decided to reclaim the section cleared by the fire and use landfill to build a new warehouse. There were numerous references to 'Meechai's infamous attacks on the King in the foreign press' and to 'the likelihood of a fifteen-year sentence.' There was also a little gossip column article on Admiral Wuthiwat's eighth cycle party which was to take place on the next day and was to have been the social event of the year. 'The Christians say the sins of the fathers are visited on their sons. What about the sins of the son on to the father? Who will go to the Admiral's party and risk the curfew? Wait and see.'

CHAPTER 12

In the early hours of Tuesday morning, the Prime Minister flew back to Bangkok with the King. They landed on the Royal Palace grounds, where General Krit was waiting to greet them at the foot of the aeroplane steps. The Prime Minister immediately lifted the curfew. 'We shall proceed,' he declared, 'as if nothing has happened.' Overnight the various divisions around the country had withdrawn into their barracks and their generals had ceased broadcasting.

Field spent the morning out on the dikes of the golf course, stamping around, trying to think what to do. He tried to make himself feel better by blaming Espoir, but failed. How could you blame someone for whom you had already felt contempt when you put your life in his hands? In any case, everything was back to square one. The moment he left this little water-enclosed fortress, Somchai's friends would be on him again. And now there was no newspaper article to wait for, no reason to wait for anything. All he had accomplished was to get Woodward thrown in jail. He walked and walked in the sun until his skin trembled with dehydration and the afternoon clouds assembled, then dropped their monsoon rain. Field looked up resentfully and trudged back through this downpour to the clubhouse, where he asked Paga if she would lend him her car.

'What are you going to do, John?' It was always unexpected, the way she managed the curiosity of a mother superior, distant yet concerned.

'I don't know.' He stared at her expressive, impatient face, thinking that it was none of her business, then suddenly said,

'Yes. I'll go to the old man's dinner. That's what I'll do. I can't stay here. You keep Ao for me. Keep her out here.'

Field made two stops on his way into town. One to buy shells for the pistol he was still carrying and the other at his own house to change. The road down to the Oriental Hotel on the river was largely under water. The hotel itself sat temporarily on an island with the Chao Phya washing right up to the lower doors. Just inside the lobby there was a large hand-painted sign:

'WE HOPE YOU HAVE NOT BEEN INCONVENIENCED BY OUR COUP D'ETAT. HAVE A NICE STAY IN BANGKOK.'

By the time Field got there and climbed to the ballroom on the first floor, most of the guests had arrived. There hadn't been a soldier, armed or unarmed, downstairs and there were none upstairs either. He stood at the door and studied the crowd, seated twelve to each round table. There were several senior officers, all of them in civilian dress; Prem shirts in fact, silk with little upright collars and open necks, named after the current prime minister, who had made the style semi official. The navy was there in strength as well as the old foreign community, most of the key bankers and businessmen and the deputy ministers.

There was a pattern to their seating. Each of the Admiral's eight daughters presided over a table with her husband. The husbands in turn had gathered around them the most important guests from whatever field they themselves were in. The most prominent of the eight was the daughter who had married the eldest son of the owner of the Siam Bank, a Chinese Thai businessman of the old school, who sat there with his son, his daughter-in-law and the owners of the other major banks, all seven of them Chinese Thai. All together they controlled enough money to break the Thai economy. The Admiral's daughter was separated by an empty seat from the Siam Bank's new president, Pong Hsi-Kun, who was also General Krit's money man. All ten men were in navy blue silk suits, cream silk shirts and heavy silk ties.

At a table not far away Amara sat with people who had no power, but came from famous families and knew everyone.

Other 'lesser' tables were scattered around the room, each within reach of one of the daughters.

An occasional latecomer slid in round Field, who stayed in the doorway in full view. After all, they had all turned up, he thought, so with luck whoever had been tormenting him would be there. Perhaps by presenting himself as a target at the right level, he would discover something.

Why they had come was hard to guess; perhaps out of a macabre curiosity to see the effect on the old man of his son's arrest; or they had been drawn the way men are drawn to executions, idly, easily, without considering what will actually happen. This was also the first event since the failed coup that had the promise of amusement. When the flow stopped, there were four chairs still empty in the room; one next to Pong and three at a table in the centre of the room, where the Chief of the Naval Staff sat with a very old man, a former Naval Chief slightly younger than Admiral Wuthiwat.

Field heard whispering behind him and turned to find General Krit coming up the stairs with a dozen members of his staff. They were in uniform, but he wore a plain Prem shirt, like a flag of loyalty. The General hesitated at the door. His eyes burning, no doubt from the brandies he had drunk to give himself the courage to come. His normally calm, easy way was cut up into sharp movements. He was too agitated to notice Field. Instead he ordered his staff to wait downstairs, took a little breath, hunched himself down into a humble pose and slipped forward into the ballroom. He hadn't gone more than a few metres before the room fell silent and everyone turned to watch. Then the son of the owner of the Siam Bank, Admiral Wuthiwat's son-in-law, jumped to his feet in respect and his wife followed suit. The entire room followed them. But Krit pretended not to see. He slipped into his place between Pong and the Admiral's daughter and apologized to her for being late. He didn't say what had held him, but the assumption was that restoring full order in the capital was keeping him busy. Conceivably, this might have included interrogating her brother, Michael Woodward. The owner of the Siam Bank, his son and the seven other bank owners came round the table to greet him personally, while Pong kept his head down, as if he were too modest to admit that Krit's victory was his own. It had been worth the crowd's while coming just to see this consecration of power and money, the essential combination. It meant that Krit had manoeuvred his way into the coup, through and out of it on a rising curve. A moment later he was heard saying, in a voice just loud enough to carry, that children such as himself owed great respect to men like Admiral Wuthiwat, who had served without failure. This was repeated round the room. All in all, it was a masterly performance.

A moment later Field heard the sound of a European voice and turned. It was the hotel manager leading the Admiral slowly up the stairs. Apart from Michael Woodward's wife on one arm and his head boy on the other, the old man was alone. At the top he shook off both and said to the manager, who was blocking his way, 'Buzz off.'

Admiral Wuthiwat looked very frail. Much frailer than he had over lunch at the British Club. He had encased himself in an antique uniform, white with an inordinate amount of braid, much of which was his right not just by virtue of his naval rank. He had also been made a nobleman with the title of Phya by King Rama VII in 1930, two years before the first coup ended the absolute monarchy. It was not the sort of thing you wore to a birthday party, particularly your own. For two years he had been able to call himself 'Sir Clear Water Tactics'; then the revolution had done away with titles. The collar was a bit too big, his own neck having no doubt shrunk, but he clasped the sword case with a great force and strode forward, his daughter-in-law following just behind. The entire room stood. He stared straight ahead until he was at his place, where he sat slowly beside the Chief of the Naval Staff. The man tried to say something to him but was ignored. Michael Woodward's wife slipped down, leaving the last empty place between her and the Admiral. Wuthiwat fixed his eyes on the plate directly before him. He was trembling. There was a hum of curiosity, a general delight among the guests that they had come, because something was clearly going to happen. Five minutes later the waiters began bringing in the first course. They had advanced almost to the tables when the Admiral stood up and barked out in the commonest of Thai, as if giving an order to enlisted men.

'No food! Take it away!' They retreated in confusion while the old man examined the room. His gaze paused for a moment on each of his daughters, in particular the one sitting next to General Krit. Then he drew his sword in a single rasping effort and laid it on the table before him. Two glasses fell over. 'I am the King's man!' He said this in a loud voice, having switched his diction from that of the streets to the almost obsolete Court Thai. Not only that, it was Court Thai with a most elegant of accents. 'I have always been the King's man. I came to this country as little more than a boy and I served the King. In 1912, when few of you were born, I began to serve. I served him and I fought for him. My name was Wuthiwat. The King rewarded me for my loyalty by giving me a title. Phya Prichacholyuth. In 1932 the coup took away the King's powers, but I held the navy ready. He knew I would have fought to protect his absolute position. He told me not to. I am a loyal man, not a proud one. I did what he told me. I gave myself to the King to be used by him. I did not attempt to use him.' He paused, his eyes slipping for a moment into vague reflectiveness; then he focused again, surveying the room. 'All of this is true.'

The other old admiral at the table nodded his head in agreement.

'In December 1941 the Japanese landed here. We had to use all of our ingenuity to protect the country. To avoid slaughter. On the twentieth of December one of my daughters fell gravely sick.' He pointed to the woman married to the Siam Bank and seated beside Krit. 'That one.' The finger no longer trembled. 'She required an immediate operation. That or die within hours. There were many fine Thai doctors but in my absence she had been taken to the Bangkok Nursing Home where the only doctor left was a German. Dr Steuben.' Wuthiwat pointed across the room to an old man. Steuben bowed his head. 'Dr Steuben was a Nazi. In those days he drove around Bangkok flying a swastika and when he found my daughter on his table he refused to operate. Why? Because she is part Jewish. On principle he wished her to die. I went to the hospital with my gun. I put it at his head and I told him, you operate or I'll kill you. If she dies I shall also kill you. I loved my daughter as I loved my King, but that day I vowed that eight daughters was not enough; that I needed a son who would serve the King. Not as a sailor. But as a doctor. This empty seat,' he gestured at the chair beside him, 'belongs to that son. He is in prison tonight. That man,' he pointed slowly at Krit, a few yards away, 'put him there.

'My son is the King's man as I am the King's man. Who does not believe it? Who does not believe it?' He picked up his sword from the table with difficulty and agitated it above his head. 'Take this blade and strike me, any of you, strike me down if you do not believe it.' He glared around at the audience and no one moved. He pointed his sword at Krit.

'That is an ambitious man. That is a general who buys and sells. That is an usurper of power and it is he who has made a scapegoat of my son to cover his own disloyalty. Does anyone deny this?' His sword was still pointed, but he moved his eyes slowly over the guests. 'Anyone?' Krit's eyes were fixed on the point of the sword. He was frozen in his place while Wuthiwat searched the room for any sign of protest. There was none and so his stare came back to the General. 'Tomorrow morning . . . if my son is not free, I shall kill that man. I am old, but I shall kill him. And I shall do it in the King's name.' He gasped for breath and clenched the table to keep his balance, then attempted to put his sword back in its scabbard. In the end Meechai's wife had to help him.

He shook off the woman's arm and strode, as best he could, out of the room, with her following behind. Field bowed to him when he went by, but the old man saw nothing. He grasped on to the stair railing and was helped down the stairs by his head boy, who had been waiting there.

No one else moved. A minute went by. One of the Admiral's daughters, the one married to a senior finance official, rose to her feet and walked towards the door, with her husband trailing nervously behind. One after the other, the daughters followed, at a growing crescendo, their husbands behind them, until seven were gone; all, that is, except the girl seated between Krit and the Siam Bank. She was edging away from the General and staring at her husband for guidance, but he had his eyes on his own father, the owner of the Bank. Everyone else in the room was looking nervously about, uncertain whether to stay or leave. They had come as voyeurs. The Admiral had turned them into participants. Amara jumped to her feet and exhorted her table, 'Well, get up then! You're not staying, are you? Ahha! You're not so ambitious any of you.' She seized Tanun's arm and sailed out with the rest of them following. There were more wellborn but powerless Thais scattered at other tables and they followed, trickling out from here and there.

Amara saw Field in the doorway and stopped. 'Hello, Johnny boy.'

'I thought Krit was your kind of general.'

'Ahha! Of course he is. But friends come first. There are lots more like him. We buy them cheap. No worry. Your little girl is fine, if you want to know.'

He gave her a kiss. 'No problems?'

'Oh yes, but I set my dogs on them. Don't worry, Johnny boy. I look after my guests.' She floated away after a friend.

Field turned back to catching as many eyes as he could, although no one seemed very interested in him. The rest of the guests stayed seated. The soldiers didn't want to alienate Krit. The businessmen needed the soldiers. And the foreigners would be bankrupt without government co-operation and business. Krit was staring round the room, fixing them all to their seats.

But then the old retired admiral at the head table pulled himself up and mumbled loud enough for the people at the surrounding tables to hear, 'Wuthiwat is the King's man,' and stalked slowly with a limp towards the door. Seconds later the current Chief of Naval Staff was following hard behind to catch his arm. Immediately, every other sailor got to his feet and moved in a flow. There was then a pause, which ended with a fuss in a far corner where Dr Steuben, the ex-Nazi, was pushing out his chair. He stumbled over to Krit's table, bowed to Wuthiwat's daughter and offered her his arm. She leapt at it and left her husband behind. Within seconds the rest of the *farangs* were pouring out, horrified at having been outdone in a public moral dilemma by an ex-Nazi.

The room was now more than half empty and the old owner of the Siam Bank took a careful look around to weigh who had gone and who had stayed. Being Chinese in Bangkok, it was very important not to stand out unnecessarily. Particularly on the wrong side. He whispered to his son, who was still staring after his wife, by then disappearing down the stairs. The two men got up quietly, avoiding a glance at Krit, and were followed by the seven other bankers. That left Krit alone at his table with Pong Hsi-Kun, who had turned his back on the General and was watching his own respectability disappear from the room in the person of the Siam Bank. With a little click of his tongue he got up and followed them. He kept his eyes on his feet to avoid seeing Krit and so got right to the door before noticing that his way was blocked. He looked up at the last second directly into Field's eyes and, as the image registered, he abruptly lost control of himself. It was as if he were going to faint. It lasted only a second. He recovered, shuffled to the side and went on down the stairs.

'How simple,' Field whispered out loud to himself. 'Why shouldn't it be simple? Why shouldn't it be the most obvious person?' He watched Pong disappear with hurried little steps. 'Why not?' He looked back into the room, where there were no more than fifty men left, all army officers. General Krit sat emptying his brandy and soda without looking at any of them.

Field spent the night in the Dusit Thani, where his friend on the reception desk gave him a room without any registration formalities, lest he be traced. Early the next day he went in a taxi to Pong's compound on a lane off Sukhumvit, not far from his own house. He waited there in the back of the small Toyota for half the morning before Pong came out in the rear of his Mercedes. It was a stretch model and easy to follow as it moved at a slow even pace through the traffic towards the railway station. There, Pong stopped at his old office, in a building that was shaped like a crouched tiger, to offset the bad luck of being faced by a myriad of oncoming roads and oncoming railway tracks. Again Field waited downstairs. It struck him that while following was better than being followed, at some point he would have to work out what else to do. Pong reappeared just before lunch and was driven back past the University and Lumpini Park before heading up Wireless Road, off on to a lane, and disappearing inside the Polo Club. Field kept his taxi, but stopped at a hole in a wall cum restaurant just before the club entrance. There they served fried garlic and sticky rice with fried chicken and green papaya salad. The chicken was grilled on the street. Rolls of toilet paper sat on the tables in place of napkins.

He was on his second helping when the Mercedes came back out. Someone was in the rear with Pong. A woman. Field stood up to see her. It was Amara, with her hair carefully pulled up and placed on top, as it was during the day, and her constant laughter. Then the car was gone. He was certain it had been Amara. But surely not. It didn't make any sense. She couldn't be the woman at the centre of something like . . . And he had delivered his daughter right into her house. He went back to his seat and ordered a beer. Then he had another and went to the telephone at the end of the lane, from where he called Amara's house. Songlin sounded annoyed with him. She was cooped up, she said, surrounded by water, as the area hadn't drained at all, and missing all her university courses. Nothing had happened since the night Amara's driver picked her up. She had seen no one. Field asked her about Amara setting the dogs on to intruders. Songlin knew nothing about it.

There was a boy hawking the afternoon papers out in the middle of Wireless Road among the jammed cars. He was shouting Krit's name. Field threaded his way out, bought a paper and went back down the lane to his seat. The General's activities covered most of the front page. There was a photo of him at the central prison early that morning. He had gone there personally to release Dr Meechai Wuthiwat and to apologize to him for the confusion which had led to his arrest. He had also handed over to Woodward one million *baht* in cash as a personal present to the fire victims of Klong Toey, so that they might rebuild their houses. He then accompanied Woodward to the slum, where he instructed the soldiers holding the burnt out area in favour of the Port Authority to let the people build new houses on their old land.

All of this was witnessed by a horde of journalists, who followed him on from there to Supreme Command Headquarters, where he submitted his resignation as General Commanding the First Division and also requested release from his officer's commission. There was an hour's delay over this request, because it required royal approval, and when that was granted he was driven off in a small family car – an old Fiat probably used in normal times for household errands – to say farewell to his family. There were eye-witness accounts of this particular scene, but no photos were allowed and there was therefore no confirmation of the tears that General Krit's wife apparently shed. One photographer had climbed a garden wall and managed with a telephoto lens to get a picture of him leaving his house wearing simple civilian clothes. In the background were two servants holding open the main doors. Behind them, one could make out a wide hall and the shapes of two large buddhas. Field thought he recognized them. The journalists followed Krit in a cavalcade to the river near the Grand Palace, where he took a simple, but private, launch upstream. Policemen forcibly restrained anyone from renting boats to follow until he was out of sight. A short press release was distributed on the dock, explaining that he had gone to a monastery inaccessible by land and there he would enter into the monkhood in order to reconsider his whole life.

'Holy Christ,' Field said quite loud. 'This is turning into a circus.'

He reminded himself that it was Pong that mattered, and now Amara, and got into his taxi. They began working their way towards the headquarters of the Siam Bank on Sathorn Avenue, a good three-quarters of a kilometre above Mrs Laker's East-West Trading Company. The rain started a few minutes later and by the time they got there the stagnant canal running down the centre had overflowed. The Siam Bank had built itself a new marble tower thirty-five storeys high, floating on deep set piles. The land all round, however, had sunk below normal road levels. The taxi paused as it approached the site and the water grew deep. Field made him pull over to the side to wait until the rain stopped. From where they sat he could see the Mercedes already parked up under the sweeping overhang of the building, near the row of front doors. Pong had no doubt made it back just before the canal overflowed. It was typical of the Bangkok rich that they would ensure their building didn't sink, but not do anything about the land they had to cross to reach it.

Half an hour later the rain stopped and Field urged his driver on towards the building. They were still fifty metres away when the motor began to sputter. Field jumped out into knee deep water and strode on until it reached his upper thighs. He paused and considered the kinds of diseases that might be caught by allowing this murky liquid to seep up through any of his orifices. There were various worms, some of which could attack your liver; and, of course, there was hepatitis. But Field decided these didn't matter – he was already infected. The pain had become so constant that he no longer thought of it as pain; more as a background noise to his life. Something moved on the surface of the water a few metres away. He looked closely and saw it was only a rat, a large rat in fact, swimming quite peacefully away from the bank, its mouth open, its teeth grey. Field splashed water to make it alter its course, then started forward again. After a few yards the cement beneath his feet began to rise, hung as it was at a steep grade round the edges of the bank tower.

He marched straight through on to the white marble of the ground floor, leaving a trail of water behind him. The sound of his socks slopping inside his shoes with each step made him stop to consider his next move. If he waited where he was, Amara would sooner or later descend from above and they would have their confrontation. He looked around. The guards on the doorways were already eyeing him. He let his gaze roll up to the cathedral-like ceiling. The building resembled any bank tower anywhere in the world. He pushed the elevator button and once inside pushed the square marked thirty-five. It was the top floor.

The guard upstairs asked for his name and he in turn asked for Pong Hsi-kun. This wasn't the proper way to come calling on the President of the Bank of Siam, but Field suddenly felt it was appropriate. He was kept waiting on the wool carpet scarcely four minutes before being ushered through wood-panelled halls to an ante-room, then a boardroom, then an office considerably bigger than the ground floor of Field's own house. Pong was a great distance away at the far end and behind his desk, with his forearms flat on the blotter and his hands clasped. There were a number of gold rings on the fingers. Pong smiled and his large teeth shone in the light.

Field walked forward, leaving a trail behind him as he wound his way across the carpet among elaborate pseudo-French furniture, each piece gilded and styled after all the Louis combined. When he was close to the desk, he took a long stare at Pong, who was in a grey silk suit, a heavy cream silk shirt and a thick silk black tie; the sort of clothes you could wear in Bangkok only if you never strayed beyond air conditioning. Field swivelled slowly to look round. One wall was windows looking down on to the wide river that Sathorn Avenue had become. Another was wood panelling with a number of doors cut into it.

'So Amara's gone.'

Pong blinked through his glasses, but only once. 'Mr Field likes to surprise. No. She is not gone. She has not been here.'

'You left the Polo together.'

Pong nodded. 'Yes. And I dropped her off on the way back. Had you agreed to meet her in my office?'

Field didn't know where to go from there. He dropped into one of the two leather armchairs before the desk and felt water squeezing out of his trousers. In the air conditioning, it was quite suddenly cold and clammy water.

'A charming woman,' Pong volunteered. 'I wouldn't have thought I'd have liked her. Not society women. No. I prefer them a little more basic.'

'This was your first meeting?'

'Oh yes. She telephoned me this morning. There is a young army brigadier I admire. I think I could help him with his career now that my friend Krit has retired. And your friend Amara is his first cousin. So we're all going to lunch together.'

'And what does Amara get?'

'You're very nosy, Mr Field. Why don't you ask her?'

'Sure. I will. I came about Somchai.'

'Somchai?'

'Somchai. Thai. Vientiane. A question of drugs, I believe. And a Canadian couple murdered.'

'Ah. That couple. Yes, I've heard about that. But the rest, no.'

'It doesn't matter, Pong. Just listen. I'm not going to do anything. I'm not going to talk to anyone or publish anything.

I didn't see. I don't know. So take the dogs off. Just leave me alone. All right? I'll leave you alone. You do the same for me. I don't care what you push or how. Just leave me alone. Is that fair?'

'I am leaving you alone, Mr Field. You're the one who has come here. I do realize that if you look at poor Krit's reputation, and even mine in my early days, you might jump to some conclusions. I don't know what conclusions exactly. But that was all childhood games. Fooling about. Look at this place.' He waved his pudgy arms around at the office. 'I'm not interested in seedy little deals.'

'Six tons of heroin a year isn't seedy and it would scarcely fit into your office. I haven't seen the vaults in this palace, but I'd say the income on that kind of tonnage would nicely fill them.' Field reined himself in. This was not what he had intended to say. 'Anyway, I don't care.'

'Neither do I, Mr Field. I think you've come to the wrong place.'

Field nodded impatiently. 'That's why, with all of this to keep you busy,' he waved at the office around them just the way Pong had, 'you had me ushered in so fast. Well, relax, I haven't come to threaten you. I just want you to forget me.'

Pong pushed a button and a secretary opened a door in the distance. 'Willingly. Good-bye.' He didn't get up.

Field noticed there was a dark stain all the way down the leather chair he had been in. So much the better, he thought, and listened to the sound of his sodden socks on the way out.

He waded through to the shallows of the road, where the water had continued rising while he was inside to such an extent that taxis were no longer high enough off the ground to move in that part of the city. Field managed to pick up a bus. It took him half-way home, standing all the way with his head twisted over to one side beneath the low ceiling. On Rama IV he found a taxi and reached his house after dark through a foot of water. There was no sign of anyone waiting in the road for his arrival, which surprised him. Perhaps he had succeeded in calling them off. He gave the cook's grandson a fresh lecture on security, locked all the doors himself, ate some scrambled eggs and went up to bed, where he locked the bedroom door and lay down with his revolver. He was unable to sleep for some time, until he decided that it was Ao's absence which bothered him. This conscious knowledge seemed to help and he dozed off.

At three a.m. he was thrown into the air and landed on the floor along with his bedding. He lay in a daze as the sound of an explosion began to reconstruct itself around him. He grabbed for his pistol – it also was on the floor – and eased open the bedrom door. A terrible smell rose to meet him.

'Cook! Cook!'

He went on calling from above until the watchman and the cook appeared at the foot of the stairs.

'Yes, mister?'

'What do you mean, yes mister? Can't you smell it? Oh shit.' He ran downstairs and switched on the lights. Everything seemed perfectly normal apart from the stink. There was a toilet under the stairs, nearly under his room. As he came up to the door he could scarcely breathe. 'Come here.' He called the watchman over. 'Open this door.' The boy held back. 'Come on! That's what you're paid for.' Field waved him forward and himself retreated. 'Go on, for Christ's sake.'

The boy warily turned the handle and pushed. A putrid smell overwhelmed them and muck began to slide out through the opening. Inside they could see a dark mess and fragments of porcelain. The septic tank had exploded under the weight of the flood water.

'Shut it!' Field shouted. 'Shut it!' He deliberately went back upstairs and waited till he was at the top to call instructions down to the cook. 'Tell your grandson to clean it up. Now.' Then he went into his room, turned his fan up to top speed and went back to sleep.

By morning the whole house was saturated with the smell, but Field woke up feeling happy. He felt as if the rains would stop, the flood would go down and Pong would vanish into nothingness, along with his drugs and his partners. He looked down at his underwear, pulled it away and examined the suffering parts. Even that would disappear. And the sun would shine.

He was still daydreaming when the cook came to the door

to say a police officer and another man were downstairs asking for him. The first thing to go through his mind was Songlin. He threw on some clothes and ran down. The 'other man' was an immigration official in a polyester Prem shirt and scuffed shoes. He handed over a letter – an expulsion order in fact – which took effect in seven days. Field read it twice.

'I have a six month visa,' he said lamely.

'Your thirty-eighth six month visa I believe, Mr Field,' the immigration official commented. 'That has been revoked.'

'Revoked. What for?'

The bureaucrat indicated the police officer. 'I am under instructions from CID.'

He looked at the policeman more carefully. There was a flaccid quality about him. His body was pushing out gradually against the unpliant artificial material of his uniform so that the belly and the backside appeared unnaturally contained. There was an air of favours done and favours received about him. 'You're from CID?' There was no reply. 'I'm supposed to be a danger to internal security? Come off it. What danger?'

The policeman said nothing and the official smiled kindly. 'I suppose that any explanations would have to come from a higher level.'

Field read the expulsion order again and looked from one man to the other. 'Oh, for Christ's sake.' He stared around vaguely in a circle and to himself said, half out loud, 'I don't want to go. I want to stay.'

The official overheard this. 'I suppose, Mr Field, that you could attempt to return on the basis of tourist entries which, providing you remain in the country less than two weeks on the occasion of each visit, require no visa. In such a case you would simply arrive at the airport from abroad.'

'You mean fly in and out every ten days?'

'You could try that.' His tone indicated that he meant well.

'And would my name be on some black list at the immigration counter?' Field asked quickly.

'I couldn't say. That wouldn't be my section. There is a special section to administer those questions.' He moved his eyes slightly off Field.

'So my name has gone into the book?'

'As I say, I don't know.' There was a silence during which the official managed a quick glance at the *farang*. 'Perhaps. It's conceivable.'

'So why would I try?'

The official made no comment, but slid in embarrassment towards the door, followed by the policeman. Field walked away from them over to his porch and stared out at the grass, strewn with mud from daily flooding, and the *klong* sitting stagnant and flush with the land. 'I won't go.' When he looked round they were gone. 'I won't go.'

He dialled Henry Crappe at home and told his wife to wake him.

Crappe came on protesting, 'If you interrupt my rest, the quality of my composition . . .'

'One question. Where did Krit go?'

'You are seeking valuable information.'

'I'm pressed, Henry. Where did he go?'

Crappe sighed, 'I understand that our General chose to ride against the current. Upriver, that is. Wat Chalerm, past Nonthaburi.'

'Thanks.' Field began to hang up.

'John. Listen. You wouldn't happen to want to buy some sugar, would you?'

'What?'

'Some sugar. The coup was so rapid, I overstocked.'

'Keep it for the next one, Henry.'

'Sure. Sure. But I have a lot invested in dry goods now. Too much for a man of my means.'

'We'll talk, Henry.' Field hung up, changed and went out himself to find a taxi. There was a small Fiat waiting by the gates of the compound and when he was fifty metres down the lane on his way to Sukhumvit it began to follow slowly. Field stopped to look back. At this point they might be anyone. CID men keeping an eye on him, making sure he didn't run away. On the other hand, that was what they wanted him to do, providing it was across a border. Or they might be Pong's men. He considered asking them for a ride, but instead moved on to the sun-struck side of the road and walked ahead to Sukhumvit where he got a taxi down to the river. The driver switched on a cassette the moment Field jumped in. A voice shouted at him from among guitars – 'Born in the USA! Born in the USA!' Field reached across the back of the seat and slammed the reject button. Sathorn Avenue was almost dry, but the Siam Bank still lay surrounded by its own deep sea. Pong's grey stretch Mercedes was already parked beneath the overhang, along with two others in black; a colour distinction which marked the owners' cars. Further down the road Mrs Laker's compound sat like a large square island, with dikes all the way round it and a short elevated bridge leading to the outer world.

He left the taxi near the river ferry stop at the bottom of the avenue. The new bridge just downstream hung like a dark shadow in the sky while Field walked out on to the dock for the Chao Phya Express. A moment later the small Fiat drew up and a man got out from the passenger side. It was hard to say what he was. He might have been a policeman. He might have been a hired gun of the superior kind. There was certainly a slight bulge behind pulling against his loose shirt. Other passengers arrived every few minutes until there were twenty or so waiting in the shade. Only Field stood right out on the dock in the sun.

Fifteen minutes passed before the boat came charging into sight from down river. It was low in the water and painted white with red trim. Half of the sixty or so seats at the bow were full and a few monks stood beside the engine at the stern. Seconds before its bow collided into the dock, the rope boy blew his whistle urgently. The pilot cut the engine, threw the motor into reverse and twisted the wheel. The stern miraculously swerved to within a yard of the landing and the rope boy jumped off to brace himself against the pull of the boat long enough for the crowd to flow down on to the dock, which they sent into violent rocking. Glued one to the other, they leapt across the space to the stern and filed up to the seats. Field waited with his legs braced while they all pushed by, his eyes fixed on the man from the Fiat, who was also hanging back. When they were alone on the dock and scarcely a yard apart, the boat boy whistled at them impatiently and moved to leap back to his boat. Field smiled at the man from the Fiat and nodded at the boat boy, as if to say he and his friend had decided not to take the trip after all. The boy whistled and, as the pilot threw his engine into forward, leapt for the stern. Field abruptly leapt behind him, grabbing on to a railing. The man had been prepared for this manoeuvre and followed on his heels, but Field reached out as if to pull him aboard and instead shoved him back with the jolt of the charging boat. He landed in the water.

The boat boy looked round in surprise, but Field laughed and so the boy laughed, taking it all as a joke. There was a seat near the bow, just behind the pilot, who was fiddling with a transistor radio roped up beside him. He came upon *Made in Thailand* and turned the volume up full. Field slouched down and leaned out so that the water splashed up on to his shirt and covered his face in a fine spray.

They swerved up the river from side to side, dodging cross ferries and lines of barges, while long-tailed boats roared out of nowhere and sped on ahead. The Express made its way up past the seven old river churches, remnants of an incompleted missionary dream, the Grand Palace, and Wat Mahattat where the relic dealers gathered. Moments later the modern cement buildings disappeared and the wood houses built out on to the water took over, with their rusted tin roofs and their steps down into the river. Women were sitting here and there at the bottom of these steps, in the water up to their shoulders and washing themselves. At each stop a group of small boys in shorts would clamber on to the roof of the Express and throw themselves off into the turbulence as the boat roared away. There was nothing in Field's mind all this time, well over an hour up to the last stop, nothing but the refrain, 'I won't leave.'

The last stop was at Nonthaburi, not far from the prison he had been to a week before. He found a long-tailed taxi tied near the other end of the dock and climbed down into the fragile craft, which scarcely rose above water level. At racing speed Wat Chalerm was just five minutes further upstream on the other side. A deaf mute boy sat on the boat landing with a small birdcage, waiting to sell its release to someone who wished to earn merit. There were three elegant wood *salas* a few metres in from the river and behind them a white wall in the Chinese style and behind that three small temples, two of

235

them in ruins. The monks' houses were further on, near the stupa, beneath the thick shade of trees. They were simple wood huts raised over the edge of a *klong*, which was more like a jungle stream. Each house had a small garden before it; flowers and rocks, each of them varied by the tastes of the individual monk who planted his own plot. There were no vegetables. It would have been wrong for a monk to become involved in his personal survival.

Field wandered around under the trees until he saw a man dressed only in his lower robe, washing clothes in the *klong*. The man turned at the sound of feet and smiled softly, 'Mr Field, good day.'

It took a moment to recognize General Krit, with his hair and his eyebrows shaved off, standing barefoot in a *klong*. But it was more than that. His face had changed. The fire was gone from his eyes. 'Wait in there until I finish.'

Field climbed up into the monk's house. There was one room, bare except for a mat and a set of robes folded in a corner. The dark wood made it cool and a breeze blew across through the screenless windows. There was a sound of rinsing and of water moving outside.

When Krit came up, he moved slowly to change into his clean robes. The skin of his chest was smooth and hung slack like that of an old man. He sat down opposite Field to look at him with a distant but not unkind lack of interest. His robe was dark brown, the colour of the strictest orders.

'Very convincing,' Field grumbled.

The expression on Krit's face changed to one of indulgence. 'You know the phrase: few men cross to the further shore. The others run back and forth on the river bank.'

'It's a five *baht* trip.'

Krit laughed. 'That's why I took the brown robes. We are not allowed to touch even one *baht*.'

'You can afford to go clean. No. Look, I'm sorry. It doesn't matter what I think.'

'Nor I,' Krit said. 'This is an attempt I am making. Yesterday I threw off power, family, money, even brandy, Mr Field. That was all a good stunt, wouldn't you say? A good show. Then I came out here, where I was freed of my clothes and my hair and after that I went down into the *klong* to wash everything away. That was what I felt. Everything being washed away. It was quite unexpected, in fact. I assure you, it was. So now I shall try and I shall see. But I'm tired of all the other stuff. I think that is the truth of the matter. Not bored. Tired. I don't want it any more.'

'I need your help.'

'And I would help you, but frankly I no longer have any tools at my disposal. Nothing. Not even Pong.'

'You know about this Lao drug trade?'

'Vaguely.'

'Vaguely? What does that mean? You know about it?'

'At a distance. I remember your press approach very well: generals live from the drug trade. Well of course we do. But so do our business partners. And frankly, I've rather lost interest in it over the last couple of years. As you said, I can afford to lose interest. But the businessmen cannot. I was quite happy with my nest egg. They, however, like cash flow. That is their dream. Perpetual cash flow. I'm just a soldier. Comfort is all I wanted. So who is using whom in such a case? I have never understood that last point.'

'I saw Pong yesterday. He gave me the same line. He's above it now.'

'Well, that might be true, but then his rise into the arms of the Siam Bank is very recent, whereas this Lao business is not. And then, one fact does not contradict the other, no more than banking contradicts heroin.'

'Whatever. The point is, they have goons after me.'

'That again is not a contradiction. The Siam Bank is respectability. Whatever you know is a threat to that respectability.'

'And now my visa has been revoked.'

'Has it? Has it really?' Krit smiled, unable to hide some admiration for such a simple move. 'Well I wouldn't have thought of that.' Then he recovered his dignity. 'Go, Mr Field. Go. Perhaps they are offering you safe passage out.'

'I don't want to go. This is my home. That's why I need your help.'

'You know about revenge here. It can be sudden or it can be long term. It can be apparent or hidden. If you leave and you are quiet, perhaps they will let you alone. If you stay, they will most certainly come for you one day. And you won't even know from which direction they will come. Even now, your expulsion may be a preparation for something else. Suppose you die tomorrow. They will say, look, this man was playing about in the underworld of Bangkok. We expelled him for lack of solid evidence, but he was eliminated by his enemies before he got out of their hands.'

'I don't want to go.'

'All right. Perhaps that is your karma. Perhaps you are meant to be killed. Certainly your death is your own property. It belongs to you while you are alive. So if you wish to invoke it, that is your business. But why not just take that weapon from your belt and do it yourself? Of course, that is not good Buddhist advice, nor Christian, but I would think it is a better way than to wait for some unknown hand from some unknown source. Look, who has organized your expulsion? It might be Pong or it might be the Laos via some other circuit I don't know. Whoever has done that might not be the same one who is trying to kill you. He may be horrified to learn you are going, far away and safe. The dealer, for example . . .'

'Somchai.'

'Is that his name? Ah yes, the one who didn't go to jail. I remember that. Now, he may not want you to leave. I have heard, for example, that there was a killing in the slaughter-house a few nights ago. His brother. That might involve a separate case for revenge. And the American woman. What about her? What does she want in all of this?' Krit was watching while he talked and so must have seen the surprise in Field's eyes, but went on as if he had seen nothing. 'That was an element which always baffled me. Why would a successful *farang* trader become involved? Frankly, I preferred not to know.' The bells of the Wat rang for eleven o'clock prayers. Krit stopped to listen to them. It was a restful, reassuring sound. 'When I was a Colonel, I spent some months in the States on a course. Fort Benning, Georgia, to be precise. The Parachute School. After that I worked with them through the Vietnam business, and really, I came to understand the Americans less and less. Perhaps it has to do with dogma. You

Christians, you put dogma at the centre of your religion and, by association, at the centre of everything else. Every statement for you is true or false. Every action is right or wrong. Your salvation depends upon acceptance of the true faith. No? Isn't that it? The true statement. As a result you lose your benevolence towards those who refuse your truth. And then, of course, you kill them. Very abstract, all of that. Terribly, terribly abstract, except for the actual killing. Our violence is much more personal. We don't believe any positive statement can be true. They are all false. Just by stating them, we make them false. So if we must kill, we kill out of passion or out of need. These people, they need to kill you. Perhaps if you go quickly, you will remove the need. But the American woman, she is a great believer in truths. I have met her, oh you know, I have done business with her over the years, but I don't understand her at all. She is always for. Always against. Always certain. Certainty is a terrible distraction for the human mind. Certainty always obscures clarity. So now I am here where there are no certainties and no distractions and I cannot help you. Not with your visa. Not with anything. Really.' He gave Field a sympathetic smile. The smile was a bit rusty, but perfectly genuine. 'Now I must go for the prayers.'

Field's confusion was such that he meekly followed him down the wood steps to the scrub grass. The garden before Krit's house had not been worked in some time, except for a corner in which the earth had been freshly broken that morning and the hoe was leaning against a tree. When he looked up, Krit had disappeared behind the wall of the central temple. He could hear them chanting as he walked down towards the river, where the deaf mute boy with the bird was still on the landing stage. Field gave him ten *baht* and took the cage which he held up near his eyes. It was a cube fifteen centimetres high with a solid bottom and top and wood bars round the four sides. One of them had a section that could slide up. The imprisoned bird was an ordinary sparrow.

'And if I let you go, will you come back, eh? Is that it? Is that the kind you are? Let me see your eyes. Has he got you on opium, eh? Will you fly in a circle and right back into the cage? I want to know.' The bird stared out at him, impassively. Field slid the bars up, but kept his face close, so that the bird retreated against the far side. 'You don't like *farangs*, eh? Come on. Give me a kiss before you go. Come on.' He pursed his lips into the cage and made a little smacking sound at the bird, who didn't move. 'Come on. Oh, it doesn't matter.' He turned the cage round and the bird fluttered out, disappearing up into the trees above them. 'Now don't come back! Go on! Further!' He looked about for a stone to throw, but there was only grass.

Field returned the cage to the boy, who had been smiling as the *farang* tried to kiss the bird. In imitation, the deaf mute made kissing sounds with his own lips. Lurid, warm smacks, his eyes rolled up in mock passion. Field laughed and gave him another ten *baht* before climbing down into his water taxi.

CHAPTER 13

Catherine Laker was not in her office. By chatting with her Thai assistant for half an hour, Field found out that she had not yet come out of her house at the rear of the compound. Apparently she often worked from there, sending and receiving written messages via her maid.

Field went down the stairs of the old colonial house and out through the maze of tractors and road building equipment and gas pipe lining. Here and there in the mud there were remains of the garden that had once covered the grounds; broken bits of glazed pots and old paving. The cement wall built close around Mrs Laker's house was an exact square, each side ten yards long and four yards high, painted white. The broken glass and bare electric wire on top glinted in the sun. Field went round once. There was a single steel door with elaborate locking devices and no outer handle. Beside it was a bell and a voice phone. Above that a suspended camera. He pulled some paper from his pocket, held it in sight of the camera, as if he were delivering a message, and waited with his head turned away. It was a good thirty seconds before a voice came with a metallic ring through the phone system.

'Who is it?'

'Documents.'

'I can't see you. Turn your head.'

Field recognized Mrs Laker's voice. He turned towards the camera and attempted to look friendly.

'What do you want, John?'

'I want to talk to you, Catherine.'

'Not today. Not now. I am unwell today.'

'It's urgent, Catherine. I've got to see you.'

'What about?'

'The Lao business.'

There was a silence. Then Mrs Laker asked, 'What about it?'

'My expulsion. They're fucking throwing me out, Catherine.' He waited, but there was no answer. After a minute he called into the box, 'Catherine. For Christ's sake, open up.' There was silence.

He looked round. Three Thais were coming towards him out of the forest of tractors. They were groundsmen. Then he saw that they were carrying metal bars. He stared at them for a moment, until it was clear that he was their object of interest. They were only ten yards away. He began stepping backwards towards the road. They weren't rushing at him, but they were coming fast. He turned and started at a half run through the mud, with them following at the same distance.

The day's rain was about to start as he came out on to the road and the only transport in sight was a *tuc-tuc*. He told the man to take him home. He didn't negotiate the price. The three men watched him go from the property line, like guard dogs. Ten minutes later the rain started and Field let down the clear plastic curtains around him. They fell short and the aerodynamics of the machine brought all the water down the curtains on to the seat and from there on to the floor. It didn't really bother him one way or the other. The driver was playing Thai rock on his radio. Field considered telling him to turn it off, but he looked out at the traffic jamming cosily in around them until they were stationary. 'Turn it up!' he shouted. Nothing moved for a quarter of an hour.

When Field got home he noticed there were two cars parked in the lane near the gate. No one was inside them, but that meant nothing. He went through the kitchen door and shouted for a beer, which he took out to the covered porch. The canal was only just beginning to overflow for the day. He looked up into the trees in search of the white squirrels, but there was no reason for them to be around in the rain. He wondered where they went, then shouted for another beer. The whole business was ridiculous. That was what he kept saying to himself. He went in and dialled Henry Crappe at home.

'I have it all, Henry. I have all the names.'

'Can you call back later? I am writing a piece.'

'Henry, this is slightly more important than the most screwable dancer of the week.'

Crappe must have been taking the time to think about that, because he was silent for a moment. 'One,' he said slowly, 'I am a quality word craftsman. I can assure you of that. You do not chuck my columns on the bottom of a birdcage. Two. Another journalist was shot this week in Chaing Mai. This year's national score is therefore already above previous annual levels and we are only in the ninth month. So, I'd like to hear your story, John, only don't count on me. Three. I suspect that the real reason for your call is to negotiate the purchase of my dry goods at a cheap price. I consider that an improper exploitation of my friendship. In all three cases, would you mind if we communicated later?'

Field slammed down the phone, took a third beer and went back to the porch. The water was now up over the ground everywhere in sight. Two cobras swam out from beneath the house and slithered up on to the boards at the far end of the deck. They moved around neatly until they were parallel and facing out at the sea as if Field were not there.

'Hello again,' he said. 'Can I get you a mouse or something?' He looked off in the same direction and saw a movement through the trees. There was the outline of a man. At least he thought there was. And when it stopped moving, it was invisible. He leaned forward, staring. No. There was nothing. A moment later he saw something move again. 'Oh shit,' he mumbled and shouted in Thai, 'Go away. Get out of here.'

The cook heard him and came through the door to see what he wanted. When she saw the snakes she gave a little squeak.

'Where's your grandson? Send him round. Go on. Hurry up.'

The boy appeared and waded out to the trees where he found nothing. Field went back to drinking until suddenly he had the sensation he was sitting for target practice. It was crazy to be sitting there. He got up so suddenly that the cobras shot into the water. Once inside behind the wall of glass and screen the same sensation remained. There were no curtains that could be pulled. He walked round his chairs examining them. No.

He couldn't sit there. So he locked the sliding door, took some bottles from the fridge and went upstairs. At eight he made the cook bring him his dinner in bed. 'This is ridiculous,' he said out loud. 'Stupid!'

He went down into the main room and stumbled through the darkness to find the photograph of his father in the Rockies. It was hard to make out the figure. He went into the kitchen cubicle, out of sight from the windows, and switched on the light over the sink so that he could examine it closely. There was a pleasant look on the young man's face. A pleasant and intelligent look. It was funny that his father had never done anything with his life. Field held the photo higher and examined all the details. He found some things he had never noticed before. A small bird behind him on a branch. A watch chain seemed to be wound round the hand he had half in his pocket. Field had no memory of the watch. It should have come to him. He was the only child. He went over to the phone where slowly in the darkness he dialled Barry Davis at home. Davis had guests for dinner. Other diplomats probably. You could hear them in the background.

'I'm dying,' Field said.

'Come tell me about it tomorrow. I'm in the office from nine.'

'Sure, Barry. I'll send my ghost.'

There was a silence while Davis thought. 'All right then. Come over now.'

'I can't, Barry. I don't think I can go out the door. No. I can't. I shouldn't have come back home.'

'You're not drunk, are you?'

'That doesn't change anything.'

'No it doesn't. I hear around town you've been making trouble.'

'Trouble?'

'Being unwise.'

'Where do you hear that?'

'Don't be stupid, John. I hear it. You know Bangkok.'

'So, Barry?'

There was another silence until Davis sighed. 'All right. I'll come over after my dinner. Is that okay?'

'That's fine, Barry. It's all your fault anyway.'

Davis hung up.

At midnight Field was woken from a sweating sleep by the sound of arguing outside. It was the watchman blocking Davis's way. Field shouted from his window that the man should be let in, then got back under his sheet, if only to disguise how diseased he was.

Davis stamped up the stairs and glowered at him. 'You have a good voice for a dying man.'

'I have to go home, Barry.'

'Home?'

'That's right. Expelled.'

'Well, get on a plane.'

'It's not as simple as that. Sit down.' When he had finished he saw that Davis was still listening, eager for more. 'In the next episode, I die.'

Davis nodded. 'I heard there was some trouble at Laker's house. They've complained to the police about you trespassing. As you are Canadian, the police informed us. Apparently you threatened the lady.' He examined the room until he saw the stock of beer Field had brought up. He took one and sat back down on the bed. 'They say that if she insists they will have to charge you.'

'I doubt it. I might say something public before they get me into a cell where I can expire.'

'We could protest to the Foreign Office about your expulsion.'

'You could. It wouldn't do any good, but you could do it. It would be a friendly gesture. It would show contrition. Useless but friendly contrition.'

'I'm sorry, John.'

'You said that last time you came calling. Now, if I am going, I am not going alone. There are three of us. I want to take my daughter.'

'You have a child?'

'That's correct. And these friends I've made, thanks to you, have already been to see her.'

'Who is the mother?'

'A Thai.'

'And how old is the girl?'

'Eighteen. I want to adopt her and take her.'

'No deal, John. Sorry. Under the old immigration law she's Thai no matter what you do and under the new law you could adopt her, but it doesn't apply to someone that age. And you want to take her mother?'

'God no! Listen, this girl is at Chulalongkorn. We're not talking about some dancer on Patpong.'

'But she lives with her mother?'

'Sure. I support them both.'

'Well, does the girl want to go?'

Field shrugged. 'I don't know. I haven't asked her. She doesn't have any choice, does she? She's not suicide oriented.'

'Just shut up and listen. She probably doesn't have a passport. So you get her a passport. You bring her to the office with her mother. With. You understand. And the mother says she can go.'

'I can't get that bitch to do anything.'

'Well you'll have to, otherwise we could both be up for kidnapping, etc. So you bring them to the office and I'll give her a Minister's Permit. I can do that on discretion in an urgent case. That will get her beyond the controls of the Immigration Act for one year. You can work out the rest once you're home.'

'We'll be back here before then.'

'All right. Who is the other one?'

Field tried to look nonchalant. 'A girl. Seventeen.'

'Another daughter?'

'No. A friend.'

'What is she?'

'I told you. A friend.'

'And?'

Field felt like an idiot. He looked up to find Davis watching him with a professional air. Suddenly he felt quite beyond this sort of conversation. 'She's a little whore, Barry! That's what she is.'

'Well nobody is going to hurt her. Not over drugs anyway.'

'I know that. But she needs me so I'm taking her.'

'Not with my help.'

Field said as calmly as he could, 'Don't go Northern Irish on me, Barry. I'm taking her.'

'You listen. I could make a human or moral argument about a dirty old man who's been through every dancer in the city. The only difference between the others and this one is that this one is the latest. And when he's got her across the Pacific and he's grown tired of her, what happens then? Once a week we get some ageing idiot like you coming in to the Embassy with his little number that he'd kind of like to take home.'

'You don't understand. She isn't a number.'

'I'm not interested, John. The fact is that the only way someone like that can get in is under the Immigration Act. She hasn't got family to sponsor her. She hasn't got qualifications to get a job, apart from leg spreading or go-go dancing. And she fails on the character test. On top of which I have no discretionary powers because there are no extenuating circum-stances. She's just John's latest lay.'

'She isn't!' Field shouted. 'You don't understand.' He gath-ered his sheet around himself and got up to fetch the envelope with her papers, to show that she was a special case.

Davis shouted after him, 'If you want her so much, marry her. I can't stop you bringing in your wife.'

'Marry her?' Field stopped at the door and turned round.

'Yes. Marry her. Let me see. I've just done your new passport. You're forty-four, right? That's only twenty-seven years older than her.'

'Fuck off, Barry.'

'Marry her. Then you could bring her in on a Thai passport. You, as her husband, can sponsor and guarantee her. We have a little interview at the embassy; coffee, cookies, polite ques-tions: Your family background, miss? Sorry, madame. Rice, you say? Your education? Washing bodies? How interesting. Then all we need is a medical to make sure she isn't riddled with VD and, Bob's your uncle, the happy couple are on their way home in time for the turning of the leaves.'

'Sure.' Field hadn't moved from where he stood. He pulled the sheet tighter around him. 'That's a good idea. I'll marry her.'

Davis looked as if he might choke on his beer. 'Divorce is a little more complicated at home than it is here, you know.'

'We're talking about marriage, Barry. Not divorce.'

'I can't believe it. You? A seventeen-year-old whore. You can buy girls like that on contract. You don't have to marry them.'

'Same thing,' Field said.

'Eh?'

'It's the same thing. They're both contracts.'

Davis pulled himself to his feet. 'You bring both girls into the office. I look forward to it.'

Early on Friday morning Field walked out of the compound. No one was waiting in the lane. He strolled along towards Sukhumvit Road, looking periodically behind, and when he reached the intersection he put a hand out to hail a taxi. While he was negotiating the price to Paga's Country Club a man walked up close to him. Field whirled around violently. The man seemed surprised and veered away. When Field turned back to the taxi, it was gone; the driver no doubt had thought the unfriendly movement meant his offer was rejected. Field stared round behind himself again. The man had gone on up the street without looking back. 'Calm down,' Field whispered, 'Calm down,' and hailed another taxi.

He arrived hours later at Paga's clubhouse to find her son across a table playing cards with Ao. They were alone in the *sala* and laughing childishly over their game. Field watched them from the entrance, looking for signs of something more than a game. The boy was nothing. Anyone could see that; just a shadow of his mother. Ao looked up and came running to embrace him.

'Where you been, John? Why you not come back?'

'I am back.'

'Long time, John. Paga and me worry.'

He looked down at her face transformed by a smile. There was nothing hidden behind it. Nothing he could detect. Just honest pleasure at seeing him. 'Come on, Ao. I want to talk to you.'

He led her out through the grove of eucalyptus towards the dike running around the golf course and up on to its ridge. Beyond, the rice paddies were so inundated that you could not see through the floodwater the pattern of the mud walls separating them. Field walked a way in the mud and turned to find Ao pressing to keep up, her sandals in her hands and her toes spread wide for balance.

'Just like your village?' Field asked.

'My village not like this, John. Never flood.'

'Would you like to go back there?'

Her eyes lit up. 'We go visit?'

'No. I mean would you like to go live there?'

'No!' She stamped one of her bare feet violently. 'Too much dirt. No cars. No nice bathrooms.' She looked around for inspiration to save her. 'No fans, John. No doctor. You not send me back.'

Field could feel the full morning sun on his head. He loved it beating down through his hair and his clothes and his skin, down through his flesh to the bones. 'Well then, would you like to marry me?'

Ao looked at him as if he were crazy. 'Why you want to marry me?'

He was infuriated by the question. 'I just do.'

This abrupt reply didn't upset her at all. 'You don't need to marry me. You got contract.'

'I want a better contract.'

She nodded. That made some sense. 'What for, John? I sick. You sick. Doctor say I can't have baby. What you want me for?'

'I want to have you with me.'

'That's okay, John. I'm not going any place.'

He tried to see if this was a joke, but her expression was earnest. 'I am, Ao. I'm going home. And if you want to come with me, we have to get married.'

'Your country?'

'Yes.'

She nodded vaguely. 'I know about Canada. It's near United States. We talk about sometimes in hotel, before you take me. We heard some girls get married to *farang* and go home with them. It's nice there?'

'Sure it is. At least it used to be twenty years ago. Big mountains, Ao. That's where we'll go. You see this flat water out here? Well, we'll go to a place which is the exact opposite. Thousands of gigantic mountains. Trees everywhere. Gigantic trees. Everything new.'

'New,' Ao echoed, as if this word were magic.

Field laughed. 'New bath tubs. New cars. New air conditioning. New everything. All clean.'

'When we go, John?'

'As soon as I marry you.'

'OK. We go now?' She laughed and started running down the mud bank on to the fairway.

Field slid down after her, caught up and threw her over his shoulder. 'Right now. I'll carry you there.'

She laughed and struggled and gave him a squeeze on the nape of his neck. A noise made them look up to see that Paga had appeared in a golf cart from out on the course. Ao slipped down and ran over to meet her. He watched their excited conversation quickly turn into an argument, so he walked on back to the clubhouse. Paga overtook him in her golf cart, with Ao in the passenger seat.

'You can't do it,' Paga said. 'You need her parents' permission.'

'What!' Field stopped walking at that. 'You've got millions of children in factories. You've got twelve-year-olds in brothels. You've got contracts on children's lives and I need her fucking parents' permission.'

'I know, John. You forget. I used to arrange group sex and marriage tours for Germans. Girls under twenty need permission. That's a technicality. I could get her older age on new ID card if I pay, but she looks too young. Don't worry. I'll go up to the village and negotiate for you. Not too expensive. If you go, very expensive.'

'They're expelling me, Paga. Thursday morning.'

'Okay. No problem. My son drive us up over weekend. Lots of time. You stay here.'

They left in the evening to avoid driving twelve hours in the heat. Field hung about alone over his meal in the empty *sala* until the mosquitoes drove him back to his monk's house. There was no noise from the other platforms around him. Perhaps the monks had some secret to sleeping quietly. Perhaps it had to do with giving up all desire. Field lay very still and listened to the sounds outside. There was no pleasure in it, he realized. Every movement was like that of someone sent to kill him. He hadn't seen a car persistently following him out on the road, but then what could he see? What could he know? And the more he thought of Paga taking Ao away so quickly, the more he wondered if he had missed something. Was someone else playing another game? Paga for example. Or Davis. What was Davis really doing? Field thought about that. Why, for example, was he the only diplomat to be left in Bangkok so long?

Field slept badly, Mrs Laker breaking twice into his dreams, a patronizing, back-combed, menacing figure, and he awoke with a start in the morning to find Paga's father standing just outside, his shaved head level with the floor on which Field slept, staring in at the *farang*. It was a stare impossible to interpret. Field sat up and raised his hands to *wai* the old man, who turned and walked away.

Small groups of golfers appeared over the weekend, which made Field increasingly nervous, to the point where he couldn't sleep. And when, on Monday afternoon, Paga and Ao had not reappeared, he left a note with the old monk and walked out along the dirt road to the highway, where he caught a bus into town.

CHAPTER 14

'The colonial queue barger. You're just in time, old boy.' Woodward indicated a mountain of packages on his desk. 'Your salvation perhaps, though don't count on it. I've had a look through and there's nothing here very different from what your nasty strain has been gobbling up.'

'So you're back at it, Michael?'

Woodward smiled indulgently. 'Going to prison for a few days doesn't get one out of work. Nor does fame. I was a potential regicide. Now I'm a hero. I would imagine they think they have bought me off; that now I'll act as they wish. A good little boy from now on. However, by tomorrow they'll have come to their senses and I shall be known once again as a pest. I hear you were witness to my father's performance. High comedy, everyone tells me.'

'Sure,' Field agreed. 'But comedy is harder to pull off than tragedy. And tragedy doesn't suit this place, certainly not Krit. Certainly not your father.'

'Either way, the old man has been in bed ever since, with all eight daughters and my wife ministering to his ego. A wonderful antidote to sickness and death. Ego, I mean. Pull them down. Come on.' He pointed his swab at Field's trousers. After a quick look at the greenish stains on the underwear, he added, 'You could do with a bit of ego yourself.' He twirled the swab in. 'I also hear they are throwing you out. With my newfound glory, I might be able to get the order reversed.'

'I doubt it, Michael. I'm going to need something far more unlikely: a medical clearance for Ao. I'm taking her with me.'

'How bizarre, old man.'

'I'm marrying her.'

'You are? Well I ought to tell you that I really can't see much hope of clearing up either of you. I mean, I can't see much of the old matrimonial carnal bliss ahead. Not really. I don't like to say that, being an optimist about medicine's ability to cure, but you're not doing well, old boy, and neither is she. Quite apart from her being sterile, which I haven't confirmed but hardly need to.'

'Will you do the medical?'

'Not unless you force me.'

'I'm forcing you. Medical perjury is nothing beside regicide. I can't take her with me otherwise.'

'I don't particularly see why you should. What about your daughter?'

'I'm taking her too.'

'It sounds like a recipe for disaster to me.'

'Well, will you do it?'

'I suppose so.'

Field smiled with relief. 'You see, Michael, how the criminal habit takes hold.'

'I'll make some calls about your expulsion.'

'Sure.' Field didn't really believe it was worthwhile. 'Listen, did you see that mongoloid kid at the fire? The boy who kept running back to save things. Is he all right?'

'Tak? Of course I saw him. He's a hero now. Remember you were talking about missing the one moment that counts. Well, he seized his. He'll be a hero forever down there.'

'Good.' Field sat shyly in his chair.

'What's the matter?'

'To tell you the truth, I'm kind of at loose ends. I'm afraid to go home. I can't really go anywhere else. There's this fucking old lady locked up in a fortress pulling God knows what strings. I mean these bastards, I see them behind every tree and I don't even know if they're there.'

Woodward looked on sympathetically. 'Let us say that you are sick. I shall give you a room here, but we won't inscribe your name up on the roll of honour in the entrance.'

Field went with relief to the room they assigned him, up on the second floor, and sat in a wicker armchair out on the covered porch to wait for the afternoon rain and Ao to come. He was woken from dozing in the same position by something tickling his nose. He lurched up, covering his face for protection.

'I have it, John.'

'Don't frighten me like that.' He saw the girl's smile. She was soaked from running the few feet between the car and the porch. 'Where is Paga?'

'She say good-bye. She not like hospitals. She not like Bangkok. She get good price.' Ao handed over the paper with which she had been tickling him. 'She pay my father for me. She make you present. Two thousand *baht*.'

Her complete self-confidence swept away his fear, or rather, his depression, which was worse than fear. Suddenly he felt all the decisions had been made. He could deal with whatever happened.

Early on Tuesday morning he went with Ao out to Amara's house. For the first time since the flooding had begun, her whole district was drained. They followed a servant in under the deck and across the open ground floor where the murals and tiling had all been destroyed. Amara came running from her bedroom. 'Ahha, Johnny boy. Have you come for your treasure?' Then she focused on Ao and lost some of her enthusiasm.

Field pointed out at the dry land. 'No water.'

Her humour came back. 'The miracle of the handshake and the pumps. Ahha! Not a *baht* out of my pocket. Oh no! After dear General Krit was left to dine alone, I heard that in any case his friend Pong was already on the outlook for new blood. The next generation, you see. And surprise, surprise, I have a cousin, a little brigadier, who is perfectly mediocre and avaricious. Everyone says he's a natural leader. A man of the future. So much so that he is hard to get to. Hard to approach. Or should I say expensive? Anyway, he is certainly pompous. And he has always said he doesn't like Chinese bankers. I assumed he meant that he hadn't yet found one generous enough. So I, concerned about my foundations and my tiling, rang him up and gave him lunch at the Polo with Pong Hsi-Kun. Slogging, Johnny. Slogging. There's not much wit in bankers and soldiers.

I believe part of their brains are filled with dreams of cash and the rest is empty. Anyway, the next day the pumps started pumping. Songlin!' she shouted.

'I need to talk to her alone, Amara.'

'Ahha. More drama. How exciting. Then I'd better take your friend here off for a biscuit. Do you eat biscuits, dear?'

Ao smiled happily. 'You have Coke?'

'I live on it. It is very good for the runs, though quite addictive. Songlin!' She put an arm through Ao's and led her downstairs to a pavilion by the *klong*.

Songlin appeared a moment later in her blue and white uniform and raised her hands together. He went straight to her and took her arms gently, then let them go. 'I have to ask you something.'

She cut in, her manner bolder than he remembered. 'Amara has told me all about your problems. She says they are throwing you out of the country because you were honest.'

'More or less. She knows already?'

'Amara says everyone knows. She says you're too stubborn.'

Field looked at her curiously. 'Maybe. Anyway, once I've gone, I'll be far away. In the Rockies, I think, in Alberta, and the same people might still try to hurt you. Maybe not. Why should they care then? But I don't want you hurt.'

'Maybe I should come with you.'

'That's not what I intended. You should stay here.'

Songlin ignored this. 'I'll come back. When do we go?'

'Well, there's one other thing. That girl. You met her.'

'Ao? I met her at your house the day you threw me out.'

'Yes. Well, she's coming too. In fact, I have to marry her to get her in.'

The mask of teenage assurance broke on Songlin's face. Field guessed it was shock. She made an effort and asked, 'Is that the only reason?'

'Well, no,' Field said slowly, 'I suppose I think it's a good idea anyway.'

'That's a relief,' Songlin said and made an effort to clear her confusion. 'When do we go?'

'Thursday morning.'

'Two days! I'll need a passport.' She ran over to the stairs and down.

'Among other things,' Field said, but she was gone.

Amara came back up leading both the girls. 'What a wonderful idea. What a nice girl.' She looked at Ao with genuine pleasure. 'As to your age, I shouldn't worry.'

'I'm not,' Field said.

'Girls make such a mistake marrying young men who are still swallowed up by Eros. Ahha! Eros — the animal drive propels a man, makes him interesting, passionate, concerned. That's what girls like. Ahha! But it also disguises the real person, hides it, covers it. And then, when the deed is done and a few years have gone by, the animal drives dissipate like a cloud swept away on the wind. And what have you got left? Ahha. You can ask me. Not much. Maturity is a silly word. What it means is that the man can't have five orgasms a day. Why? Because his mind has cleared. So, good for Ao. She'll get the real thing.'

'Very real,' Field agreed.

Amara decided that she would personally put everything in order. She cancelled her day and marshalled her driver to take them off to the passport office, near the Royal Palace. There she ignored the thousands of people queued outside beneath an awning and carrying packages of food to give themselves strength. Some seemed to have slept on the spot. They were all emigrant workers going off to build roads in the Middle East or work in hotels or do other menial jobs. Students and other people middle class or above passed by a more personal route. Amara had a nephew in the passport service and he had passports for both girls within an hour.

'Now for the wedding,' Amara kept saying in the car. 'Ahha! Johnny boy. Now for the wedding!'

They had been heading for some time towards the government office on Sukhumvit, where Field was registered and therefore should be married, when Ao whispered shyly to Amara, 'You know Khun Veectoreea?'

'What?'

'Khun Veectoreea?'

'She got a massage?' Field asked.

'Girls at hotel say she famous to make children. She has statue in Bangkok. I like to give something.'

'Ahha!' Amara thought about that. 'Queen Victoria! Yes. Yes. Of course.'

'You know her?'

'I know her statue.'

'Can we go first?'

Amara ignored Field's moan and looked at the girl with genuine curiosity. 'You won't need much help with fertility. Ahha.'

'It's all right,' Field broke in. 'We can stop near the gate.'

At the next traffic light, Ao crawled half across Field to wind down the window and shout to the children running back and forth selling garlands. She made him buy a dozen of the longest and within seconds they were overwhelmed within the confines of the car by the sweet, hypnotic smell of the jasmine. When they pulled up before the grille of the embassy compound, Ao pushed Field ahead and jumped out. A Gurkha sentry watched suspiciously while she pressed her face between the bars. The statue was half-way across the grounds towards the elegant sweep of the Ambassador's residence.

'I want to go in,' she said. No one seemed to hear this, so she turned to Amara who was looking on from the car. 'Please, can I go in?'

Songlin climbed out and added in Thai, 'Let's go in. I've never been. Please, Amara.'

'Why not? Why not?' Amara scribbled a note to the Ambassador's wife and handed it through to the Gurkha. Ten minutes later the gate was opened. Ao ran ahead across the lawn to the foot of the Queen's pedestal, which itself was almost as high as the girl.

There were a few damp garlands around the neck and one over her Orb. Victoria's Sceptre and Orb were at the very heart of her reputation as a goddess. It didn't take great imagination to interpret them as sexual symbols; although there was a joke about the great globe-shaped Orb of State in her left hand being so large in comparison to the phallic-shaped Sceptre in her right. The punch line was that it had to be big as she held only one. The alternate, more serious, punch line was that

Khun Victoria had the power of fecundity, not of pleasure. The Sceptre was merely a useful tool. It was the solitary great Orb that delivered the seeds of children.

'I too small, John. You do it for me.' She shouted back at Field and the other two women who were catching up.

Field shrugged and took the garlands before climbing on to the stone platform. As he reached up to slide the flowers over her head he caught a glimpse of someone watching from an upstairs window in the residence. 'Well, why not?' he said and balanced on the bronze knee to get them over the crown. When he climbed down, Ao was still staring up, dissatisfied.

'What's wrong?'

'Only flowers,' she said. 'I should bring more.'

'The English like flowers.'

'Not enough, John. I should give more.'

'Here,' Amara pulled at a finger on her right hand and managed to twist off a small gold ring. 'Here. Give her this.' Ao held back from taking it. 'Go on. Ahha! Go on. I think she likes gold too. Go on. It could make all the difference.'

Ao took the ring and began climbing up on to the statue 'Help me, John. Help me.' He gave her a push, which got her up to the platform, but when she reached up, she slipped down the bronze lap into a pile, like a baby in Victoria's arms. She started again, this time placing her feet on Field's shoulders and holding a bronze arm for balance. This put her own head just below the Queen's. She held up the ring for Victoria to see and climbed part way down to where a large, pudgy, left hand was turned palm up to hold the Orb of State. Ao managed to jam the ring on to the end of the smallest finger. Field glanced towards the Residence again and saw an upstairs window crowded with heads haloed by back-combed hair. The outline of each resembled Mrs Laker. He started, so that Ao, on his shoulders, gave a little cry, 'Hey, John! Stop that.' He looked again. Of course it was his imagination at that distance. In any case, Mrs Laker didn't go out to lunch. She didn't even eat lunch. But the silhouettes stayed with him after Ao had come down to say some prayers on the ground. What difference would it make, he reflected, whether Mrs Laker came out or not. All she had to do was telephone from her bunker. They could kill him. They could expel him. She didn't have to move.

'That should do it,' Amara said and waved towards the window filled with watching heads, whose silhouettes disappeared abruptly.

The afternoon rain began before they reached the district office way out on Sukhumvit near Soi 54. Amara refused to come in for the ceremony and she made Songlin stay with her.

The marriage bureau was in the corner of a large office on the first floor where six ceiling fans created a constant shuffling and rattling among the light documents piled up on all the desks. Two pretty girls were in charge. They sorted out all the documents Field handed over and began copying them into books. Ao sat before them watching every stroke, while Field was jammed into the corner up against a rusted filing cabinet. There was a small vase holding four chrysanthemums on the desk. He fixed his gaze upon these. Somehow they reminded him again of Mrs Laker. He didn't want to leave Bangkok. He looked up at Ao, excited like a child. He didn't mind marrying her, but he didn't want to leave. When it was done they had to sign a declaration that they were single and a male bureaucrat of a superior level glanced over everything before wishing them *Yue dee mee suke*.

Ao took Field's hand discreetly when they were climbing back down the stairs, but he allowed her to hold it for only a moment. Somehow he felt abruptly free, as if he had done everything he could for other people and now he wanted to be alone, so he put Ao back in the car with Songlin and told Amara to look after them until Wednesday morning when they would meet at the Embassy.

He went off to deal with Songlin's mother, whose permission was still needed, and the meeting was as unpleasant as he had imagined it would be. He promised her everything; continued support, a cash settlement, he even tried to explain what was happening, but the woman could not forgive him for having made her a victim of his own innocence eighteen years before. Now he was completing the damage by doing what she had always known he would do one day; he was taking away her daughter.

With the promise that she would come to the Embassy the next morning, repeated until there was no doubt, he went back to his bed in the Bangkok Nursing Home, where he allowed the guilt that Songlin's mother had projected on to him to run its full course.

The meeting at the Embassy turned out to be a painless affair, partially because Amara had insisted on coming and had dominated Songlin's mother. There were no tears and no sudden reversals. She also seduced Barry Davis who, like most well brought up Protestant boys, was particularly susceptible to a beautiful woman if she was better brought up than he and elegant as well.

Again Field asked Amara to keep the two girls for the rest of the day and the night. He said he would meet them at the airport the next morning. When they had disappeared in her car, he abruptly felt alone without particularly wanting to be. He dodged across the traffic of Silom Road and wandered off into the back streets on the other side. Hunger surged up, so he bought himself a little coconut pancake from a man grilling them by the road, then wandered on. He was almost surprised to find himself suddenly on Sathorn, just across from Mrs Laker's compound. He walked down the avenue far enough to get over to the other side via a raised crosswalk and approached her property carefully. The groundsmen weren't in sight. He walked quickly to the elevated bridge, ran across and off in among the piles of gas pipe lining.

He waited. No one came. There were no sounds. No voices. Field looked around and began working his way in towards the bunker. The tractors provided almost as good cover and he ended up behind a road grader. From there he had a clear view on to the wall surrounding her house and its single entrance. It was about fifteen metres away. He stared at the broken glass and electric wire running round the top. There was no one in sight. He crouched down in the mud and waited. Twenty minutes or so passed before a young man in a white shirt and tie came across from the direction of the office. Field recognized him as a junior shipping clerk. He had a file with him and he rang the bell.

Almost immediately Mrs Laker's voice came over the phone

system asking him to wait. He smiled obediently at the camera. After a minute's silence, the steel door opened and a stout Thai maid came part way out. She was over sixty. She took the file and gossiped for a moment with the young man. It was probably her fresh air for the day.

Field walked quickly out from his hiding place. So quickly that they didn't see him until the last minute. He grabbed the maid by the neck, pulled her outside and went in himself, locking the door behind. The wiring for the bell was fed through and down the face of the inside wall. He gave it a yank and it ripped free. The whole thing had taken less than ten seconds. There was the muffled sound of two voices shouting behind him.

A metre wide passage ran all the way round between the wall and the house, which was also built of cement and also painted white, without windows. There was again only one door and it was open. He went carefully through into a small living room and closed the door. The muffled cries disappeared. Everything inside was American and made of artificial material; a polyester symphony. The walls were panelled in imitation wood. Two bouquets of plastic flowers sat on coffee tables. Through the lamp shades, protected by cellophane wrapping, a soft light of permanent night shone.

There were two doors within the room, both open. A voice came from the one straight ahead. A feminine, girlish voice. Field went off to the left through the second and into a dining room/kitchen so clean that it appeared never to have been cooked or eaten in. He came back towards the voice.

'Yes, of course, dear. I agree entirely. I'll do that this afternoon.'

Then there was a silence. Field crept closer. Through the door he could see a large portrait of an elegant, thinnish man with a broad smile. He had an engaging look which shone out of the terrible painting and past the streaked imitation wood frame that enclosed it. Two spotlights were trained on to the canvas from the ceiling. On a table just to one side was the silver urn which contained the ashes of the man Catherine Laker said was not her husband.

'I hadn't thought of that. What a wonderful idea,' the voice said.

Field slipped to one side to get a broader view and saw a bathroom door. That accounted for the entire house. He paused a second, then pushed himself forward into the room. Catherine Laker was sitting up on the bed in a blue nylon satin dressing-gown edged with nylon frill and staring at the painting. She was alone. As she turned, a flash of fear went over her face and then was gone.

'What are you doing in here?' Her voice had lost any hint of girlishness.

'I want to talk to you.'

'Go and wait in the office.'

'No.'

'Where is my maid?'

'Outside. Locked outside.'

She paused and looked him over carefully. 'Well, John, what is it?'

'Who were you talking to?'

'Norman.'

'Norman?'

She pointed her untanned fingers and arm at the painting. 'Norman.'

'Oh, right. How is he? How's Brazil?'

'Peru. He is absolutely fine; in fact, much better since I freed him of that imposed organic body. He likes to have the ashes near to remind him of his freedom. I'm very grateful to you, John, for your help in the whole business. Norman is grateful.'

'Great.' Field looked up at the painting. It clearly was not of the green man he had seen in the casket. 'Listen, how often are you two in communication?'

'Every morning. We always have a good talk after breakfast. His advice is what makes East–West Trading work.' A romantic edge came into her voice. 'Do you know, the company is our child.' She looked up expectantly, then harshly. 'Well, what do you want, John?'

He pulled out his gun and threw it on the bed. 'I want you to kill me.'

262

She stared at the pistol lying just beside her on the pink polyester sheet. 'I don't understand.'

'Kill me. Your partners in Vientiane killed my two friends. Your partners here and yourself have been trying to kill me. And now you've got me thrown out of the country. Well, I don't want to go. In fact, I won't go. So kill me.'

She put a hand out to pick up the gun, but drew away at the last second in confusion.

'You need advice, Catherine? All right. Ask Norman for instructions. He's an efficient type. He'll tell you to kill me.'

She looked up at the painting and back at the gun.

'I've never seen you so quiet, Catherine. Maybe you don't talk to strange men in your dressing-gown. You're shy. You want me to turn my back, then you can shoot me in it. No?'

'Stop badgering, John.' She shook herself primly. 'I didn't do all these things. I had nothing to do with most of them. You're such a clumsy man. You always get in the way. You never look to see where you're treading. You've been out here twenty years and you still blunder around like someone off the plane yesterday. I don't have to kill you. Someone else will. Now get out. And take your gun with you.'

Field leaned over and picked up the pistol. It was cool from lying on the polyester surface. He walked down to the end of the bed and looked carefully at the painting. He lifted the cover of the urn. Only then did he realize he was trembling, shaking, in fact, so violently that he couldn't keep his grasp on the lid. It fell on to the carpet. He looked down inside the urn. There were bits of bone among the ashes. But the shaking had spread through his body and suddenly he lost his focus. The grey matter filled into colour and he saw Diana again, butchered on the floor, the colour of the sliced flesh raw before his eyes. He began to retch and turned round violently to stop himself. 'No point in being distant, Catherine. You ought to get cosy with the people you talk to.' He picked the urn up by its base and, without letting go of it, flung the contents at Mrs Laker. When the cloud settled there was a fine dust all over her and her bedspread.

She screamed, looking wildly around, and screamed again, a violent prolonged sound, then tried frantically to brush the ashes out of her hair and off herself. The sound could be heard echoing around inside the thick walls. She got up on her knees on the bed to push it all into a pile. Bits of the bone were recognizable as hip and skull. One of them was caught in her hair. 'Stop, John! Stop now! Get out! Get out!' She shouted but did not look up. She was too busy pushing the ashes into a pile.

Field dropped the urn on the carpet. 'First you tell me what the problem is.' He slipped the safety off the gun, pointed it at an eye in the painting and fired. The explosion echoed round the house and she started screaming again. He put his finger in the hole of the eye and jerked it down, ripping part of the face.

'Norman had nothing to do with it! Leave him alone! Oh.' She went on screaming and sweeping up the ashes. 'Oh. We'll have to leave here, you know. We'll all have to leave. Look what I've done in this country. Look how hard I've worked. But the Vietnamese are going to come. Oh yes, they're coming. And they'll be in Bangkok so fast when they come. And the Thais, they won't resist. I know they won't. They'll collaborate, just the way they did with the Japanese. And we'll have lost it all, John. All of it to the Communists. The great liars. You know that. You tell me why. I knew it was all going to end long ago. Norman told me. After the Tet offensive. You remember. We won the Tet offensive. I don't like war, but it was a great victory and our own press turned it into a defeat. Now you tell me why, John. What's wrong with winning? And these Communists, look at them,' she pouted her lips in hatred, 'they want to sell all of that heroin to us. Six tons every year. When I heard about that I knew what to do. I had to get proof. Proof that even our press couldn't turn around.'

'You went into the drug business to expose Communism?'

'And these Thais. These Thais who will sell out their country to the Vietnamese. All of them. All of them corrupt. Filthy. Filthy. People don't understand that, John. All of this filth. This filth. We're going to lose it all.'

Field went over to her and sat on the bed with the pile of ashes between them. It was still thick in her hair and in her eyebrows. Even like that, without her full public façade, she was very beautiful. He pulled the piece of bone out of her hair.

'Listen carefully, Catherine. I don't want to leave. I want to stay here. Will you get my expulsion annulled?'

'We're all going! You don't understand.'

'Just for now, Catherine.' He said it as quietly as possible. As calmly. 'Just until the Vietnamese come. Then we'll all go. Will you do it?'

'I can't. It's not me. I can't do anything.'

'Well, fuck you!' He jumped up. 'Tomorrow morning everyone in Bangkok will know about your master plan. If I'm going, you're going with me.'

'You don't understand.'

'You're right. I don't.' He threw the gun back on the bed. 'So if you won't kill me, kill yourself.'

Field didn't look at her again. He ran through the front door and closed it behind him. There were voices on the other side of the enclosing wall. He shoved the outer door open hard and the crowd drew back. They were all the employees from the office and the ground staff and, of course, the maid. Thirty or forty of them. He let the gate close behind him. They surged forward to catch it, but too late. Apparently none of them had a key. In the confusion Field slipped through them and ran towards the street. As he went he heard a muffled report and realized he no longer had a weapon. 'Too bad,' he thought, 'too bad.'

He leapt into a taxi and took it down to the river where he jumped on the Express boat and rode it upstream as far as it went, with his head hung over the side down near the water, the sun and the spray on his face. And when the afternoon rain came he made no effort to protect himself while the flaps of canvas were lowered and raised and the monsoon somehow crept through the barriers to soak all the passengers. The ride back down was a mournful slide, too easy, too much with the current, as if the will of the river and of the tides were chasing him on faster and faster, on and on, down to the Gulf of Siam and away from the East. But the Express stopped near the new bridge and Field took a taxi up to the Grand Prix, where he had a last beer without saying it was the last, and then took another taxi and told the driver simply to drive, anywhere in the city, but to keep moving. So he drove all night, awake most of the time. Dozing periodically, only to be woken by the tyres splashing into flooded streets, or by an explosion of honking at a disputed corner.

In the full darkness he went back to his own house for a last time and told the taxi to wait. There was still a sense around it that people were lurking, that movements of branches had meaning, but he locked himself in and went upstairs. He was no sooner in his bedroom than he wondered why he had come. There was nothing there he wanted. Nothing. He prowled around like an intruder before stamping downstairs. Nothing. At the last second he went back into the main room and stared at the photograph of his father for a good minute. Then he snatched it up violently and smashed the frame against the shelf. The glass shattered and the baroque carving fell in two pieces to the floor. He bent over and carefully picked the photo up from among the splinters. This he slipped into an envelope along with his papers and went out to the waiting taxi.

He was already at the airport when Songlin and Ao arrived. Amara had not come in. She didn't like airports. She had, however, taken them shopping and they were both in light cotton dresses that took them far away from their blue and white uniforms. Field checked the two girls and himself in on the Hong Kong flight. They would stop one day there; long enough for him to deal with his money, then fly on to Vancouver and Calgary.

A wall broken by three openings separated the airline check-in area from the row of passport officers. Field put the two girls before him in a queue. There were two Japanese ahead of them. He gazed back at the main hall where there was a confusion of passengers. It was still a Bangkok crowd. Songlin went through, her passport stamped, and they were processing Ao when he looked back again and saw a poorly dressed man coming across the check-in hall in his direction. He recognized the type immediately. A lean, dissatisfied look, loose clothing. A curious way of walking, as if invisible. Field refused to focus on him. Ao was finished and was going through, laughing and talking with Songlin. He threw his passport and tax clearance on the counter. The officer looked at it all carefully. He referred to his books, where no doubt he found a reference to Field's expulsion, because he looked up again suddenly, in an unfriendly way. Then he began checking through the passport and papers again, with much greater care. He was a meticulously groomed officer, his hair smoothed back, his sun-glasses surely a hindrance in such lighting. Field considered pointing out that he himself was only leaving because they were forcing him to go, so if his papers made this impossible he would be delighted to stay.

Instead he glanced back and saw that the man had just come through the low broken wall a few yards away. He wore a cheap white shirt which hung down outside his trousers. He had his right hand in beneath, grasping something. Field looked back at the officer to appeal for help, but there was no help in the eyes hidden behind the dark glasses. He looked round again to shout, but the man was already up against him. Field raised his hands to seize the hidden object.

'Khun Field,' the man whispered into his ear, 'Dr Meechai couldn't come. He sent this.' The man pulled out a thick envelope.

Field trembled so that he could hardly grasp it. He violently ripped the paper open and found two pages inside. One was a list of the results of his last antibiotic test. The other was a scribbled note.

'Good news, old boy. The expulsable are no longer expulsed. All is forgiven. Celebrate over lunch. I'll wait for you at the Home. Love, Michael.'

He read the note again and looked at the officer, who had just stamped his passport, then on at Songlin and Ao waiting for him. He shook his head and bent over the counter to scribble on the sheet at the bottom. 'Too late. The curtain is rent. See you.' He handed this back to the man, whom he suddenly recognized as his guard from the slaughterhouse. 'For the doctor. For Khun Meechai.'

The man took it and pulled out from his belt a package wrapped in newspaper. He smiled encouragingly.

'Thank you.' Field took it, picked up his papers and went through.

It was a cloudy day, the first when the monsoon rain had fallen in the morning and it would no doubt go on into the afternoon. They rose into the sky through the beginning of the downpour, Field with his seat back and his eyes closed.

The safety belt sign was no sooner off than a stewardess reached over to wake him. 'Sorry, sir. A passenger in First Class would like to see you.'

Field climbed over Songlin to the aisle, thinking too late that if someone wanted to see him, they could come back to Economy. It was George Espoir, buried in the London *Times*.

'John!' he said, catching his breath as if he were surprised to see him. 'How marvellous. Come. Sit down.' The cabin was largely empty. 'What would you like? Champagne?'

Field shook his head.

'Well, I've done it. Got all I needed, much thanks to you and your strange, if you will forgive me saying so, strange friend. I am sorry that I wasn't able to use your story. It was very good, but you know the papers just didn't want another drug caper. Not another one, they said. There must be more to the place than that.'

'Sure. No problem.' Field was getting up to leave.

'But I do think I'll be able to give this book an unusual aura. Something different. Somehow to get at the sickness of our time. The confusion. The dissolving of moral boundaries. Oh, say, do you want one of these?' He pulled out a package of durian moon cakes. Only the edge of the fruit's strong smell was there.

'Too early.'

'You like them, do you?'

'Sure.'

That seemed to relieve him. 'Say, I saw you checking in. Looks like you have a little extra baggage.'

'What?'

'Two girls. Ha, ha. Are you staying in Hong Kong? I've got a little research to do there. Don't suppose you know anyone in the Jockey Club, do you? I want to check that out.'

Field shook his head.

'Doesn't matter. Home ground all of that. Lots of us left there. Come on. Have a taste. No?' He held a tart up and bit into it carefully. 'Very strange. Oh, I don't suppose you're free tonight? Dinner. Whatever. Bring your two birds along. I mean two's too many for one, wouldn't you say? I wouldn't mind getting into either of them.'

Field excused himself and went back to his seat, where he sat down between the girls and considered sending Ao up to join Espoir in a toilet. There she could pass her diseases on to him. Then he thought of the durian cakes. If you drink beer with durian in its pure fruit state, your stomach blows up and can explode, unless it is punctured first. He wondered if there was enough durian in the cake to produce at least indigestion. All he had to do was go back up to first class and suggest they have a beer together. In the midst of this thought he saw Espoir coming down the aisle towards them.

'Hello, girls. They're beautiful, John. Come on. Don't be selfish. I'll buy us all dinner. Then we'll split this little harem in two and retreat to private places.'

Songlin looked up at Espoir, hanging over her, and said in English, stilted but without accent, 'Are you addressing my father or my step-mother?'

'What?'

'In either case, a man of your age ought to be more conscious of how ridiculous he sounds. Now go away. Go on.'

Espoir had melted back behind his curtain before Field took hold of Songlin's arm. 'You speak English?'

'Of course I do. Everyone does. I'm sorry, but there was no point in obeying you.'

Field laughed. 'No. As it turns out, none at all. So you'll fit right in.'

'I shall stay for a while, to help you get settled. Then we'll see.'

'That's right.'

The plane burst up through the top cloud level into a perfectly blue sky. Ao, who had never been in a plane, had not looked away from the window. Suddenly she jumped around, 'Look! The sun! The sun!' and went back to staring. It was large and red on the horizon.

Field squeezed by Songlin and went along the aisle towards the toilets. With him he carried his envelope of papers. In the other hand he had the package left by the slaughterhouse man. He asked a stewardess at the rear for matches and lined up before the cubicles, which were already full. There was a little turbulence that could be felt in the tail, so he kept his feet spread.

The stewardess came over, concerned, 'It's forbidden to smoke in the toilets, sir.'

'Of course it is,' he replied. 'I collect match boxes.'

An Indian came out of the door before him and Field went in. There was fresh mud encrusted on the toilet seat in the form of boot treads.

'Oh shit.' Field moved to clean it off, but suddenly gave up and instead pulled down his own trousers, hung them on the door and climbed up on to the seat where he balanced his feet carefully on the tread marks of his predecessor and crouched. There he emptied his papers and his father's photograph from the envelope on to the counter and looked through them one by one until he came to the sheet which proved his purchase of Ao. He pulled out a match and lit the contract over the basin, just below the *No Smoking* sign. It was cheap, yellowish paper that flamed into nothing in seconds. Then he unfolded the new medical results hand-delivered to the passport counter by Woodward's friend. All the tests were bad. He had gobbled up every antibiotic. At the bottom Woodward had scribbled, 'Sorry.' Field shrugged. It was expected.

He unrolled the slaughterhouse man's newspaper package. Inside was a handful of deep fried pork crackling. Field laid this out on the counter beside the basin and picked up the photograph of his father, which he studied as he ate the crackling, piece by piece.